A CHILD IS MISSING

Seven-year-old Phoebe Ho's parents searched the neighborhood when she did not come home from school.

No one had seen her for hours.

No one had seen her at school.

No one knew where she was now.

But everyone in the small community wanted to help. As the police interviewed the parents and neighbors, scores of volunteers joined search parties, and distributed flyers with Phoebe's picture. As the hours, then days, passed and the slim leads didn't pan out, the search intensified.

Someone must have seen Phoebe.

Someone must know where Phoebe was.

Someone did.

And when he finished with Phoebe, he tossed her tortured body into a ditch and drove home.

WHETHER IT'S A CRIME OF PASSION
OR
A COLD-BLOODED MURDER—
PINNACLE'S GOT THE TRUE STORY!

EVIL SECRETS

KATHY BRAIDHILL

Pinnacle Books
Kensington Publishing Corp.

http://www.pinnaclebooks.com

PINNACLE BOOKS are published by

Kensington Publishing Corp.
850 Third Avenue
New York, NY 10022

Pinnacle and the P logo Reg. U.S. Pat. & TM Off.

First Printing: December, 1996
10 9 8 7 6 5 4 3 2

Printed in the United States of America

This book is dedicated to my mother, Laura Braidhill.

ACKNOWLEDGMENTS

I would like to thank the lawyers, the DA investigators, and the dedicated detectives with the South Pasadena police department and the Riverside County sheriff's department for their assistance in reliving the painful details of this case. I thank San Diego police detective John Flynn, investigator Patrick Birse, Bill Molina, and investigator George Hudson, for their time and support; Avry and Randy Budka and Shannon Williams, for cheerleading; and my family and friends, for their enthusiasm.

CHAPTER ONE

It was cupcake day at Arroyo Vista School and little Phoebe was in a hurry to get there.

The thirty-five pennies she had saved to buy a cupcake jangled in her bright red Hello Kitty bookbag as she scampered alongside her mother this cool December morning. At 7 years old, Phoebe thought school was a great place to play with her friends. She liked socializing and the once-a-week indulgence of shopping for sweets at school. Like her teenage sister, Jennifer, Phoebe was already getting choosy about her clothes, but their mother didn't mind indulging them. Every school morning, Sharon Ho and her two daughters stood in front of their open closets and discussed their outfits while the girls' brother, Damon, and their father, Kenneth, tried to grab a few more minutes of sleep. While Jennifer's tastes ran to the junior high school style of the month, little Phoebe clung to certain pieces of clothing and was partial to wearing them in layers whether or not they matched.

Phoebe's choice this morning was to pair her favorite red and blue shirt with a long-sleeved sweatshirt and light pink stirrup pants. Even though wintertime is never too chilly in southern California, Sharon insisted that she wear her jacket, a vibrant red, green, and blue, with letters and a cartoon character on the back.

The wrangling over what to wear took longer than usual this morning, and Phoebe was going to be late to school if she didn't hurry. Damon, who was in the fifth grade at the same school, had just sped away on his bike. Her cousin Lana, with whom Phoebe usually walked, was already 100 yards ahead.

Sharon walked with Phoebe halfway, since it was only five blocks and the streets of South Pasadena were safe, filled with moms driving carpools and suburbanites commuting a dozen miles south into downtown Los Angeles. A cluster of small, historic houses on the west side of the city formed South Pasadena's oldest neighborhood. All the houses in those dozen blocks backed up to a crisscross of alleys used by delivery trucks for ice, milk, and coal at the turn of the century. The mayor lived just around the block, and many of the city's other prominent residents lived nearby. It was the kind of neighborhood where almost anything out of the ordinary sparked a phone call to police. Phoebe's walk to school took her past neighbors who would watch out for her as she skipped and sang.

The small town sits just north of LA's industrial sprawl, a handy drive for the middle managers and executives who can afford homes in one of the pricier middle-class suburbs surrounding downtown. South Pasadena mirrors the rest of the area in attracting a large population of well-to-do Asians.

Like most immigrants, Sharon and Kenneth had recently moved from Taiwan to find a better life for themselves and their children. To save money, they were crammed into

Ken's parents' tiny home, kitty-corner from the home of Ken's brother and his family. Ken's brother was the pastor of a local church, and the Hos quickly made friends in the community and with others in the congregation. But they had little time for a social life. The couple worked backbreaking hours during the week selling shoes at an outdoor swap meet in the seaside city of Redondo Beach, an hour's drive away. On weekends their children joined them, and Phoebe usually went along unless her parents wanted her to stay home with her grandparents. Unlike her brother and sister, who were old enough to realize the swap meet was work, Phoebe enjoyed the excitement and bustle, socializing with customers, visiting with the other vendors, playing around the stacks of shoes, and impressing everyone with her willingness to help. Most of all, she enjoyed the pleasure of being around her parents and siblings all weekend.

The couple was as ambitious as they were hardworking and were trying to save enough money to buy their own home and eventually open a shoestore in town.

Sharon sighed as they came to the end of the short alley that opened onto the street behind their house. It was Thursday, and while that meant a restful weekend was approaching for most people, Sharon knew her busiest days lay ahead. The day was going to be a long one—they had a load of shoes to pick up and then the forty-mile drive to the swap meet.

As Phoebe pranced in the morning chill, Sharon pulled her sweater tight around her shoulders, then stopped to fasten the child's jacket. Sharon knew it was time to go, but she hesitated, torn between wanting to walk Phoebe the rest of the way and returning to the house to load the van. Sometimes it was hard to let Phoebe go. Phoebe was her unabashed favorite, the one who slept in her parents' bed, partly because Sharon wanted her to, but also to save space, since the entire family had to sleep in one bedroom. Sharon and Ken and Phoebe were on a mattress on the floor, while Jennifer and Damon had bunk beds. Ken's parents used the other bedroom.

Phoebe was the one Sharon bragged about most. It was Phoebe's classroom art adorning the walls of their small home, Phoebe's bright paper decorations hanging on their small Christmas tree, Phoebe's photos in her wallet, and stories about Phoebe dotting Sharon's conversation.

When they reached the end of the block, Sharon stopped and Phoebe ran ahead. Sharon turned to go, then turned back to see her daughter skipping toward school, her shiny black hair bouncing with each step. Sharon called out, "Aren't you going to kiss your mother goodbye?"

Phoebe ran back to her mother, grinning a gap-toothed smile. It had been only a few days since Phoebe had lost her two front teeth. The youngster wrapped her arms around her mother and delivered a wet kiss to her cheek.

"'Bye-'bye."

Sharon watched for a moment as Phoebe headed to school, then turned toward home. Her husband was waiting for her and they had a long day ahead of them.

Phoebe had gone barely another block when she shouted ahead to her cousin, who turned around to see Phoebe running toward her. Just then the schoolbell rang. It was 8 a.m.

"Phoebe! Come on!" she yelled.

After a moment, Lana turned and ran the rest of the way to school.

Ann Parnell still had a dishtowel in her hands when she went to answer the front door. With eight kids, she always seemed to be fixing a snack or a meal or cleaning up. She looked through the picture window of the living room but the sun had just gone down and she could see only the shadowy forms of two people standing on the porch. She reached for the light and saw the parents of one of her daughter's friends. Something must be wrong for them to be out there like this, she thought.

"Hello," said the man. He extended his hand and introduced himself as Ken Ho, Phoebe's father, in thickly accented English.

"We are the parents of Phoebe Ho. We don't know where she is. Did she come here?"

Ann's heart leapt to her throat. Ken Ho had apparently left his home looking for his daughter without a coat in the chilly evening, and Sharon was shivering in her thin sweater. Susan held the door open and invited them in, then called out for her third-youngest child, Emily, to come downstairs. Emily was Phoebe's playmate. They were the same age and in the same class. Out of curiosity, the rest of the children started drifting downstairs, and soon the whole brood was with the Hos, who were sitting on the couch in the living room.

She knew Phoebe was one of the smallest children in Emily's class. She came over frequently to play and jump on the trampoline in their backyard, a magnet for the neighborhood kids. Susan knew most of their parents, but it was the first time she had met Phoebe's. She asked her sons and daughters if they had seen Phoebe at school that day.

"I saw her at recess."

"No, she wasn't there."

"Phoebe was with a lady pushing a stroller."

"She was on the playground."

Sharon and Ken looked somewhat confused by the jumble of responses, but the kids seemed to remember her having been at school that day, which meant there was a chance she was still at a friend's house. They just had to figure out

which one, and the Hos' language difficulty was probably
making that task a bit tougher. Ann still felt terrible with
this girl's parents sitting on her sofa on a very chilly night,
unable to find their daughter. It must be a horrible feeling.
She hoped nothing bad had happened. She tried to think
who else would know if Phoebe had been at school that
day. Had they tried phoning the school principal or the
teacher to find out if she'd been there?

The Hos said they had been driving and walking around
the neighborhood looking for Phoebe but didn't have the
phone number for her teacher. Ann assured them she would
help them out. She called a friend who knew the teacher's
home phone number, then called the teacher. Her husband
said she was having dinner at Kathleen's, a restaurant in
Pasadena. Ann phoned the restaurant, explained that she had
an emergency, and asked the hostess to page the teacher.
She glanced over at Ken and Sharon Ho, sitting motionless
on her sofa, their eyes trained on her. Within minutes, the
teacher was on the line. Ann said the Hos had come looking
for Phoebe and wondered if she remembered whether Phoebe
had been in school that day.

No, she was pretty sure Phoebe had been marked absent,
the teacher said, but she couldn't be absolutely certain. The
teacher wanted to know why. Ann felt helpless. A little girl
had been missing all day and she was going to have to be
the one to break the news to her parents. Ann told her that
Phoebe had not come home after school, that her parents
were worried, and that they were continuing to look for her.

Ann's mind drifted to the times she'd seen Phoebe laughing and playing with Emily. She wondered if Phoebe had
even made it to school.

She told the Hos the teacher had reported Phoebe absent.
They thanked her and got up to leave, and Ann walked
them to the door. She didn't know what to do except to try

comforting them, saying that Phoebe would probably turn up. It was such a shocking thought that a child in their neighborhood would be missing. Ann lived only a block from the Hos. Foul play was the last thing on people's minds here.

It almost wasn't far enough to get up to full speed on a bike; it was only five blocks from school to home. Just when you got started, it was time to stop. Damon wheeled up to the house, leaned his bike against the garage, and took his homework out of his bookbag. He should have done it right after school, but his parents had given him permission to visit a friend that afternoon. Once darkness had hit at about 5 p.m., Damon had headed home, hoping to beat his parents to the door. He saw by the van parked in the driveway that he was too late and braced himself for a scolding. He walked into the kitchen, but before he could round the turn toward the living room, he saw his grandparents hunched over the kitchen table, looking very worried.

"What's wrong?" he asked them in Chinese.

"Did you see Phoebe today?" his grandfather asked.

Sometimes Damon saw his younger sister at school. But today he hadn't.

It sounded like his parents were in the other room, talking on the phone to his aunt and uncle. Since it was such a small house, Damon could make out a few words. His parents had walked to the homes of Phoebe's playmates to see if she'd been playing there. A friend's parents had helped track down Phoebe's teacher, who'd said she'd been marked absent. Sharon had jumped into her car with Jennifer and driven around each block in their part of town, getting out to call Phoebe's name.

His mother had been crying and his father was sternly silent.

Damon couldn't believe it. Where could she be? It was like her to become enchanted with make-believe and lose all track of time. Even at 7, Phoebe had quite a social life and loved playing with her friends. But Damon and his sisters had been raised to obey their parents, and Phoebe didn't have permission to be out after dark. Damon heard the anxiety in his parents' voices and knew something was very wrong. He felt ashamed he had spent the afternoon playing and had not been there to help look for his younger sister. But why Phoebe? What would someone want with his sister?

Born of Taiwanese parents but raised on American soil, Damon knew the cultural barriers to asking the police for assistance, since that represented a loss of face: it meant you couldn't solve your own problems and had to go outside your family for help. But his parents had embraced their new country, had eagerly learned English, and were working very hard to make a new life here. They clucked their tongues at the high crime rate in the United States, but he knew they'd do anything to get Phoebe back.

Damon immediately felt responsible. His mother often asked him to watch out for his younger sister and to make sure she got to school and back, even though he always rode his bike. This morning, he had torn out of the house because he was late and hadn't even seen her walk to school.

He scanned his memory and tried hard to think. Had he seen her in the schoolyard that day? He didn't remember seeing her today in particular, but it was hard to tell because there wasn't anything to distinguish today from any other day . . .

Then something jogged his memory. It was a few weeks ago, and he had wheeled into the front yard on his bike just as Phoebe was getting out of someone's car—one he didn't recognize. He had scolded her because their parents had always told them not to get into the car of someone they didn't know very well. Phoebe was very friendly, almost too trusting, and it was hard for her to understand the concept of danger. Everything had turned out all right that day, but Damon knew it was possible—Phoebe could have climbed into someone's car.

Damon wondered if his parents knew.

In the next room, he could hear them dialing the phone.

Officer Gabriel Thierry rolled his patrol car up to the small wood-frame house, radioed the station to let them know he'd arrived, and walked toward the front door. A former reserve officer for the department, he'd worked as a supervisor at a private security firm before becoming a full-time police officer earlier that year. Despite a lack of experience, he had the advantage of fifteen years of martial arts weapons training, which gave him light, quick movements despite his solid, square physique. He had been on patrol for just a few hours when the missing child call had come at 5:42 p.m. Since he was closest to the call, he'd told the dispatcher he'd respond. It had been a typically slow day in South Pasadena. The police force prided themselves on keeping a small-town feel to the city, a citadel of safe suburbia surrounded by the worst violence modern urban life had to offer. To its south were the murderous rampages of Los Angeles gangs. Its neighbor to the north and east was Pasadena, known worldwide for its cheery Tournament of Roses Parade on New Year's Day, but its bloody gang violence had achieved notoriety. The eastern neighbor was San Marino, another tiny, idyllic city of mostly mansions whose quiet population of millionaires and heads of corporations rivaled the residents of the better known Brentwood and Beverly Hills. South Pasadena was the closest residents would ever get to a midwestern town. The neat, well-trimmed houses lined up row after row in neighborhoods on either side of the main street, Fair Oaks Boulevard, which still had a drugstore with a soda fountain. There were lots of businesses, like the barbecue place and the antique stores that had been there for decades. The newer businesses, like the specialty gourmet grocery stores, coffeehouses, and trendy import boutiques, mixed with older ones in the retail business district.

If there was ever any trouble, it was usually rowdy kids having a loud party, an occasional drunk, bickering couples, or loitering homeless people. The residents were willing to pay more in local taxes to have their own police department instead of contracting for police services with the county sheriff's department. The difference made for a painfully small force with antiquated equipment. But each of the twenty-two sworn officers, from the patrol cops to the detectives, went to work proud that the residents preferred them over the county sheriffs and put out extra effort for the people who paid their salaries.

As he walked up to the small porch and knocked, Thierry felt no sense of urgency at the missing child report. Though he'd never handled one himself, he knew from his training and by talking to other officers that a kid in such cases usually winds up hiding or fast asleep in a bedroom closet or playing at a friend's house, or will sometimes come strolling through the front door while an officer is still interviewing the panicked parents. There are also the runaways, who eventually wander home after a few days. He also recalled from a police academy class that there could be a number of serious reasons why a child might be missing, such as child abuse, or if the child was stuck somewhere, like in an abandoned refrigerator, and couldn't get out. He kept these things in mind as he interviewed the family.

Sharon Ho let Thierry in and introduced her husband. An older couple sat in the small living room along with a teen-aged girl and a boy about 11. Sharon immediately offered the officer tea and cookies, but he politely declined.

Notepad in hand, he ran through the list of questions while taking careful note of the tiny house and its contents, the attitude of the parents, and the demeanor of the other two children. He asked the parents the basics and Sharon Ho provided most of the answers. Phoebe Hue-Ru Ho was born November 27, 1979. She stood just under four feet tall and weighed forty pounds. She had black hair and brown eyes, was missing two front teeth, and had a scar on her chin and another scar on her left thigh from an iron burn. Thierry frowned slightly and looked at the parents for a moment, but they gave no indication that they were at all embarrassed about her scars. He moved on.

She was last seen at 8 a.m. that morning, on her way to school. She was in second grade at Arroyo Vista School. When she didn't come home after school, Sharon got in her car and drove around the neighborhood, calling Phoebe's name. With the help of another parent, they had phoned her teacher and was told Phoebe had never made it to class. Phoebe had been carrying a red bookbag.

Thierry couldn't help thinking the little girl was going to walk in the door any minute. The parents would first hug her, then scold her, be thankful she was safe, and ask where she'd been all this time. Nevertheless, he quickly launched into the next set of questions, designed to figure out if this seven-year-old had anything on her mind that would lead to her whereabouts. Had she been punished lately? Was she doing well in school? Did she have any other problems with school? Had she ever run away from home before? Did they know of any reason she might run away? Had she been sick? Was she depressed about anything? Had she been moody the past few days? Had she had any disagreements with any of her friends? Did she ever seemed depressed?

The whole time, he observed the parents to gauge their reaction. It had been ten hours since they had last seen their child. Were they anxious or upset? Sharon and Kenneth Ho seemed disheveled and rumpled, wearing casual after-work clothes. Sharon looked as though she'd been crying, but she was composed when she spoke with Thierry. Neither of them seemed alarmed, but that didn't bother him. People react differently in front of a police officer. Some parents get hysterical if their child is gone for five minutes. Others stay calm in front of an officer in a uniform and a badge, but break down in front of their family as soon as he leaves. This couple seemed calm and concerned, not frantic. Maybe they, too, believed she'd come through the door any second.

Something else struck Thierry as he was talking to them: though Kenneth was more proficient in English, Sharon had taken control of the situation and was answering Thierry's questions. Thierry worked closely with Asians for 15 years in connection with martial arts, and he knew that the culture dictated that women stayed in the background when dealing with strangers, while men most often did the talking. It was even more unusual that Sharon had been taking charge in front of her husband's parents in their own home. Thierry made a mental note for future reference.

After collecting the information from Sharon, the next move was to conduct a preliminary search. If Phoebe had been playing hide-and-seek, it was safe to say she'd won. The problem was finding her hiding place.

He started right where they had been talking, in the tiny living room. Still keeping an eye on the parents, Thierry looked behind the couch, under the coffee table, and behind chairs. It didn't take long; the room was tiny. As Sharon and Kenneth walked him through the house, he couldn't help noticing the big cardboard cartons of athletic shoes in individual boxes. He saw the two small bedrooms. Still mentally scanning for signs of child abuse or neglect, Thierry noted the condition of the house. It was extremely small and cluttered, but he saw nothing that would indicate neglect. Both children seemed well groomed and were clothed in ordinary schoolwear. Everyone seemed fine emotionally, as far as he could tell. He went outside, wriggled under the crawl space, and shined his flashlight around. More shoeboxes. He went back inside. Thierry and the parents had looked under all the beds, in all the closets, in the kitchen cabinets, behind every chair, and in the tiny space between the ceiling and the roof, and they'd literally beaten the bushes and shrubbery in the small backyard. No Phoebe.

Thierry ran through his mental checklist. There was no swimming pool within eyesight for a child to have fallen into; no garage, basement, or attic to hide in; and not much of a backyard. He unholstered his radio.

"We're UTL on the missing juvenile," Thierry told the dispatcher, using the police acronym for "unable to locate."

In a heartbeat, Commander Michael Ward came on the line.

"Status?" Ward said.

"UTL on the missing juvenile," Thierry repeated. "Nothing on the premises search. No signs of 415 or 278," he added, giving the codes for a family disturbance or child abuse, which might explain a child's absence.

He could hear Ward sigh. He confirmed the Ho address and said he was on the way and to stand by with the family in case she showed up.

Thierry heard Ward tell the dispatcher to activate the emergency call-up plan on a "critical missing." That meant

all officers were to drop what they were doing and report
in to help with a full-blown search for a missing child. Like
most other police agencies, their department assigned top
priority to a missing child.

Ward had someone call and ask the larger and better
equipped sheriff's department to assist with a canine team
and handler. He asked another dispatcher to call the Sierra
Madre search and rescue team. All available personnel,
including on-duty firefighters, volunteers, reserves, and
police explorer scouts were being recruited. Even the dispatchers in the tiny police department were coming out to
help while the receptionists handled the police and emergency lines.

Thierry knew police procedure dictated that Ward first
follow up on his interview with the family before assigning
a team of detectives to take over the case. Ward would ask
similar questions, trying to find some morsel of information
Thierry had missed, in hopes of shedding light on Phoebe's
whereabouts. Ward, assisted by other officers, would also
scour the house and yard, then broaden the search to include
a few neighbors. The next step was to initiate a neighborhood
grounds search. That was going to be tricky. Phoebe lived
in the oldest section of the city, with turn-of-the-century
homes backing up to a series of intersecting alleys.

It had been an hour since the couple had reported Phoebe
missing. It had been 12 hours since her family had seen her.
Ward didn't want to waste a single minute before activating
the emergency call-up plan.

If Phoebe was playing with a friend, she should be walking
in the door any second. As Thierry waited for his supervisors
and the rest of the officers and assorted helpers to arrive,
he wondered if the family had any idea what their house
would look like in a few minutes. While every other family
on the block was sitting down to dinner, this family would

soon be overrun with supervisors, officers, detectives asking questions, a search and rescue team, and bloodhounds and their handlers, all sniffing into every aspect of their life, looking for some angle on the girl's disappearance. He prayed she was simply having dinner with one of her friends, or even playing hookey. He looked at the couple, sitting next to one another. Kenneth seemed distracted, fidgiting slightly and staring into space. Sharon was very quiet and seemed to be staring at something on the wall. Thierry glanced up to see what she was looking at and saw a ceramic imprint of a foot with designs around the edges and the deliberate childish printing of the artist—Phoebe.

CHAPTER TWO

The doctor told him he should be sitting down doing paperwork, not out messing up his shoulder running down crooks, but Detective Bill Molina was a bullheaded ex-Marine and he didn't care. Cop work was what he lived for, not chasing paper across a desk. Molina wanted to be a cop so bad he'd spent 4 years marking time as a collection manager at a bank until they'd dropped the height requirement to five feet six inches and he could apply to the South Pasadena police department. Before that, he and three of his buddies had enlisted in the Marines. After three tours of Vietnam, he was the only one who hadn't come home in a box. What did he care about his damn shoulder?

He got the radio call on a hot summer night—a carful of kids pulling donuts in Garfield Park. He pushed the pedal of his black-and-white cruiser and sped over the soft grass to where the kids' 357 Chevy carved another double-circle with its extra-wide performance tires. He heard the faint peals of laughter turn to taunts as they caught sight of him.

The Chevy's deep-tread tires threw patches of sod as the kids tried to speed away, but the fancy suspension got stuck on a sprinkler head and they jerked to a halt. Molina was already roaring straight at them and he had a split second to decide whether to hit a tree or slam into the cherry Chevy with the custom paint job. The kids were gone when he came to, but the tree didn't have a scratch. They impounded what was left of the Chevy.

Molina was in and out of surgery for eight months with doctors trying to patch together what was left of his shoulder. They wanted to tinker with it some more, but Molina was itching to get back to work. No problem, the doctors said, as long as you stay in the office. Molina's boss, Lieutenant Joyce Ezzell, who headed the three-person detective bureau, went along with the doctor's orders and assigned Molina to light duty. But for the month he'd been back to work, the only time Molina had ever seen the office had been at the beginning and end of his shift. He knew that the twenty-eight-member department—twenty-nine, if you included the chief, the dispatchers, and the civilian employees—needed all hands on deck, and he was certainly happy to oblige. Molina had his own cases to work, anyway. When Detective Kent Stoddard had asked him that afternoon to help him chase down some punk, Molina had never given his bad shoulder a second thought.

Stoddard told Molina the details of the case as they walked out to the parking lot behind the station to get an undercover car. They had three choices—a repainted, recycled patrol car, the chief's old car, or a blue 1970s Chevy Malibu the city manager used to drive. They took the Malibu. Stoddard was also a twenty-year veteran of police work who'd joined the department as an officer after working for the Los Angeles police department as a fingerprint expert. But unlike Molina, the balding detective distanced himself from police work. He thought the best police work was done at the station, not by wearing your heart on your sleeve.

Stoddard and other officers had watched this kid grow up at the wrong end of a pair of handcuffs. Molina had also seen him around and might have even arrested him once. He'd gone from kid stuff—truancy, loitering, and petty theft—to more serious crimes, like marijuana use and possession. At the ripe age of eighteen, he'd committed his first grown-up felony. He had robbed a friend of cash, jewelry, and stereo equipment and then smacked him in the face. It was a dead-bang case because the victim knew him. All they had to do was bring him in. Stoddard got behind the wheel of the Malibu and drove west toward a Los Angeles neighborhood called Eagle Rock.

Four hours later, the two detectives were almost out of places to look. The Malibu was dogging as it rumbled up and down the steep streets of Eagle Rock to the suspect's girlfriend's house, his buddies' houses, and his apartment. Nothing.

"Attention all units. Critical missing. Asian female. Seven years old. Approximately three feet ten inches tall, forty pounds."

They had to get back to the city. Without a word, Stoddard turned the Malibu back toward South Pasadena and Molina picked up the radio microphone to call in that they were on their way. Time was of the essence. Molina muttered that they'd probably find the little girl before they did their local hoodlum.

The dispatcher told them Commander Ward was en route to a command post they were setting up at Arroyo Vista School.

"We're on our way. ETA about fifteen minutes," Molina said. Looking for Stoddard's suspect would have to wait for another day.

As Stoddard and Molina breezed over surface streets in post-rush hour traffic, the shop talk ended. As veteran officers, they had both handled missing children reports, and each time the kid had surfaced a few hours later. They always hoped for the best but prepared for the worst. A missing child was every parent's nightmare. Stoddard and Molina each had two children and they worried like any other parents, sometimes even more, because they were exposed to the more sinister aspects of life.

Agent Mark Miller walked to the office and grabbed markers, notebooks, clipboards, a handheld police radio, flashlights, batteries, masking tape, and an engineering map of South Pasadena showing the address of every house, every business, every empty lot, and every park, street, alley, and private drive. He piled everything in a box and took it out to his patrol car. Miller's job was to establish the command post and coordinate the patrol officers for a ground search for Phoebe Ho. Since the lost girl was last seen headed to Arroyo Vista School, they would set up there. Ward had already arranged with school officials to have a janitor open up the school auditorium. It was 7:30 p.m.

After Officer Thierry's initial interview and search, Ward and Lieutenant Douglas Brown did the routine follow-up interview with the Hos and searched the house a second time. Ward then sat down with the family and prepared a list of Phoebe's friends who lived nearby. Two patrol officers were sent out to do a cursory check on those friends while Brown called the school attendance clerk. Both came up negative.

Ward and Brown drove back to the station, leaving the officers at the house in case she came home or they heard anything.

Tall and bearded, with a robust sense of humor, Ward was uncharacteristically somber as he ordered Miller to set up the command post and conduct a thorough canvass of all neighbors who lived between Phoebe's house and the school. On a city map, he and Miller marked off Phoebe's route from her home to the school and expanded it by several blocks in each direction. They would blanket sixteen streets—roughly two dozen square blocks, three city parks, the railroad tracks just south of the school, and the school itself.

Ward walked over to the dispatchers' bank of computerized phone equipment and asked them to call in every available person for the search, an unprecedented move for the small department. He wanted all on- and off-duty officers, all reserve officers, all teenage explorers, and anyone else they could get their hands on, including firefighters who weren't busy. Ward retreated to his office at the rear of the stationhouse to call the Sierra Madre search and rescue team and the Los Angeles Search Dog Association. Both had trained bloodhounds that typically tracked lost hikers in the hills, but these dogs were often used to find missing children. Within the hour there could be several teams of dogs at Phoebe's house to trace her scent.

Since this incident was happening on his watch, Ward wanted things done right. He had just been promoted from lieutenant to commander, and he wanted to see what kind of advice he could get from the large neighboring agencies— the Los Angeles police department and the Los Angeles County sheriff's department, both of which had missing persons units. Larger agencies like the sheriff's department often advised small city police departments faced with complicated cases or unique types of perpetrators. It wasn't unusual for the sheriff's department to step in and take over a kidnapping or homicide investigation. The sheriff's homicide unit, which handled nothing but murders, had more detectives than a small city's entire department. The sheriff's department also boasted one of the largest and most sophisticated crime labs in the country, with a staff of criminalists capable of analyzing anything from bloodstains to fingerprints and tire marks.

If this was as serious as it seemed, there was no one on the South Pasadena police force with experience in a crime of this magnitude. His department would need all the help it could get.

Miller was also experiencing some firsts, he thought, as he drove the short distance from the police station to the school. In his four years as a police officer, he had never established a command post, nor could he recall an incident so grave the commander was calling in every available person. It seemed out of character for the community.

Miller, a two-striper in charge of the patrol division, had already gone home after working the day shift when he was called back in, and was the first officer to show up at the station. He and his wife, a CHP (California Highway Patrol) officer, on crutches from an on-duty injury, lived only a few blocks from the station, across the street from where the lost girl had gone to school. They could look down on the playground of the school from the backyard of their home, which sits on a hill. His wife, who was the adviser to the teenaged explorer post for the department and had grown up in South Pasadena, went to the station and helped the dispatchers phone explorers and pitched in any way she could. Miller was close to earning a bachelor's degree in administration of justice at a local university and this was like the class he had just completed in crisis management. But with the limited resources of their small department, staging an effective ground search would be a real challenge. Even if all the patrol officers showed up, that only gave him a dozen uniforms. There were twenty reserves, but he expected to see only a handful. There might be another half-dozen explorers, and who knew how many, if any, firefighters would respond to the call? The trick would be to put them to the best use he could, which meant teaming sworn officers with explorers and reserves.

The janitor had already opened up the auditorium and turned the lights on, and he was waiting outside in the hallway when Miller parked his cruiser. He unloaded the equipment and thanked the janitor, who stayed to help him set up few tables and chairs at the front of the auditorium, next to the elementary school's child-sized stage. The officer said goodnight to the janitor, rolled out the blueprint map of the city on a tabletop, and fished out the felt-tip pens. He marked off Phoebe's route and outlined the total search area, then divided it into one-block grids. He also outlined the school, the parks, and the city library. He got out the flashlights and loaded them with fresh batteries.

He heard a car pull up, and another came close behind. Commander Ward and Detectives Stoddard and Molina walked into the auditorium. Ward had stopped at the Ho residence to pick up a photograph of Phoebe. On the way to the school, the dispatchers told Ward by radio that the fire department was at their disposal, giving them enough people for fifteen to twenty search teams.

Ward pulled out the picture of a solemn little girl holding up a big fish she had caught. "This is Phoebe," he told Miller and the detectives.

"What we have is this little girl who was last seen going to school this morning," he told the detectives. "It doesn't appear that she made it to school. The clerk marked her absent. She's in second grade, lives with her parents and grandparents on Orange Grove Avenue. Parents don't know where she is; she's gone when they get home. They do some checking and they find out she didn't show up at school. They don't know if she ran away or if she's with a friend or what. That's all we've got right now.''

Officers started to stream in the door and they gathered around Ward. He gave one of them the photo and told him to make a hundred copies to distribute during the search. Ward gave the detectives the names, phone numbers, and addresses of Phoebe's classmates.

Molina and Stoddard wrote everything down and headed back to their car to go to the Ho residence. They would do still another interview with the parents. The repetition was insurance that no one had left anything out. There was always a chance that by the third time around, some nugget of information would surface that could lead them to the missing girl.

Oh, God, Molina thought, this is serious. He hoped she hadn't been kidnapped. Experience told him that the lion's share of critical missing calls were unfounded, and he figured they might find her late that night. He automatically thought about his two kids but resisted the impulse to give them a call to make sure they weren't headed out that night. It's tough being a cop with kids, he thought, but it's worse being a cop's kid.

Molina figured by the time he and Stoddard showed up, they would be pretty tired of seeing more cops and answering the same questions, but following police procedure meant they had to be thorough. The detectives drove to the Ho residence.

The tiny auditorium became thick with uniforms and the high-energy sense of purpose that had brought them there. On- and off-duty police officers milled around with the reserves, some of whom had just come from their jobs as lawyers, insurance agents, and business owners. Teenaged police explorers rubbed elbows with on-duty firefighters, and a handful of off-duty firefighters gave up much-needed sleep to help with the search. Miller passed out the copied photos of Phoebe and the auditorium buzz grew as the teams chatted about what they knew so far about the missing girl. Miller paired the least experienced people with veteran officers, then gave each two-person team its assignment. Each team would get one square block to search. He briefed each team before it left.

The first objective, of course, was to find Phoebe. Miller asked them to be creative.

"Any trashcan, any dumpster, bushes, a hole in the ground, the back seat of cars—look in and around everything that could possibly hold a small child . . . or her body," Miller said.

The second goal was to find witnesses and lay the groundwork for detectives, he told them.

"We obviously can't search people's homes, so you need to contact every resident of every house, or any person who was at the house at the time Phoebe disappeared. Get permission to search the front-and backyards. ID all your residents. Get names, approximate ages, phone numbers, what time they were at the house. These people may be witnesses, they could be perpetrators, they might have seen someone acting suspiciously in their area. They may know something," Miller said.

"Keep track of every person at every address. Make sure you interview every person at every house, not just the one who answers the door. If there was a resident, friend, or relative who was at the house when Phoebe disappeared, get their vitals so the detectives can find them later.

"Do your best. Find Phoebe."

Even if they didn't find her, Miller told them, the search would at least tell them where Phoebe *wasn't*.

After Miller briefed the teams, Ward decided to run by the station to make another round of phone calls. A detective with the sheriff's department told him he should also contact the kidnapping unit, the missing child unit, and homicide as a matter of procedure, but Ward felt reluctant. He didn't want to call them right away as he still had hopes the girl would show up.

With the command post established and the search under way, Ward became resigned to phoning the specialized units but wished this nightmare had not visited his city. People were going to be shaken up for weeks, months, years, even if there was foul play. And with foul play, the media would be right behind, sniffing at their heels. That was one thing Ward dreaded because he'd never had to deal with reporters. It was just a matter of time before news of the search got to the press and they'd be out at the command post in record time asking questions. Ward knew he'd be stuck giving the answers. The sheriffs' deputies would also have to give him pointers on this. Nowadays, most newsrooms had radio scanners, which were receivers turned to the frequency used for police business. It was only a matter of time before someone showed up. The local press and wire reporters also made several calls throughout the day and night, asking for "notables"—arrests for serious crimes or interesting situations or those concerning famous people. Ward had never before handled press calls.

When he got back to the station, Ward stopped by the dispatchers' desks and was told more searchers were on their way to the command post. The Sierra Madre search and rescue team and their bloodhounds were also en route. Miller's wife Judi was soon bringing in pots of coffee, donuts, and blankets for the officers, who were certain to be hungry and cold on the mid-December night. Ward thanked the dispatchers and retreated to his office to make more phone calls.

But just as soon as he'd finished up with the sheriff's department, a dispatcher told him to contact Miller at the command post. A TV reporter was there wanting to interview someone about the missing girl.

Amid the bustle of blue police uniforms and olive drab explorers' outfits was a white-haired man in a sports jacket. Reporter Stan Chambers from KTLA-TV in Los Angeles walked into the auditorium just as the newest wave of eager searchers began assembling in the auditorium, exchanging stories about what they'd been doing when they got called in. Chambers drew the attention of every uniform in the place when he entered, followed by a cameraman and a soundman holding a huge, fuzzy gray microphone on a pole. Chambers, known for his 25 years as a TV reporter, had heard about the lost little girl by listening to his police scanner and wanted to talk to the person in charge.

Miller was alarmed at the sight of the news crew and felt it was an intrusion. They had a grave task at hand, and the last thing anyone needed was the press interfering with the search. Miller soon found the veteran reporter was genuinely concerned and intent on helping out.

"If there's anything we can do to help get the story out, let us know," Chambers told him. He asked Miller if they could broadcast the photo of Phoebe tacked to the bulletin board. Chambers said her photo would air on the 9 p.m. news, less than a half hour away. Maybe someone had seen her and would call in.

When Ward got there a few minutes later, Miller introduced the reporter to Ward, who gave him a brief rundown

of the facts. Ward, remembering what the sheriff's deputy
told him about using the media to help find the girl, let
the camera crew shoot Phoebe's picture. As he dealt with
Chambers, more uniforms continued to collect in the auditorium. Chambers told him he hoped the broadcast would do
some good. Ward expected the newspeople to leave, but
Chambers said he was going outside to give his live report
and would then hang around to file continuous reports on
the search. Ward thought for a minute, then said he would
allow them to set up the camera at the far end of the auditorium.

As a crop of fresh searchers arrived, Miller gave the new
troops their own blocks to search. This time, since he had
the personnel, he sent a team to cover the school grounds,
the classrooms, and the playgrounds. He assigned another
team to search the brushy area along the railroad tracks a
block south of the school. The railroad tracks backed up to
a bank of apartment buildings and some of the brush was
quite overgrown, so they'd have to be thorough.

Miller's wife and another dispatcher arrived a few minutes
later with coffee, blankets, and a huge assortment of donuts
in a big pink box and set everything on a table at the opposite
end of the stage.

By 9 p.m., the hour-old search for Phoebe was the top
story on Channel 5's broadcast. The photo of the missing
girl went out to living rooms all across southern California.
Unfazed by the scoop, other TV stations and radio, wire,
and print reporters made beelines for the command post.
The news clattered over the City News Service and the
Associated Press wire. News vans with antennas rumbled
up the street to Phoebe's house and more crowded around
the small elementary school, their tall satellite spires piercing
the branches of ancient oaks lining the historic streets. Ward
acted as the media coordinator, giving interviews to each

arriving news crew. He directed each crew to set up its camera or radio microphone at the rear of the auditorium. At the arrival of network news, a few neighbors padded out of their homes in robes and slippers against the December chill. They watched the TV reporters deliver the story of the desperate late-night search for the missing girl.

The first of the search teams began reporting back to the command post, with uniformed officers and explorers trying not to gawk as the camera crews filmed them. Some had radioed in their progress but hustled back to the command post for a quick break once Miller told them about the coffee and donuts. Others came for fresh batteries for their flashlights. So far, no one had seen anything out of the ordinary.

As the night wore on, the temperature dropped in the unheated auditorium and the mood darkened. With Ward's permission, the camera crew at the far end of the auditorium continued to roll film as the weary officers, firefighters, reserves, and explorers returned to the command post to check in and get their next assignments. The excitement of the search gave way to the disappointing reality that something serious had happened to the little girl. The nervous chatter of a few hours before vanished as the searchers nibbled donuts and sipped coffee. Those who had left their jackets behind in their haste to respond to the call-in huddled in blankets and cupped their hands around the styrofoam coffee cups for warmth. Except for some nervous laughter about curious things spotted in people's backyards, there was little talk. No one needed to tell the search teams that with every passing hour the chances of finding Phoebe diminished. All they knew was that no one had seen her. There was no sign of her at all.

The good news was that the neighbors were eager to help once they found out why the police were banging on their

doors in the middle of the night. With the increasing number
of news broadcasts documenting the search, most residents
were well aware of the missing girl. Almost every search
team told Miller that neighbors had volunteered to pull on
warm clothing and help the officers find Phoebe. Typical,
Miller thought. In that neighborhood Miller and his wife
knew a good number of the people who lived in those historic
homes. That made it even more maddening—where was
Phoebe? Who could have taken her, Miller wondered.

The Hos' tiny bungalow was overrun with officers stomping in and out of the house, turning each room inside out,
searching and re-searching every corner, every closet, the
small backyard, and the tiny attic. The phone rang constantly.
A crew had been recruited to physically crawl underneath
the home and search with powerful flashlights. Other cops
were rummaging around in Ken's truck full of athletic shoes.
The large cardboard cartons had been tossed out of the truck,
sending bright new sneakers tumbling onto the damp grass.
Bloodhounds from two different canine search teams arrived
and their handlers led the dogs around the house, sniffing
every corner of every room for Phoebe's scent. The energetic
dogs had recently returned from Mexico City, where they'd
located survivors of an earthquake, and had been successful
at finding people underwater and in burned buildings. Both
teams had already been to the command post and had located
Phoebe's scent but were unable to get a track on her. The
principal had opened Phoebe's classroom and retrieved
books from her desk, but the scent track went nowhere.
    Their luck was no better at Phoebe's house. The dogs
picked up the scent but had trouble figuring in which direction she had gone. Sharon Ho had given the handler Phoebe's
small blue pajamas as a scent guide, but it had misled the

dogs because Phoebe slept with both parents and their scent was also on the pajamas. Amid all the confusion, the canines were happily leading their handler to Ken and Sharon. The dogs seemed interested in the Christmas tree set up in the living room, which was decorated with paper ornaments Phoebe had made.

The bloodhound handler asked for another piece of clothing Phoebe had recently worn. Sharon went into the bedroom and returned with a very small pink sock. She seemed reluctant to hand it over.

It looks like a doll's sock, Molina thought. He held the door open as the handler went outside, then Molina walked to the kitchen, where he could keep an eye on the living room, where the family was sitting. He and Stoddard had finished their first and second rounds of questioning, at least for the time being. He was giving the family a breather and needed a few minutes to gather his thoughts. Stoddard went outside to radio the command post for a status check.

Molina propped against a wall of the kitchen, watching dogs and officers going every which way. On one hand, he felt bad for the family, losing their privacy in the tiny home to hordes of police poking into all their personal things. He knew it was an intrusion, particularly if you're from a different culture and you don't quite understand why all these guys in uniforms are all over your house. Ken's parents looked confused and probably felt a little helpless because everyone was speaking English, which they had difficulty understanding. Molina found it hard to read Jennifer—she just looked exhausted. Damon, though, was extremely tense. You could see it in his face. It was like he'd been caught doing something and he was really going to get it, but that was probably because he was a pre-adolescent. Ken, sitting on the couch, was cool, calm, and collected. Sharon looked like she had been crying. She had been sitting and standing and pacing and wringing her hands and clasping them together as if in prayer. At times she seemed frustrated that she didn't know enough English to get her point across. At other times she just stared into space. And Phoebe? She was definitely a very special child. There were photos of her all over the place. There was the photo of Phoebe and the fish, Phoebe at her birthday party a few weeks ago, wearing the shirt she'd disappeared in, Phoebe doing this, Phoebe doing that. No pictures of the other children. Molina thought it odd that her parents put up pictures of one child and not the other two. And Phoebe winds up missing. Being the apple of her family's eye might have made her more of a target to someone.

The language barrier had made it tough to interview the parents, since the Hos didn't speak fluent English and no one in the department knew Chinese. Damon had helped translate, and that had made their interview smoother. Even with the language difficulties, Sharon and Ken in their own way had let the police know they placed all their faith in them and were certain they could bring Phoebe home again.

Molina and Stoddard had gone over the same material with the Hos as Thierry and Ward—then went a little further, asking whether she had ever talked to strangers and whether she would ever get into a car with someone. They asked who was the last person to see her and exactly when she'd left the house. They got mixed reactions, which they chalked up to translation problems. Stoddard and Molina tried another tack. They asked if Phoebe would ever get into someone's car. Sharon said that she would, particularly if it was an Asian woman, because Phoebe would want to help. The detectives prodded in another area, whether they had any ongoing feuds with anyone in the shoe business. Ken seemed very stiff as he simply said no. They asked how business was, whether there was much competition, and if they were successful. Everything was fine, they answered mechanically. Molina thought maybe they had found an area to explore, but perhaps they needed assurance the police could be trusted. Molina decided to call it quits for the time being and give everyone a break.

Stoddard came in after radioing dispatch, bringing with him a gust of cold air. With all the traffic in and out of the small house, it was nearly impossible to keep out the chill. Despite his practice of not displaying emotion, Stoddard wore a look of concern and nodded toward the car.

"Let's give these guys a breather. We need to go by the command post," he mumbled.

Molina nodded and walked over to the Hos to let them know they were leaving but would be back within the hour.

As soon as they stepped outside the house, Stoddard and Molina saw the TV trucks crowding the street. They ducked past the media vans, fired up the Malibu, and, instead of driving on surface streets, crept through the alleys linking the homes back-to-back. As Stoddard drove across the street to the next alley, they saw a search team on a front porch holding up a photocopy of Phoebe's picture to someone behind the screen door. They arrived at the school, ringed with police vehicles and news trucks. The detectives double-parked on the wide street and headed toward the brightly lit auditorium.

"What's happening?" Molina said to Miller.

"We got nothing so far."

Molina and Stoddard exchanged glances and sighed.

Miller continued, "Everyone wants to help, but no one's seen her. It got on the 9:00 p.m. news, so people already know what's going on."

Miller filled in the detectives about the areas searched so far and told them they were collecting the officers' notepads filled with names, numbers, and addresses. Again, there were no standouts. Molina shook his head at the shoe leather that could be spent tracking down every single resident who wasn't home tonight, but was home when they thought Phoebe'd disappeared because they might know something. It'd take a platoon of law enforcement to follow up on all those calls.

Molina saw Ward at the end of the room, being interviewed by reporters. No leads yet, he was telling them. Better him than me, he thought. He and Stoddard wanted to stay as far away from the press as possible. Let the brass deal with that. At the same time, they were using the press to get the word out. If they were smart, they would use the media to plaster that little girl's face on every TV set in the state. Whoever had her wouldn't stay hidden for long. On the other hand, there was a remote chance that an avalanche of publicity like that could spur someone to get rid of her, too. Molina didn't want to think about that.

Molina glanced at his watch and winced. It was already close to 1 a.m.

Stoddard and Molina piled into the Malibu and made their way back to the Ho residence. He and Stoddard would take another stab at interviewing the parents tonight, then start fresh in the morning. Maybe getting a few hours' sleep would help them remember something.

Stoddard pulled the Malibu back into the driveway. There was so much foot traffic in and out of the house, any semblance of privacy had vanished, and they walked in the front door, which stood ajar. Sharon and Ken were still in the front room, looking tired but not frantic. Molina gave them an update on the search and watched them closely for a reaction. There wasn't any. He ventured a few more questions about their family. Were there any arguments about money? Had there been any disputes in the family business? Was the shoe business profitable? Were they happy with the money the business was bringing in? How was their marriage? Were there any marital upsets or fights that would have driven Phoebe to run from home?

Business was fine, their marriage was fine, and the money was good, Ken and Sharon answered. They insisted nothing was wrong, but it was clear their marriage was a closed subject.

He and Stoddard tried going over familiar territory. Who had seen Phoebe last? Exactly when was that? Where was she the last time they saw her? Molina kept a poker face as he heard a couple of different answers than he'd gotten a few hours ago. This time around, Ken and Sharon told him Sharon wasn't sure who saw her last and she thought Phoebe might have left around 7:45 a.m. Sharon thought she saw her from inside the house, walking toward school.

Molina took the answers down diligently but knew fatigue had gotten the best of them. Several hours ago, Sharon had told them she'd seen her daughter last and she'd walked her out to the street, and that it was closer to 8 a.m. because Phoebe was late for school. Molina glanced quickly at Stoddard, who continued to ask questions in the same vein. It was crucial to try to pin down a time, because they didn't know if she'd disappeared outside her house or down the street, closer to the school. It could be important. Hell, anything could be important. Could anyone possibly forget exactly when and where and what time they had last seen a missing child? Wouldn't a distraught parent play that over and over in her head out of panic and grief? How could she forget? Maybe they needed to try a different strategy.

Stoddard and Molina kept the questions up, gently but firmly prodding the couple, however it was impossible to pin down the time or exactly where Phoebe was the last time anyone saw her. Molina left with Stoddard still talking to the couple and went out to use the car police radio to call Ward.

"We're wrapping up for the night," Ward told him. "Get to the command post as early as you can get here."

Molina briefly told Ward their status and they clicked off the line. He looked at his watch. It was 2:30 a.m.

Miller collected the portable radio and markers, scooped the old, dead batteries into a trashcan, rolled up the map to the city, gathered up the photocopies of Phoebe's picture, and dropped everything into the same cardboard box he had brought with him.

He was satisfied the search teams had done the best job they could, but he had mixed feelings. He was glad they hadn't discovered her body, but the other side of the coin was an ominous feeling—where was she?

During the night, the officers were floating various theories, all based on speculation—she could have been killed inside a building within the search area, or she could have been held captive in that area and there was no way to search the interior of any building without a search warrant. She could have been taken a few blocks away, she could have been taken out of state, or even whisked out of the country. It was frustrating because they didn't know where to look.

As the night wore on, Miller could see the disappointment in the faces of the searchers. Finding Phoebe was a matter of pride for the small department, from the brass to the officers, the reserves, the firefighters, and the explorers. They not only wanted to assure the public they were doing everything possible, but to prove to themselves South Pasadena could not have been the scene of a kidnapping, or worse. The media had wasted no time in seizing the angle of an historic small town bewildered by a missing child.

Ward had left the auditorium minutes ago with the last search team. They would retrace their steps in the morning, the daylight giving them a better chance to spot something. A different crop of people would be at home or in the neighborhood than those they'd encountered this evening. Perhaps one of them saw something.

Miller paused before picking up the cardboard box. Phoebe's picture was still tacked to the bulletin board. He walked over to the bulletin board, gently pulled out the tack, slid the photo in between the photocopied sheets, and walked out to his car.

Tired of hanging around in the cold, dark night, the reporters were giving their cards to Commander Ward, who promised to phone them if Phoebe happened to surface in the next few hours. The search would resume in the morning, he told them, and they were welcome to cover it, given the same rules. The news vans left.

CHAPTER THREE

The phone always rang at 8:30 a.m., right after Dawn Edwards dropped off her three girls at school, and it was always her best friend, Rita Austin. This morning, the usually cheery neighbor was somber.

"There's a little girl missing," Rita said, half-shouting, half-crying. "It made the news last night. She's seven years old, and they're not even sure if she made it to school."

Dawn felt the blood rush to her head as her face turned prickly hot. Rita filled her in on the details she had heard on the news, confirmed by a friend who worked at Arroyo Vista School. Police went house to house knocking on doors until very late, and now officers were stationed at roadblocks near the school to hand out flyers about the missing girl to all parents dropping off children. A special meeting had been called for teachers and school employees later today. The teachers and the principal had been outside all morning, ushering children inside as they arrived. Rita said that another friend was told by police that detectives were going to interview all children who were in the same class as Phoebe Ho.

How could this have happened here? Dawn, a matronly woman with dark hair, was outraged that something had happened to one of their children. She had moved to South Pasadena with her husband twenty years ago. Lifelong residents joked that the couple were still newcomers. It was such a close community, it was like someone had stolen one of their children. *That's our little girl and everyone's little girl.*

"I can't believe this," she managed to croak out.

Rita told her Phoebe's route to school from her house on Orange Grove Avenue—across the alley, over to Adelaine Avenue, up to El Centro Street, and then left to the school. Melanie nodded, her mind racing, picturing the blocks in her mind. Her daughter had friends on Adelaine. There were two families from her church who lived along the route Phoebe took to school. The little girl usually walked with her brother, but she was running late yesterday, Rita continued. It was really frightening. There was no discussion about what they were going to do about it—they were going to help look for Phoebe. Dawn hung up the phone and punched the speed dial to her husband at work.

In the back of her mind, Melanie held out a hope that it was a divorce situation or a custody battle, or that some relative had picked Phoebe up and forgotten to tell her parents.

Melanie and Hugh Edwards had one girl of their own and were foster parents to two they hoped to adopt. Their home, like many in South Pasadena, was a gathering spot for their own friends and their children's friends. Someone was always stopping by to drop off kids, pick up kids, or just hang around.

Dawn reached Hugh at the PIP printing shop they owned, one of a national chain.

"There's a little girl missing," she said, then quickly told him all the details. While they both knew it was premature to assume there was some kidnapper prowling the streets, preying on children, they were both frightened. It went without saying that both would volunteer their time and do whatever they could to find that child.

Hugh hung up. When he turned around, Sergeant Miller was waiting at his front counter. Hugh knew what he was going to say before he said it.

"We've got a little girl that's been reported lost. How much will it cost to run off a few hundred . . ." Miller asked, holding up a handmade flyer showing an enlarged picture of Phoebe.

Before he could get the words out of his mouth, Edwards plucked the poster out of Miller's hand. "Not one cent. I'll have them for you as soon as I print them," he said, whirling around behind the counter to fire up the copier.

Edwards made six copies and put one on each copier. While the uniformed officer watched, Edwards unwrapped bundles of copy paper from his back room and filled the paper bins quickly as soon as each was depleted, then watched as the photo of the small child holding a big fish was reproduced hundreds of times.

MISSING: THE SOUTH PASADENA POLICE DEPARTMENT NEEDS YOUR HELP IN FINDING THIS MISSING CHILD—PHOEBE HUE-RU HO.

FEMALE, ASIAN, 7 YEARS OLD, 3' 10", WEIGHT: 40 LBS., BLACK HAIR AND BROWN EYES, MISSING 2 FRONT TEETH AND HAS A SCAR ON HER CHIN.

IF YOU SEE PHOEBE OR HAVE ANY INFOR-

MATION REGARDING HER WHEREABOUTS, PLEASE CONTACT THE SOUTH PASADENA POLICE DEPARTMENT IMMEDIATELY.

Miller leaned against the counter, marveling at how quickly word of Phoebe's disappearance had spread and at everyone's eagerness to help. Some teenaged explorers and a couple of reserve officers had shown up at the department at 6 a.m. to make photocopies on the department's clunky copy machine of Phoebe's poster to hand out to parents during the early-morning roadblocks around the school. News of the little girls disappearance had truly rocketed through the entire town. The camera crews were back and the phones at the station were ringing off the hook from the wire services, Los Angeles-area TV and radio stations, and newspapers, asking if they had found her and what they were going to do next. Residents were starting to call in, too, wanting to know if they could help. Edward's response was unquestioningly generous but typical of this neighborhood. He shook his head. And people wondered why he didn't want to work at a bigger outfit like the LAPD.

Lieutenant Joyce Ezzell flipped on the all-news station long enough to hear what the traffic was like on her way into work, then cut back to a talk show. The freeways were fairly clear, so she didn't have to take any alternate routes into the Los Angeles area. A female supervisor of South Pasadena's three-person detective unit, Ezzell was one of thousands of Angelenos who escaped the escalating real estate spiral by migrating to a rural area where a house could be purchased on a cop's salary. The downside was an hour-long drive into work.

Ezzell wanted to be a police officer for the purest reasons—to help people and protect them. The father of a good friend of hers had been a cop. She grew up listening to glorious stories about chasing criminals and putting them behind bars, and that sounded like a worthwhile profession. At 57, Ezzel had survived years of being the first female officer to penetrate the all-male enclave of law enforcement, working side-by-side with fellow officers who'd never seen a woman carry a gun and a badge. She never complained about years of not being taken seriously, doing donkey work and enduring snickering, backtalk, practical jokes, and an array of torment that today would be seen as sexual harassment. Ezzell took the flak with the job, shut her mouth, and did her work. She graduated from the police academy in 1967 the sole female. All she wanted to do was catch criminals and be a cop. When her fellow male graduates were hired as full-time officers, Joyce didn't file a lawsuit or complain because no department would hire a female officer. Even though she had academy training, she was hired only as a reserve officer at South Pasadena. The only time they called her in was when they needed Ezzell to escort a suspect to the women's jail. The chief finally offered her a job as a meter maid, promising after 2 years, she'd be assigned to juvenile, then detectives. She marked cars for 5 years until the new chief made her a dispatcher. The next new chief said, "What are you doing here? I need you out in the field!" Times had finally changed.

After years of handling drunken drivers, car break-ins, occasional purse snatchings, and home burglaries, Joyce became head of detectives. While larger police departments had separate units devoted to crimes against people, property crimes, and sex crimes, South Pasadena had Joyce Ezzell, Bill Molina, Kent Stoddard, and Gary Robbins. They split things up the way they liked. Bill was good at fraud and bounced checks. Gary and Kent had burglaries, and Joyce took the leftovers—the rare robbery and the burglaries Gary didn't want or didn't have time for.

When Joyce got to the station, it looked deserted, except for the incessant ringing of the phones.

"Where is everybody?" she asked the dispatchers.

"They're at the command post," one said.

"What command post? Where? What's happening?"

"There was a little girl reported missing last night. They set up a command post at Arroyo Vista School," the dispatcher said. "They're calling and calling and calling. They all want to help."

Joyce sighed, silently cursing Molina and Stoddard and anyone else she could think of, got back into her car, and drove over to the school. Rounding the corner to El Central Avenue, she couldn't believe her eyes. An armada of police and media had descended on the elementary school. Ezzell had never before seen such a media carnival. From the number of news vehicles, reporters, and camera crews on the scene, it looked like it was the day's top news story. This was more bad news, she thought. No detective wants to work under the glare of media and being bothered by reporters' phone calls and having suspects disappear in the midst of all the attention. No wonder they didn't have time to call her. The only good thing was that she was in plain clothes and could slip unnoticed into this mess, she thought. She pulled around to the teachers' parking lot in the back and double-parked behind one of the department's beat-up detectives' cars. Ezzell made her way through the media morass and poked her head into the school auditorium and saw police officers setting up a command post. School was still in session, despite the confusion, and it looked like the search crews were out. She shouted out if anyone knew where to find Captain Ward and was told he was in the principal's office down the hall. She headed there.

Sharon and Ken Ho were sitting on a well-worn couch. She saw no sign of Ward, but Molina and Stoddard were inside the principal's office with a school secretary who was retrieving the names and addresses of Phoebe's classmates. Stoddard and Molina told her about the previous night's search. That morning, officers distributed more than 800 flyers to parents, students, teachers, and neighbors at the school roadblocks. There was still no sign of Phoebe. Molina and Stoddard were getting ready to interview her classmates. Ezzell wanted to talk to the parents and, as was police procedure, Molina went with her. The Hos looked like they were in shock. Sharon was in a nice pantsuit and a blazer, but her face was pale and drawn and her eyes puffy from crying and lack of sleep. Ken was wearing a long-sleeved white shirt tucked into slacks, baggy on his thin frame. He looked stern and worried and at the same time, his eyebrows lifted hopefully as he greeted Molina and as Ezzell introduced herself.

Like the officers and detectives before her, Joyce had a very difficult time understanding the couple and they had an equally hard time with their limited knowledge of English, trying to answer her questions.

After a few minutes, Joyce thanked the parents and shot Molina a hard look. She asked the principal's secretary if she could use the desk phone.

"They don't know if you're asking when you last saw her or who last saw her," she said. She picked up the phone and dialed Ward's private line.

"You've got to ask the chief to call around to other departments and see if we can get an interpreter over here," she said. "Try Alhambra PD or Monterey Park. We need an officer who speaks Mandarin Chinese. This investigation is going nowhere until we can understand exactly what the parents are saying."

Ezzell told the Hos they were looking for an interpreter and to go home. There was nothing for them to do here. She left Molina and Stoddard to do the kids' interviews while she drove back to the department to make some phone calls.

No one wanted to believe there was foul play, but she had to start with the basics. The very first thing that needed to be done was to check for registered sex offenders living within city limits, then within a fifteen-mile radius. California required that men convicted of sex offenses (the number of female sex offenders is negligible) register with the police departments in the cities where they live within 30 days after being released from prison. Most of them never do it in Los Angeles County and parole agents are too overworked and understaffed to follow up. Getting lost in the urban shuffle tends to attract hundreds of parolees to the greater LA area each month, many of them sex offenders. Failing to register was only a misdemeanor. Nevertheless, Ezzell knew many sex offenders dutifully registered and it would be error to overlook such an obvious source. She retrieved the documents showing sex offender registrants from her own department, then sat down with the phone and called the police department in Alhambra, a city to the south.

As she waited to be connected with the right detective, she thumbed through the reports from her own department, looking for something similar in their MO, their *modus operandi,* the way an offender commits a crime. Nothing fit this case. Most sex offenders grabbed a kid off the street, committed the offense, then dumped him off a few hours later, sometimes on the same block. That wasn't this case. Other types of sex offenders, such as schoolteachers, babysitters, priests, scout leaders, and others who "love" children, seek continuous access to their young prey and often molest them again and again. That wasn't this case, either. She called the other departments surrounding the town—Pasadena to the north, Los Angeles to the west, and San Marino to the east and told each of the sex crimes detectives, "If you have any registered sex offenders that fit that MO, I'd appreciate you dropping some names on us."

Plainclothes detectives in a grade school classroom seemed as out of place as prostitutes at a baptism. The pint-sized desks and smell of chalk dust only amplified Molina's feelings that their role as crimefighters brought an aura of doom into a world where the worst tragedy to befall a child should be skinning a knee on the playground or forgetting lunch money. He figured the kids would be plenty hyped up by all the activity at the school. They knew Phoebe was not there today and they could see cops in uniform and reporters with camera crews crawling all over the school. The commotion was enough to distract anyone, especially the second-graders from whom he had to try extracting information. The last place Molina wanted to interview a bunch of squirming kids was in the principal's office. How could they be comfortable talking to strangers after being summoned to the principal's office, of all places? Helen Cease, the principal, was bending over backward to help out, and thankfully, she decided to let the detectives use two empty classrooms so they would have a quiet place to talk to the kids. With Ezzell back at the station, the detectives decided to split the classroom, with Molina and Stoddard interviewing half of the kids and Robbins taking the other half. To their surprise, the principal allowed the detectives to walk into Phoebe's classroom and escort the children, two at a time, into separate classrooms for their interviews.

The neatly dressed second-graders, most of whom, like Phoebe, had just lost one or both of their front teeth, wore pigtails and ponytails, jumpers and kneesocks and playground-ready designer togs. The children were eager to help, some too eager. About half said they had seen Phoebe on the playground or in class. Two girls said they saw Phoebe in the school auditorium. A few said they saw an adult approach Phoebe by the playground fence and she had gotten into a car, but the children couldn't describe the person or the car. One said it was a van. Another said it was a station wagon. One said it was a man. Another said it was a woman. No details. No descriptions. No consistency. The detectives dutifully wrote down what the children said, but these accounts contradicted the teacher, who'd said last night that Phoebe had been marked absent. The school playground monitor had told Stoddard she never saw Phoebe arrive at school and didn't see any strange people or cars she didn't recognize. She certainly hadn't seen any child climb into a car after arriving at the school.

The rest of the children said matter-of-factly that they hadn't seen Phoebe. These interviews went quickly. Did they see her the day before? No. In the classroom? No. On the playground? No. Were they sure? Yes. That was it. Next kid. Much as he wanted some clue, some thread to start an investigation, Molina figured the kids wanted to help so badly, they created a scenario they thought the detectives wanted to hear.

The hard part was trying to answer the questions from the kids: *Where is Phoebe? When is she coming back?*

Grim-faced searchers, block assignments in hand, had come trickling back into the command post, set up for a second day in the school auditorium. After one night out, it was starting to sink in that they were no longer looking for a little girl who'd lost track of time with her friends or was napping in a good hiding place. Earlier that morning, Miller had gently but persistantly raised that possibility in his talk to the search troops and pointed out that they should act as the eyes and ears of the detectives who could follow up on suspicious circumstances. He wanted everyone's hopes high and didn't want anyone to limit his search out of discouragement. As tough as it sounded, the fact that they hadn't found her body was good news because it meant that Phoebe was somewhere and any one of them could find her.

Miller gave them a quick rundown of the situation, even though most had searched the night before, and sent them out with enough flyers to cover their blocks. Their mission was to retrace their steps from last night and find people who would have been around at the same time in the morning when Phoebe'd disappeared. He sent out additional teams to search each of the city's six elementary schools, the high school, and the parks and widened the search perimeter to include the surrounding streets. Miller dispatched a particularly athletic group to search the hillside next to Monterey Road, a steep incline south of the school.

"You've got daylight on your side, folks," he told them. "Take your time. Remember, even though you might have looked last night, look again; the light changes things. Check trashcans, dumpsters, big boxes, in and around shrubbery, abandoned cars, cars on the street."

"Okay, let's go! Line up for your block assignments."

With the first wave of search teams out the door, Miller had taken the quick trip to make more photocopies of Phoebe's poster. He had left Ward to keep an eye on the news crews.

When Miller returned to the auditorium with stacks of flyers bearing Phoebe's gap-toothed grin, the Sierra Madre canine unit returned with the bloodhounds. Unable to track the scent, the handler had given the dogs a rest and wanted to try picking up a scent guide from her desk and schoolbooks.

Miller told Ward, who summoned the principal. Because of the children's natural curiosity at seeing real, live bloodhounds, the handler decided to wait until the lunch period to enter the classroom.

While they were discussing the possibilities, Miller's radio cackled.

"SAM 11 to Adam 20."

Miller reached for his handheld radio.

"Adam 20, go ahead."

"Adam 20, be advised, we've located some . . . uh, remains. Unsure at this time. Request a supervisor to respond to this location. Fifty feet south of Monterey Road, approximately the three hundred block."

Miller's heart sank. It was the hearty team he had sent to scour the brushy hillside.

"Sam 11, Miller here. What do you have? Over."

There was a pause.

"Unsure at this time," the officer repeated. "Remains. Possibly intestines, but it looks too small to be human. They look fresh. Over."

"Supervisor en route. Adam 20 10–4," Miller said, signing off. He breathed a sigh of relief. It was extremely unlikely that an animal had attacked Phoebe as she walked to school, dragged a screaming child through city streets in broad daylight and devoured her in the hills. It would have to be a pretty large animal to carry a child three feet tall. The animal who took Phoebe, Miller thought, walked on two legs.

Miller scanned the small auditorium and saw Ward being interviewed by a camera crew. He waited a few moments, then caught Ward's eye as he turned away. He didn't want to let the press think there was anything afoot. And he didn't want news crews in their helicopters trying to locate what were probably animal remains. Miller filled him in on what the search team found and Ward directed him to phone the Los Angeles County sheriff's department criminalists' team to photograph and collect the remains and have them examined by a deputy medical examiner from the coronor's office. Then they would know for certain if they were animal or human. Miller got back on the radio and told the officer and the explorer Ward's instructions to stand near their find to make certain they were undisturbed until the criminalists arrived.

Miller was about to sign off when the officer said he had something else to report.

He and the explorer had found a medium-sized collection of marijuana plants, complete with an irrigation system and gardening tools. He wanted to uproot the plants and seize the equipment, but that meant hours of paperwork. Miller knew what the answer would be but relayed the information back to Ward anyway before he got involved in another press interview.

"Mark the area and come back to it," Ward told Miller. "We've got enough on our hands now."

Miller relayed the information and signed off. When he looked up, there was a handful of teenaged boys shuffling into the auditorium.

"We heard there was this little girl missing," said a tall, brown-haired kid, not quite sure of himself. "We were wondering if you needed some help. Uh, we're football players . . ."

One of the beefier kids jumped in with, "Coach said we could do this instead of practice. We just wondered if we could, you know, go door-to-door or something."

Miller nodded, astonished at their caring and concern, at this age, for someone they didn't even know. Well, it *was* the end of football season, he thought. The teammates, arriving in groups of three and four, quickly filled the auditorium. Miller knew exactly how to put ten big strong guys, who were accustomed to working as a team to best use. There was one particularly difficult area he had wanted to search, the arroyo on the city's border with Los Angeles. The twenty-acre city-owned spread, a true wilderness refuge smack in the middle of the suburbs, had a well-groomed ballpark and soccer fields. The arroyo had horse trails and hiking paths winding up and down tree-studded hills, some leading to a tiny creek where homeless people often camped out and teenagers ditched school. There was a lily pond and a concrete wash with a pedestrial tunnel—lots of places for a small child to hide or be hidden.

"Okay, gather 'round and listen up," Miller said, repeating slowly and in greater detail the talk he had given his search troops. Then he sent the football team out the door with an experienced officer leading the way.

Miller glanced around the command post as the dejected search teams returned. One officer, seeing the youths, motioned to him.

"We found something in an alley, near a dumpster," the officer said in a quiet voice. "There was a pair of women's panties, a woman's shirt, and an adult porn magazine."

The officer had already photographed, collected, and booked the evidence at the station. Neither of them thought it had any connection to this case. If Phoebe had indeed been abducted, that kind of a person would not be interested in adult pornography. Plus, the clothing didn't match the description of what Phoebe had on yesterday morning and the clothes in the alley were too large to fit a child. But the significance of the items would be up to the detectives to decide. Miller tried getting Detective Molina on the radio, but he was out of range. He tried Detective Ezzell, who was at the station, finishing up phone calls. She thanked him and jotted down the information.

Miller turned back to his search teams and gave them new assignments.

CHAPTER FOUR

The phones at the tiny South Pasadena police department wouldn't stop ringing.

"I'm ninety-nine percent certain I saw the missing girl," a Burbank woman caller told the dispatchers. She phoned at 6:27 a.m. Friday morning, after hearing about Phoebe Ho's disappearance on the morning news. She had been at a department store the night before and saw a white male, about 65 years old, with a well-mannered Asian girl. She even noticed that he paid for his purchase with a credit card and she had commented about how well behaved the young girl had been.

A Glendale caller reported seeing a strange-looking man with a squalling Asian girl when she went to the bank. It looked exactly like the photo of the missing girl she'd seen on TV, she said, offering a description of the man, the car in which he'd been driving and the exact location of the bank.

With Phoebe's disappearance at the top of the news cycle

on radio and TV broadcasts and making headlines in most local newspapers, callers deluged the small department with reports of spotting the gap-toothed girl in grocery stores, a private storage facility, at the airport, in cars, in department stores, in parking lots, and walking down streets all over the greater Los Angeles area.

Every 20 minutes or so, a dispatcher would collect a stack of phone messages about Phoebe sightings and deposit them in front of Ward, who was helping the dispatchers with the phone calls at the front desk. They fielded twenty to thirty calls per hour on the average, with intense periods of fifty to one hundred calls per hour. As the day wore on, reporters also phoned, sometimes on the hour, to find out whether she had been found and if there was any news at all. Calls from the press went to Ward, who wanted to keep them away from the detectives so they could work unhindered. In quiet lapses between calls, Ward squirreled himself away in his office, phoning larger agencies for advice on how best to handle the disappearance. There had never been an incident like this in South Pasadena, and Ward didn't feel the least bit awkward asking for advice. The chief had phoned around to the other police departments to line up a Chinese-speaking detective. The police department of Monterey Park, whose residents included a large population of Chinese residents, had immediately assigned one of their best, Sergeant Bill Yeung, to assist full time. He was already re-interviewing the parents at their home with detectives Ezzell, Molina, Stoddard, and Robbins.

There was no way Ward's small department could investigate all leads. Granted, some were farfetched, but out of one hundred reported sightings, one might point them in the right direction. The department just didn't have the man resources to immediately chase them down, and that frustrated him. As the number of phone calls climbed, Ward

created a special form to save time taking the reports, and
assure all the details about what was seen and who saw
it would be gotten. Ward routed the forms to the watch
commander directly overseeing the investigation, who then
decided whether to radio Ezzell. It would be up to her to
decide which should be pursued on the spot.

Ever since last night with the first search, he could sense
this case was different. In his 20 years with South Pasadena,
he'd never seen a more determined group or seen the community lend such overwhelming support. However, without
training in handling citizen calls for help or crimes in progress, Ward couldn't allow citizen volunteers to answer police
phone lines. He had taken down their names, but hadn't had
time yet to figure out how to put them to best use. There
was also talk of a reward fund. That was good news.

The bad news was that they were no further along than
when Phoebe was first reported missing. They had no witnesses, no credible sightings, no solid clues. It was 2 p.m.
and no one had seen this youngster since yesterday morning
at 8 a.m. Miller had radioed in a few minutes ago to report
he was wrapping up the command post. The football players
had turned up nothing in the semi-wild arroyo. Miller had
thanked the volunteers, the explorers, and the dispatchers
and released them from their duties.

The dog handlers who tried using Phoebe's schoolbooks
as a scent guide said the bloodhounds lost the trail just
outside her classroom because too many people had walked
through the doors of the classroom since the last time she
was there.

As soon as he broke down the command post, Miller said
he would drive through town with a core team of officers
to distribute flyers. Miller told Ward he'd found a generous
local printer who was giving them an unlimited number of
photocopies of Phoebe's picture and the "missing child"

poster. He was headed down to the printer to pick up another 1,500 flyers and planned to distribute them throughout the city streets and just beyond its borders. All school staff, the gas, water, and electric workers, trash collecters, the street and parks employees, firefighters, postal workers, every single open business, and citizens on the street would get a poster. There weren't too many places for someone to take a child if her photo was on a poster and plastered all over town. When he got back to the station, he would deliver the names and addresses of residents for the detectives for follow-up interviews; including those who weren't there at the time of the previous two searches.

Ward answered a call from the coroner's investigator, who had collected the intestines on the Monterey Avenue hillside. He was positive they had come from an animal, but he would examine the specimen at the lab and file a more complete report.

That was a relief, Ward thought, reaching for his radio to tell Ezzell about the findings.

"Commander Ward!"

A dispatcher jumped out of her chair and ran over to his seat at the dispatch center clutching a report form, hastily filled out.

"We have a caller who is positive she's seen Phoebe. She's absolutely insistent that she's at the Sears store in Alhambra right now!"

"Are they on the line?" Ward asked.

The dispatcher pointed to the blinking light on Ward's phone. He punched the button, picked up the receiver, and spoke with Al Solis, the department store's operating manager.

"Ward here."

"It's Phoebe—the missing girl," Solis said, almost stuttering, in an excited voice. "We have a customer who saw her. I've got store security guards looking now. How soon can you be here?''

Ward signaled for the dispatcher to contact Miller by radio at the command post to send a team of officers to the store in Alhambra, a mile or two outside the city limits. To Solis, Ward said it would be a matter of minutes before they arrived.

"Is your customer there?" Ward asked.

"She's with our store security officers now," Solis said. "She didn't see the male suspect because she was focusing on the girl. She did see the back of his head and his clothing, his hair, and his build. She's absolutely positive it's Phoebe Ho."

Ward, grinning, flashed a thumbs-up to the dispatcher and asked Solis to direct the security guards to seal off the exits immediately and delegate one employee in each department to monitor the changing rooms, particularly in the children's department and men's clothing. Ward told Solis he was sending out a search team and bloodhounds as soon as possible.

As he hung up the phone with one hand, he reached for the radio on the other to Ward call Ezzell. When she answered, he used police shorthand to ask her to step out of earshot of the Ho family, whom she was reinterviewing with Yeung, the Mandarin interpreter.

"Subject reports missing at Sears department store in Alhambra. Witness has positive ID. Patrol en route. Supervisor requested."

Even over the static of the radio, Ward could hear Ezzell's sudden intake of breath. "Stoddard en route. Status report on family. Ken Ho advises he had a dispute with a competitor. Molina and Robbins are en route to the Rodium swap meet in Redondo Beach," Ezzell said.

Ward signed off and picked up the phone again, this time

dialing the number of the Los Angeles County sheriff's department. He'd spoken with the sheriff's department watch commander who had offered to lend a few deputies from their specialized search and rescue unit. Ward was hoping they could deploy the unit for the Sears search. He would have to run over to the Hos' house and pick up a scent guide for the dogs, then meet them down in Alhambra, which bordered South Pasadena to the south. Ward's pulse pounded with a double dose of hope as he waited a few seconds for the sheriff's watch commander to get on the line. The tip from Ken Ho about a disgruntled competitor could explain Phoebe's disappearance, or she might be a few short miles away in a department store. This could end today, he thought. She could be home tonight.

The blue Chevy Malibu still hadn't quite recovered from climbing the hills of East Los Angeles as Molina pushed hard on the accelerator. It was 45 miles to Redondo Beach. Friday afternoons in the greater Los Angeles area usually meant slowing to a crawl over the most heavily traveled freeways. As a precaution before they left, Robbins reached into the back seat, grabbed the rotating amber police light with a magnet on the bottom, and stuck it on the roof of the car. He whooped the siren a couple of times to test it, wincing at the loudness as he flipped the switch. It was an incongrous noise coming from a 1970s muscle car.

Molina wove the groaning Chevy at a healthy clip through freeway traffic, turning over the recent developments in his mind. Ten minutes ago they had squat, and now they had a lead—possibly two. Molina decided to reserve judgment on the department store sighting. He knew people were phoning the department after spotting any Asian girl with a pageboy haircut. There were probably thousands of little girls who resembled Phoebe in Southern California.

Joyce had already checked for sex offenders. South Pasadena showed none living within city limits. They were still waiting to hear back from several departments, but Joyce had told him that most registered sex offenders didn't have an MO like this case. As a broad category, child molesters dump their victims within a few hours, or, in rare cases, the next morning. In the worst possible scenario, they would be looking for a body. Molina angrily pushed that out of his thoughts. They were going to find this little girl. The business angle was the better lead. Molina felt frustrated at not realizing earlier the motive for revenge over a bad business. If the detectives had known about Chinese culture, they would have asked. Maybe Sharon and Ken hadn't considered that possibility, either.

Before they'd left to go to the swap meet, Yeung had filled them in about dirty tricks in Chinese business culture, when the wounded party masquerading as an ordinary businessman acts as a money launderer for gangs or has underworld connections. One common form of retribution is to kidnap the other person's firstborn male child or sometimes their entire family and hold them for ransom. Perhaps this hadn't occurred to the Hos because there had been no ransom demand. Also they'd kidnapped the youngest *girl,* not a son. But anyone close to the family might have gleaned that Phoebe was the favorite child and therefore the one the parents would miss most. Molina felt anxious and a bit antsy to get going on this because so much time had passed since Phoebe's disappearance.

The Hos had also told the detectives through Yeung that Ken had another brother living in West Covina in addition to the one who lived near them. Molina hadn't had time to interview them. Making a list in his mind, Molina wanted to tackle that next. They might have some insights or other information the parents had not considered. The uncomfortable aspect of the business dispute angle was the potential contact with the Chinese underworld. There was not much gang activity in South Pasadena, other than occasional incidents that overflowed into their city limits or young wannabes who hung out with gang bangers and ditched school, committed petty thefts, and smoked marijuana. If international hoodlums had snatched Phoebe, their department was going to need a lot of help. He put that next on his mental list. He'd have to coordinate with Ward to research that if they turned up empty on the Sears search. They would need to contact the FBI and gang experts from the Los Angeles police department and pick their brains. Also, Yeung should be able to help them out.

As he got closer to the swap meet, Molina felt his tension build. All this was just speculation. There could be a gang connection. Or it could be a child molester. Or she was kidnapped by some nutcase who wanted a young child. It could be anything. Until they had more information or something pointing them in the right direction, they would have to keep every possibility in mind. He just didn't want this little girl to get away.

Molina pulled the Chevy into the swap meet parking lot. At mid-afternoon, it was getting a pre-holiday surge of business. Cars snaked around the parking lot, their drivers staking out shoppers laden with bulging plastic bags so they could swoop into their parking spot when they left. Like most swap meet sites in Southern California, the Rodium had once been a drive-in movie theater. The business office was located in the former snack bar in the dead center of an enormous lot of black asphalt.

Molina and Robbins hurried past blaring boom boxes, racks of clothing, boxes of housewares, cosmetics, snakeskin boots, frilly little girl's dresses, dried flower arrangements, and framed posters to the office. Discreetly showing his badge to the blond, big-haired manager, they got the number and the directions to the booth run by the competitor Ho had named, Henry Wu. The manager confirmed that Wu was registered to sell that day and the next.

Molina was not a tough-talking cop. He always used his head to outsmart the crooks, or sheer bullheaded stubborness to wait until they did something stupid. He and Robbins quickly found the booth and saw an Asian woman amid tables laden with open-faced cardboard boxes of unlaced athletic shoes. Same business, same swap meet, Molina thought. He wondered how bad the business dispute had been.

Wu wasn't there. They spoke with his sister, who said in halting English that he would be back the next day. Nothing more could be accomplished until they could get Yeung to interpret for them.

Shaking their heads, Molina and Robbins walked back to the beat-up Malibu. With the darkness of dusk approaching, they were caught in a flood of shoppers behind the wheel, inching their way to the parking lot exit, then navigating through the rush-hour deluge.

Stuck in traffic, Molina's mind was racing. They still had an enormous amount of work to do. Maybe it was time to back up a little and do the routine interviews that had been put on hold—the interviews with Ken Ho's brother and sister and their spouses, and the more detailed interviews with the Ho's other children, Jennifer and Damon, and the grandparents.

As soon as the Malibu got within range, Molina picked up the radio and checked in with Ward at the station to let them know they'd stuck out—temporarily—at the swap meet. He could tell by the tone of Ward's voice that Phoebe hadn't turned up at Sears, but Molina asked anyway.

"Negative," Ward said.

No use telling each other they were disappointed.

As the only unmarried detectives in the four-person detectives' unit, Molina and Ezzell teamed up. Without spouses to worry about them working too late or too long, Ezzell and Molina devoted night and day to finding Phoebe. They chased a series of tantalizing leads, only to find their hopes crumble as they hit dead end after dead end. When they caught up with Wu, the shoeseller at the swap meet, he cooperated completely, fully admitted the business dispute, and seemed genuinely concerned by Phoebe's disappearance. He even offered to help, if there was anything he could do. Between them, Molina and Ezzell had 35 years of experience, and they agreed that this man didn't have anything to hide.

With no other active leads to follow, Molina and Ezzell decided to backtrack and interview more of the extended Ho family members in hopes of uncovering something they had overlooked, or finding some clue Kenneth and Sharon Ho had been too distraught to consider. In the rush to hunt for Phoebe, and lacking an interpreter, Phoebe's grandmother, and Phoebe's brother and sister, had somehow been neglected. The detectives first sought out Kenneth Ho's two brothers and two sisters and their spouses for routine interviews. Phoebe's aunts and uncles confirmed that she was indeed the most-loved child and anyone who wanted to hurt the parents would target Phoebe. They also said Phoebe was well-mannered and a well-adjusted child who would not become friendly with strangers.

The interviews with the Ho family members who were

living under the same roof with the missing child proved to be frustrating. In separate interviews, Jennifer, Damon, and their grandmother disagreed with Sharon Ho and each other about when they last saw Phoebe. The grandmother said she got up at 6:15 a.m., made rice soup for her husband, and left the house at 7:30 a.m. without seeing Phoebe or Sharon. Damon said he got up at 7:40 a.m. and saw his mother helping Phoebe get dressed. He thought Phoebe left the house between 7:55 and 8 a.m. and he had biked to school without seeing her. Jennifer said she got up at 7 a.m., and insisted that she had helped Phoebe get dressed because her parents were not home, but then blanked out on when Phoebe left for school. The detectives gently prodded each of the family members, telling them that their stories didn't match. With Yeung interpreting, the detectives went over and over their versions of exactly what happened that morning, but none of them could give a more precise account of those crucial few minutes. Ezzell and Molina were familiar with the tendency of victims and eyewitnesses to vary widely in their accounts of the same event. Since Sharon Ho couldn't remember exactly when she kissed Phoebe goodbye, the lack of detail left detectives without anyone who could say precisely when Phoebe was last seen alive.

The detectives tracked down the neighborhood residents who weren't home when the search teams were hunting for Phoebe. An elderly woman who lived a few houses from the Hos appeared to have seen the young girl with an Asian woman that morning leading her by the hand. That didn't appear out of the ordinary—it was probably Phoebe's mother. But something didn't fit. The place on the street where she said she saw Phoebe with the woman was different from the point where Sharon Ho said she walked with Phoebe and kissed her goodbye. The discrepancy was about a block. The detectives were also unable to nail down whether or not she recognized the woman as Phoebe's mother because the elderly woman was a Dutch citizen who didn't speak English very well and had been in the country only a few months visiting her daughter.

Detectives thought they had a break in the case when Thomas Ho, one of Kenneth's brothers, reported that he'd received a phone call from an Asian male speaking in broken English asking if he had reached the family with the missing girl. When Thomas Ho said that it was his niece who was missing, the man hung up. Five minutes later, Damon Ho said he also got a phone call from a male Asian speaking in broken English asking if he had reached the Ho family who had the missing child. When he said that it was, the caller asked to speak to Damon's parents. Damon told him that they were not home because they were out looking for his sister. The caller then hung up.

Thinking they had finally heard from the kidnapper, the detectives scrambled to quickly set up a tape recorder to the phone line as well as a phone tap to trace the caller's location. A South Pasadena patrol officer was assigned to keep guard and make certain that either Sharon or Ken was at home in case they heard from the kidnapper, but the mysterious caller never phoned again.

Distressed after days passing with no word of her youngest child, Sharon Ho, in desperation, visited a fortune teller, who told her simply, "You don't look so good." The Hos' business suffered, as they needed to make themselves available whenever the detectives had questions. They temporarily suspended their business operations. Sharon drove Jennifer to surrounding cities where they would blanket malls, grocery stores, and neighborhood shopping centers with the missing child flyers. Neighbors often saw Sharon driving very slowly down the street with her windows rolled down in the December chill, calling Phoebe's name. At night, Sharon wept until she fell asleep. An intensely private person, Kenneth found it difficult to think of events or situations to tell the police that might have some connection to Phoebe's disappearance. Yeung, a Hong Kong native who came from a family of police officers, spent time with Kenneth to earn his trust and make him feel comfortable with him, in hopes something might spark his memory.

Finally Yeung triumphantly reported to the detectives that Kenneth mentioned another competitor—with whom he'd had "serious business problems" two months ago—who might have kidnapped Phoebe. Since it was well known that she was his special child, this would be a way of hurting him and his family very much, he told Yeung.

Dean Cho was also in the shoe business. Fired for embezzlement by one former employer, he was being sued by another former business partner and was in danger of losing his house to a creditor over a $20,000 debt. The deadline for the foreclosure on his home was December 31. Although Kenneth had turned it down, Cho still carried a grudge over Kenneth's being chosen over Cho for a lucrative sales position with another shoe company.

The detectives' first contact with Cho had been curious. Edgy and alarmed at the police visit, Cho had said he was still working for the company something, Ezzell and Molina knew was no longer true. He also tried to point the finger at the woman he said was still his employer, Mrs. Lin, by saying she "had information that would help them out." Cho warned the detectives that she distrusted the police and wouldn't cooperate with them. But even more curious than Cho's suspicious attitude was the enormous warehouse he leased just 10 minutes from South Pasadena, in San Gabriel. It was 9,000 square feet and stood virtually empty, save for a few boxes of mixmatched shoes and old, unpopular styles. Up to his neck in debt, accused of embezzlement at two companies, and facing foreclosure of his home, for what reason was he paying a monthly lease on a huge warehouse? After a lengthy interview with Mrs. Lin, who turned out to be helpful, not hostile, as Cho had warned, both detectives thought he had a motive and the means to abduct Phoebe.

Molina and Ezzell decided to set up a surveillance of Cho and returned to the station to make the arrangements. They would begin at 7 a.m., when Cho said he had a business appointment in Marina del Rey, a seaside city.

"Nothing like this has happened here before."

Lee Prentiss, mayor of South Pasadena, looked out over the crowd of residents, parents with children, reporters, and news crews gathered around him at the press conference at Arroyo Vista School. He was outside the school on the grass. Next to him was state senator Art Torres of Los Angeles, South Pasadena police chief William Reese, and other city, county, and state officials to announce the Find Phoebe Reward Fund, headed by George Brown, who was there with representatives from the Adam Walsh Child Resource Center, letting the mayor make the announcement. Hugh Edwards had torn himself away from his copy machines long enough to put on a tie. He was there with his wife and their two girls. It was 3 p.m., and parents who came to school to pick up their children lingered to see what was going on and learn if there was any news about Phoebe.

"Our crime rate is one-third the rate of Los Angeles, and we are proud of that," the mayor continued. "For this to happen on our quiet streets with our fine police force has amazed us, but the entire community is resolved to find her."

Torres stepped to the microphones and said he would do "anything in his power to help reunite young Phoebe Ho with her family."

He and the other politicians spoke about finding the scoundrel who had abducted the innocent schoolgirl and made a plea for funds from the community to the Find Phoebe Center.

Brown told the crowd that the outpouring of support from local churches and individuals was funding the reward and also being used to defray the expenses of the Find Phoebe Center. The next step would be to set up a storefront and a hotline, but more donations would be needed.

After looking at Edwards, who he knew was making thousands of copies at his own expense, Brown added that the funds were specifically for the storefront and phone lines and that PIP franchises locally and throughout the Southland were donating their time, money, and paper.

"Every PIP location will be shutting down commercial production on Friday to print one million posters in English, Spanish, and Chinese. We're still working out the details, but we're hoping that the Boy Scouts and Girl Scouts will then help in distributing the posters to every home, every business, every shopper, every apartment complex, every office building, every government office in every city in southern California," Brown said.

Principal Helen Cease told the solemn crowd that for the past several days, she and the teachers had held assemblies for the children and made the teachers available after school in case the youngsters wanted to talk.

Looking directly at the TV crews, Cease said, "Many children are confused by the presence of the media and don't know what's going on. We are talking to the children and identifying those who we think may need individual counseling."

The school superintendent said students from nearby schools in the district were also getting counseling and warned parents to be particularly attentive to problems their children might have during the upcoming Christmas vacation.

Sharon and Kenneth Ho, looking haggard, stood nearby. Sharon dabbed at her eyes with a pink tissue and the couple thanked the residents, shook hands with the politicians, and even shook hands with reporters to thank them for covering the event.

Ward wanted to talk to both detectives, so Ezzell looked around for the coffeepot. It was a trick she learned after years of being female in an all-male workplace. With the front lobby overrun with reporters, they would think she was just a secretary, not the lead detective on the case, and ignore her. She picked up the coffeepot, walked past the frenzy at the front counter, and found Molina talking with Ward near the dispatch counter, where phones were ringing constantly.

"Now we're getting the loonies," Ward said, holding out four of the phone report sheets.

"We've had four psychics call today. Two had dreams about Phoebe and one had a vision. One sees some guy in a white helmet standing over a motorcycle, one sees an elderly couple in a older house with aqua trim and Phoebe holding a rust-colored washcloth over a bump on her head. This one sees a male suspect, twenty-five to thirty, in a red or yellow van with curtains and an old red Victorian house. This lady has a vision about Phoebe being abducted by a guy with a 'pretty face.' She gives a location at a duplex in the city—on Pine Street.

"They're all yours, folks."

Ward handed them to Ezzell, who told Ward about the surveillance set up for the next morning on Dean Cho. Detectives from Alhambra and San Gabriel were on board, as well as sheriff's deputies. The chiefs were also throwing in undercover cars. He would be contacting the FBI to see if they had an expert on the Chinese version of the mob.

A dispatcher walked up and handed the next batch of messages to Ward. He divided them into thirds and as they thumbed through the forms, Molina pulled out one and read aloud, "Yellow sweatshirt, white shoes, and a pink headband behind the Pasadena Nissan lot on Colorado Boulevard. I'll go on this one."

Ezzell, still holding the coffeepot, sighed and asked Ward for the form with the report from the psychic about the "pretty boy."

"We'll do more follow-ups tonight after we check these out," she said. "Keep in touch."

It was over almost before it had begun.

From the way he drove his Toyota sedan, Cho seemed to know he was being tailed. With his wife and their toddler in the car, he screeched out of his driveway at 9:20 a.m., jumping from lane to lane in heavy traffic, before getting on the freeway going west. Molina and Ezzell were alone in separate cars, as were two additional officers. They avoided the radio, in case he was watching any of their cars. Cho stayed in the fast lane. One of the officers tried to maintain a steady pace but wound up in front of him when Cho slowed down. He suddenly lurched right across the lanes, slammed on his brakes and pulled off on the right median strip, where state transportation workers in orange vests were trimming shrubbery and picking up trash.

The police helplessly passed him. When they were able

to turn around and return, Cho was gone. Unable to reach Molina by radio, Ezzell and the other two undercover units went back to the station to regroup.

Molina had been able to get off at the very next exit and found a gas station where he could watch Cho, who had approached one of the orange-vested workers. He was able to get back on the freeway when Cho did. Cho headed north, the opposite direction from Marina del Rey. Molina kept up with him as long as he could, but Cho threaded the Toyota smoothly through mid-morning traffic and Molina couldn't keep him in view. He headed back to the station.

This guy was it, Molina thought—wasn't he?

Molina suspected Cho bore the consciousness of guilt to spot the officers tailing him and the ability to evade all four of them. A San Gabriel undercover officer was assigned to watch Cho's house. Ezzell and Molina asked for more back-up officers from other departments. If they were going to do a surveillance, they'd need twice as many officers and a more comprehensive plan to accommodate Cho's hardball driving tactics.

Ezzell and Molina called Yeung to contact Sharon and Kenneth Ho and bring them back to the station to press them for more details about Cho and the dispute with the family. Cho was acting suspicious, but the motive seemed to lack something. There had been no ransom demand, so what was he planning to do with Phoebe? Maybe the family could tell them something. Ezzell coordinated with Ward to do a follow-up with the FBI's Chinese mafia experts to find out what they could about Cho and whether this MO of taking a family member and mutely keeping him or her for several days fit any familiar pattern.

Kenneth and Sharon looked drained but anxious, and the

detectives were exhausted but keyed up at the prospect of finding a real, live suspect who could lead them to Phoebe. The detectives asked them about Cho. Had he ever been to their house? Had he ever met Phoebe before? Had he ever showed her any special attention? What were the details of the dispute? Did Cho ever make any threats?

A frantic knock at the door interrupted the interview and Ward popped his head in the door.

"'Scuse me, folks," Ward said, motioning with his head to Molina and Ezzell. "I've got to talk to the detectives for a moment."

Outside in the hallway, Ward spoke fast and low.

"We have a confidential informant who says Phoebe is at a house in Los Angeles. He's positive. I've already contacted the LAPD. They're sending the SWAT team and back-up officers.

"Wear vests," Ward said, as the detectives rushed past.

With as much composure as Molina and Ezzell could muster, they stuck their head in the door and explained that something had come up and they had to leave for a while, but they would be back. The Hos stared back, searching their faces, but the detectives knew Yeung would translate for them and explain. Despite their desire to tell the Hos what they knew, they could not, just as they could never share with them details of the investigation. Molina and Ezzell grabbed their equipment and headed toward Los Angeles.

"It was a male Hispanic," Ward told them over the radio. "His exact words were, 'I do not want to get involved. I do not want to have anything to do with this, but your missing little girl is at a house in Ulysses Avenue. She is definitely there.' A patrol officer cruised by and spotted an Asian female matching Phoebe's description through the front window," Ward said.

Molina pushed the accelerator down, the siren blaring. He cut the siren a mile from the house. As they pulled up to the curb two houses away, Molina could see three LAPD black-and-white patrol cars parked near the house and a SWAT team maneuvering into position behind the open patrol car doors.

Molina and Ezzell drew their weapons and crouched behind their open doors. Ezzell grabbed the rifles from inside the car, kept one, and slid one across to Molina. In camouflage gear, the SWAT team had automatic long-range weapons strapped to their backs and held handguns at the sides of their legs. They snaked along the shrubbery by the neighboring houses on either side of the modest stucco home, staying out of view of the front window. Everyone moved quickly to avoid having neighbors coming out of their houses to gawk and alert the suspect inside. The SWAT officers continued moving along the side of the house. Two officers stayed along one wall and four more stationed themselves on the porch; two each on either side of the front door.

Straining to look inside the house, Molina could see an Asian man and a young girl just sitting down to dinner. The man was eating soup. With the other officers in position around the house, the SWAT team officer knocked on the front door. The man came to the door.

Molina felt himself gulping for air. Just behind him was a young girl. It was Phoebe!

The SWAT officers moved in, ordered the man to kneel, then lay him flat on the floor, facedown. Molina and Ezzell and the other officers rushed into the house and Molina grabbed the young girl by the hand and hustled her outside.

Safe outside, he knelt down to look at her.

It wasn't Phoebe.

The girl started the cry. Molina felt like crying, too. He took the youngster by the hand and led her back inside the house. He managed to croak, "It's not her" to Ezzell, the SWAT team, and the officers outside.

Molina and Ezzell apologized to the man and the little girl, explaining that there was a little girl missing who looked very much like his little girl. Molina was not surprised when he said that he knew about Phoebe's disappearance and understood they had the best intentions. The fact that the man was such a nice guy made Molina feel even worse.

The detectives thanked the officers and the SWAT team and they all left.

Driving back to the station, it was very quiet. Molina felt himself choking up. He wanted to find this girl. Most of all, he wanted to beat this guy at his own game. This unknown person. A lousy child kidnapper. Some scumbag who snatches innocent kids off the streets. He wanted the girl back, and he wanted the guy behind bars.

Molina and Ezzell walked back into the station, dumped their gear, and went back into the room where the Hos were waiting. Molina saw them searching their eyes, but he put on his practiced, detached demeanor and picked up on the interview where they left off.

There wasn't much more to say about Cho than what Kenneth had already told them. By now, Sharon thought someone had picked up Phoebe and taken her to a nice home and would give her good food and good clothing.

As Yeung translated her words into English, he included his own observation that she was suffering severe stress and depression. It was probably making her say things that didn't sound right.

Molina and Ezzell nodded and did their best to comfort her. They were finished with the interview for the time being and told the Hos that they could go home and should rest.

The two detectives returned to their desks and sorted through the latest messages. The psychics were in one pile, the sightings in another. Ezzell showed a phone message from Mrs. Lin, Cho's ex-employer, to Molina as she punched in the phone number.

Ezzell wrote down an address and agreed to meet Mrs. Lin there in 30 minutes.

"Let's go," Ezzell said. "Mrs. Lin remembered she has an empty house in Hacienda Heights and Cho has keys to it. It's a big house and it's in a remote area. She's meeting us there."

With the detectives halfway out the door, the phone rang again. Ezzell picked it up. She frowned as she wrote down three names, three addresses, a license plate number, and a date. Ezzell hung up and gave the paper to Molina.

"That was Sergeant Dennis Hanby from Alhambra PD. They have a registered sex offender by the name of Ward Bland. He has a previous arrest for molesting and torturing a young boy.

"Hanby said he's a handyman for a Gary Thayer and rents out a room in his home in San Marino. Bland has an Asian girlfriend or wife. I'll take an officer with me to check out the house. You go see what Mr. Bland has to say," Ezzell said.

Back at the police station by 5 a.m., Ezzell and Molina compared notes. They had everything in place for their surveillance of Cho to begin in 2 hours. Curiously enough, Cho had asked Mrs. Lin to meet with him at her office and she'd immediately phoned the police. She agreed to wear a body wire that would tape the conversation and transmit it to officers listening in the next room. If she ran into trouble, the officers could be there in seconds.

Mrs. Lin's large house in Hacienda Heights could have sheltered Phoebe and her captor. Her tenants had moved out unexpectedly, leaving the electricity and heat still working. Other than a floor lamp and an old mattress, the house was empty, and a thorough search of the surrounding hillside showed no sign of Phoebe or anything unusual. If she had been kept at the house, there was no trace of her there now.

Molina updated Ezzell on what he'd found out about Bland, whose name was actually Warren James Bland, not Ward Bland.

Molina never got to see Bland, but he spoke with Gene Thayer, the elderly father of Bland's employer, Gary Thayer. The younger Thayer was a firefighter in San Marino who had a side business of painting and light construction and repairs. Bland was one of his workers. The elder Thayer, who was renting out a room to Bland, didn't seem interested in talking to Molina and gave minimal answers. The only thing Gene Thayer said was that Bland left for work each day between 7:30 and 8 a.m., returned home to shower at 5 p.m., then went out again until midnight or 2 a.m.

When he asked if Bland went to work every day, Thayer said, "Well, he leaves here every day around 8 a.m. I can't say he goes to work."

Ezzell and Molina decided to speak to Bland the next day, after they had the surveillance up and running and after they had taped Cho talking to Mrs. Lin.

At 5:30 a.m., officers from San Gabriel and Alhambra started arriving to review the strategy for the surveillance. Two of those were on the previous day's chase and they discussed various techniques to keep a lock on a suspect in crowded road conditions. Then they tested the handheld radios and surveyed the freeway maps to discuss who would take which off-ramps in the event Cho pulled the same stunt he had before—stopping on the freeway shoulder.

At 6:30 a.m., they headed down to Cho's house to start the surveillance, but the detectives were unprepared for Cho's ambition. He was already gone. The Toyota and his blue Dodge van were not parked in front of his house.

Determined to slam shut all loopholes, Ezzell sent one detective to the Rodium swap meet, another detective to the La Mirada swap meet, and another to the Gardena swap meet to see if he was registered at any of those places to sell shoes that day. She summoned another team of undercover officers to watch the house and wait for Cho to get home, and sent Molina to check on the Dutch lady and on other residents who had been gone the first morning of the search.

Earlier, one of the detectives had told Ezzell that three streets had been left out of the first night's search. This was as good a time as any to go back and correct that, Ezzell thought. She pulled out the maps and called the sheriff's department for a deputy with a bloodhound.

The dispatcher interrupted Ezzell's call to tell her Warren Bland was on the line. "He said his parole officer asked him to call. He wants to come in and see you."

Ezzell knew that wasn't true. Molina had talked briefly to the parole officer, as well as Thayer, and specifically asked that he *not* call. They wanted to catch Bland at home.

"Take his number and tell him we'll call him back," Ezzell said.

"I already asked and he wants to talk to you. He wants to be interviewed. He says he'll hold until you're done," the dispatcher said.

Ezzell thought this was odd. Why was he so eager to come in to see detectives? To prove he had nothing to do with Phoebe? They had their hands full already with the investigation of Cho heating up. It seemed ill-timed.

"Okay," she said, then finished with the sheriff's supervisor. He agreed to bring a canine officer and a bloodhound to the South Pasadena station in 30 minutes.

As soon as she hung up, the dispatcher transferred Bland's call.

"Lieutenant Ezzell, this is Warren James Bland," he said. "My parole officer said you were looking for me, and that it had to do with the disappearance of the little girl. I had nothing to do with it and I want to come right now for an interview."

Now? I don't like this at all, Ezzell thought. His voice sounded gentlemanly but stubborn, like a senior citizen demanding to see his grandkids. It was 10 a.m., she was meeting with the sheriff's canine unit in a half hour, they had to do the search, and they had to coordinate the surveillance of Cho and then the conversation with Mrs. Lin. They were already looking at two other child molesters and there was nothing to tie Bland in to Phoebe's disappearance. This was just inconvenient.

"I can't do it now," Ezzell said. "Why do you want to come in right now?"

"One of your detectives was at my work asking embarrassing questions and my parole officer said you were asking about me in regard to this little girl that's been all over the news. I'm working at a good job and I want to keep it.

"I don't want any more officers coming around and asking questions, so I want to come in and get it over with. What time can you see me?"

He was persistent, Ezzell thought. She tried to think of a time. If he came in too early in the afternoon, the press would probably still be hanging around. But she didn't want his interview to interfere with Mrs. Lin, who was coming in at 5 p.m. to be fitted with the body wire by detectives. Cho was coming to see her at 6:30 p.m.

"How about . . . 3:45 p.m.?" she said.

"I'll be at the station at 3:45 p.m. Thank you, Lieutenant," Bland said, emphasizing "Lieutenant."

Well, Ezzell thought, maybe he got riled up about detectives snooping around his work. Or he has some other good reason to push his way in to the police station.

She was halfway out the door when her buzzer sounded again.

"Ezzell," she said.

"I have a Mrs. Lin on the phone for you. She says it's urgent," the dispatcher said.

"Put her through."

Mrs. Lin's melodic voice came over the phone. "Hello. I thought this was important. Mr. Cho just visited with me. He says he's leaving the country for good. He's going back to Taiwan. He says he's not coming back."

Ezzell's mind was racing.

"Did he say when he was going?"

"No, he didn't," Mrs. Lin said.

Green shirt. White pants. Beige jacket. His slicked-back hair was the dishwater gray of an aging blond. Warren James Bland in his all-polyester outfit struck Molina as an aging rummy you'd see at the track who can't accept getting old, but still fancies himself a ladies' man. Bland was strangely, calmly composed. Something about this guy gave Molina a bad feeling.

Molina and Ezzell walked him to an interview room. Bland reminded the detectives it was they who had approached his parole officer about the missing child. In a practiced fashion, Bland recited the most recent additions to his résumé. He was released from state prison for child molestation in January 1986, and was working for Gene Thayer's son, Gary Thayer, as a handyman-painter.

Ezzell asked him, "Where have you been working the first two weeks of December?"

"I've been painting Pat Haden's house in San Marino," Bland said, with a hint of a twinkle in his eye. "You know him, he's the former football player. Played for the Rams.

"I just finished that job today."

Molina long ago had learned to resist the temptation to roll his eyes or show any reaction to things people said to him. It was one hell of a convenient alibi, if true. He stayed blank-faced.

"What were your hours for the first two weeks of December?" Ezzell asked.

"I always leave the house at 7:30 a.m., drive over to the Winchell's Donuts at Huntington Boulevard and Garfield Avenue for breakfast, then I drive over to the Hadens' house, which is only a few blocks away.

"I always get there between 8:00 to 8:30 a.m. On Monday, I'll start at Mrs. Miller's house."

"Do you have a girlfriend?" Ezzell asked.

"Yes, her name is Evie, and she lives in West Covina. I only see her on weekends. During the week, after work, I go to AA meetings. All of my problems in the past were caused by alcohol and now that I don't drink anymore, I don't have any more problems," Bland said, referring to his child molestation convictions as "problems."

"Are you going to talk to my girlfriend and the Hadens?" Bland wanted to know.

"I probably will," Ezzell said.

"Well, my girlfriend doesn't know about my past, and neither do the Hadens," Bland said. "All they know is that I once had a drinking problem."

This is all just too rehearsed, Molina said to himself. He's probably had a lot of practice talking to cops over the years. But listening to Bland made Molina want to take a closer look. He was disturbingly icy.

Ezzell wrapped up the questions and the detectives said goodbye to Bland.

"This guy bugs me in a big way," Molina said as soon as Bland was well out of earshot.

"Same here," Ezzell said.

Molina and Ezzell knew their hands were full. The detectives on swap meet detail had checked in hours ago by radio—Cho was nowhere to be found. The Rodium was going through a change in recordkeeping and couldn't say whether Cho was selling shoes that day. The business offices in La Mirada and Gardena didn't keep records of sellers who did not have permanent spaces. A walk-through of the swap meets showed several Asian families selling various types of shoes. Without having seen Cho for themselves and without a photo of him, the two detectives strolling through the swap meets couldn't say whether Cho was at either swap meet selling shoes or not. The team watching the house said Cho hadn't shown up. Ezzell sent the detectives on swap meet detail to relieve the two watching Cho's house.

With Cho ready to leave the country, they had to revise plans again and perhaps bring in the FBI in an active role to track Cho if he left the country. Ezzell had assigned an officer to call the airlines to find out which carriers flew to Taiwan and how often they departed from the Los Angeles International Airport. If she didn't get cooperation from the airlines, she was prepared to get a judge to issue a subpoena to force the airlines into telling them whether Cho had booked a ticket for himself and a young girl to Taiwan.

It was 5:30 p.m. Mrs. Lin was in a back office with detectives Stoddard and Robbins, who were hiding a tiny microphone and microcassette recorder in her clothing. They were teaching her how to activate it just before she met with him, as the cassette would record only for 60 minutes. Molina and Ezzell were making final surveillance plans with the other two detectives. This time, they couldn't lose sight of him.

The detectives watching Cho's house radioed Ezzell.

"Subject just pulled up in the blue Dodge. Looks like his wife is driving the Toyota. Over."

Cho was back. Now was the time to put the surveillance plan to the test.

"Stand by. Back-up units are on the way. Subject should be headed to next location," Ezzell said, referring to Mrs. Lin's place of business. "Back-up units and primary surveillance units are ready if he changes plans. Over."

Everything was in place. They were cutting it close. Mrs. Lin was going to drive back to her place of business and wait. Stoddard and Robbins would stay with her and be ready by the time Cho was scheduled to arrive.

Ezzell and Molina would be in separate cars and join in the active surveillance only if Cho decided not to show at Mrs. Lin's. They would drive roughly the same route in the same direction, but on parallel streets, so Cho wouldn't see their cars.

The phone on Ezzell's desk was ringing again.

Molina got to it first.

"This is Detective Mike Lackie from the Riverside sheriff's department. We think we have your missing girl . . ."

Molina caught Ezzell's eye and motioned toward the phone, grinning.

"We wanted to confirm the ID. She has on pink pants, a red jacket with green sleeves, and white sneakers. The coroner has taken her to the morgue and we need someone to make an ID . . ."

Molina froze and his throat felt like someone had twisted it into a knot. The tears were already rolling down his face when he handed the phone to Ezzell.

CHAPTER FIVE

Someone is looking for this little girl.

Detective Michael Lackie stood on top of a fire truck in the dark, damp December chill trying to get a better look at the tiny figure lying in the drainage ditch. The criminalists hadn't arrived yet to process the evidence and clear a path to the crime scene. Lackie surveyed his latest murder case from the fire truck, parked on the blacktop to avoid destroying footprints or tire tracks in the dirt shoulder that might have been left there by the killer. A clanging gasoline generator powered the portable lights illuminating the embankment below. From the top of the truck, Lackie adjusted the lamps to aim them squarely at the child-sized body, throwing light on her clothing. Lackie's first priority, behind preserving evidence at the scene, was to identify the body and notify the frantic parents. This was his fourth child murder in as many years, and it wasn't getting any easier. Wherever they found a child's body, there was usually an armada of law enforcement on the hunt and parents spending sleepless nights worrying about their youngster. Lackie recalled something about a missing little girl from the suburbs of Los Angeles. He would have a deputy check the missing persons bulletins as soon as he got a firm description.

After 13 years as a police officer, Lackie had worked the homicide unit for 6 years and was considered one of the best in the Riverside County sheriff's department. He'd never planned to be a cop, but in the mid-1970s, when he'd graduated from high school, the economy was in a slump, and working for the government meant steady work. His father, a theater manager, warned him not to go into the movie theater business. Lackie needed no convincing. His cousin was the chief of police in a nearby city and other relatives were police officers. Being outside and working with people as a cop seemed like the bright side of government work, where most people wind up chained to a desk in a cubicle.

Lackie wanted to get this girl moved as quickly as possible to the morgue to allow a criminalist to process the body for trace evidence. He couldn't gamble on finding an eyewitness who saw anyone dumping a body or commiting the murder. He figured with this case, hairs and fibers clinging to this dead child's clothing, or even cigarette butts, shoeprints, or soda cans could help them identify the murderer.

Except for the people who'd found the body and firefighters who'd responded to the scene first, no one, not even himself, had been permitted to approach the body until the criminalist arrived. He knew they were on their way, but he hoped they would come soon. The night was damp and a storm was moving in. He didn't want to get caught in a deluge that would destroy evidence.

Lackie pulled out his notepad, looked at his wristwatch, and wrote down the time. It was 5:37 p.m. The body had been discovered at about 4:30 p.m. He moved along the edge of the fire truck to get a better view. He could make out the girl, lying on her left side, her face in the dirt. Her arms were splayed at the odd angles one would expect if she had been hastily tossed from a car and rolled down the embankment, but he made no assumptions. The first thing he had long ago learned about investigating a murder was to start with a blank slate. He didn't know if someone had walked her down into the ditch and killed her there, or killed her elsewhere and walked down with the body, if she had been thrown, or if she had been tossed on top of the embankment and rolled down the small slope. He thought he saw dirt on her clothes but would make no note until he knew for certain. Red jacket with a design on the back, turquoise sleeves. Pink leotard-style pants. White tennis shoes. From that distance, he could see no weapons or obvious wounds.

Thorough and meticulous by nature, he was a detective who favored the art of detecting with a scholarly touch. Everything was important, anything could be significant, and it all needed to be documented. He typed all of his reports single-spaced. He recorded what he found and to whom he had spoken at each stage of the investigation and the time everything happened. Lackie's genuine love for the English language made him popular with prosecutors who praised his reports, written plainly but in fanatical detail.

Lackie pulled out his pocket temperature gauge and took note of the air temperature, 59 degrees, and wrote himself a note to take the ground temperature once the crime scene was cleared. He noted the air was a bit damp, the dirt and roadway were dry, the fog was starting to roll in; it had rained two days ago, and showers were forecast for that night. There was no wind, and visibility was good. One time Lackie had been stung, and that was once too many. It was a murder trial where the body was found on a cold concrete slab in an enclosed room. While it is commonplace to take the ambient air temperature, Lackie had failed to take the temperature of the slab, the temperature next to the body, and the temperature of the air coming from the heating system because the suspect's defense attorney thought all those temperatures were critical to pinpoint the time of death.

The suspect's lawyer had tried to poke holes in the entire case based on that, waving Lackie's police report in front of the jury, saying his investigation was shoddy and those details *should* have been noted, but weren't. The jury didn't buy it and convicted the guy, but Lackie was determined never to let it happen again.

The episode only strengthened the detective's resolve to immerse himself in the crime scene, study the clues, impose a zero tolerance on mistakes, and gather the facts into an airtight noose to convict the sorry creeps who kill, particularly those who kill kids. He couldn't soothe the pain of parents burying children who suffer violent deaths, but he satisfied his sense of justice by nailing down every possibility so that the killers didn't get away with murder.

In his notes, Lackie wrote that a body of a young man had been found several months earlier a few yards from where this girl had been dumped. That case quickly closed and the suspect was in custody, but he put it down anyway. Turning around on top of the truck, he could see, in most directions, desolate desert. Off to his right, as he faced the embankment, were the distant lights of civilization. To his back were the freeway and the off ramp the killer probably drove on to dump the body. In a remote area like this, he wasn't likely to find any eyewitnesses.

Lackie had grown up in Riverside when the desert terrain attracted retirees, large families, people who liked solitude, and an odd smattering of outlaw biker gangs. In recent years, the ugly duckling desert had blossomed into a boomtown. Because of its three-digit summertime temperatures and smog-ridden air, the high desert offered cheap and plentiful real estate. Suburbanites from Los Angeles County had migrated en masse, as had light industry, manufacturing plants, and service businesses. Nicknamed the Inland Empire, building and construction were at an all-time high. The building boom made Riverside County one of the fastest-growing areas in the country. Despite the growth, there was plenty of undeveloped land. Next to some of the newest, nicest tract homes and closed-gate communities were acres of emptiness. On the average of once a month, the sheriff's homicide unit responded to calls from campers or rock climbers who found a body. Most of the time, days, months, and sometimes years passed between the time the luckless person was killed and the time another individual found him, making identification of the person difficult and an investigation and collection of clues nearly impossible. Scavenger animals, insects, and the ravages of the sun, wind, and heat quickly decompose bodies and destroy evidence before investigators can gather it. Miraculously, this body apparently had been dead for just a few hours before an off-duty security guard, Larry Scarberry, had found her. A patrol deputy, who had immediately sealed off the crime scene with yellow tape, had briefly interviewed Scarberry, who was temporarily down on his luck and living out of his car. He worked nights guarding a nearby housing tract construction site. During the day, he walked along various highways with a big, plastic trash bag, gathering aluminum cans and glass bottles and turning them in for cash at recycling centers.

Glen Avon, the unincorporated county area where the girl was found, was a semi-rural area, another piece of desert being consumed by housing tracts and trailer parks. After finding the body, Scarberry had dropped his bag of cans and bottles so he could find his way back to the body and run to the nearest phone at a board-and-care home for the elderly about a mile away. Three nurses and a receptionist came back with him to see if they could resuscitate the girl, but she was obviously dead and they made no lifesaving attempts. A crew of firefighter-paramedics were the first emergency personnal to show up. One of them ran down the embankment and put his fingers against her neck to check her pulse but felt none. He also grabbed her arm to see if he could rouse her, but the entire body moved. To Lackie, that meant she was probably in full rigor mortis, meaning she had been dead for about 12 hours.

Finding an intact body relatively soon after death was a good sign, because it meant there was a chance of finding trace evidence that would be more likely to lead them to the killer.

The watch commander notified Lackie, the on-duty deputy district attorney, a team of criminalists from the state Department of Justice, a crime scene photographer, and back-up patrol officers to block off the street and keep spectators and motorists away from the crime scene.

Lackie climbed down from the fire truck and he saw the coroner's van arrive. The criminalists' truck was already there and he saw criminalist Faye Springer get out. That was a relief. If this was going to be a circumstantial evidence case, she would be the first person he would choose to process the crime scene. She was the best in the state for analyzing trace evidence. Springer had built a solid reputation as a hair-and-fiber analyst over the years, particularly after helping police nab a serial killer the press dubbed the trash bag murderer for his fondness for bagging his victims in Hefty bags. Lackie felt comfortable stepping back so she could work, leaving him free to study the crime scene without second-guessing her decisions or worrying if all the evidence was collected properly.

Lackie summoned a deputy, asked him to review the missing persons bulletins, then briefed the new arrivals.

Springer went back to her truck to get her tools. The photographer went with the criminalists to take the standard orientation pictures of the area, the body, all shoeprints, including the bottoms of the shoes belonging to Scarberry, the civilian witnesses, the firefighters, and the first patrol officer at the scene. The criminalists were going to remove all other trace evidence and clear the area to allow Springer to get close to the body. The deputy Lackie had assigned to contact the national bulletins returned and they spoke quietly.

"It looks like the missing girl from South Pasadena. Her name is Phoebe Ho," the deputy reported.

It was going to be a long night. Lackie assigned Sanchez to oversee the criminalists and take the temperature next to the body while he called the South Pasadena police department by phone. Lackie never used his police radio to broadcast critical information about a homicide case because the local newspapers, wire services, and TV stations have police scanners and routinely listen to the airwaves. Lackie wanted to let the criminalists work without interruption. He was not going to have the press mucking up his crime scene.

Faye Springer never planned on being a criminalist, much less walking around tumbleweed-strewn fields at dinnertime plucking debris off dead bodies. As a college student, she'd had a natural affinity for math and science, but she'd resisted going to medical school because everyone else was pre-med and she wanted to do something different. On the eve of graduation, she spotted a want ad for a technician's job at a state forensics lab. She had no idea what forensics was, but it sounded interesting. Springer was hired and she spent

2 years in toxicology, (testing blood and urine for drugs and alcohol) and testifying mostly at drunk-driving trials and hearings for parolees who failed random drug tests. They started giving her more difficult and unusual cases, such as looking for poisons or prescription drugs in the blood and bile of homicide victims. Later she was cross-trained as a criminalist in hair and fiber analysis, tire tracks, toolmarks, and firearms, but it was in trace evidence that she excelled. After several years, she and two other criminalists were sent to Riverside County in the early 1970s to start a new crime lab as part of a state expansion program.

Over the years, Springer resisted getting into management because she liked the problem-solving aspect of her work. But processing a crime scene at a homicide often meant stretching the workday into the wee hours of the morning.

Sometimes Springer worked all night, sometimes it was her criminalist husband's turn. Since they worked at the same lab, each knew when the other would be tied up with a crime scene. Springer didn't mind the long hours. But one of the hardest aspects was working literally face-to-face with those who have succumbed to violent deaths. Kid cases were the worst. Springer learned to push her emotions aside and concentrate.

The obvious, best approach to the body was to walk about 75 feet down the road to make certain they didn't destroy the killer's shoeprints or tire tracks in the dirt shoulder, cross the dirt shoulder, walk down the embankment, cross the field and then make left turns until they approached the body from the center of the field. Kits in hand, Springer led the way as they kept their eyes on the ground and stepped carefully, their breath making small, foggy clouds in the night air. They walked silently, looking for shoeprints, drag marks, or any signs of trampled brush. Springer noted there was no indication anyone had walked in the brush for some time. As the group got closer to the body, she motioned for the photographer to take pictures at regular intervals. When they got within six feet of the body, Springer saw a number of footprints in the soft dirt, a beer bottle in a brown paper bag, a cigarette butt, and a crumpled foil candy wrapper. She pointed out each item to the photographer, who took photos from where he stood as the criminalists gave them a number and wrote them down on an evidence list. Sanchez drew out a rough sketch of the body with the shoeprints and the evidence around the body. Sanchez made a second sketch mapping out the crude dirt terrain of the drainage ditch and where the body lay in relation to the embankment. Afterwards, the photographer got closer, taking photos of the body and the other evidence from various angles.

The criminalists then went to work. He measured the distance each item was from the body and mapped that out on the sketch. He did the same with the footprint impressions in the soft dirt. Conscious of the prediction for rain that evening, the criminalist was thorough, but did not waste time. With everything mapped out and photographed, the criminalist donned Latex gloves and carefully picked up the cigarette butt and the candy wrapper, placing them in separate bags. He picked up the Budweiser beer bottle in the paper bag, poured about two ounces of liquid into an evidence container, then placed the bag, the bottle, and the liquid in separate containers. Each bag was marked with the evidence numbers corresponding to the numbers on the sketch of the crime scene. The bags were taped shut with evidence tape and the criminalist initialed each bag.

Springer carefully spread a plastic tarp next to the small body in the dirt, unpacked her evidence kit, and took a closer look at the child's face. Her eyes were closed and her straight black hair was messy and streaked with dirt. Ants were crawling on her face and had left small red bite marks on her cheek. Small dirt clods clung to the little girl's jacket, hair, and face. Her light pink pants were streaked with dirt, probably from when she'd rolled down the embankment. There were several inch-long hairs and fibers on her jacket and what looked like a little furball on the bottom of one shoe. There were also tiny white spots on her clothing in a sporadic pattern. Springer found a few on her pants, a couple on her jacket, and some on her shirt. She had no idea what they were.

From her kit, Springer removed a smaller box of instruments and removed a roll of scotch tape and set aside a stack of individually wrapped plastic petri dishes, tweezers, and Latex gloves. Crouched near the girl's outstretched hand, Springer put on her gloves, pinched off a small piece of tape, and gently pressed it against the girl's left hand, then stretched the tape, sticky-side down, over the open mouth of the petri dish. She could fit four lengths of tape across each petri dish. Then she fastened down the lid of the petri dish and taped it shut to secure each one. For each bit of evidence removed, Sanchez wrote down the time it was removed on a crime scene evidence report. Springer moved around the body, taking tape lifts of the hands and wrists, each side of the face, the back of the jacket, the pants, and the front of the T-shirt under the jacket. When she moved to the little girl's feet, she noticed the tiny white tennis shoes were fastened with velcro instead of shoelaces. She pulled off another length of tape and lifted the whitish fuzz ball from the bottom of the right shoe.

When she was almost through, she told the technician to summon the coroner's investigator so they could expedite the processing of the body at the morgue. The last bits of evidence she took were samples of soil and vegetation from near the area. Sanchez took the temperature of the ground next to Phoebe's body. It was 61 degrees.

The coronor's investigators carried the metal gurney, over which was draped the red plastic body bag. They took the same route as the criminalists, leaving the gurney several feet away from the immediate crime field. They carefully laid the red plastic body bag on the ground, lifted her up, tucked her inside, and zipped up the bag.

No one spoke because no one could speak.

Five detectives were crammed into the blue Malibu for the one-hour-and-fifteen-minute drive to Riverside County. Molina sat in the back, his arms folded against his chest, looking out the window at buildings wreathed in Christmas lights. He choked back tears and tried to get rid of the burning knot in his throat. It was hard for him to accept Phoebe's death and realize there was nothing more they could do for her. Before they'd left, Lackie had told them scant detail—the killer had dumped her body down an embankment adjoining a street. This vile person had used her up and tossed her away like a careless motorist who pitches a beer bottle from his car. Molina leaned his head against the window and tried not to think about the seven days and nights they'd spent searching for her, looking in all the wrong places, while the killer held this innocent second-grader captive before extinguishing her life. This little girl was dead and their focus must shift to finding the child-murdering wretch.

Stoddard drove. In front with him was Ezzell, also silently grieving. Molina shared the back seat with Robbins and Dennis Hanby, the Alhambra detective. They had asked Hanby to come with them for two reasons—his expertise in the occult, and his knowledge of Bland, the person they had planned to start tailing. Their first stop would be at the crime scene, where Ezzell, Robbins, and Stoddard would assist Lackie. Hanby and Molina were going to the morgue to make the identification of Phoebe. Hanby could also help Riverside in assessing whether Phoebe's body showed any signs of ritual abuse.

Lackie told them he had learned the body was probably Phoebe Ho's from the clothing she had on. The plan was to have the South Pasadena detectives first to identify the body, then phone Yeung so he could personally notify Sharon and Kenneth Ho.

Each of the detectives knew the investigation now was in Lackie's hands. When Phoebe was kidnapped from South Pasadena, it was their case, but the body and crime scene were in Riverside County, so the sheriff's department now had jurisdiction. That was fine with the detectives. Their tiny department hardly had the resources to work on the kidnapping, much less a murder.

Mike Lackie introduced himself at the crime scene and briefed them before Molina and Hanby left for the morgue.

Phoebe looked like she had been in a concentration camp for a week. Her nude body was laid out on the cold metal coroner's gurney, face up, her face red from bug bites and her stomach concave from dehydration and lack of food. As soon as he walked in the room, Molina could see the red lines encircling her neck, her wrists, and her ankles like track marks. He concentrated on figuring out what had made such marks so he didn't have to deal with the horror of realizing what Phoebe had endured for days before her death.

Molina sucked in his breath. "That's her," he said to Hanby, his voice scarcely a whisper. "That's her."

Faye Springer was crouched over the body with a magnifying glass and tweezers while a technician took photos. She straightened up and introduced herself. Molina managed to croak out, "Bill Molina, South Pasadena police. This is Dennis Hanby, Alhambra PD."

As was his duty, Molina removed the photos of Phoebe from his jacket pocket and walked over to the table, looking from the photos to the little girl lying on the gurney and back to the photos. He just had to make sure.

Molina turned to Hanby and nodded, unable to speak. Hanby left the room to phone Ward at the department so he and Yeung could make the formal notification to Sharon and Kenneth Ho.

Before the detectives arrived, Springer had started her evidence collection at Phoebe's right foot. With tweezers, tape, glass slides, and petri dishes by her side, the criminalist had peeled off the sock, turned it inside out, and plucked off a long dark hair. She told Molina she pulled a grayish-white hair from the bottom of Phoebe's right foot. And there was something else.

"She was dressed wrong," Springer said. "On her right foot the pants' stirrup was next to her skin and the sock was pulled over it. But on the left foot, the sock was on the foot first, and the stirrup of the leg was pulled over the outside of the sock."

As soon as she took off the left sock, Springer told Molina she had noticed tracks resembling crow's feet around the ankle and had them photographed. They were imbedded so deeply into the skin that she could probably take a plaster cast of the marks.

There was also an intact pubic hair with the root attached taken from inside her panties, as well as other hairs.

"She had a lot of blue and green fibers on her clothes that look like carpet fibers and some reddish fibers on her skin. There are also a lot of these little dots. See?" Springer pointed.

Molina bent over Phoebe's frail form and followed Springer's gloved finger to an area on Phoebe's thigh. Almost too small to see, the tiny white dots didn't seem to follow any pattern. He shook his head.

"What do you think they are?" Molina asked.

"I'm not sure," Springer said.

In quiet tones, the detective and the criminalist discussed the marks on Phoebe's body. Springer said the track marks around both wrists and ankles looked like they came from a plastic cable tie, like the kind used in construction work, or used in lieu of handcuffs by police, where one end of the tie is inserted into a slide and the raised ridges on the tie form a one-way ratchet that can be pulled tighter, but must be cut off to be removed. The marks formed almost perfect circles around her wrists, including the slide mark of the cable tie, but the marks appeared only on the outsides of each ankle. The tie marks formed a complete ring around her neck, leaving hideous red tracks. It appeared she'd died after being strangled by the cable tie, but that determination would have to be made by the coroner. Springer told Molina she thought she would be able to make plaster casts of the ligature marks.

Molina winced as he looked at the angry marks on both sides of the little girl's chest. Hanby returned from making the phone call and was looking over his shoulder.

"That is definitely a Bland trademark," Hanby said.

The room was so quiet that Molina could hear himself breathe. He and Springer stared at Hanby:

"What are you talking about?" Molina said.

"That's what he did to his last two child victims, a little boy and a little girl. Bland used pliers and a surgical tool to pinch them . . . to torture them," Hanby's voice trailed off. "I'd say he is a real strong suspect in this case."

If Bland had magically appeared in that room, Molina would have had no qualms about killing him. He wanted the guy dead. There was no reason in the world why a little girl should ever have to suffer like this.

Springer broke the silence and said Phoebe had been sexually assaulted. Although the coroner could tell them for certain, it appeared as if she had not been given food or water for several days. She also didn't appear to have any defensive wounds, such as broken fingernails or scrapes, bruises, and cuts on her hands and arms, which would indicate that she had tried to fend off the attacker. That would not be unusual for such a small child, Springer said softly. She had other bruises and scrapes that seemed to have come from being tossed down the embankment that had probably occurred after she had been killed.

Molina bit his lip and ignored the tears welling in his eyes. The cruel truth was that someone—very possibly Bland—had abducted and relentlessly tortured, raped, and sodomized this forty-pound child while she was bound at the hands and feet, starving and emaciated for a week. And the evidence leading them to that person lay in the minute pieces of evidence being removed from Phoebe's body. He watched silently as Springer painstakingly plucked off each tiny piece of evidence, placed it on a glass slide or in a petri dish, sealed and labeled the evidence, sterilized the tweezers, and moved to the next item. The technician wrote down the time on the evidence sheet when each item was removed. After tweezing off the larger items visible to the naked eye, Springer used the tape to take lifts from every area of her body, front and back.

As she finished up, the technician brought a hand-held lamp over to the gurney. He turned on the lamp, then switched off the room lights. The smaller lamp glowed with a purplish-blue cast. Springer passed the lamp over Phoebe's body, looking for deposits of bodily fluids such as semen or saliva.

Momentarily transfixed, Molina stared as spot after spot on Phoebe's skin glowed under the lamp's bluish light. He could see smeary fingerprints and handmarks where she'd been manhandled. Unfortunately, there was no known technique to lift fingerprints or palm prints from human skin. As the technician held the lamp, Springer collected the stains by moistening a sterile swab with distilled water, rubbing the cotton patch over the area, then putting the swab with tweezers in an open glass test tube. With the help of the technician, Springer turned Phoebe over onto her stomach to collect tape lifts from the back of her body. Molina suppressed a gasp as he saw the angry, purplish tearing between her buttocks, indicative of repeated vicious sexual assault.

As one of the last procedures, Springer ran a brush through Phoebe's hair and collected the evidence from the brushings. Then she clipped Phoebe's fingernails with scissors and collected them in separate envelopes, one for each hand. When she finished up, it was 11:30 p.m. Springer had spent 2 1/2 hours collecting evidence from Phoebe's body at the morgue.

Molina turned to leave with Hanby. He needed to phone the department to find out whether Ward and Yeung had notified the Hos about the death. They agreed that they would not tell them about the sex abuse and torture until after the coronor had made an official finding, and only if Ward thought it was necessary to tell them.

Molina's portable radio crackled.

"Molina. Ezzell here. Do you read?"

"Yeah," Molina said, momentarily abandoning radio regulations. "We're at the morgue. It's her. Over."

"Riverside homicide is taking over the investigation and Lackie wants to debrief us. They're taking us over there now. Do you need directions?"

"I can find it," he said.

For 4 hours, Ezzell, Molina, Robbins, Stoddard, and Hanby drank hot black coffee and told Lackie everything they knew. Ezzell did most of the talking. They told Lackie about every clue, every lead, every suspect, every surveillance, and every serious tip that was phoned into the department. It had been exactly one week since Phoebe had been kidnapped, and the killer had either been conscientious enough to cover his tracks, or just lucky. Lackie had a lot of catching up to do. He took exhaustive notes and asked detailed questions of the detectives while one of the Riverside sheriff's dispatcher kept their Styrofoam cups brimming with coffee. Since he was a stranger to their city, they told him about the small-town atmosphere, the type of businesses, the dearth of serious crime, the growing immigrant communities, and their neighboring cities.

At 4 a.m., the detectives wearily left the station in the chilly darkness, climbed into the Malibu, and headed back to South Pasadena. In a few hours, Lackie would be in their backyard and the detectives were hoping to catch a few hours' sleep. The late-night session cemented the resolves of detectives from all of the agencies to work together. Now that the sweeping search for Phoebe had come to a heartwrenching end, the hunt for her killer had begun.

Phoebe's tiny pink and white casket sat below the altar of the chapel at Rose Hills Memorial Park surrounded by cascades of baby's breath, miniature pink roses, sprays of lilac, and white orchids, all swathed in pink ribbons. Phoebe, wearing a pink lace dress, clutched her Barbie doll, also wearing a frilly, pink dress. A fluffy, white plush teddy bear and a plastic bear bank were by her side, along with a small American flag. The funeral director had tenderly made up

Phoebe's face, erasing the ugly red marks left by her attacker, giving her a lifelike glow and a child's rosebud lips.

"Who can truly bear such sorrow?" the Reverend Felix Liu cried out to more than 500 mourners packing the chapel. Neighbors stood next to city councilmen. Volunteers who staffed the twenty-four-hour hotline at the Phoebe Ho Volunteer Center held hands with schoolteachers. The funeral for the little girl who'd disappeared on the way to school one day attracted the mayor, the school superintendent, the police chief, and an array of city dignitaries. The pews were full of people and an overflow crowd stood along the outside edges and in the back of the church. Muffled sobs and sniffles echoed as Liu's voice rose.

"It is a terrifying fact when the heart is full of wickedness, a person can do anything. Why, at Christmastime, can the Lord allow us to experience the deepest grief?"

Sharon and Kenneth Ho, both in black suits in the front row, sobbed and clung to each other and Kenneth's brothers and their wives. Phoebe's grandparents hung their heads and wept.

Even though Phoebe met a violent death, her abduction mobilized hundreds in the community in a groundswell of faith and hope, Liu continued. "We can see that love survived. She had only seven years of life in this world, but she made an impact on many people's lives."

Molina and Ezzell, in black, sat in the pews. It was all Molina could do not to sob. Ezzell's stoic expression didn't reveal that her heart was being ripped in half.

The detectives were there to scout for suspects, but they were overcome with grief and couldn't help but mourn. Lackie and two other Riverside County detectives were also out in the crowd. Their mission was to look for anyone unusual, someone who didn't appear to be with anyone else or simply looked out of place. The Riverside County detectives videotaped the funeral and stood where they could surreptitiously tape the crowd.

Dawn and Hugh Edwards sat grim-faced next to their two children. Holding her fidgeting daughter with one hand, Dawn dabbed at her eyes with a tissue, then handed the pack of tissues to her husband, who was sobbing harder than she. Rita Austin was also crying. Ann Parnell and her brood of youngsters squirmed through the service. Reporters were also sprinkled through the crowd, scribbling notes from Liu and observing the crowd reaction. Several crews of TV cameras, banned from the chapel, waited just outside for the family to exit and make their way to the gravesite.

The service and eulogy lasted three hours. A line formed for mourners to file past Phoebe's casket. Sharon and Kenneth Ho walked slowly to the casket as if they were holding each other up. Sharon held a white handkerchief to her face and looking into her daughter's casket, collapsed in screams, moving her head from side to side, her arms flailing. Everyone froze, heads bowing as her cries of agony filled the church. Kenneth and his brothers came to either side of her and together they carried Sharon outside to a black limousine. The TV reporters seized the moment, directing the camera crews to zoom in on the violently grieving mother. Molinas turned to scout for a Riverside County detective. He and Ezzell had been watching a strange-looking guy who looked like he was there by himself. They wanted the detective to take a photo of him so they could ask people if they knew who he was and why he was there.

The limousines carrying the family and a caravan of cars followed the white hearse to the sunny hillside where Phoebe would be buried. Rows of folding chairs and a portable microphone system and speakers had been set up to accommodate the crowd for the graveside service. Molina found it too difficult to approach the gravesite and viewed it from afar. He had the instant photograph of a supsect in his coat pocket and was going to show it to one of the neighbors who knew most of the people in town. It was a long shot, he knew. He and Ezzell continued to look through the crowd for anything unusual. Molina felt the lump tighten as Liu gave the service. For Phoebe's final farewell, mourners plucked single flowers from the arrangements and dropped them into the grave until pink petals covered her child-sized casket. Sharon knelt by her daughter's casket and wrapped her arms around it as tears streamed down her face. Kenneth and his brothers gently pulled her away and sat her in one of the folding chairs. The mourners said their goodbyes to Phoebe, then paid their respects to Sharon and Kenneth Ho and filed away. As the last mourners left, the couple remained seated at the gravesite, leaning against one another.

CHAPTER SIX

Detective Lackie had no trouble finding the Ho residence. All he had to do was look where the TV cameras were aimed. Lackie and Officer Bill Yeung parked down a separate side street and walked up to the house. Neighbors streamed in and out of the small house, bringing bouquets of flowers, covered dishes, and sympathy cards. Reporters with camera crews stayed on the sidewalk, interviewing mourners. The detectives brushed past the media but hesitated at the front porch. Lackie didn't bother knocking because the front door stood wide open to accommodate the constant traffic.

On the way over to the house, Officer Bill Yeung had warned Lackie that the couple was taking Phoebe's death particularly hard. Sharon had become hysterical when he went over to notify them of the death late the night her body was found. Previously, Kenneth had told Yeung that he had grown to like him and after she was found, had planned to make him one of Phoebe's godfathers. Yeung was extremely touched by that. Ward had waited until that morning to hold a press conference to notify the media about finding Phoebe's body in Riverside.

Lackie poked his head in the door and spotted the grand-mother, who was greeting neighbors. Since he couldn't see Kenneth or Sharon, he asked Yeung to ask the grandmother if she would find them. She ushered the detectives into the small living room, where people were standing shoulder-to-shoulder. Flowers occupied every surface of the room. By turning his head to one side, he could see the kitchen counters laden with food. Looking in the other direction, he could see the doors to the small dining room and the bedrooms. Kenneth came out of one of the rooms, but he couldn't see Sharon.

Yeung greeted Kenneth and introduced Lackie. With Yeung translating, they talked briefly and quietly in the corner of the living room. Kenneth seemed oblivious to the people crowding the room. He agreed to lead them in to see his wife.

Sharon was lying underneath the blankets on the bed her daughter used to sleep on, softly moaning. As a homicide investigator, Lackie often had to conduct lengthy, difficult interrogations of grieving family members, and it pained him. But he had a job to do. He found that survivors wanted answers about the crime, and by cooperating with him their own questions were satisfied. Kenneth was asked to rouse her to talk with them. Sharon burrowed her head in the pillows, saying, "No, no, no, no."

After considerable coaxing, she was convinced they needed to know some things about Phoebe's clothing in order to find the person who'd killed her. Sharon agreed to talk about the clothing, but nothing else. She very slowly pulled herself up from under the sheets and sat on the edge of the bed, her face wet and swollen from crying.

In gentle tones, Lackie repeatedly reminded her that they

needed her cooperation to catch the assailant. Lackie needed to establish a rapport with Phoebe's parents. While this was far from an ideal situation, he was used to introducing himself to grieving relatives for long interviews. The Hos were already familiar with the South Pasadena detectives and he wanted to get to know them as well. Molina and Robbins would be coming by in another hour to gather fibers from the family's carpets, rugs, and blankets to use as comparisons for the fibers collected from Phoebe's body the night before.

Lackie needed to clear up a discrepancy in the clothing description the couple had initially given South Pasadena police. The couple told the police about the jacket and the long-sleeved sweatshirt and the pants, but Faye Springer had undressed Phoebe the night before and found she had also been wearing an extra shirt. It was extremely important to find out if they had overlooked an item of clothing she had worn that day. If the killer had placed an extra shirt on her, it would give them a unique signature for a particular sexual predator and give them at least one piece of hard evidence to begin tracking and trying to find where he had obtained it. On the other hand, the killer might have kept one of Phoebe's shirts as a trophy, as pedophiles often do, and that would give them something to look out for once they had a suspect. Sharon eventually gave him a detailed description of the shirts she was aware of and pulled out several of Phoebe's colorful pint-sized shirts.

She said Phoebe often wore several shirts, such as undershirts or T-shirts, polo shirts, or pullover sweatshirts. Sharon could not remember exactly how many layers of clothing Phoebe had on that morning and said she probably wore several layers because it had been cold that day. The only shirt she remembered was a blue and yellow pullover shirt she had been wearing under her red and green jacket. As she stood holding up the tiny shirts, Sharon burst into tears and trembled as she held them to her face.

Lackie wanted to finish the interview quickly and changed the subject by asking Sharon if her daughter had been carrying anything with her to school.

Sharon told Lackie about the red Hello Kitty bookbag and the pennies she had saved for cupcake day. Phoebe might have had some schoolwork in the bag, but she wasn't certain.

Lackie wanted to ask her if Phoebe would ever go along with a stranger, but Sharon became extremely disturbed at that suggestion and started sobbing and mumbling.

Lackie and Yeung withdrew from the room and her husband shut the door, saying he would be out in a minute. When he emerged Lackie and Yeung interviewed him, talking softly in the hallway. The living room was still full of people and there was just no other place to talk. Lackie asked what Phoebe usually carried in the bookbag and Kenneth said she usually carried crayons and her homework, but she often took it to school empty because she liked the bookbag. Lackie asked some general questions about Phoebe's personality and was told she was "overly friendly." If some stranger asked her for help or distracted her somehow, it was very possible she would go along with him, Kenneth said solemnly. He seemed as if he didn't want to admit that to himself or to the detectives. Kenneth added that his wife had repeatedly warned her not to be so friendly with people outside the family. Lackie noted his answer was quite different from what the couple had earlier told South Pasadena detectives. He figured Phoebe's death had brought the couple closer to the disturbing circumstances of her disappearance and death.

Lackie asked Kenneth about whether she could be lured away by someone offering candy or a snack, whether she knew her address and how to phone home, her attitude toward school, and what she had been instructed in regard to handling strangers.

Looking haggard and leaning against a wall in the hallway, Kenneth said he had absolutely no idea who had done this to his daughter and no one had approached him for a ransom demand. While there were some people with whom he had business disputes, none of them gave any indication they were involved in kidnapping and murdering his daughter.

At that point, Molina and Robbins arrived. That provided a convenient break and Lackie asked if they could remove some carpet fibers from the house. The grandmother, who recognized Molina and Robbins, motioned for them to enter and they made their way to the hallway. Lackie kept talking to Kenneth while Molina and Robbins went from room to room, taking carpet samples. The last room was the bedroom, where Sharon was still curled up. Kenneth opened the door first, then led the detectives in to gather samples. Sharon was still crying and they gently took a few fibers from the blanket Kenneth said that Phoebe had used. All four detectives quietly said goodbye, and Lackie left his business card so they would have his phone number.

Lackie had no eyewitnesses. He had no suspects. He had no idea where the kidnapping had taken place. That trail was long cold. He had no idea where the killer had kept Phoebe for a week. The crime scene in Glen Avon had yielded no tire tracks and no shoeprints. He had no finger-prints. The only bits of evidence he had to connect Phoebe to her killer were packed in petri dishes—the hair and fibers plucked from her body and her clothes.

He'd never understood what sickness and torment drove killers to slaughter helpless children. This case was dis-

turbing to everyone who heard about it. The media had
jumped all over the news of Phoebe's death, but as Christmas
drew near, they seemed less interested in filling their newscasts and front pages with details of a child sex killing. But
Lackie wanted publicity. He needed the media to get the
word out about the killer. While Phoebe's body held a reser-
voir of circumstantial evidence, it would take Faye Springer
a few days to examine everything and give him some kind
of a lead. In the meantime, he needed help from the public.
He wanted someone who'd seen a vehicle, a license plate,
a face, a name. Someone had to have seen someone with
this little girl. Lackie was truly hoping to find someone who
knew of a child sex offender who was living or working in
Phoebe's neighborhood or had simply been seen there.

Lackie had set aside his other cases to work exclusively
on finding Phoebe Ho's killer, and so had Springer. He last
spoke with her the night before last at the crime scene.
Lackie knew her reputation well enough to let her alone.
She knew this was a priority hot-pursuit case in which he
would need some lab sleuthing to help point him toward a
suspect. It usually took a few days to process the clothing
of a murder victim and analyze trace evidence before she
came up with some preliminary conclusions. He knew she
would call him in a day or so, as soon as she had something.

Hair and fiber cases were not popular with most investigators, who pride themselves on wearing out shoe leather
finding a key eyewitness who breaks their case. But sometimes luck is on the side of the murderer, or the perpetrator
is extremely careful not to be seen. Solving the case then
depends on the forensic scientists and criminalists. Lackie
liked those kinds of cases. Eyewitnesses sometimes don't
show up for court, get intimidated or scared away, can't
describe the exact lighting in an area, forget who and what
they saw between the time they talk to police and the time

the trial rolls around, and often don't survive withering cross-examination by crafty defense attorneys. Hair and trace evidence doesn't forget. Instead of an eyewitness, the jury sees an expert criminalist in a crisp suit who has usually testified hundreds of times before. Nothing beat the emotional impact of a witness pointing a finger at a squirming defendant in the courtroom, saying, "He did it," but Lackie knew the evidence in Springer's hands would be around for years, if it took him that long to find a suspect. Lackie would have preferred a fingerprint, a palm print, or a shoeprint, but he didn't have that in this case. Phoebe's body was also very strong evidence. There aren't too many people who torture and sexually molest children, then kill them. Given his limited knowledge of pedophiles, he sensed even this was unusual. That area would have to be pursued aggressively.

Even without a specialized background in child sex crimes, Lackie knew the torture-killing was not the work of Chinese terrorists or a business rival. He didn't blame South Pasadena detectives for aggressively pursuing such a theory because they didn't have any idea which way to turn. Like him, they had been frustratingly short of clues. But now that Phoebe had been found, Lackie knew it was the work of a man with a history of sex crimes against children.

Lackie's first priority had been to retrace the South Pasadena detectives' steps and redo the search in Phoebe's neighborhood, knock on every door, and talk to every resident. It was tedious and repetitive, but Lackie wanted to be thorough.

The combined forces of the South Pasadena detectives and Riverside County sheriff's deputies combed the streets, knocking on each door, taking names and phone numbers, asking to search in backyards, scanning alleys, and looking behind dumpsters, this time specifically for Phoebe's red bookbag and homework papers she might have been carrying. Nothing of Phoebe's was recovered and no one had seen Phoebe forcibly removed. Some of the residents burst into tears at hearing of Phoebe's murder. While they had been alerted to her disappearance by officers the week before, they were sickened and saddened at learning she had been ruthlessly killed.

There was just one lady, a Dutch woman, who seemed promising and who South Pasadena detectives had tried to interview. Lackie was having the same sorts of difficulties coordinating a visit with her when her daughter was home. He had started tracking down an interpreter who could help him interview her.

Lackie had already phoned the FBI, the LAPD, and the Los Angeles Sheriff's Department and sent national tele- types asking for help in profiling this particular killer and for names of potential suspects who shared the *modus ope- randi* of a progressive child molester. One sex crimes expert with the LAPD who specializes in profiling offenders con- firmed that it was extremely rare for the usual child molester to kill his victim. The overwhelming majority of sex offend- ers assault their victims and either let them go or kill them within 24 hours. The person who committed this crime was not a new offender, since raping, torturing, and killing a little girl is rarely a first violent offense. The man who killed Phoebe, the detectives suggested, had a history of molesting and torturing children, perhaps of both sexes, and had most likely been diagnosed as a mentally disordered sex offender. That investigator suggested that the killer had a ''long and persistant'' sex crimes history against children for whom murder would be the next escalating step of violence.

Lackie had also spoken with experts in child pornography and prostitution and was told that a seven-year-old child would be too young and that starving a subject would not serve their interests. One experienced investigator told him that snuff films, where young children are killed, are mostly the stuff of fiction and this type of violence was not tolerated, even among child pornographers.

To protect himself and safeguard his investigation, Lackie had lined up interviews with some of the registered sex offenders, including Bland. Stung by clever defense attorneys more than once, Lackie was very careful not to focus solely on Bland but was deliberately keeping the field of suspects wide to avoid being accused of pinpointing one man for the crime.

As expected, nothing had come of the ongoing surveillance of the Pedley Road crime scene. He'd had deputies watching the area, looking for residents, motorists, and others whose normal business took them past that area, and no one had seen anything unusual. He was going to keep the deputies there for one more day at least.

The other messy matter to deal with was the plethora of phoned-in leads from South Pasadena. The tiny department had been inundated with callers phoning in tips—psychics who "saw" the crime, people troubled by homeless men mumbling to themselves on street corners, and busybodies eager to turn in their oddball or surly neighbors. Now his department was getting the calls. Lackie had created a tip sheet and assigned several detectives to prioritize the leads and chase down those that seemed most promising.

He was planning to meet with Ezzell to review the lists of pedophiles paroled to South Pasadena and nearby cities and learn what those who had been interviewed had said to the detectives. Shortly after Phoebe disappeared, Ezzell said she had phoned the state Department of Justice for a list of recently released child sex offenders and was perturbed at not having received it by now.

Lacking resources, Ezzell had instantly eliminated those who did not live or work or have relatives or friends within a ten-mile radius. Now that the child's body had been found fifty miles from her home, the parolee's proximity to South Pasadena was no longer an issue, considerably broadening the geographic scope of their search for the killer. The net they cast to snag Phoebe's killer would have to be extremely wide until he heard from Springer about a solid lead.

Faye Springer was already headed down the freeway to the crime lab as the sun came up over the San Bernardino Mountains. The dedicated criminalist wanted to put in a few hours of work before her twelve-year-old daughter's gymnastics meet that afternoon. The day before had been hard for her, harder than usual. She had taken refuge in one of the evidence examination rooms at the back of the lab to sort through Phoebe's clothing and let the inner turmoil settle. Throughout the day, whenever she shut her eyes for a moment, she saw Phoebe's face. It was the same chilling reaction Springer experienced despite working on more than 300 homicides. Springer had needed the entire day to allow the disturbing images to subside, quite a difficult task as she pored over the dead girl's clothing. It wasn't until the end of the day, when she had repackaged the clothes and was lifting them up to a shelf, that she realized what had been bothering her. She had flashed back on the night before, lifting Phoebe's body from the cold, damp field, and recalled that it was similar to the weight of her own daughter. She had pushed that aside so she could work.

The first thing Springer wanted to tackle in the lab was the stain she had found on Phoebe's pant leg. It was undoubtably semen, but she had to test it. Getting a result could take several days, but she would have some preliminary results within an hour. She would phone Lackie as soon as she found out.

Springer eased the Buick station wagon into the parking

lot of the crime lab. Located on the same hilltop as the Riverside County Sheriff's Academy, the door to the lab bore the title "California Department of Justice, Bureau of Forensic Services, Riverside Laboratory" on a small sign. The entrance was hidden halfway down the walk obscured behind a cement-block fence. Purposefully nondescript, the two-story brick building shared space with the sheriff's academy, which had classrooms on the upper floor.

Springer flipped on the lights and walked through the silent lab to the evidence freezer. Unlike other criminalists, who sometimes wore headphones and listened to music or radio talk shows as they worked, Springer preferred quiet while she worked so she could better concentrate. She unlocked the evidence freezer where they kept blood and bodily fluids shed during violent crimes on bed linens, axes, firearms, towels, huge hanks of carpet, and clothing. All of the items were stored in brown paper bags and bore bright red and yellow evidence seals. She took the bag containing Phoebe's pants from the freezer and put the bag on the counter while she put on a sterile smock and Latex gloves. Since she'd found a potential stain just on the pants, Springer had put only the pants into the freezer. The first lab test she had to do was to see if proteins from semen could be detected. That kind of a test was routinely performed on an entire garment or bed linens, for example, to locate hard-to-find stains. She spread butcher paper on a wide table, laid the pants on top, covered the bottom portion of the front left leg with a single layer of special reactive paper, then brushed a clear chemical solution on top of it. Any semen stain will render a purplish blob. Springer methodically tested the entire pair of pants and found, after a half-hour, that there was just one stain she had already identified.

This was at least one nugget of information that could help identify Phoebe's killer. With sterile scissors, Springer cut out the small area containing the stain and carefully wrapped it to preserve it. She carefully rolled up the tiny pale pink pants with the wrapped-up stain and put them back into the paper bag and put the bag back into the locked freezer, then put away the rest of the test equipment. It would take another half day to extract the sample from the cloth, which would have to wait until Monday. Next week would probably be consumed with running a battery of tests on the stain to identify the blood type and other genetic information of the killer. The problem was, the stain looked fairly small and there might not be enough of it to run the full complement of tests.

The next task would take more time than she had that Saturday, but she wanted to start examining the hundreds of fibers and hairs pulled from Phoebe's body and catalogue them. She knew it would take days, maybe a week, to sort out similar fibers, human hairs, and animal hairs, and separate what was important from what was irrelevant.

She went to the evidence locker and looked for the two cardboard boxes she had put there Thursday night. One contained the evidence removed from the field and the morgue the night Phoebe's body was found. The second box held the hairs and fibers she removed from the clothing yesterday. She took the first box down and carried it to an alcove off the main trace evidence room, where there were two microscopes and a stereomicroscope, which allows the analyst to use both eyes and provides a distortion-free three-dimensional view of evidence. Springer broke the evidence seal and unpacked the box, removing the first dozen plastic petri dishes, and set them down on the counter.

Springer's first step in any trace case was to take a rough inventory and find out what the victim picked up, group the evidence into broad categories, and then compare the findings with the victim's own environment to see if any of the hairs and fibers can identify a location or a perpetrator. Do the hairs have characteristics commonly associated with a Caucasian, Asian, Hispanic, or black individual? Did the fibers come from upholstered furniture, an Oriental rug, a nylon carpet, an angora sweater, a camel's-hair overcoat? Were there animal hairs? And in most cases, were there tiny chips of paint or plastic from the environment? Since every surface people come into contact with is painted or coated, tiny chips too small to be seen with the naked eye constantly flake off and stick to clothing and skin. Springer pulled out a blank evidence sheet and a petri dish across which were suspended four tape strips holding fibers plucked from Phoebe's jacket. For her initial look, Springer inverted the clear petri dish and looked at it under the microscope one tape strip at a time, scanning for whatever caught her eye.

A tiny fiber magnified hundreds of times resembles the thick stalk of a plant, with the strong light of the microscope making it appear sheer. Human hairs look like translucent tubes in light brown, yellow, red, or black, with the shaft and inner parts of each hair standing out to the trained eye. Carpet fibers are recognizable because they are bigger than most fibers. The end of a carpet fiber—a cross-section— looks triangular, like a three-cornered hat. Springer quickly identified several blue and reddish-rust fibers that looked like they came from a carpet. She also saw white cotton fibers that looked like they came from a wide-weave fabric. From her own experience, she knew those fibers didn't come from Phoebe's own clothing and were too large to come from thin T-shirt material or a thin gauze. The ubiquitous ragged-edged paint chips were present as well. There were just a few rare cases where Springer didn't find paint or some sort of plastic. As she examined the chips, she saw what appeared to be varying shades of white. She also saw rounded globules of paint looking like lopsided baseballs.

That usually occurred when someone had used an aerosol can. She made a note of that, writing that she would have to do more tests to confirm the nature of the substance.

The most critical aspect of trace evidence cases was deciding which of the hundreds of fibers collected were relevant to the case. The carpet fibers seemed immediately important to Springer because it was obvious they didn't come from the dirt ditch or from Phoebe's own house, although she would have to do some comparisons later to confirm that assumption.

Turn-of-the-century criminalists reasoned that someone who enters a room leaves a little of himself behind, whether it's a shoeprint, clothing fibers, soil from one's shoes, or a few naturally shed hairs. Modern criminalists found that two objects rubbed together will exchange material, one to another. The longer and the more intense the contact, the more trace evidence will be deposited. If Springer could find where Phoebe had been held captive, there was a good chance they would find Phoebe's hair, and fibers from her clothing, which would help nail down the case against the perpetrator. The kidnapper already had a considerable head start. By the time Springer and Lackie put together the trace case, identified the suspect, and did a search of his home, he would have had plenty of time to clean up. But the detective and the criminalist had one advantage. Many times, contact with an assailant is typically brief—a few hours, or sometimes minutes. Phoebe had been held prisoner for an entire week, allowing the fibers from her own home to rub off and be deposited in the perpetrator's home and allowing time for Phoebe to pick up foreign material on her clothing and skin. The dirt field where her body was dumped was an unlikely source for stray hairs and carpet fibers, meaning it was more likely the carpets and hairs came from the kidnapper and his environment.

Petri dish by petri dish, Springer catagorized the hairs
and fibers in her mind. For the eventual criminal trial, she
kept a running commentary of her observations on an evidence form. Most of the carpet fibers were rust or blue.
There were a few animal hairs and some of Phoebe's own
hair, the whitish cotton fibers, and the expected chips of
paint. Springer knew she had to leave soon and had time to
examine a few more petri dishes so she could lock up the
lab and leave in time to attend her daughter's gymnastic
showcase.

She had quite a few more petri dishes to go, but the
analysis was going quickly because she had a rough idea
of what had been collected. Noting that the next group of
tapings came from Phoebe's pants, Springer slid the petri
dish under the microscope and immediately spotted a human
hair. That was one of the most exciting finds so far because
it most likely came from Phoebe's killer. Through the clear
plastic of the petri dish, she saw what appeared to be a limb
hair, not a head or a pubic hair, typically used for comparison. Hairs are not like fingerprints because they cannot be
inextricably linked to one person, but certain similar or rare
characteristics can be compared. Although it was encouraging to find a hair, limb hairs have less evidentiary value
because they lack much of the inner structure contained in
head and pubic hairs. But there was something odd, as if
there was something stuck to it. Under the microscope, it
looked like a translucent fiber with a big, black basketball
glommed onto its side. It was one item from among the
hundreds she planned to separate and mount on a slide for
a more thorough examination.

Springer had time for one more group of petri dishes
before she left. This group contained taped lifts from the
jacket. Under the microscope, Springer saw what looked
like little footballs with long spikes sticking out from each

pointed end. Almost invisible to the naked eye, there were quite a few of the little whitish footballs. Springer recalled seeing clusters of tiny dots on Phoebe's skin and a few on her clothing. She thought it looked like paint, but she wouldn't know for certain until she ran a few tests to make certain. Whatever it was, Phoebe had been practically caked in it. During her examination, Springer counted nine different shades of paint, mostly varying shades of white, gray, and some light pink and blue. According to the laws of trace evidence, whenever there is a large quantity of a fiber or some other sort of trace evidence, it is certain the victim had a lot of contact with it. Springer spent a few moments writing down what she saw, then picked up the phone to call Lackie. She wanted to tell him about the preliminary results on the semen stain and let him know one preliminary clue—it was likely that Phoebe had been around someone who worked with paint.

CHAPTER SEVEN

Lackie picked up a signed search warrant at 8:46 a.m. on Saturday, January 3, 1987. Two hours later, he and a law enforcement convoy of detectives, criminalists, and evidence technicians knocked on the front door of Warren James Bland's home in Alhambra. Gene Thayer opened the door. He wasn't surprised at seeing detectives at his doorstep and didn't bother to read the warrant. Since one of his sons was in jail, he knew the police didn't even need one to search a parolee or his house. Without even asking, he volunteered that Bland was down the street, helping a neighbor repair his roof, but he wasn't certain where. Lackie asked Sanchez to find him.

The police had been out to Thayer's house a half-dozen times in the last week to interview Thayer and his other son, Gary, about Bland and the missing girl, and they both figured this was the next step. It didn't change Thayer's mind about Bland.

"I'll cooperate. Search all you want. I still think you got

the wrong guy,'' Thayer said. His other son, with whom Bland had become acquainted in prison, was serving a life sentence for murder, Lackie had learned.

Lackie nodded thanks but didn't waste time trying to convince Thayer. Lackie and detectives in both counties had spent the last 16 days running down every paroled pedophile, every child sex offender, and every pervert who could have had reason to be near South Pasadena on the day Phoebe had disappeared. They had painstakingly re-interviewed every sex offender first contacted by South Pasadena detectives and traced the steps of recently released pedophiles from lists sent to them by the state Department of Justice. Lackie had been pulled away from Christmas Eve dinner to the drunk tank in South Pasadena to interview a borderline mentally ill transient that detectives had thought was good for Phoebe's murder. On Christmas Day, Lackie had been called to take a look at a child molester rolling through Riverside. Two days later, San Bernardino deputies had phoned at 3:30 a.m. to check out a miserably drunken fool with a past prison record of kidnapping and rape. One ex-con child molester Lackie had decided not to interview was so elderly and infirm he couldn't walk. Lackie was, however, very interested in a two-time child molester who worked three blocks from Phoebe's school, as well as the school's head custodian, who school officials hadn't even known had a past history of child molestation.

Each man could account for his time, verifiable by independent time cards, fellow workers, employers, or other witnesses. Nothing connected any of them to Phoebe Ho. None of them had anything close to the criminal history that rose to the level of torture, sexual slavery, starvation, and strangulation of a seven-year-old girl. Even after checking and re-checking the accounts of the school custodian and the paroled child molester who worked near the school, no one had had access to Phoebe as she walked along El Centro Avenue to school in South Pasadena—except Bland.

In his own handwritten log, Bland could not account for his whereabouts between 7:45 a.m. and 8 a.m. on December 11, when Phoebe was abducted. During the entire week Phoebe was gone, the family for whom Bland was painting complained that he rarely showed up on time, took extremely long lunches, and often left well before his 5 p.m. quitting time. His last work site was just over a mile from Phoebe's school and several work sites were less than two miles from her school. Bland's girlfriend, a Vietnamese woman with three children, said Bland normally spent time with her on the weekends, but she could not account for Bland's time on the weekend after Phoebe had been captured.

Bland's twenty-five-year career as a sexual predator of women and children set off alarms with Lackie and everyone else who had reviewed Bland's prison file, a criminal curriculum vitae fat with reports from former prison officials and parole officers. By Lackie's calculations, Bland had spent more time behind bars on sex offenses than he had lived as a free man.

The horrific crimes against Phoebe were chillingly similar to two of Bland's previous child molestation offenses. In 1976, Bland picked up an entire family—mother, infant, son, and eleven-year-old daughter—then shoved everyone out of the car except the girl. He sexually assaulted her, using needle-nosed pliers and vise grips to torture her during the attack, then let her go hours later. Imprisoned for that offense, he was released in 1980 and kidnapped a ten-year-old boy the same year. The boy was also tortured with vise grips, pliers, and wire during a more prolonged sexual assault. Bland was paroled for the latest offense in January, 1986. Lackie had spent hours talking with experts who specialize in profiling child sex offenders, and they all agreed child molesters rarely kept their victims more than a few hours, and very rarely tortured them. They did offer a bit of advice—that unique *modus operandi* was probably the work of an intelligent, experienced sex offender who had been in and out of prison and who inflicted an increasing amount of violence on his victims. More important, the experts noted, this type of career criminal would deliberately change his MO to avoid detection.

Again and again, the profile seemed custom-suited to Bland, most notably the similarity of torture. Before the crimes he had committed against children, Bland was found guilty of a series of rapes against adult women from 1959 to 1960. He was convicted of a second series of more aggravated rapes against women in 1968. Over the years, Bland's victims had gotten younger and more vulnerable and he had subjected them to greater humiliation, pain, and degradation.

The words written by Bland's parole officer in 1969 stuck in Lackie's head: "The defendant is a Dr. Jekyl and Mr. Hyde. Seven years at Atascadero have prepared him for every interview and diagnosis. He can play humility, remorse, open-faced candor, and earnestness with Oscar-winning facility. He can be a model employee, punctual probationee, regular churchgoer, and doting sibling. But when alone at 2 a.m. he becomes Mr. Hyde. He has stabbed a man, raped at least three women and tried to rape others. He appears incorrigible and his dangerousness has increased since his early crimes. Society is saved only while the defendant is incarcerated."

The previous week, Lackie had learned Bland's latest brush with police had come earlier that year. Just weeks after Bland was released from prison in January 1986, he had been arrested for shoplifting a ten dollar pair of needle-nosed pliers from a hardware store. He had $71 in his pocket.

A few days ago, Springer had completed the tests on the

stain from Phoebe's pants and come up with some general genetic markers that were identical to Bland's, based on prison records of his blood. There wasn't enough of the stain to do a full complement of tests to further narrow the genetic characteristics.

The paint balls covering Phoebe showed she most likely had been near someone who worked around paint. None of the other subjects matched that criterion as easily as Bland, who painted for a living.

Lackie shook his head. He didn't need to convince Thayer. He needed to convince twelve jurors. Bland had the motive, the opportunity, a few genetic markers, and a criminal history. Lackie was ready to arrest Bland for the murder of Phoebe Ho, but the deputy district attorney with whom he was working wanted more than a similar MO and a window of time. If he couldn't put together a solid case in 2 days, he'd have to let him go. The next step would be to weave together the threads of trace evidence for a direct link from Phoebe straight to Bland. This would be a case where you connect the dots and pin the tail on the child killer, he thought. The fibers from this victim go to that murderer.

It had been 16 days since Phoebe had been found dead. Lackie silently hoped that Bland had kept Phoebe for at least some of the time in his room, but this was not realistic, since Gene Thayer lived there and was probably home during the time when Bland was working. A skilled ex-con wouldn't be that careless. The next best possibility was that Bland's car, clothing, blankets, and carpet could still bear traces of Phoebe's hair and fiber. Lackie knew he would be extremely lucky if they found that evidence, since years in prison had taught Bland how to cover his tracks. Some things were Crime 101 textbook stuff, like making sure no eyewitnesses see you, wiping off fingerprints, getting rid of your shoes so police can't trace shoeprints, and stealing a car to use for crimes. However, a sick addiction shared by many child molesters was to keep some kind of a souvenir from each victim. From Phoebe, Bland might have kept her Hello Kitty bookbag or some of her homework papers. In addition, few child molesters thought to vacuum out their cars, strip out all the rugs and carpeting of their cars and houses, or get rid of blankets. And Bland couldn't change the structure of his hair.

The search warrant sought all items, from which fibers, and paint samples could be gotten, as well as head, limb, and pubic hair from Bland, his saliva, and his blood.

Gene Thayer swung open the door to the green stucco house with the white trim and stepped aside. Faye Springer, Bill Molina, Joyce Ezzell, Gary Robbins, Ken Stoddard, James Blum, Bland's parole officer, an evidence technician, a criminalist, and three Riverside detectives descended on the house and garage. Lackie earlier had assigned duties to each person. Thayer pointed out Bland's room and mentioned that several boxes and bags of goods lining the walls to his room belonged to him, not Bland. As the detectives searched, the evidence technician took photographs of everything, inside and out. Bland's primer-gray 1972 Datsun was not in the driveway.

As the officers crossed the threshold, Sanchez returned and told Lackie he'd found Bland fixing a roof across the street and down a few houses. Lackie walked across the street to where a stack of shingles and some tools were visible on the roof.

As he rounded the corner to the backyard he came nose-to-nose with Bland.

"Are you with the police department?" Bland asked. "I've been expecting you."

He was sweaty but quite well groomed for Saturday chores. He wore khaki pants bearing a hint of a crease and a short-sleeved madras shirt revealing aging blue tattoos on each forearm and unbuttoned to show a few curly gray chest hairs. His clean-cut attire was marred by a ragged, purplish scar running from his ear and disappearing toward his collarbone, the result of an ambush by another inmate while he was on the toilet. The dirty, prison-made shank and medical neglect had contributed to the garish scar. Bland was dabbing his brow with a rag.

Lackie could see the Datsun parked on the grass behind the neighbor's house, out of sight from the street. He glanced at the license plate to make certain it was the same one.

Lackie introduced himself and before he could show him the search warrant, Bland explained that he was helping his neighbor, Fred Thompson, re-roof his house and peppered the homicide detective with questions and complaints.

"What are you going to do with me today?" Bland asked. It was hard to tell whether he was worried or annoyed.

"Well, I'm here to search your home and your car and I also need to speak with you," Lackie said, showing him the warrant.

"You can search to your heart's content, Mr. Lackie," Bland said, settling into an uncanny calm and cooperative mood. "I'll help you in any way possible.

"I need to talk to you as soon as possible because there's some things I need to tell you," Bland said, lowering his voice as he walked with Lackie back toward his house like they were good friends.

"This thing has caused me a great deal of embarrassment with my friends, and I, I need to ask you for a couple of favors because, well, this has been real embarrassing for everyone," Bland said.

"You've ruined it for me and you've caused Gary Thayer, my employer, a lot of problems. I can't do jobs for him anymore because everyone who hired him to do jobs are now mad because you've been out questioning them about me.

"I'm just glad you came out here today to get this thing over with."

Watching Bland chatter on, Lackie observed him grow more confident, like he was challenging him, making Lackie even more suspicious about what they might find. He was just like Ezzell and Molina had described—a real cool character, cocky and bluffing the police like it was his special challenge. Most ordinary folks became extremely unhappy about having their homes turned upside down in a police search. Bland had become institutionalized after living most of his life behind bars without privacy, a process that had stripped him of the capacity to feel indignant about the intrusion.

Lackie wanted to get the formalities of the search out of the way and get his team busy with the search. He performed the official function of serving Bland with the search warrant. He also stated that Blum, his parole officer, was invoking the right to search because he was a parolee. As a triple layer of protection, Lackie asked Bland to sign a "consent to search" form. Almost with a flourish, Bland signed the form. For most detectives, this might be overkill, but Lackie wasn't taking any chances that the trace evidence and fibers would be tossed out on some technicality by a defense attorney complaining about an improper search. That was his entire case and he knew it. It was going to be done right, three times over.

Bland walked over to the garage, unlocked the padlock, unlocked his rollaway tool chest, and pointed out a few of his personal items, like furniture, paint cans, car parts, and sealed cardboard boxes. For someone out of prison just under a year, Bland had a lot of tools.

Carrying an evidence kit like a briefcase, Springer headed

for Bland's bedroom, looking for carpet and cotton fibers of the type she'd found on Phoebe's body as well as dropcloths splattered with paint.

With everything unlocked and the remainder of the search team at work, Lackie asked Bland to come with him to the station for an interview.

"After we talk, I want to take some evidence from you, like hair and saliva, things like that," Lackie said.

Bland reiterated that he would be cooperative and was "eager to get things going so that this whole thing can get cleared up."

Before he got into the car, Lackie put the handcuffs on Bland, who submitted, but complained about having a bad back. Even for the short ride to the South Pasadena police department, Bland said he would be uncomfortable in the back seat of the detective's unit. Lackie resisted the temptation to roll his eyes and slammed the door shut on Bland in the back seat. Lackie drove and Detective Patrick McManus sat in the front seat of the four-door Ford sedan. Bland's parole agent, John Blum, followed in his own car.

On the way to the station, Bland pressed Lackie for information: what they were looking for, what information they had, and what they were going to do with his car.

Lackie recited to him the boundaries of the search warrant and decided the rest should go on tape once they got to the station.

Lackie, McManus, Blum, and Bland sat down in an interview room of the South Pasadena police department. Lackie took off the handcuffs, got some coffee, lit a cigarette, turned on a tape recorder, and listened to Bland explain where he was from the day Phoebe was kidnapped to the day she was found dead.

Bland, in a friendly tone of voice, said he'd always gone by "Jim." He said he usually got up by 7 a.m. and was at

Winchell's getting donuts and coffee by 8 a.m. or so, then
went to his worksite, depending on where he was painting
or doing minor repair work. Most of his time that week was
spent at the Haydens' in San Marino, painting the interior
and exterior. Bland said he quit at 4:30 p.m. or 5 p.m.,
went home to clean up, and went to Alcoholics Anonymous
meetings in different cities every weeknight. Bland said he
typically stayed until midnight or 1 a.m. Weekends were
reserved for Evie, his girlfriend, who lived 15 miles away
with her three children.

Lackie kept the interview easygoing and friendly as he
questioned Bland about his work schedule every day during
Phoebe's capture. Bland kept asking to see his logbook, a
yellow legal pad on which he kept track of his working and
weekend hours. Using the honor system, Gary Thayer paid
Bland based on the hours he said he'd worked. But the
logbook had been confiscated a week earlier during the
investigation and Lackie told Bland he wanted him to speak
from memory instead of referring to his own notes.

Lackie started pushing Bland gently, probing his failure
to write down the AA meetings in his logbook until the day
Phoebe was found dead, his extremely long lunch hours,
and the discrepancies in his workday compared to the times
the Hadens said he'd started and ended work. Evie also
said he wasn't with her during the weekend Phoebe was
kidnapped but still alive.

On some of the critical days, Bland explained that he'd
spent one of his long lunch hours talking to "a lady cashier"
at the Arco station.

"She's kind of cute. I'm a rascal," Bland said, with a
wink and a chuckle. "I've been going in there constantly,
uh, regularly, I should say, getting Cokes and then donuts,
snacks and stuff like that."

On another day, Bland claimed he chatted with a 7-Eleven

clerk until the wee hours after one of his AA meetings. He said he couldn't remember the name of the cute gas station clerk or the convenience store clerk, but volunteered one fellow he spoke with at an AA meeting was named "Bill."

"A couple of times I've been out until 2:00 a.m. I got talking to a couple of people and God, I mean it, it was 2:00 a.m. or 2:30 a.m. Time . . . time gets away from me.

"I don't . . . I can't tell you the exact dates on that, because I can't remember it."

Lackie had watched Bland that day go from being mildly nervous to calm and confident in a relatively short period of time, a personality flip-flop not so dramatic as the one described by the 1969 parole officer, but certainly a confluence of emotions. Bland, in his own way, was trying to be charming and acted as if being searched and interrogated by police for the horrendous sexual assault and killing of a little girl were chores to be crossed off on his Saturday "to do" list. Lackie thought Bland was exhibiting the classic pedophile's attitude that there was nothing wrong with molesting children because he was somehow driven to it and that he had somehow rationalized his behavior. Lackie wondered how Bland wove his girlfriend into this tangled web.

"How are you getting along with Evie?"

"Right now?" Bland asked back.

"Tell me about right now, today."

"Right now, today, I am a big embarrassment to her. Evie came into this country and she put herself through school and educated herself and, uh, the people that she associates with are pretty well-to-do people, and they're coming around asking, 'What's going on with Jim?' and it's at the point where I'm an embarrassment and she wants to break up."

Lackie thought that was very interesting that Bland would

admit to that. He also remembered they'd had a fight before Phoebe was reported missing.

"Okay, Evie is the kind of a girl who likes to spend money when she hasn't got it to spend. I'm talking about the hairdo, the nails, and what have you, and I thought more should be given to the bills and the food in the house, and I got all over her case one day and that really kicked it off, then suddenly, it's my family, you're not a part of this family, Jim, you don't offer your opinion in things like that.

"That was the gist of it and from that point on, every little thing I did was irritating to her and we just about broke up."

"When was that?"

"It's, uh, been a while back. Two months, I guess, when all this started."

"During December?" Lackie wanted to nail down the time.

"We had a couple of ups and downs. A couple of them. It was just, you know, it was yell at each other and then, I usually get mad and slam doors, you know, it's my big thing. I walk out and stomp around a little bit."

"Are you going to try to marry her?"

"I want to."

"Do you think that's possible?"

"No, I just don't know. We have had some . . ."

"Well, prior to us coming on the scene, was that a possibility between the two of you?"

"Yes, yes."

"Was it a serious possibility?"

"When her divorce was final and things had settled down a bit and we had more money, and she had some room to breathe, I think, I had every feeling to, to pursue it.

"You meet people every now and then in your life that really, for lack of a better word, ring your bell. And she rang mine. She's everything I wanted. I wanted a responsibility to her, the kids, the home.''

For someone who had had to guard his emotions so completely behind bars in order to survive, Bland was either putting on a convincing performance or he was actually expressing true regret at losing this woman. Bland apparently saw no connection between his feelings for Evie and the failure of the relationship so close in time to the crimes against Phoebe. Lackie recalled that one of the LAPD sex crimes experts mentioned that offenders feel they are ''forced'' to commit crimes because of stress from work demands, or problems with women. Bland seemed anxious and strained at recalling the tension with his girlfriend, but he seemed not to worry about revealing that to police. Lackie felt the fighting and stress with Evie, who is Asian, in the assault on a vulnerable Asian victim was a key motivator for the crime.

Lackie decided to slowly start squeezing Bland.

''Do you sign in there at the meetings? I understand that sometimes records are kept at some of the groups, if we have to prove that you were there,'' Lackie said.

''No,'' Bland said. ''There's no sign-in with names or anything. You've got to understand that in Alcoholics Anonymous, everybody deals with you, unless people volunteer their last names, the anonyminity, you know, the last names, the people you are talking with are judges, police officers, doctors, attorneys.''

When pressed about the gaps in his work hours by Cindy Haden and the gaps in weekend time with his girlfriend, Bland called Hayden ''uptight'' and ''flighty'' and claimed both she and Evie were mistaken. Then he remembered that he might have had a paint job that weekend, but he wasn't sure and wanted to look at his logbook.

Lackie pushed a little harder, saying the wide time gaps

"make us highly suspicious that you could have easily been with this little girl."

Bland had little reaction: "Uh-huh."

"We know that on more than one job you've been inaccurate as to the times that you've arrived and the time that you've left because we went to—"

"Not by much," Bland interrupted.

"We obviously have done our homework. We went to these people because we saw in your log, it looked like you're pretty consistant, eight-thirty a.m. to five p.m., eight-thirty a.m. to four-thirty p.m. most every day. We go out and contact these people and they're telling us Jim, 'No, I never saw him that time, he always got here real late,' you were never punctual, there were days you promised to show up, but you didn't and it became quite clear in looking at your log that it's somewhat fabricated . . ."

"It's inconsistant and this is causing you concern. Now I know why you're still, you know, looking at me. I see what you're saying, yeah," Bland said.

Bland asked to see his logbook again and said the people in whose homes he worked wouldn't necessarily keep a watchful eye on his hours, but Lackie decided to change gears.

Referring to Lieutenant Ezzell, Lackie asked if she had told him that "some of the things you've done to some of your victims" were identical to "what happened to Phoebe. That's one of the problems I have here."

"No, she didn't. No one said that. Now I know, okay."

Lackie asked Bland if he'd ever driven on the 60 Freeway or Pedley Road, the off ramp where Phoebe's body was found.

Bland gave a long, rambling answer, saying that he had driven the freeway, but hadn't taken that freeway "very far."

"We just have this great amount of time in the morning and in the evenings that we just have problems with. Where you say you've been places and have been working at locations and been with people and we just can't show it and it's very likely that maybe you weren't. And we have some other little problems.

"You know the girl's got white paint on her," Lackie said.

The detective waited, holding his breath, watching as Bland looked down.

"Nobody's said that . . . oh, I see. I was painting. I see what you're saying. That's why you're looking at me," Bland said.

"It looks real bad," Lackie said.

"It does," Bland agreed.

"With the evidence we got from the little girl and with the things we know about you and what happened to her, it just gets worse. The gaps get wider and the evidence narrows and starts pointing at you. So I decided to come and talk to you to see . . ."

"Well, what does it come down to?"

"Well, it comes down to whether or not you had anything to do with the little girl," Lackie said.

"I doubt if you'd believe me if I told you, but I didn't," Bland said.

"I just want you to understand that you're in real trouble," Lackie said, speaking slowly. Most people by now would have stated their innocence in no uncertain terms: they didn't do it, period. Bland seemed almost reluctant to distance himself from the crime. Perhaps his warped sense of values made him abhor lying.

"Sure I am, God," Bland said, his frank and congenial tone gone. He sounded frightened and his forehead glistened with sweat. Lackie sent Bland's parole officer on an errand just to get him out of the room and then told Bland he wanted the truth and he didn't care about busting him on any penny-ante parole violation.

"If there's any way that you could have been spotted near the girl, if you've been around the girl, been near the school . . . if there's anything like that, I've got to know about it," Lackie said.

To Lackie's surprise, Bland admitted painting an apartment complex one and a half blocks from Phoebe's school.

Bland said he wasn't aware how close it was to Phoebe's school.

"Well, it's getting worse. If we go and prove that you did it, you know you're gonna go to jail," Lackie said.

"You got the hell scared out of me right now. I'm not gonna lie to you."

Yet still, Bland didn't blurt out that he hadn't had anything to do with the girl.

"Are you aware that through your blood we can exactly show if you had any contact with this girl?" Lackie asked. "What kind of explanation will you have if we say that it's your fluids that are on her clothing or on her body?"

"There are no explanations," Bland said, his voice becoming unnaturally calm. "If something like that happened, it's bullshit, you know, that's how I feel, but you know, anything you want to do, I'll go along with it."

"Are you sure you haven't had any contact with the girl at all?"

"No, sir, I haven't."

"Would it shock you to tell you that we can prove that you did?"

"Yes, it would. It really would. It makes it sound like I'm it."

Another lukewarm denial. Lackie decided to give Bland another chance to blurt out that he had nothing whatsoever to do with Phoebe and told him that he would be better off admitting to the crime rather than having the police and a prosecutor go through the time and trouble of putting on evidence at a trial.

"We'll have to play these tapes to the jury where you're lying about all these things when we can prove absolutely you did it, that'll look terrible," Lackie said. "Obviously, if you come in and admit to this . . ."

"I know what you're saying," Bland said.

"It's just like with the other crimes you've committed. You know how that works," Lackie said.

"I know. I know what you're saying," Bland said.

After two and a half hours, the interview ended and Lackie transported Bland to a local hospital so that a registered nurse could draw his blood and procure a saliva sample. Lackie also retrieved head, limb, and pubic hair from Bland and put the hairs in a plain white envelope to give to Faye Springer.

As Lackie pulled up to Bland's house, a tow truck driver was hoisting Bland's Datsun onto its two front wheels as Detective Sanchez and Springer chatted nearby. Its doors were sealed shut with red evidence tape. As the car's rear end angled upward, Lackie could see the load of junk filling the car shift forward into the front passenger compartment. Papers, notebooks, paint supplies, tarps, and tools filled the car up to its doors. The car was too full for Springer to sift through at the scene and she wanted it hauled back to the sheriff's impound yard in Riverside. Lackie glanced over at Bland, still in the back seat, and saw his face harden and turn ashen.

"Will I be able to work tomorrow, or, I mean, on Monday?" Bland had asked, as they were driving him back to his house.

"I don't see any reason why not," Lackie replied.

"Okay, I'm not leaving the area. You know I'm not gonna run anywhere. Jesus. You know my paranoia is not way up in the air.

"You know what my routine is. I'm never far away."

"Evie, this is Jim."

Evie Kingston had just put her children to bed and she was lucky enough to grab the telephone on the first ring. She walked with it into her bedroom, pulling the long phone cord behind her. Petite, with her jet black hair neatly pulled back in a long, straight ponytail, Evie was not really in love with Jim and she had been trying to cool off the relationship, but he was sweet and generous to her and her children and she liked having him around. But having homicide detectives nosing about asking questions had made her grow more uncomfortable. Even though she couldn't see him hurting a fly, the persistence of the police in pursuing Jim gnawed at her. She could tell he was trying to sound upbeat, but he sounded worried.

"Is everything okay?" she asked cautiously.

"The police were here today with a search warrant. It's bad, Evie, it's real bad. They really want to get me for this Phoebe Ho thing. They took away half my clothes, they took the sheets and blankets off my bed, the towels out of the bathroom, and interrogated me at the police station for hours. I don't even have a car.

"I really need to see you. I hate to be a burden to you, but can you come and pick me up?"

Evie hesitated, torn. It wasn't such a big favor to come and get him, given all the wonderful things he had done for her and her children during the 8 months she had known him. Long before the police had started poking around they'd had problems. The first whiff of trouble had come when he told her about his past criminal conviction. He'd said he had been drinking at a party and gotten "out of control" with a woman who turned out to be a seventeen-year-old girl. When his parole officer suggested that might not be the extent of his criminal history, she'd told him she didn't want to know the rest of it since the way he treated her was good enough for her.

They had met in June when she lived down the street from him in Alhambra and he had come over to fix her garbage disposal. They had wound up talking all night at her kitchen table. Within a month, he had moved in, and he confessed he had fallen hopelessly in love with her. He had bought her an expensive watch and a ring and showered attention and gifts on her children. He took them to nice meals at expensive restaurants and to Disneyland, Knott's Berry Farm, and Magic Mountain. He had talked endlessly about how much he loved his "instant family." She had been a little surprised but flattered, and she figured her love for him would grow over time.

The first real glitch had come when his parole officer told her Jim couldn't live at her house because he was not allowed to be around children without supervision. It had been an unnerving experience to have a loved one's parole agent have a say in their lives. She still didn't want to know the full extent of his criminal history but figured it was bad enough for the parole officer to get involved. She had kicked him out of the house, then moved to another city with her children. He had followed her undaunted, coming over every night after work. The relationship had begun to deteriorate, with petty arguments over money and his always being at her house. She had resented him telling her how much money she spent getting her nails done or buying new clothes, although he had never hinted that she was a bad mother. She had begun to feel pressured and felt like his nightly visits were an intrusion, particularly his heavy demands on her for sex. He had told her he had a "heavy sexual appetite," but she had begun to get the feeling that the gifts and nice dinners were just compensation for her to provide him with physical affection. She loved being around him and genuinely enjoyed his company, and her children loved being around him, but she sensed something was wrong with how he constantly pushed himself into her life. She finally told him she wanted him to visit only two or three nights during the week.

Jim had balked but seemed to take this new restriction as a challenge. Instead of visiting her, he went to her sister's house or went to the home of mutual friends during the week, talking about how much he loved her and wanted to marry her, telling them about the fights they'd had and discussing strategies on how to win her back. He was constantly doing them favors, like fixing their cars or building a backyard deck, all for free. Evie had found herself wondering why he was talking about marriage with everyone but her. She found it preposterous that he would be thinking of marriage when they had known each other less than a year, with the last few months the most troubled for them as a couple.

Jim had quickly worn out his welcome. Despite the favors, Evie's family and friends complained that Jim was always dropping by and hanging around their homes. Evie again had to act like a disciplinarian and cut the number of visits he made to her and her relatives and friends. She had then limited his visits to once a week, just on weekends. Their fights intensified and by late November the relationship had cooled.

Then, in mid-December, he had suddenly proposed as they were sitting outside her house in her minivan. He had pulled out a ring and pledged his eternal love to her. When she had politely declined, Bland had asked her if she was using him and what he could do to patch up their relationship so they could wed. He'd burst into tears and cried off and on as they talked into the night.

Evie remembered that their conversation became somewhat disjointed and he started saying unusual things, such as the fact that he was the "last eagle" of his family, which she thought meant that he was the only child in his family. He'd also said he wasn't proud of what he was doing, and Evie didn't ask what he was talking about, assuming he had done something wrong.

The most disturbing moment had been when Bland mentioned nightmares he'd been having about going off to war and watching as Soviet soldiers tortured Vietnamese women, using pliers to squeeze their breasts and inserting things into their genital areas. Evie had been too shocked to ask any questions about his dream and changed the subject. Unnerved, she'd thought it was a good time to call it a night.

She had continued to see him somewhat sporadically during the first few weekends of December, until she learned that the kindly, generous man she'd once lived with and was still dating was suspected of killing a little girl. In the past few weeks, the police had been questioning her and her family and friends to verify Jim's whereabouts and if they had noticed anything unusual about his behavior during the first few weeks of December. Evie and Jim had visited friends and relatives on Christmas Day. Pressured by the sexual demands on her in the midst of their stormy relationship, she broke up with him 2 days later.

As was his way, Jim had tried worming his way back into her life and the on-again, off-again relationship had weakly resumed.

Now Jim was pleading with her to pick him up and Evie

felt sorry for him. She couldn't believe he'd had anything to do with such a hideous crime.

"I'll come and get you," she said.

Holding hands, Evie led Jim into her darkened house, keeping quiet so she didn't wake her children. The couple cuddled on the couch the way they used to do. She was curled up almost in his lap and he had his arms around her and was stroking her hair, talking quietly. He reached into his pocket, pulled out a letter, and held it out to her.

"This is for you," he said, as she looked up at him with wide eyes.

"Don't open it now," he said softly, kissing her on the forehead. "If the police ever arrest me or if something should happen to me, . . . open it then.

"I'm just afraid the police are going to try and make me a suspect in this case," he said. "I can't believe the way they're coming after me, but I'm worried about the effect this is having on you."

"I don't want to know the details. I don't want to talk about it," she said. "I wish this whole thing would just go away."

Even though he was the target of the police, Jim comforted Evie, soothing her with kind words and kisses. For a moment, she thought that it was wrong of the police to intrude into their personal lives and allowed herself to believe that if not for this investigation, things between them might be different.

Six cardboard boxes now had hair and fiber evidence. Springer had pulled carpet and fiber samples from every rug, floor covering, and carpet she could find at the Thayer home, where Bland rented a room. She had taken stained clothing, stained blankets, stained towels, and stained rags.

They had towed Bland's car to the police impound yard. Emptying and examining the debris-filled Datsun had consumed the entire day. Springer and Sanchez carefully cataloged every item, culling fibers and hairs and other trace evidence from the car's interior. She also found paint-splattered dropcloths. There was so much to analyze, she decided to start looking for the distinctive blue carpet fibers and then the rust-colored carpet fibers, because there were so many of them found on Phoebe's body and she had a vivid recollection of what they looked like. Then she would look at the dropcloth fibers, then at Bland's hair.

Within a few hours, she knew the carpet fibers from the house didn't match. An hour later, she had one hit on a car carpet fiber. It wasn't a fiber from the car's own carpet because that was mildewed and deteriorated. The matching carpet fiber had come from a clump of hair and fiber found in sweepings of the car floor.

The drop cloths did not match, nor the paint, nor the fiber. Springer pulled out the white envelope into which Lackie had put Bland's hairs. Almost on sight, Springer knew the hair found on Phoebe's foot was Bland's. Looking through the microscope, she easily made out the distinctive "dog-bone" cross-section called "troughing," common in African American hair, but extremely unusual in Caucasian hair. She planned to do a more extensive examination of the fibers and the hairs, but she knew she had one hair and one fiber whose characteristics matched those found on Phoebe.

She picked up the phone to tell Lackie the news.

"This is Faye," she said, speaking quickly. "I got a couple of hits. A fiber from Bland's car and a hair."

She waited while Lackie absorbed the information.

"Faye, I'm going to have to call you back," Lackie said. "Bland is gone."

CHAPTER EIGHT

Evie looked up from her desk and saw Jim standing there. He looked pained and tired. She was furious. After a dreamily romantic night on Saturday and a pleasant, leisurely day together on Sunday, she had driven him over to her best girlfriend's house to fix her car. He'd borrowed Susie's car, promising to return it in two hours, but instead had brought it back at 2 a.m. Susie had waited up all night and was so distraught over his taking her car she'd called in sick (she worked for the same nonprofit charity as Evie). To Evie, this was the last straw. She didn't want to have anything more to do with him, given what he was doing to her friends and to her.

''What are you doing here?'' she asked. ''Why did you take Susie's car?''

''This is the last time you're ever going to see me,'' Bland said, his face drawn in a melancholy frown. ''I'm going away.''

Evie at first couldn't have been happier, but she immediately felt torn. His hang-dog look made her curious, but she said nothing.

He came around the edge of the desk and knelt by her chair and took her hands in his. She was aghast at the display of affection at her office and felt her co-workers were staring at her. They would soon know from Susie about Jim's escapades with her car, and she knew she would be faced with somehow having to explain why her boyfriend, who was being questioned about a murder, had borrowed her best friend's car for 8 hours on a Sunday night.

"I just wanted to come by and tell you that I love you very much and to tell you goodbye," Jim said. "You won't be seeing me in the near future. I might be dying. I expect to die.

"Remember those forms you got for me to change my name back in October? I filled them out and I'm changing my name. I ordered new ID in the name of James Sterling and Charles St. Germain. I'm going to change my name and to everyone else, Warren James Bland is as good as dead.

"This is the last time you're ever going to see me," he said, tears coming to his eyes.

Evie was not happy about this whole scene being played out in her workplace and was confused by his claims that he was dying. He certainly hadn't said anything of the sort over the weekend, and she couldn't understand why he felt he needed to come to her office with a big display like this. It seemed he was making his last round of goodbyes, but he didn't elaborate on why he thought he was dying. Evie thought it was ridiculous and maudlin and wanted him out of her office and out of her life.

"Jim . . . you're going to have to leave," she said. "I heard what happened with Susie's car last night. I don't understand what's going on with you. I . . . I just can't handle this."

Right before her eyes, Jim burst into tears. He started blubbering about the police following him around and not having anything to do with Phoebe Ho and some other things she couldn't quite make out. Evie was astonished and her face grew hot with embarrassment at the scene he was making. She felt guilty for making him cry. But he had no right to come in and disrupt her and everyone else at work.

"Jim, I'm sorry. I'm really sorry. I can't deal with you coming here. You'd better go. I don't want to see you anymore. I want you to leave," she said. She got up out of her chair and walked him over to the door.

"Goodbye, Jim," she said, shutting the door.

Within a half hour, he called her back on the phone. Without tears, in a calm voice, he told her again that he loved her and her children and that he would miss them.

"I won't see you again. This is my last goodbye," Jim said. "I'm sorry for the embarrassment I caused you and your friends. Goodbye."

Evie hung up the phone, shaking her head.

The elderly woman's voice was hushed.

"Maddy, can you come over? Jim Bland is here. He's asleep and I don't want to wake him. I'm scared."

Frightened and frail, Celia Blake was whispering, curled up under the blankets with the phone to avoid waking the sleeping ex-con in the next room.

Maddy Jordan couldn't believe her ears. She knew her ex-son-in-law had been out of prison for months but thought he was living at Gene Thayer's house. Maddy couldn't figure out why he was imposing on her good friend, whose advanced age made her extremely vulnerable. He probably knew the poor woman was half senile and in poor health.

"I'll be right over, dear, don't you worry," Maddy said,

reaching for her car keys. "Just stay where you are. It won't take me more than a few minutes to get there."

Maddy herself getting on in years, never liked Bland when he was married to her daughter, Norma, and she cared much less for him now. He'd dropped in on her back in January when he'd gotten out of prison the last time and was nosing around, asking for Norma's address and phone number. Of course, she didn't give it to him. Norma had long ago divorced him and she was remarried, living in another state. Norma never wanted to see that man again. But for years, Maddy had acted as a buffer between her daughter and Bland, with him mailing her letters to mail to Norma. She didn't know what he wanted with Celia Blake, who was her roommate's sister, but she suspected he was up to no good. Celia was petite and fragile to begin with, and now she was starting to lose her mental capacities, even though Celia was just a few years younger than she. She probably had let Bland into her house because she recognized him. She knew Bland was a criminal but probably couldn't remember the kinds of trouble that had gotten Jim Bland locked up.

Maddy pulled her car into Blake's driveway, made her way up the sidewalk, and knocked on the door. As Celia opened the door, Maddy could see past her to Bland sitting on the couch, where he had apparently spent the night, his hair uncharacteristically mussed.

"What are you doing here?" Maddy asked, taking a stern tone. "What's going on?"

Bland looked up at her with sad eyes and a downturned mouth like a child's.

"I just wanted to see you and Celia before . . . well, I wanted to surprise you, Grandma. This may be the last time I see you. I won't be around much longer," Bland said, his voice low, calling her "Grandma" the way he did when he was married to her daughter. Maddy was not persuaded by this show of affection.

"What are you talking about? You know you shouldn't have come here and bothered her like this," Maddy scolded him. "She doesn't want you here and you have no business being here."

"I'm dying," Bland said. "I've got bleeding ulcers. I'm losing weight. I just came to say goodbye."

Maddy paused. He looked fine to her. After years of dealing with the ex-con, she was suspicious of everything Bland said.

"Well, get dressed. You're not going to die here."

Maddy turned on her heel and hunted for Celia while Bland got ready. She would give him a ride out of town and drop him off and be rid of him. He had a lot of nerve, showing up at Celia's house.

Celia was in the kitchen fixing tea and toast. She was a bit shaken up and Maddy comforted her. They sat and chatted and drank tea until Bland was ready. Celia told her that he had come over on Sunday night to pick up some papers. Maddy didn't know what she meant by that, but she just nodded. He left and returned the next night without a car and asked to borrow her car to go shopping and Celia had agreed. When he came back to her house, he simply spent the night. Maddy was incensed that he would take advantage of someone whose faculties weren't up to par. She patted Celia's hand and said she would take Bland away and she didn't have to worry, but to never, ever let him into her house again. She said it several times so that Celia would remember.

When she went back into the living room, Bland was ready to go and said he wanted to go to the bus station. Maddy was happy to oblige.

"What were you doing at Celia's? I thought you were living at Gene Thayer's house."

"My friends have turned against me. I didn't have any other place to go. I was just looking for a place to stay. I didn't mean her any harm.

"I guess I was just drawn to my old neighborhood. I've always had very fond memories of this area," Bland said.

Maddy remembered Bland had committed some of his crimes here in Long Beach, too. He used to be a very happy resident of the bars and restaurants. He used to have lots of friends at his old stomping grounds down here, and she wondered why he didn't look them up instead of taking advantage of a defenseless old woman who couldn't turn him away.

"My mind's really been clouded over for the past few days," Bland said. "I went to Mother's grave and spent a few hours down there, just to get some peace. I don't think I'm going to be here much longer."

Bland asked a few questions about Norma, but Maddy didn't answer, except to say that she and the kids were fine. The children were no relation to Bland; they were from Norma's second marriage.

Jim knew better than to ask for her phone number and address.

"You can give me a letter, if you want, and I'll give it to her," Maddy said. "You know I'm not going to give you her address." The thing she feared was that Bland was going to somehow track her down, but he had absolutely no idea of the address, although he knew they were living somewhere in the Chicago area. If he wanted to, he could probably make a serious attempt to find her.

"I've been much more at peace at the church I'm going to now. I need to find a church down here now."

Maddy looked over at Bland, wondering if he was drunk.

He didn't look drunk and he didn't smell drunk, but he was acting very strangely, almost as if he was delusional. She carefully avoided indulging his talk about death and dying because she didn't think he was ill, much less on his death-bed. All she wanted to do was get him out of the car and out of her hair.

As she drove past a Salvation Army thrift store, he asked if they could pull in because he wanted to buy some tennis shoes and some clothes. Maddy at first resisted, but then gave in, thinking he would leave after he got what he felt he needed.

She sat in the thrift store parking lot for 20 minutes while he bought the shoes and some pants and shirts. On the way to the bus station, Bland complained about not having any transportation and said he was taking a bus into Los Angeles. She didn't really listen because she wasn't interested in his plans. She knew he was down on his luck, but she didn't feel sorry for him.

Before he got out of the car, she again told him to never, ever go to Celia Blake's house again and extracted a promise that he would not step foot in her house again.

He agreed, saying, "I'm leaving town for good. I've got to regain my health."

As he got out of the car, Bland got back in and sat down, pausing.

"Grandma, I've done something terrible."

The remark gave her a chill. She sensed that for the first time that day he was telling her the truth, and she had no idea how to respond. She didn't want to know what, if any, other crime he had committed, and the remark just hung in the air.

"Let's pray," Maddy said. She bowed her head and said her prayer. But something felt wrong. She opened her eyes and looked over at Bland and shuddered. Bland had a horrible, vacant look on his face. It wasn't an expression she had ever seen before. He was eyeing the keys to her car. As the seconds ticked away, she wondered if she had the strength to push him out of the open car door and stomp on the gas.

"I won't be taken alive," Bland said, abruptly getting out of the car and pushing the door closed.

Maddy slammed her foot on the accelerator, the tires squealing as she peeled out of the parking lot and away from Bland. He's either going to commit suicide or get in a shootout with the police, she thought.

This time, Celia was screaming when she phoned Maddy.

"He's back! He came back!" she shrieked. "I don't want him in my house! Get him out!"

Maddy, frightened for her friend, banged the phone back onto the receiver, lunged for her car keys, and drove frantically to Celia's house, parking the car askew in the driveway and halfway on the front lawn, fearful for what Bland was doing back at the house. She hoped and prayed Celia was all right.

The door was slightly ajar. As she stepped inside and ran toward the sound of Celia howling, she caught a glimpse of Bland running out the back door. She walked quickly to the back of the house and stepped through the back door in time to see her ex-son-in-law hoist his paunchy, middle-aged frame over the fence into the neighbor's backyard.

She turned to comfort Celia and asked her what had happened.

Thin, frail, with snow-white hair and dark eyes, Celia was breathing heavily and held on to the furniture for support as she staggered over to the couch to sit down.

"He came back and he told me to leave the back door open, in case he had to leave," she said. "He went right into the bathroom and he was in there for a long time, so I called you.

"I was so scared. Why does he keep coming back?"

Celia was nearly hysterical with fright and didn't want to sit in the living room. Holding each other by the arms, they walked through the house and locked the back door, checked to see that all the windows were shut and locked, then peeked into the open door of the bathroom.

The white tiles around the sink were splotched with dark brown hair dye. The bottle had been dropped in haste on the floor, its contents staining the chenille rug and linoleum floor. Bland had used her fluffy white towels to blot the dye and one towel still hanging on the rod bore his smeary handprints. The dye had spilled into the sink, staining the pristine porcelain.

It was obvious that Bland was trying to change his appearance by dyeing his hair and by purchasing clothing and shoes, but Maddy didn't know why. It didn't matter. It seemed that Bland was gone once and for all and she wanted to comfort Celia, who was nearly hysterical with fright. She sat her down in the living room with some tea to get her calmed down, then went back into the bathroom and picked up the ruined rug and towels. With a bucket and sponge, she wiped the stains off the tiles and the sink and the floor, then went back into the living room to check on Celia.

"I don't think we'll ever see or hear from him again," Maddy told her.

Celia was still shaken up, so she didn't ask her in detail what had happened. Maddy told her this time to call the police if she should see Bland at her front door and showed her how to dial 911 and repeated over and over that she needed to phone the police.

Maddy left and suddenly felt exhausted at having to deal with Bland twice in one day and lay down to take a nap.

* * *

Out of the darkness, Warren James Bland walked from the shoulder-high bushes surrounding Celia Blake's front yard to the unlit front porch and knocked gently. His newly dyed dark brown hair was combed into a thinning pompadour. He had on the dark blue sweatshirt, brown pants, and sneakers he had purchased hours earlier. As Celia opened the door to see who was on her porch, he easily pushed the door opened and walked inside, towering over the frail elderly woman.

Bland pulled the door shut.

"I don't want to hurt you," he said, backing her into a corner of the front hallway. "But I will.

"I want you to get your car keys because I need to borrow your car. And I need your gun. Get your gun."

Petrified, Celia couldn't move. Her eyes darted around, but her mind was fuzzy and she was unable to speak or think clearly. She wanted to call Maddy, but she was afraid of what Bland would do if she tried to get to the phone. She started to cry. Bland kept talking, thinking she was simply reluctant.

"Hurry up! I'm on the run," Bland said, his voice getting louder, more urgent. "The police are looking for me right now. They think I killed Phoebe Ho. I'm a wanted man.

"I wouldn't want what happened to her to happen to you. She was tortured. I wouldn't want that to happen to you."

Sobbing silently, Celia looked up and pointed. Bland backed away a few inches and she staggered over to a sideboard, opened the drawer, pulled out a two-inch, blue steel gun, and offered it to Bland, her head bowed.

Bland stuck the gun in the waistband of his pants and covered the waistband with his sweatshirt. Using a chair for support, Celia leaned over her desk and picked up her car keys.

"Don't tell the police I was here," Bland said, backing out of the house. "Tell them I had nothing to do with Phoebe Ho. Don't tell the police about this. They want me for the Phoebe Ho case. But I'll be long gone."

Bland left, slamming the door shut behind him.

Celia stood stock still, listening to the sound of Bland fumbling in her garage, starting up her blue 1970 Toyota and driving away. She wanted to call Maddy, but she was afraid Bland would somehow find out and carry out his threats. Instead, she sat down on the sofa, in shock and confused.

"I told him the worst possible thing he could do was to run," Gene Thayer told Lackie. "He was very worried after you guys left on Saturday and cleaned out this place. He didn't have a car and I loaned him mine, but that didn't do it for him.

"He couldn't understand what you were trying to do after coming out and searching and going through all of his things, then leaving without arresting him."

The old man was sitting on his couch, wheezing. A small, dried-up Christmas tree was still sitting in the corner of the room, its tinsel glinting on withered branches in the noon sun. Thayer had called Lackie early Wednesday morning, 4 days after the search, to let him know about Bland terrifying Maddy Jordan and Celia Blake. Just after getting out of prison in January, Bland had given Thayer's phone number to Maddy during one of his brief visits and she had phoned Thayer to see if Bland was there with Blake's blue Toyota. Celia had finally told Maddy early Wednesday morning about Bland taking her car and gun. After being somewhat gruff with Lackie in the beginning, Thayer was downright chatty and cooperative, perhaps because he began to see Bland for more than just a friendly ex-con. He hoped Thayer and his son, Gary, would open up a bit more than they had in the past.

Lackie had spent Wednesday morning in the office phoning Bland's ex-wife, Norma, to let her know Bland was armed and dangerous and possibly headed her way. Lackie notified the FBI's wanted fugitives unit, sent out an All Points Bulletin over the national crime network and let Long Beach police know about the theft. He had gone down to Long Beach that afternoon to interview Maddy and Celia.

It was now Thursday and Lackie was learning how Bland's brazen demeanor had melted into hysteria and fear after the police search. Lackie had figured Bland's tough-guy cockiness was a facade and was interested to learn how Bland could assume different masks for his purposes.

"I told him not to worry about it. If he had nothing to do with Phoebe Ho, then there was nothing to worry about," Thayer continued. "I just told him to do his normal routine and let the police sort things out. That was what his parole officer, Blum, told him. Go about your business until you guys finished your investigation.

"I said if he was that worried, maybe he should see a lawyer, but, you know, being an ex-con and all, with the kind of background he has, he can't expect the police to ignore him when there was this murder so close by," Thayer said.

Bland had calmed down on Sunday, but by Monday, he seemed to have come to the conclusion that he had to run. Thayer urged Bland to just borrow his car, go to work, and follow his normal routine, but Bland had called that afternoon in a panic, saying he was being followed by police.

Lackie didn't interrupt, but he knew that was true. He

had assigned Molina to tail Bland on Monday, but he'd lost the surveillance within a half hour by driving to a store in Thayer's car, walking in the front door and out the back leaving the car in the parking lot.

"I told him to come home and just sit tight, but he started talking about taking off and hiding somewhere because he was afraid the police would come and arrest him," Thayer said. "I tried to talk him out of it, but he acted like he had no other choice.

"I told him to go talk to someone at the public defender's office and he said that he would, but he called back later and said the lawyer told him the police would arrest him because he was on parole and hold him until they finished the investigation.

"That didn't sound right and I told him so, but Jim said the cops were constantly following him, so he had to leave the car in the parking lot. He said he would leave the keys with Bert O'Reilly. He's a mutual friend.

"Well, after I heard that, I figured he was going to take off. I couldn't talk him out of it. Now he is probably going to be arrested because he stepped over the line and left town. I guess that's a guaranteed parole violation.

"I kept telling him over and over that it was the absolute worst thing he could do, but he wouldn't listen. I haven't heard from him since, so I assume he's in hiding."

Thayer matter-of-factly told Lackie that he didn't bother telling the police that he suspected Bland was on the lam, figuring it was Bland's problem and not something he wanted to get involved with.

Lackie thanked Thayer and started to walk out the door, then thought of one more question.

"Did Jim ever admit or deny being involved in the Phoebe Ho killing?" Lackie asked.

"One time, I asked Jim if he did it and he was noncommittal,'' Thayer said. "He kept telling me, 'I'm in big trouble, I'm in big trouble,' but he wouldn't say what that was. All he would say was that he didn't know anything about Phoebe Ho. It didn't make sense. He never outright denied killing her.

"I was always convinced Jim had nothing to do with this, but now, of course, I have some second thoughts. I don't know why he would go on the run if he didn't have anything to do with that little girl.''

Lackie thanked Thayer again and headed out to his car. The old man seemed almost eager to share any tidbit that might help. It was quite a change from his previous attitude of protecting Bland. He wondered if his son, Gary, would respond the same way. Lackie mentioned that he was on his way over to his house to talk to him, then waved goodbye and drove about two miles to Gary Thayer's home in San Gabriel. The middle-aged, brown-haired man opened the door and invited Lackie inside.

It was the first time Lackie had met the younger Thayer, who bore a strong resemblance to his father. Thayer introduced his daughter and her husband, Lois and Peter Carver, who were also living in there. Molina had interviewed Gary Thayer briefly once and had asked to examine his records to verify Bland's work hours on particular days and at particular times, but the detective had found Thayer extremely reluctant, claiming he didn't keep such detailed records. Thayer had also mentioned that his customers got upset when they learned that a convicted ex-felon had been working at their homes, and that they were being interviewed by homicide detectives.

Mindful of the presence of his daughter and her husband, Lackie started off the interview by telling him that the best way to satisfy his investigators was to be as open and cooper-

ative as possible so they would no longer have a need to come
back to probe him or his customers for more information.

"You employed Bland, so you're involved in this anyway,
since it is clear to us that he had the victim under his control
while he was still working for you," Lackie said. "If you
want to lessen your involvement, just be as honest and up-
front as you can with us."

"I am making myself available for you now and I have
been always cooperative," Thayer said with an edge to his
voice. "But I am tired of your investigators pressuring me
and my customers. They are complaining about being questioned by your people about having a criminal in their houses,
and to tell you the truth, I've lost a lot of business as a
result of all this.

"I had no idea what Bland was up to or what his criminal
history was or that he was some kind of child molester, and
if I'd have known that, I never would have sent him out to
people's homes where they had little kids," Thayer said.

Thayer was probably mad, more at himself than at the
detectives, at having been conned by an ex-con, Lackie
thought. He tried to defuse the tension by gently asking a
few questions about what Thayer had known when he'd
hired Bland, the nature of Bland's painting and repair skills,
and other general background information.

Thayer still insisted that he didn't have any detailed
records to show Bland's work schedule on the morning
Phoebe was captured and the week she was missing, but he
told Lackie he had given Bland $254 on Christmas week
as a combination of several days' pay and a small bonus.

He said he was pretty bad at keeping records but relied
on Bland's own accounting of his hours for his paychecks.

Lackie questioned Thayer in detail about the records he
did keep, such as the purchase of materials and the checks
from his customers, his tax records, and which apartments

and homes Bland was working in during December, when Phoebe was missing, whether the residences were occupied when Bland was doing the work, and if Bland had keys to those places.

Thayer couldn't recall and said repeatedly that he didn't have any specific records to rely on except for bills for materials, which would remind him whose home was being worked on, then comparing that with paid invoices from customers.

Lackie didn't expect too much to come from Thayer's roundabout records search and instead asked Thayer about the brown van parked in front of his house. Lackie knew that Bland had a fondness for committing crimes in and around cars and that his most recent known child sexual assault had taken place in a van he had borrowed from a friend.

Thayer said Bland occasionally used it to pick up materials for painting or light construction.

All four of them walked outside to look at the Dodge van. Thayer rolled back the sliding door and Lackie immediately saw rust-colored carpet on the floor of the van. As his eyes adjusted to the darkness of the van, Lackie saw mismatched carpet pieces covering the walls and the ceiling, boxes of tools, cans of paint, a hand-made bench at the rear, and some dust marks on the window of the rear cargo door, just above the bench. Squinting, he made out the ghostly outline of a child's bare foot. Lackie froze, feeling an involuntary shudder. He slammed the door shut and turned to Thayer and the Carvers.

"How often did Bland use the van?" Lackie asked.

"Well, I remember he used it, I think, in the last week of November and again in the second week of December," Thayer said. "I had him pick up some paint for a job and a door for the Hadens. You know, he's got so much stuff in that Datsun of his, he can't fit anything else in there.''

"I remember when he used it," said Lois Carver, a petite woman with shoulder-length brown hair. "He came to the house really early one morning and asked me for the keys. I think it was the first or second week of December, um, December eleventh sticks in my mind for some reason."

Before he could question her further, her husband broke into the conversation.

"I remember that. The afternoon before that happened, he asked Gary if he could use the van and he said no, but Bland came by the house the next morning really early, like at about six a.m., knocking on the door real soft, like he was hoping Gary wouldn't hear and could talk Lois into giving him the keys. I remember it because he asked Gary first, then it's like he went behind his back to get Lois to give him the keys."

Peter Carver also couldn't remember the exact date, but he thought it was the second or third week in December.

Lois said she was home when Bland brought the van back in 4 hours, at about 10 a.m. or 10:30 a.m., but was a little surprised there were no materials in the back, which he said he needed to pick up.

Peter said Bland used the van a second time about a week later, but that time, he got permission from Gary.

"Jim took the van keys at about 1:00 a.m. and said he had to pick up a tall ladder, like a metal extension ladder, and some paint. He came back, well, it was around seven p.m. and he gave me the keys and I went and looked and there wasn't any ladder in there and I didn't see any paint, either."

"Oh, God, I just remembered something else," Lois said. "There was one day when Bland came over to do some work in the dining room and he started yelling about Evie, that it was her fault for causing his predicament or something and he was mad about the police investigation.

"I just remember that he was upset and ready to blow up. He was yelling that he wished that he could get a gun and shoot someone. It was really weird and I was a little scared at the time. I didn't think he meant anything by it, but I did leave a little early for an appointment to get my nails done."

"When was this?" Lackie wanted to know.

"It was December twenty-first because that was the day of my last nail appointment," Lois said.

Lackie turned to Gary. "Did Mr. Bland ever have any reason to use plastic cable ties? Were they needed for any job that he did?"

"I don't use them and I don't know anything he would use them for," Thayer said.

"Did he keep any of his tools or equipment here?"

"Not really, just a few dropcloths in the backyard," Thayer said.

Without missing a beat, Lackie yanked out a "permission to search" form, filled it out to include the van and the backyard, and asked for Thayer's signature.

"We're going to have to tow the van to Riverside so our criminalists can go through it," Lackie said, "but I need a search warrant first. You understand there may be important evidence in there, so no one can go into the van until after we've gone through it and taken out trace evidence and other things like that.

"There may be someone out very late tonight, but it'll probably be next morning before I get a search warrant together and a judge to sign it before we can tow it."

"No problem," Thayer said, adding that he drove a white truck, so it wouldn't hurt his business not to have the van for a while.

"Okay, where are the dropcloths?" Lackie asked.

Thayer pointed to the side of the garage. "Over there."

Lackie collected the tarps, placed them in brown paper bags stored in the homicide unit for collecting evidence, then went back to the van. Lackie collected carpet fibers from each portion of the van, scraped some paint from the paint cans, and took samples of paint from the cans, said his goodbyes to Thayer and the Carvers, and made a beeline for the Riverside County crime lab.

While Springer was making the comparisons, Lackie drove back out to the San Gabriel Valley for a visit with Evie to see if she had heard anything from her wayward boyfriend. Far from protecting him, the diminutive Asian woman seemed genuinely frightened of Bland and told Lackie she never wanted to see him again. She ushered Lackie into her home and said that she was expecting a locksmith that evening. She had grown so fearful of Bland, she wanted to change the locks on her doors and on her minivan because he had duplicates of all her keys.

"He gave me this on Saturday night, after the police searched his house," Evie said, handing Lackie two sheets of yellow legal-sized paper with Bland's old-fashioned hand-writing titled "To be read only in the event of my demise or arrest."

"It's like a combination suicide note and will," she said, shaking her head. "I don't know why he would give me something like this.

"I don't want it. You keep it. I don't want anything to do with him anymore."

A child's cry interrupted the conversation and Evie excused herself to see which of her three children needed her attention. Lackie took a moment to skim the letter.

It started out like a traditional love letter: "You are an exceptional lady . . ., You have brought forth in me, even in this short time, emotions that I was afraid to ever feel again . . . At this time, I find myself practically accused of this murder that we talked about," Bland wrote, then described the search of a few days before. "They took me to the police department—asked me all kinds of questions, there appeared to be a number of discrepancies in my written records of the time during the week of the crime, what I said and what other people have said . . . he told me that paint was found on the girl . . . all makes them look more at me. He said he had physical evidence that puts ME with her . . .

"They took samples of my hair, saliva tests, impounded my car—I do not like what's happening or the direction this thing takes, you must know down deep inside that I have NOT done this horrible thing that I am practically being accused of."

In the rest of the letter, Bland bequeathed a watch and ring to her and told her that she and her children were beneficiaries in his life insurance. Following that was Bland's flowery farewell: "My heart and spirit shall always be with you. I shall always love you. Be happy, stay beautiful."

With her children in the next room, Evie sat down on the couch, and in a hushed tone of voice, unloaded all that she knew about Bland, including his bizarre dream of torturing women. Lackie questioned her closely about it.

"Did he ever directly deny having anything to do with Phoebe Ho?" Lackie asked.

"No," Evie said, after thinking for a moment. "No, he never did. I asked him just one time after it first came out that he was being investigated for the murder and all he would ever do is just say that he didn't know anything about it.

"He was worried about the police search a lot, but in looking back on it, he almost seemed more worried about the impact it was having on me. He wanted to know how I would react and what I was going to tell the police . . ."

Evie stopped in mid-sentence and the last phrase hung in the air. When she looked up at him, her eyes were moist with tears.

"I thought the police were intruding on our relationship at first, we were having so many problems to begin with. I just wanted it all to go away. I could not believe that he had anything to do with this, that the man that I was dating was, somehow, . . ."

Lackie patted her on the shoulder, trying to comfort her in the only way he knew how and completed the thought in his mind: the man she was dating was a killer.

Lackie made the long drive back to his office at the sheriff's department in good time since rush-hour traffic had long subsided. He hoped Springer had a comparison by now, but he had plenty of paperwork to keep him busy until she was ready to call him with a result.

Lackie plopped down at his desk and focused on two piles of paper. One was a stack of reports from detectives assigned out of his department and from South Pasadena who had been assigned to look into all the locations where Bland had written in his log that he had worked. Lackie methodically read the reports, noting that some were places of business where they had no repair or construction work done, they didn't recognize a color photograph of Bland, and they weren't familiar with the Thayer Construction Company. Some of Bland's purported "clients" had been dead more than a year, some people who didn't exist, and more than a few were friends or relatives of Evie's who'd met Bland once or twice. Interestingly, Evie's relatives had strong negative reactions to Bland after meeting him at a party or at a holiday dinner but couldn't put their finger on why he gave them the creeps. Of the homes, apartment buildings, and real estate offices where Bland actually did work, several said they had fired him because he'd shown up late, left early, performed shoddy work, or purchased the wrong color paint. A few who were bona fide customers were satisfied with his work, but most said he rarely put in a full day, never working more than a few hours at a time.

Asked to scout for the blue-and rust-colored fibers found in abundance on Phoebe's body as well as a place where he could have held a small child for several hours or several days, the detectives said Bland's workplaces didn't yield much, other than an empty, boarded-up garage, a warehouse selling used engines imported from Japan, and an empty apartment in a multi-unit complex in Alhambra. The detectives were following up on those possible leads.

The second stack of paperwork was a compilation of lists from the state Department of Justice of sex offenders paroled to Los Angeles County. The DOJ agents had said it would be useless to give the entire list of names because over 30,000 mentally disordered sex offenders were released to Los Angeles County each year. Lackie had asked the DOJ agent to create categories and send him the names of those who fit into each by category: those who had committed crimes against children and who had been paroled in the past 2 years to Los Angeles County—179 names; those with a certain child sex conviction who had been paroled to six southern California counties—234 names; and parolees with child sex offenses in Los Angeles County who had the genetic markers Springer had found in the semen found on Phoebe's clothing—48 names. Each of the lists included Warren James Bland. When the geographic area was narrowed to the San Gabriel Valley, the list of parolees with at least one child sex conviction who carried the identical genetic markers carried on Phoebe's clothing dwindled to three. Of those, one was African American in his twenties with black hair, the other was a Hispanic in his twenties with black hair. The final name on the list whose hair was the same gray color found on Phoebe's body was Warren James Bland.

The ringing phone seemed rather loud in Lackie's quiet office.

"Okay, we've got hits on these fibers," Springer said, her voice sounding rather perky at 9 p.m.

"The rust-brown carpet fibers from the van match twelve of the rust-brown carpet fibers on the victim. Paint balls from the tarp fibers from the Thayer backyard seem to match the paint balls and the fibers in their shape and color and fiber type, but I'll have to do some more analysis on those.

"I want to go through the van myself. There's a good chance she was in there for some time because she had so many of those fibers on her. She could have left some hair, blood, any other kind of trace evidence. I'll bring a print expert with me to lift that footprint and any fingerprints that might be in there."

He knew it. They were starting to close in on the physical evidence. Adding it all up in his mind, there were these fibers, the few fibers from Bland's car, the matching hairs, and hopefully, the matching fibers from the dropcloths, as well as the matching genetic markers in the semen stain on the panties.

"Thanks," Lackie said. "I'm going to write out the search warrant for the van and try to get it signed tonight. Can you go out there tomorrow?"

"Absolutely," Springer said. "Let me know what time."

CHAPTER NINE

"May I take your order, please?"

Bland, a neatly pleated fast-food hat over his dyed hair, smiled at the pretty forty-something woman on the other side of the counter. His name tag read "Thad." He brought her burger, apple pie, and Coke on a tray and asked if she needed help to her table.

"It's pretty slow right now," he said hurriedly, when she hesitated. "I've seen you here a couple of times this week. Do you work somewhere close by?"

Bland took the tray and walked around the end of the counter and brought it to a booth with orange cushioned seats, then stood chatting with the woman as she sat down. At 2:45 p.m., the lunchtime crowd had long since died down. The McDonald's in the northern San Diego suburb of Pacific Beach seldom attracted many hungry sunbathers in mid-January, even though it was warm outside. A cluster of teenaged employees huddled around the cash register to gossip about their newest co-worker.

"What's with the crusty dude picking up the women?" said Robert, a tall, skinny surfer with thin hair toasted to a whitish-blond by the sun and saltwater.

"You're jealous," Roger said, laughing.

"He's a suave Alaskan babe magnet," Robert said, strutting behind the counter as the others giggled. "I bet he gets laid this weekend."

"He can't! He'll smear his make-up!" snorted Ginny, a punk-rocker whose hat didn't hide her half-shaved scalp, shock of purple hair, and multiple ear piercings.

"God, I thought it was just me. He wears eyeliner like Michael Jackson. Weird!" Debby chimed in.

"Well, he said he just left his wife," Roger said. "Maybe he wore her clothes, too."

"I got the story that he's getting screwed out of his two-million-dollar business in Alaska," Ginny said.

"No way! He told me he was an engineer!" Debby said.

"Dude lives out of his car. Some millionaire," Robert said.

"He has a millionaire's name—'Thaddeus Sterling,'" Ginny said.

"Well, he should spend some cash to touch up his dye job," Roger said. "His roots are showing."

"Why don't you show him your fine dying technique, Ginny?" Robert said.

"Oh, shut up. He's coming!" Ginny said, sliding back to her end of the cashier's counter.

Bland sauntered back sporting a big grin and paused near Debby, also a cashier.

"Don't you ever smile?" he said to her.

"No," she shot back, as Robert and Roger snickered back in the kitchen.

"Hey, anyone know when Carla's working next?" Bland asked about the store's night manager.

No one responded.

"I'm outta here," Ginny said as the clock hit 3 p.m. She grabbed the hat off her head and ran her hand through the only side of her head with hair on it, fluffing the violet-tinged locks. "See ya."

She walked through the kitchen and down a set of stairs to the employee locker room and quickly slipped out of her polyester uniform and into her street clothes. She zipped up the back of her flip skirt and was bending over to lace her black boots when she felt like someone was watching.

Bland was leaning against the open doorway, his hands in his pockets. Ginny glanced at him, but he openly stared with a vacant look different than anything she'd ever seen. His intense gaze made her feel like a bug being fried under a microscope. Her first inclination was to angrily wave her hand in front of his face and say, "Hello, I'm changing in here, get the hell out," but his moody silence melted her frosty indignation.

"What is your problem?" she said, as fright dropped her voice to a whisper.

Silence. Ginny remembered that she had closed the locker room door when she'd come down to change. It was a small room with just one entrance, and he was blocking it.

"How old are you?" he asked, his voice oddly calm.

"Sixteen," Ginny said, her voice shaking.

"Where do you live?"

Her panic skyrocketed, bringing a rush of adrenaline. She glanced at her backpack still in the metal locker and she realized one boot was still unlaced. She considered running, but gauged her chances against a man twice her petite frame. It seemed as if many minutes ticked by, but it was only fractions of a second as she tried hard to think, her feet rooted to the cement floor. A wave of terror descended on her and she grabbed her backpack, banging her hand on the metal edge of the locker door and pushed past him, her wobbly legs forcing the heavy boots up the steps two at a time.

"I have to go," she said, shaking and fighting tears. She didn't feel safe until she was behind the wheel of her car, the Dead Kennedys cranking on the stereo, surrounded by other motorists on the streets of Pacific Beach.

"Hey, Jim. Right on time, buddy. Got your hot chocolate and jelly donut." Brett Cross had just finished putting the sprinkles on the iced donuts and was arranging maple bars and apple fritters next to the freshly baked bear claws and glazed twists in the glass display case.

"Call me Thad."

Bland put ninety-five cents on the counter, took a sip out of the paper Winchell's cup, and took a ferocious bite out of the jelly-filled donut.

"What?"

"Just call me Thad from now on."

Cross, a tall, thin man in his late thirties, didn't question Jim, or "Thad," as he now insisted on being called. Even though he was the donut shop manager, he was a fairly new addition to the coffee klatch of regulars at Winchell's, which was in the same minimall as a McDonald's, a dry cleaner's, a one-stop photo developer, and a frozen yogurt shop. From the time Cross first met Jim—or Thad—he'd talked incessantly about changing his identity. Cross had the guy pegged as a harmless transient, one of the more intelligent and literate he had met. Cross had once worked as an orderly in a mental institution peopled with residents of varying degrees of psychological and emotional incapacities and had learned that people sometimes told white lies to smooth over a rough background. He knew "Thad's" story about recently

moving from Alaska to Pacific Beach didn't jibe because
Cross had relatives living in Alaska and Thad didn't know
squat about life there. Cross also didn't think Thad was an
engineer or that he had run a big company, or that he'd left
a wife of 28 years and three daughters. Cross figured he had
stumbled on a stretch of bad luck and was looking for a
fresh start, so Cross swallowed the inconsistent stories to
afford Thad a little dignity.

Still, Cross couldn't help but wonder about his background. Thad was the cleanest homeless man he had ever
come across, always having nicely combed hair, a fresh
shave, and neat, clean clothes. He was certainly smart
enough to figure out he could filch a free shower at the
campground down the road, or clean up at one of the nicer
gas stations that had hot water and well-stocked restrooms.
Even the kids Thad worked with at McDonald's had figured
out he was sleeping in the blue Toyota parked in the back
alley behind the minimall parking lot.

Cross sometimes wondered what he had done for a living
and why he was out on the streets. He seemed like a proud
man, and Cross admired him for taking a minimum-wage
job flipping burgers to get back on his feet. Despite his
tough times, Thad always had a smile on his face and seemed
cheerful and upbeat. On the other hand, he sometimes discussed odd topics, like his obsession with changing identi-
ties, but Cross figured it was part of some internal struggle.
Perhaps it was tied to his homelessness and he wanted to
change that part of himself by leaving his old persona and
bad habits behind.

Thad blended in well with another of the regulars, Frank
Schroeder, whom he learned was drawing a social security
income. Schroeder, who looked far older than his 65 years,
had been hanging out at that Winchell's for so long, the
regulars called him "Mr. Winchell." When Cross became

manager, the outgoing manager told him having Schroeder around was like having an unpaid employee and an in-house booster who brought in customers as some of the regulars came in just to chat with Schroeder. He was always there if you needed someone to talk to. In fact, when Cross stepped in and took over the store, Schroeder was right at home behind the counter, ringing up donuts and coffee at the cash register, filling him in on when all of the regulars came in and what they usually ordered, and even keeping the early-morning bakers on their toes. Schroeder provided companionship during some slow stretches behind the counter.

From Schroeder's self-appointed position as the official greeter, he welcomed Thad into the donut shop gang. Better a donut shop than a bar, Cross thought. Maybe swilling booze had driven Thad into homelessness. Cross's wife, Joyce, sometimes joked that the bakers put something in the donuts to attract the mental cases, but Cross was happy to provide a safe harbor, and the customers seemed to like the atmosphere. Thad had a definite social bent and had invited the Crosses out to dinner at one of the nicer seafood restaurants a few nights ago, then insisted on paying the bill—a lonely man, hungry for companionship and too proud to let someone else pick up the check, he thought. Cross was floored by his generosity, but his wife took an instant aversion to him. Joyce couldn't quite put her finger on it. She wouldn't be happy when Cross told her that Jim wanted to be called "Thad" from now on. Maybe he could explain it to her.

Cross was willing to humor him. On such a glorious, sunny January afternoon, it was easy to be tolerant. Schroeder had gone home to spend a few hours with his wife and would probably be back by evening time to catch the late-night rush, so it was just him and Thad. In the early mornings, young surfers straggled in to pick up donuts to fuel their predawn rides and some came by afterward for a late-morning sugar rush. If they were lucky, a few of the local gals would whiz by on their rollerblades, showing off winter tans in swimsuit tops and short shorts. Fortunately, it never got too cold in Pacific Beach.

"Where's Frank?" Thad asked.

"He went home for a few hours. He should be back in a little while," Cross said. He looked at Thad, munching on his donut and wiping the jelly off his chin. His hair seemed noticeably darker than it had been a couple of days ago. When he'd first started coming around a few weeks ago, his hair was reddish with white streaks in it. By God, Cross thought, he was hard-driving enough to keep up his appearance. He was a bit curious, though, about the black eyeliner Thad wore, but it wasn't that noticeable and Cross didn't want to embarrass him by asking about it.

They people-watched and chatted about the weather, customers, Thad's day at McDonald's. The talk rolled around to changing his identity. Cross listened to Thad ramble, hoping it would be therapeutic.

"I need to get some different ID, maybe in a different name . . ."

A motorcycle with no muffler roared past, drowning him out.

"What?" Cross asked.

"I was just saying," Thad said, "I was wondering about how to get legal paperwork for a motorcycle, you know, a used motorcycle that didn't have paperwork. Maybe one that had been sitting for a while and didn't have legal registration anymore."

"I guess you just take it down to the DMV," Cross said. "Why, are you planning to get a motorcycle?"

"Well, I've had my eye on one," Thad said, chuckling. "You know, I used to race motorcycles when I was a kid, long before you were ever born. We were real daredevils back then. Me and some friends used to race at, uh . . .''

"Over that Alaskan tundra, huh?" Cross said with a quick wink.

"They broke down so much, we were really grease monkeys, that's for sure," Thad continued without missing a beat. "But they were nothing like the machines they have now. All that firepower. We probably would have killed ourselves if we'd had that much on two wheels . . .

"Speaking of firepower . . ." Thad said, his voice trailing as two bikini-clad teenagers entered the store.

Made Amazon-tall by rollerblades, they wheeled up to the counter, parking their impossibly long, freshly tanned legs directly in front of Thad's line of sight across the shop. The girls chattered while they discussed whether to split an apple fritter or if they each should each get one and whether the diet Coke they'd had earlier would nullify the calorie-laden confections. Cross, waiting for them to decide, smiled at the youthful indecision and rolled his eyes in Thad's direction, but found Thad's attention entirely consumed by the girls. He sat stock still, staring, visibly looking the young girls up and down. Cross at first was amused, but as Thad continued openly staring and getting a bizarre look on his face, Cross became annoyed and began to feel somewhat protective of the girls. Most men early on learned to control themselves, and this was strange behavior. It wasn't unusual at all for men to walk around in swim trunks or women to wear bikinis in this area. You just got used to it. Cross was distressed to see Thad behaving oddly.

Cross prompted the girls to hasten their decision and offered them a special—"Buy one, get one free"—to get them out of the shop. They happily rolled out of the shop, each one with an apple fritter. Thad's head turned and he watched intently as they gracefully rollerskated down the street. Cross waited impatiently until Thad turned his attention back to him.

"I need to get a girlfriend," Thad said, his voice husky.

Cross was disgusted and didn't know what to say. He was glad the girls didn't notice and get freaked out. Fortunately, Schroeder came in.

"Hey, where've you been? Everyone's been asking for you," Cross said.

"Gotta spend some time with the wife," Schroeder said.

"Bring her down, then," Cross said. "I run an equal opportunity store here."

Afternoon business started to pick up and a few regulars came in to get bakers' dozens. Thad and Schroeder kept the customers talking and happy.

"Good God!" Thad muttered. "That's just what I need!"

Cross glanced up and looked at Thad, whose head was turned in the direction of the parking lot. Two police officers had parked their motorcycles out front and were ten feet away, heading straight for the front door. Cross watched as Thad appeared to panic. He jumped to his feet, looked around as if he wanted to hide, then sat back down again. He turned his chair away from the door, and in a final, panicked flourish, declared, "I need to use the restroom!"—and locked himself in the men's room.

Helmets in hand, the officers entered the store, their leather boots and Sam Browne gun belts making crunching noises as they walked. The portable radios on their hips squawked and each officer instinctively reached to turn down the volume. The officers made their way to the front of the short line and both ordered coffee and a donut, then took their food to one of the tables. Cross thought of Thad huddling in the men's room and wondered why he was hiding. He couldn't figure out what was bothering him these days. Maybe he'd once had a bad experience with the police.

The officers took their time with the donuts and the stream of customers was fairly steady. Schroeder helped behind the counter for a while. Thad remained in the bathroom.

The men in uniform finally got up, tossed out their trash, and went outside, put on their helmets, and took off. The dull roar of the motorcycles died out and the shop was empty. Schroeder was chatting about something and Cross looked at Thad, who had finally emerged from the restroom.

"I hate those fucking pigs," he muttered to no one in particular.

Cross was astounded. Thad had always been the most polite of gentlemen and he had never before heard him swear. He didn't say it loud enough for Schroeder to hear, however, and Cross continued talking to him. Maybe he would talk to Thad later and find out what that was all about. Heck, cops were some of their best customers. Cops and donuts just went together, and that built-in safety feature was one extra reason that tilted him toward Winchell's rather than other fast-food places. He was starting to wonder if his wife was right about Thad.

Schroeder was rattling on about something and he tried making a minimal response when the phone rang.

"Winchell's, may I help you?"

"Hello, is Frank there?"

"Uh, let me see. He may have stepped out for a minute," Cross said, sighing.

Cross cupped his hand over the mouthpiece. It was Wanda, Schroeder's sister-in-law. Her husband, Leo, was Frank's brother. When he had died about a year before, she had begun calling Frank incessantly, and it had been getting worse the last few months. It was making Frank's wife crazy. Wanda had been barred from calling Frank at home, so she constantly called him at the shop.

"It's Wanda," Cross said, whispering to Frank, holding the phone receiver toward him.

Frank shook his head and backed away. He was the second person in his shop that afternoon who looked like he wanted to escape.

Frank's gaze landed on Thad, who was sulking at his table. No one had told Frank about the name change.

"Jim," he said. "Why don't you talk to Wanda? She's a nice woman. She's recently widowed, you know, kinda lonely.

"She's got two kids . . ."

Thad's eyes widened. He rose out of his seat, purposefully walked across the shop with a grin, and plucked the receiver from Cross's outstretched hand.

"Hello, this is Thad, a friend of Frank's," he said with practiced smoothness.

They were sipping the last of their wine when the waiter brought the check.

Cross reached for it, but Thad was quicker. He hardly glanced at it, then reached into his pants pocket, pulled out a wad of cash, and peeled off four twenty dollar bills as Cross, his head slightly tilted back, gaped over the top of his wineglass.

"It's on me," he said, waving his hand at Cross, who feebly reached for his wallet. "I like to socialize. It gets pretty lonely, now that I'm pretty much on my own down here."

It was the second time he had bought them dinner, and an expensive one, at that. Maybe Thad was trying to appease Joyce, who had been quiet most of the night. She'd told Thad she had a headache, but Cross had argued with Joyce about going out with him, particularly after he'd told her about his name change. She'd said there was something about him she distinctly didn't like. He hadn't even told her about his reaction to the teenaged girls or the motorcycle officers. Cross wanted a chance to talk with Thad about that first.

"Well, thank you," Cross said. "You know you don't have to do that."

"It's my pleasure, really," Thad said. "I enjoy that. Nothing like a good meal with good friends."

Joyce kicked him underneath the table as Cross said, "Are we all ready to go? I think Joyce might need to lie down, with her headache and all."

"So soon? It's so early. Gee, I don't know what I'm going to do with myself the rest of the night," Thad said pleasantly.

Cross thought of the poor guy sitting in his little blue Toyota for hours on end until it was time to slide the seat back and fall asleep. Joyce was drinking from her water glass.

"Well, would you like to drop by for a little while?" Another hard kick from Joyce.

"Oh, I'd love to!" Thad said.

On the way home, with Thad following them in the Toyota, Cross told Joyce that she could simply go into their room and lie down if she didn't want to talk to him.

"Why not indulge the guy? He was nice enough to pay for dinner, you know," Cross said.

"I just don't want that man in my house," Joyce said. "I don't know what it is about him. And now this name change. Something about him gives me the creeps."

"All right. You can escape into our room and I'll sit and talk with him awhile and then call it a night, how's that?" Cross said.

As soon as they pulled into the driveway, Joyce retreated

Warren James Bland, 9, in San Antonio, TX during a visit with his older half-brother. (*Photo courtesy John Isaacs*)

Bland with his parents Carl and Hava Bland in Reseda, CA. (Photo courtesy John Isaacs)

Bland and his mother. He never posed with his parents without making a face. (*Photo courtesy John Isaacs*)

Already six feet tall, a twelve-year-old Jim (right) poses with his father and mother. (*Photo courtesy John Isaacs*)

Bland with his grandmother in Los Angeles, CA. (*Photo courtesy John Isaacs*)

Considered a daredevil motorcyclist, the 17-year-old Bland (left) and his friends raced at the Saugus Raceway. (*Photo courtesy John Isaacs*)

Bland, 18, and his first
wife, 16, in 1955.
(*Photo courtesy John Isaacs*)

Bland sexually assaulted
his wife on their wedding
night. She fled in terror
shortly after this
photo was taken.
(*Photo courtesy John Isaacs*)

Torture marks from pliers and vise grips on 11-year-old Paul Corday's chest from a December 1980 assault by Bland. (*Photo courtesy Riverside County D.A.'s Office*)

April 1977 California prison ID card issued to Jim Bland while he was serving time for kidnapping and assaulting an 11-year-old girl. (*Photo courtesy John Isaacs*)

CALIFORNIA
DEPARTMENT OF CORRECTIONS

CALIF PRISON
B20205A
W J BLAND
4 5 77

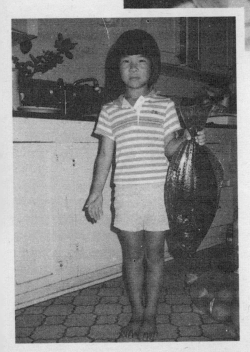

Phoebe Ho.
(*Photo courtesy Riverside County D.A.'s Office*)

Photo of Phoebe Ho used on the thousands of missing child flyers distributed during the search.
(*Photo courtesy Riverside County D.A.'s Office*)

At her seventh birthday party a few weeks before her abduction, Phoebe Ho wore her favorite shirt, the same one she was wearing when she disappeared. *(Photo courtesy Riverside County D.A.'s Office)*

Wanted poster circulated after Phoebe Ho's body was found. *(Photo courtesy Riverside County D.A.'s Office)*

WANTED BY:
RIVERSIDE COUNTY SHERIFF INVESTIGATIONS
FOR: INVESTIGATION 187 P.C.

REFER: ER86352074

COIS BYRD,   SHERIFF

SUSPECT INFORMATION

NAME: BLAND, WARREN JAMES
AGE: 51   DOB: 01-22-36
SEX: MALE   RACE: WHITE
HEIGHT: 6'0" WEIGHT: 180
EYES: BLUE HAIR: BRN & GRY
TATTOOS/MARKS:

AKA: STERLING, JAMES
PHYSICAL TRAITS:
PRESCRIPTION GLASSES

LAST KNOWN ADDRESS:
ALHAMBRA

OCCUPATION: PAINTER
VEHICLE: '70 TOYOTA COROLLA
MAKE/MODEL: 4 DOOR
COLOR: LIGHT BLUE

LICENSE: 314ASU STATE: CA.
FELONY VEHICLE IN N.C.I.C.

WARRANT INFORMATION

COURT: PAROLEE AT LARGE
WARRANT #:
BAIL: NONE
EXTRADITION APPROVED: YES
NCIC #:

ARREST AND NOTIFY
RIVERSIDE COUNTY SHERIFF INVESTIGATIONS

4129 MAIN STREET
RIVERSIDE, CA. 92501
REFER TO: INV. LACKIE/SGT. SZELES
AT (714)787-2066
24 HR NUMBER (714)787-2444

ADDITIONAL INFORMATION

SUSPECT WANTED FOR INVESTIGATION OF THE KIDNAP OF 7 YEAR OLD PHOEBE HO FROM SOUTH PASADENA ON 12-11-86. VICTIM FOUND DECEASED IN RURAL AREA OF RIVERSIDE COUNTY ON 12-18-86. VICTIM WAS SEXUALLY MOLESTED WITH DEATH DUE TO STRANGULATION.

SUSPECT ALSO SOUGHT FOR QUESTIONING IN SIMILAR DEATH OF WENDY OSBORN; ABDUCTED 1-20-87 FROM PLACENTIA AND FOUND DECEASED ON 2-1-87 IN CHINO HILLS AREA OF SAN BERNARDINO COUNTY.

SUSPECT POSSIBLY ARMED WITH HANDGUN.

The Alhambra, CA house Bland rented is only a few miles away from Phoebe Ho's home. *(Photo courtesy Riverside County D.A.'s Office)*

Los Panches, the San Diego Mexican restaurant where Bland was chased, shot, and captured. *(Photo courtesy Riverside County D.A.'s Office)*

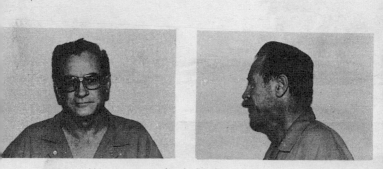

Warren James Bland's booking photo.
(*Photo courtesy Riverside County D.A.'s Office*)

Phoebe Ho's body was found in a dirt ditch in
Glen Avon, CA on December 18, 1986.
(*Photo courtesy Riverside County D.A.'s Office*)

Paint chips in the jacket Phoebe Ho wore when she was abducted were used to link Bland to the crime. *(Photo courtesy Riverside County D.A.'s Office)*

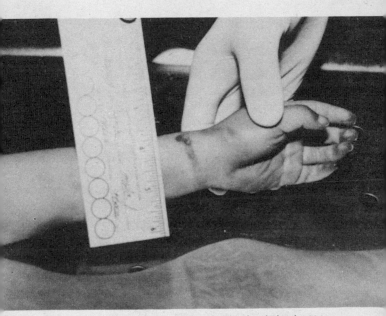

Wrist marks from cable tie used to bind Phoebe Ho.
(Photo courtesy Riverside County D.A.'s Office)

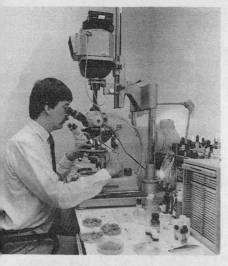

Microscopist Skip Palenik who matched hairs and fibers found on Phoebe Ho to Bland and his drop cloths.
(*Photo courtesy Skip Palenik*)

Riverside County Superior Judge Gordon Burkhart.
(*Photo courtesy Riverside County D.A.'s Office*)

Riverside County District Attorney Cregor Datig.
(*Photo courtesy Riverside County D.A.'s Office*)

Riverside County District Attorney Investigator George Hudson.
(*Photo courtesy Riverside County D.A.'s Office*)

into the house and Cross stood outside in the dark, talking with Thad for a while. Joyce was kind enough to flip on the porch light. His next door neighbor's light went on soon after that and Cross saw him open his garage door and wheel out a motorcycle with a "For Sale" sign on it.

Thad followed his line of sight and seemed to scrutinize the bike, a year-old, top-of-the-line Kawasaki.

"That's a nice bike," Thad said. "Have you ever seen him ride it?"

"He rides it once in a while," Cross said. "He takes good care of it. He's always tinkering with it, messing around with it. It's not too loud, either."

"Do you think he lets it sit out there all day long with that 'For Sale' sign on it?" Thad asked.

"No way," Cross said. "He put an ad in the paper. That bike stays locked up in the garage."

"Oh," Thad said flatly. "I need to get another car, something bigger. I'm also in the market for a gun. I've got a .22 right now, but that pea-shooter wouldn't hurt a flea."

"Well, I guess you could go to a gun store," Cross said.

Thad walked over to his car, opened the driver's side door, and pulled out a tiny blue steel, .22-caliber revolver with a two-inch barrel.

"Look at this thing," Thad said. "I hate to go through all that rigamarole to get a gun. I don't believe in it. I'm a firm believer in firepower."

He likes saying that, Cross thought to himself. He wasn't a gun nut and wasn't familiar with the terminology. He looked gingerly at the tiny gun. Thad put it away and then pulled out a pair of handcuffs.

"Ever try getting out of a pair of these?"

Cross was starting to get a little antsy. Good thing Joyce was in the house. His shins couldn't take anymore swift kicks.

"Can't say that I have," Cross said.

"Ever heard of Houdini? I love magic and the mystic. Here, put these on me. Go ahead. I have a key."

Cross had used handcuffs on unruly patients at the mental institution where he'd once worked, and he was a little puzzled at Thad's desire to be handcuffed. He complied, ratcheting the cuffs down around his wrists, then snapping them tight.

In the semi-darkness, he watched Thad rotate his wrists, working his forearms, and felt almost embarrassed for him until he heard a clicking sound and Thad sprang out of the cuffs, holding them aloft like a circus performer.

Cross stood there with his mouth agape. Like a polished lounge act, Thad tossed the handcuffs in the back seat and pulled out a rope, saying he also knew how to escape from tied ropes. With the flick of his wrist and a few loops, Thad showed him several knots, narrating as he worked, explaining that during World War II, the Japanese soldiers in the Pacific would tie a slip knot around a prisoner's neck, then loop it around their wrists and ankles. The more the prisoner struggled, the tighter it would draw the noose around the neck, slowly strangling the captive.

Cross was uncomfortable with these displays and tried to draw a close to the conversation, but Thad was on a roll with the bizarre party tricks. He tossed the rope back into his car and dug around in the glove compartment looking for something else to show him. Cross glanced at the clutter in his back seat and looked squarely at a pair of girl's peach-colored panties. The seams were cut out, splaying the panty legs open, and clothespins were attached to the fabric of the crotch. To make matters worse, they were sitting next to a porn magazine.

Cross squinted a bit harder at the back seat and rubbed his eyes. He couldn't believe what he was seeing.

"Here it is," Thad said, pulling out some paperwork.

Cross took the papers in his hand. It was a birth certificate and a Department of Motor Vehicles computer printout, both in the name of Leo Schroeder, Frank's recently deceased brother.

"Where did you get this?" Cross asked.

"Frank's wife sold it to me for $100," Thad said. "Now, all I need to do is go to the DMV and get my picture taken and I'll have a driver's license, too."

"Gee, look at the time! I should probably check up on Joyce. It's been real nice seeing you," Cross said, shaking Thad's hand. "Thanks for dinner."

He shut the door to his house, went to the kitchen, and stood in the dark looking out the window until he saw Thad pull away in the Toyota.

It was going to be a long drive to Escondido, Bland thought, sliding behind the wheel of the Toyota. Wanda probably wouldn't mind if he showed up a bit late; he would just tell her he'd worked the second shift. She wasn't too bright, anyway, like the rest of the people in this area. That was good for him, though. No one seemed suspicious. Bland prided himself on his clever techniques.

He had thought long and hard about absconding, as he preferred to put it. He had picked out two names for himself, "Thaddeus Sterling" and "Charles St. Germaine." He thought both names sounded dashing, like characters out of bodice-ripper novels. He had pieced together the names out of books but couldn't remember exactly who those characters were, just that they were superior gentlemen and had lived their lives with honor, unlike him. He admired that but knew he couldn't change his lengthy criminal past. It was all he knew. He didn't want to go back to prison and didn't want to think about what would happen if he was ever confronted by a police officer.

One of the many books he had devoured while in prison was written by an ex-FBI agent who discussed how to change your identity and disguise yourself with subtle techniques, like using eyeliner to make your eyes look deeper. He sat in his car every day and carefully applied the eyeliner, just like it said in the book, but the tube he had taken from Evie's bathroom was almost dry. He made a mental note to see if Wanda had any. He had shaved his moustache at Celia Blake's house, chuckling to himself that the cops would never think to look for him clean-shaven, since he had worn a moustache for almost all his adult life. The other telltale characteristics were also disguised, like his gray hair dyed to a dark brown. He was going to need more long-sleeved shirts, though, to keep the tattoos on his arms covered up. The tattoos were the word ''Gearbox,'' a reference to his mechanical ability, a rose with a dagger through it, and the names ''Marty'' and ''Babs.'' He also had a huge eagle on his chest, but he never went out in public without wearing a shirt. The tattoos he'd received in prison were of such poor quality and were so old, the once-crisp lines had run together, blurring the shapes and making them no more than bluish blobs on his arms. Since abandoning parole, as he liked to put it, he wore long-sleeved T-shirts all the time, even under his McDonald's uniform. But he needed more changes of clothing.

He also needed a bigger car. He had hot-wired the black van owned by the McDonald's manager a few times, but that was risky. The first time he'd done it was before he'd started working there. He hadn't known the manager lived only six blocks from the restaurant. He'd chuckled as he'd heard her complaining about the radio being changed to a different channel and finding the ignition wires dangling down. She should've been happy he'd returned it. He might have to use it again, but it was getting risky. He'd had a run-in a few days ago with Ginny, but she had run out before he'd had a chance to talk with her. Later he'd had an encounter with the cute cashier, Debby. He knew she was headed down to the locker room and had gotten there before she had. He'd been very excited. He'd dropped his underpants around his ankles as if he was changing and waited until she walked in. She hadn't screamed. She'd just walked out and apparently hadn't told anyone. Afterward, he'd been real cool and come up to her later and asked why she hadn't stuck around. He'd have to try something different next time.

He stuck to side streets and drove carefully within the speed limit. The last thing he wanted to do was wind up in the can for a lousy traffic violation. The Toyota was taking a beating with the miles he was putting on it. It had been sitting in the old lady's garage so long, he'd had to give it a tune-up. He didn't have the right tools because the cops had grabbed everything in the search, but he was pretty good at improvising in a pinch. He wished he had a bigger car, but he wanted to plan that acquisition in a little more detail. Getting rid of the Toyota would be no problem—it was about an hour to the Mexican border and he could sell it for a few hundred dollars and the cops would have no way of tracing it. But for the time being, he was stuck driving the damn thing. He used a car cover to shield it from prying eyes and had long ago stolen license plates and dumped the original ones, but it was still risky to keep it. He'd been looking for a motorcycle and fancied the sports model that Cross's next-door neighbor was selling. He'd have to scout around and check out the neighborhood, maybe take it for a test run.

His mind drifted to how much he had scared the old lady,

but she didn't need the car. Celia Blake was in her eighties, half senile, and not physically capable of driving. And what was she going to do with a gun? That's why he took hers! It was easy. All he had to do was ask for it. If he hadn't been chased out of there by the other old bag, it would have been a perfect place to stay for a few days. She lived there alone and the cops would never have looked for him there.

He admitted he took advantage of her, but he had needed a place to stay. Just like with Wanda. Now he understood why Frank palmed her off on him. It didn't take any more than a couple of dinners out with her and her two kids before she was wrapped around his little finger. She waited until he got back to her place every night. It was a lot better than sleeping in the car and showering at a campground, but boy, was she dumpy. And stupid. She was even letting him take naps with her kids.

Staying at Wanda's was perfect for him right now. One, it was quite a distance from where he worked at McDonald's, and two, there was absolutely no way for the cops to connect her to him.

His next move was to get a different job with less visibility. The run-in with the motorcycle cops at Winchell's had made him panic. They also came into McDonald's with a fair amount of frequency, but so far no one had recognized him. The cops down in this part of the state were pretty stupid anyway, he thought. They didn't have any reason to go looking for him. He had been checking out the U-Haul rental place a few blocks from McDonald's, thinking it would be a good place to work. It was less likely to attract cops and it was off the main boulevard, so it had much less visibility to traffic. The pay was slightly better and he would get to work outside, cleaning out the backs of the trucks. He had lied through his teeth on his McDonald's application and hoped he could use the reference from there to boost his U-Haul application.

Despite shacking up with Wanda, he was feeling heartsick for Evie. He feared he had alienated her forever. There was still hope in his heart that if he could stay clean—not get caught for anything, and put down roots somewhere, maybe he could send for her. It was a farfetched wish, but his desire for her always seemed to be with him. The real test would be if he could get a partner to help him out on some of his extracurricular projects he had in mind. He had heard Thomas Kemp, an old buddy of his, had also broken parole and was also on the run. He figured he would stay at his mother's house in Seattle, so he wrote him a letter on January 28. Without spilling the beans, he wrote, "This letter comes with the utmost urgency!!! Tom, you and I have talked about many things previously, which I would very much *now* like to put into operation *at the earliest possible date!*

"For me, life has hit the proverbial fan—and I mean to tell you, it's serious!! I am currently hotter than a fire-cracker," Bland wrote. "I have a number of two-man operations lined up and I need you. You, Tom are the only one that I've trusted and you are indeed a good friend!

"The enclosed address is a mail drop—*safe!* If possible, please respond just as soon as it is possible. I know that *we both need the money badly!*

"I would appreciate, Tom, if you would treat this letter with the utmost confidence and please destroy it and the envelope just as soon as you can." Bland had given him his alias and the address to a private box he had rented at Pacific Beach Mail Box, but signed it, "Always your friend, Jim Bland."

It had been several weeks since he'd sent Kemp the letter and he had been visiting the mail drop every day. He was counting on Tom's reply to get some cash. He had been doing some jobs, but it was way too risky for him to keep going like he was down here. He watched as Cross gaped at his roll of twenty-dollar bills. Bland knew he ought to be smarter and keep a low profile, but sometimes he couldn't help but show off.

He was kind of annoyed at his other prison buddies. He felt like they'd let him down. John McCarthy, who'd been released a few months before Bland, seemed reluctant to hustle. Bland had done all the work and planned out a robbery of a nudie bar on the fringes of Los Angeles County months ago. They checked it out together, but McCarthy backed out at the last minute. Christ, Bland needed money, and that would have given him the perfect boost. He had a couple of other deals lined up last fall, but McCarthy backed down from those, too, then cut off contact with him. He'd finally gotten ahold of him a couple of days ago, but McCarthy didn't want anything to do with him.

Bland had phoned another buddy who lived in the San Diego area, but he had also begged off, saying he was desperate to stay straight. He was crossing his fingers that Kemp would pull through.

On a whim, Bland decided to turn the car around. It was Friday night and he guessed Evie might be making a weekend visit to her friend who lived in a suburb of San Diego. He had an hour or two to kill before he had to get back home to Wanda. He had a hunch.

He rounded the corner. His heart quickened as he saw her silver minivan parked outside her friend's house. Bland parked around the corner, walked silently in the dark to the front porch, and knocked quietly.

Her friend opened the door and visibly blanched.

"Is Evie here?" Bland asked.

Her friend, a middle-aged man who had sponsored Evie's

immigration to the United States, turned and Bland could see Evie sitting on the couch with a photo album on her lap. He said Evie didn't have to speak to him and that she should call the police.

Evie got up and came outside to the porch where Bland was standing. She looked upset and scared. He wanted to hug her but thought she would make a noise and attract attention. He invited her to talk in the alley behind the house.

"No, I don't want to go into the alley with you," she said. "How did you know I was here? I've only been here a few minutes."

Bland could tell she was unnerved. "I followed you from your house," he lied.

"It's too risky for me to call you at home, and of course, I can't visit you at your house. The police are probably staking out your house and tapping your phone lines. I doubt if I'll be able to see you in person on your birthday, but watch for something in the mail," he said.

Evie acted like she was frozen. She stared at him with wide eyes.

"I miss you very much," he said, trying to soften her up. "I wish I had a picture of you. I didn't bring one with me. Do you have one?"

Evie just stared at him and shook her head.

"It's really good seeing you. I've wanted to meet you somewhere in LA, but it wouldn't be a good idea," Bland said. "Hey, where's that ruby ring I got you? Don't you wear it anymore?"

Bland didn't like the fact that she looked so scared.

"You know, the police are looking for me, but they're looking at you, too. They have these sophisticated electronic monitoring devices now," Bland said. "Have the police been talking to you? What are they doing?"

"The police are looking for you," she said mechanically. "The told me to call if I saw you."

"Do what you have to do," Bland said.

He turned away and walked into the darkness.

CHAPTER TEN

It was nearly midnight when Lackie's pager woke him up.

His wife hated it, but he had been sleeping with his beeper on their nightstand ever since Bland had fled. She now wore earplugs to bed, but it didn't always drown out the constant beeping. Neither of them was getting much sleep lately. A fourteen-year-old girl was missing, and Lackie had every reason to believe Bland was involved. So did authorities in the Orange County suburb of Placentia, where Wendy Osborn had been kidnapped on her way to school on January 20. The circumstances of the kidnapping were of startling significance to the detectives, who compared it to the Phoebe Ho kidnapping. It had happened while Bland was on the run. The girl was intercepted as she walked alone from her home to school early in the morning. In another unfortunate parallel, no one had witnessed the abduction. Detectives in both jurisdictions also found the location important. If one were to drive from Los Angeles County, where Phoebe Ho was abducted, to Riverside County, where her body was found, one route would take you right through Orange County. The worst part was that Wendy Osborn had been missing for 3 days without a trace.

During the month Lackie had been working on the Phoebe Ho homicide, he had received dozens of calls from detectives with recent murders in other jurisdictions to see if there were significant similarities between the cases. Lackie had checked the state Department of Justice system, a computerized database of unsolved homicides, to look for a match to the MO. If there was enough in common with a case he talked and compared notes with the detectives handling it.

When Bland fled, Lackie had put out that information over the teletype. But there was one catch. While Lackie thought Bland was responsible for Phoebe's murder, the Riverside deputy district attorney assigned to the case wasn't convinced and wouldn't file murder charges that would allow Lackie to obtain an arrest warrant. It was one thing to simply inform other agencies there could be someone in their area who might be responsible for murder. But another police department would certainly sit up and take notice—and take action—if they bagged a man wanted for murder. While Lackie considered Bland a felon fleeing to escape prosecution for murder, all he could officially say was that he was a "strong suspect." The only arrest warrant for Bland was put out just 3 days before through the parole board for a parole violation for reneging on the terms of his release by fleeing the jurisdiction. John Blum, Bland's parole agent, put in the paperwork right after Bland fled, but it wasn't processed and put into the system until recently and was distributed via teletype to all state law enforcement agencies. The teletype was routinely checked before each work shift in most jurisdictions for various tidbits, such as if an ex-con wanted for murder was hiding out on their streets. So far, there were no bites from anyone who'd spotted Bland in their area.

Lackie had tried using the media, but there wasn't much to feed the reporters. When he first got the case, he tried to sustain media and public attention by engaging them in a search for an eyewitness in the remote chance that someone in either county had seen something related to Phoebe's abduction or murder. When the holidays approached and there was no news, there was nothing to report and the headlines died. Even when Bland vanished he had dutifully informed a few dedicated reporters from both counties, who continued to call him periodically for updates on the case, but all he could tell them was that Bland had fled.

The DA was a thorn in Lackie's side. He wanted more evidence to tie Bland to the Phoebe Ho case. Of course, prosecutors always want more evidence to connect the perpetrator to the offense, preferably some unbiased bystander with perfect eyesight who can immediately identify the murderer. Both Lackie and the DA knew some of the better cases were trace cases and didn't have an eyewitness, but that fell on deaf ears. Lackie thought the DA was chicken because it was a high-profile case and he didn't want to fall flat on his face in the press and in public. No one was going to find the perfect murder scene with Bland's calling card politely paper-clipped to the body.

In a way, if he could just get the DA to listen, Bland had indeed left his calling card on Phoebe's body. The murder bore Bland's trademarks and what kept Lackie and the Placentia detectives up at night was wondering if Bland was holding Wendy Osborn and if he was using the same hiding place.

The Placentia detectives handling the Osborn kidnapping were working night and day with the same frenzy and panic as the South Pasadena detectives had the month before and had summoned the FBI for assistance.

If someone wanted to reach him this late, Lackie hoped it was good news.

It was his dispatcher. "Evie Kingston needs you to phone back. It's an emergency. She said Jim followed her down to San Diego," the dispatcher told him, then gave him a phone number with a San Diego area code that seemed vaguely familiar.

"Thanks," Lackie said, then dialed Evie.

"Jim was just here. He said he followed me here all the way from my house. I told him he had to leave," she said, speaking in a rush.

Lackie did his best to calm her down, got the address she was calling from, and told her he was going to put her on hold so he could ask the San Diego police to send a unit to the house.

Lackie dialed the San Diego authorities. It was highly unlikely that Bland would hang around after Evie had told him to his face that she was going to phone the police, but he would be derelict in his duties if he didn't call for a unit.

It was too hard to tell where Bland had been hiding out merely by taking him at face value. If you believed Bland's story about following Evie from her home in West Covina, he was still under their noses in the LA area. But that was hard to swallow for several reasons. Bland knew Evie would immediately talk to the police, so whatever he said was an obvious attempt to throw them off.

Lackie also didn't think Bland would stay within the county if he was going to flee. He could be somewhere in the San Diego area, which covered more square miles than Los Angeles, but with fewer people. He could also be hiding out in Tijuana, a Mexican border town 45 minutes south of

San Diego. The only thing he could be sure of that night was that Bland wasn't in Seattle or Chicago or Las Vegas.

Lackie quickly filled in the San Diego police dispatcher, then clicked back over to Evie.

"He asked me why I wasn't wearing the ruby ring he gave me. He wanted me to give him my picture and he wished me a happy birthday. I told him I had to phone the police.

"It makes me so upset. I now have it in my mind that he is a criminal and could have killed Phoebe Ho, and it was really difficult for me to see him again.

"He really scared me," Evie said. "He said the police were looking at me, too."

Lackie reassured her and took down the address of the friend she was staying with over the weekend, noting it was in Pacific Beach, a suburb just north of San Diego. Lackie said he would leave first thing in the morning.

Lackie took Detective Patrick McManus with him for the drive to San Diego. Since it was a Saturday, there was scant traffic and they made good time. Lackie hadn't slept too well and had been thinking about Bland's hiding place. He had slipped out of the house fairly early and gone to the station to go over some of his files and realized why the phone number Evie was calling from seemed so familiar. It was the phone number of the man who had sponsored Evie when she'd come here in the early 1970s. Evie had mentioned that she and Bland had visited them during the Thanksgiving weekend and again during the Christmas holidays.

During the 12 days Bland had taken flight, Lackie had painstakingly interviewed and reinterviewed the Thayers and Bland's friends, acquaintances, and others, like Celia Blake and Maddy Jordan, Bland's Alcoholics Anonymous sponsor, and his ex-con buddies, and he had collected their phone bills. Lackie found it interesting that Bland had fled to the area where he had visited one of his ex-con buddies who lived in San Diego. When Lackie had talked with him, he said he had heard from Bland but insisted he hadn't allowed him to spend the night. Jordan, who knew about Bland's relatives, had said Bland had a half-brother in Utah, a step-daughter in the Midwest and his own daughter from his second marriage in the Northeast. A few distant cousins were scattered across the country, but most had never met Bland because he had spent most of his adult life behind bars.

The phone records had revealed that Bland had frantically called several ex-con buddies and old friends, as if trying to line up a place to stay before he took off, but he hadn't bothered any relatives. A few of the ex-felon friends said they were on the straight path and claimed to have ignored Bland's hints about doing a "job" with him, which they took to mean armed robberies or business burglaries. Bland hadn't asked any of them if he could stay there for a while. Several of the phone calls over a period of months were to the workplace and temporary residence of Tyler Lowell, a man with whom Bland had done time in two different California prisons. Through the phone records, Lackie easily found out that Lowell worked and apparently lived out of a trailer parked on a ranch in a very remote area in Riverside County called Good Hope. The trailer didn't have utilities, water, or a phone, and phone calls to Lowell were being screened through the residents of the ranch house, who were Lowell's friends. Since Bland lived in Los Angeles County and Phoebe's body was found in Riverside County, Lackie had been extremely interested in speaking with Lowell, but Lowell, speaking through his friends, had made it extremely clear that he wanted nothing to do with police. Lowell had told his friends to tell Lackie that he was no longer working at the factory where Bland had called him and was now making his living as a truck driver crisscrossing the country and living out of his rig. The only other tidbit Lackie had gleaned came from the FBI agent working with the Placentia detectives on the Wendy Osborn kidnapping. He had learned that a longtime inmate pal of Bland's had recently fled from parole and was hiding in Seattle.

After Bland's cameo in San Diego, Lackie knew he could forget everything else. Bland was not harrassing Midwesterners, conning the elderly in Miami, or running around Seattle with his escaped prison pal.

The intensity of the murder investigation had taken its toll on Evie. She was suffering a severe head cold and looked ragged and run down. It had been two weeks since she had last seen Bland before the unexpected visit the night before and she was living life looking over her shoulder. A week after Bland disappeared, an unknown man had phoned her, saying that he was "a friend" and telling her to "be good now." She said there were "strange things" going on in her neighborhood. A neighbor told her he had seen three police officers at her house carrying shotguns and wanted to know why the police were so heavily armed. A few nights later, her son said he saw several police officers sitting in a car kitty-corner from her house. When her son went over to talk to them, they sped off, leading Evie to think they were not police officers but friends of Bland's.

"I don't want anything to do with Jim anymore," Evie told Lackie. "I don't want anything to happen to my children or to me."

Lackie sensed that she still had a very tough time coming

to grips with the fact that Bland was responsible for the murder of Phoebe Ho but still had some lingering feelings for him and did not want him hurt by the police. Lackie doubted Bland had any influence at all to command a platoon of ex-cons who would risk their parole status to harass Evie, particularly when Bland obviously still had feelings for her. It appeared that her imagination was running wild.

Despite feeling under the weather, she directed Lackie and Detective Patrick McManus as they drove around Pacific Beach, pointing out various favorite spots the couple had visited just months before.

When they got back to her friend's house, Lackie sat down to talk with Evie and did his best to convince her that the police were not staking out her home, but they were driving by her house several times each day and evening to provide extra security for her and to see if the car Bland had stolen from Celia Blake was in her neighborhood. He encouraged her to phone the police if she saw any suspicious cars or if Bland came to talk to her again.

The lengthy buzz of the security door sounded and Thaddeus Sterling and the woman in the pink muumuu entered the building, walked into the elevator, and punched the button for the fifteenth floor.

"I really appreciate you driving me down here," Florence Kramer said, clutching a plastic grocery bag overflowing with a light brown fabric. "It won't take long to drop this off."

Sterling, carrying a larger plastic bag also overstuffed with the fabric, was smooth and soothing.

"Oh, it's a pleasure," he gushed. "I just gave my old Toyota a tune-up and I think a short hop on the freeway was just what it needed."

The elevator motor stopped humming and the doors glided opened on the fifteenth floor. They walked down the unfamiliar hallway, looking at the handwritten directions, comparing the number on the paper to the numbers on the door to each apartment.

Cathedral Plaza was an apartment complex dedicated to senior citizens and run by one of the larger local churches. It was clean and well lit and the windows at the ends of the hallways offered grand views of San Diego Bay.

"You know, I don't come down to San Diego all that often anymore since I stopped driving," Kramer said. "I like Pacific Beach so much better. Everything's so close.

"I don't know where I would go for my morning coffee if McDonald's wasn't right down the block from my house," she said.

A trio of sprightly residents in golf attire walked out of a nearby unit and passed them in the hallway.

"Here it is," Kramer said, knocking on a door.

The door opened almost immediately and an elegant woman with snowy-white hair in a stylish cut opened the door and ushered them inside her studio apartment. While it was small, its huge picture window offered a wide view of the bay and the crisp white sails of the boats in the sparkling harbor. A telescope on a tripod stand was set up at the corner of an antique desk near the window.

At one end of the apartment was a senior citizen–sized kitchenette with a small bar stocked with liqueur. The other end of the apartment was the bathroom and dressing area. The sofabed was shrouded in pillows.

"Please, come in, sit down," said Ruth Ost. "It was so nice of you to stop by. It saved me from having to cancel my bridge match and getting my sister to drive me up to Pacific Beach."

"This is Thaddeus Sterling," Kramer said. "He works at the McDonald's where I get my coffee every morning.

"And this is Ruth Ost," Kramer said, pulling the mounds of beige material out of the plastic bags. "It won't take but a minute to put these on. They should fit perfectly."

"It's very nice to meet you," he said, with a smile and a nod of his head. "This is a great view."

At 80, Ost was frail but fashionably dressed and her apartment was tidy. Ever the gracious hostess, she offered her guests coffee and chocolate-covered cherries, but Kramer politely declined.

Ost walked over to the dressing area, and pulled her checkbook from her handbag.

"How much do I owe you for all your hard work?" Ost asked.

"Forty-five dollars," Kramer said.

"Is that all? I'll make it out right now," Ost sat down at the desk, and as she wrote, the sunlight sparkled on her expensive jewelry.

The glittering of diamonds and gemstones did not escape the eye of the portly ex-con. A three-carat diamond ring, surrounded by smaller baguettes, hung from the ring finger of one hand. On the other hand was an antique ring, also dripping in diamonds. A seventeen-jewel white gold watch decorated her wrist, and around her neck was draped a gold and opal choker.

Bland tried not to stare at the jewelry. He picked up a chocolate-covered cherry, peeled off the foil, and popped it in his mouth, saying, "I've always had a weakness for sweets."

He engaged Ost in small talk while Kramer bustled around the small apartment. She pulled the pillows from the sofabed, stripped off the pillow cases, and put on the new ones she had sewn.

She peeled off the old couch cover and fit the matching nut-brown cover over the sofabed, stretching the fabric and tucking under the ends.

Ost was more than happy to chat. She explained that she had learned of Kramer's sewing skills and had chosen the fabric with her sister, who also lived in the area, then dropped it off at Kramer's house just before Thanksgiving. Then she had gone on an extended visit for the holidays to her daughter's home in northern California and returned just the week before. Her daughter had given her the telescope set up by the window to watch the sailboats in San Diego Bay. Ost was showing Bland the latest photos of her grandbabies when Kramer tucked the last bit of fabric around the corner of the sofa.

When she was through, Ost stepped back to survey the new cover.

"Oh, it looks wonderful," she said. "That is a beautiful fabric. You did a lovely job."

"It only took me a couple of afternoons to sew it together," Kramer said. "I think it fits well."

"Looks good to me," Bland volunteered.

"If you don't mind, I'm going to run into the bathroom and then we'll be on our way," Kramer said. "Thad told me he got up at four a.m. to make biscuits for the restaurant. He must be really tired, and we have a little drive to get back to Pacific Beach. If we hurry, we'll miss the evening rush hour."

Kramer excused herself. When she came out after a few minutes, the kindly middle-aged man with the hair too dark for his age was writing something down at the desk by the picture window and Ost was nearby, laughing at comments he was murmuring.

"Okay. Are we ready to go?" Kramer asked.

"All right," said the smiling man. "It was certainly a

pleasure making your acquaintance, and perhaps I will see you again sometime.''

Ost was smiling as she said goodbye and shut her door.

The man who called himself Thaddeus Sterling had a lot to show his new friends. After treating Wanda, his new ladyfriend, and her children to dinner at Denny's on January 27, he said he wanted to show them something.

Driving Wanda's car, he pulled up to the curb at her house, right behind the light blue Toyota, and left the car engine running and the headlights shining on the rear of the Toyota. He got out and Wanda and her three children followed him to the trunk of the car. He pulled out a couple of rings and a brooch.

One of the rings had a huge diamond, larger than any of them had ever seen. The gemstones glinted in the bright headlights as they stood on the pavement and stared gapmouthed at the jewelry.

"I've never seen a diamond that big, except on TV," Wanda said, fixing her eyes on the solitaire ring.

"All of this belonged to my mother," her new boyfriend said. "Do you know where I can hock it? Are there any pawnshops around here where I can sell this stuff?"

"I have no idea," Wanda said.

Bland pulled a few foil-wrapped chocolate-covered cherries from his jacket pocket and handed them to her children.

"Here," he said, hugging each of the children. "I picked these up just for you."

Earlier that afternoon, Bland had promised the solitaire to Evie for her birthday on March 2.

"I have a ring I want you to have," he told her. "I've

had it appraised and it's about three carats. I want to mail it to you.''

Taken aback by his gesture but afraid to refuse him, Evie told him not to mail it because it might get lost in the mail.

He seemed not to hear and told her that she could change the setting or do whatever she wanted to do with it. Then he changed the subject abruptly and asked her what was going on with the police and if there had been anything about him in the papers lately.

Still frightened and not wanting to have anything to do with him, Evie said she hadn't been reading any newspapers, got him off the phone as quickly as possible, then called Lackie.

The next morning, "Thad" paid the ninety-five cents for his hot chocolate and jelly donut in nickels.

When Cross asked him why he was paying for the second day in a row in nickels, he just said he'd saved them up. What Cross couldn't see was the writing on the side of the paper coin roll bearing the shaky scrawl of Ruth Ost.

When Cross mentioned that one of his children had an astronomy project, Thad insisted that he had a brand-new telescope his kid could borrow.

Perplexed, Cross asked Schroeder to watch the store while he went out to the parking lot. In the trunk of the light blue Toyota was an expensive telescope, still in the box, with a scrap of fancy Christmas wrapping paper stuck to the box with Scotch tape.

Bland also showed him some rings and other jewelry and asked if he knew a pawnshop where he could sell them.

Cross shook his head, figuring it was costume jewelry.

The very next day, on January 28, the mail carrier noticed that Ruth hadn't picked up her mail from the day before.

She stuffed that day's mail in the box anyway, figuring Ruth was off on another trip.

On February 1, the body of Wendy Osborn was found in the remote Carbon Canyon region of San Bernardino County, a largely rural desert area. Her body had marks that were arguably signs of torture, though not all agreed about what the marks symbolized. She had been strangled and there were marks on her ankles and wrists that indicated restraint.

The detectives from Placentia had already been overwhelmed by the kidnapping case and lacked the resources to devote to a homicide investigation, so they turned it over to the larger San Bernardino County sheriff's department, which had its own homicide unit. When the body was found, the detectives notified Lackie, who went to the crime scene to observe while the criminalists, the coroner, and the detectives worked. The coroner could not immediately determine if she had been held for longer than a few days or if she had been the victim of multiple sexual assaults because of the condition of the body. At the autopsy the next day, Lackie and Springer saw marks on the body similar to the assault on Phoebe Ho. But the body of Wendy Osborn, at 14, was that of a young woman and bore no resemblance to a child like Phoebe, leaving some to wonder first whether it matched Bland's MO, and second, what type of restraint was needed for a prisoner who more closely resembled an adult than a child. With questions open about whether or not there had been torture, restraint, or multiple sexual assault over a number of days, the detectives from all agencies agreed they wanted to bring Bland in for a talk.

The following day, detectives from South Pasadena, Placentia, Los Angeles County, Riverside County, Orange

County, San Bernardino County, and the FBI decided to pool their efforts and form a multi-agency task force to locate Bland. The detectives from all agencies agreed to meet at 8 a.m. every morning, including weekends.

FBI agent John Kinard, brought in by Placentia detectives to assist the task force, had been helpful about finding out about the potential for Bland to travel out of state by obtaining toll records for phones Bland had used during January. He had made calls to Las Vegas and Reno and was thought to have been traveling with Tyler Lowell through Texas. Through his series of interviews with the Thayers, Lackie learned Bland had expressed interest in a vacant home the Thayers owned in Missouri, the same state where Bland's stepdaughters were residing.

With the variety of leads pointing to Bland fleeing the state, Agent Kinard filed a case with the U.S. Attorney's office. In early February, a U.S. Magistrate issued an arrest warrant for Bland for unlawful flight to avoid prosecution.

On the same day, Springer called to say another fiber from Phoebe's body had been matched to Bland. A blue fiber found in the car matched one on Phoebe's body. That made at least a dozen different fibers, one head hair, and a limb hair. Lackie immediately turned Springer's report over to the DA, who said he would consider filing charges with the new information.

On February 3, Deputy District Attorney Brian McCarville filed charges of murdering Phoebe Ho. McCarville also filed special circumstance charges of sodomy, rape, and lewd conduct with a child. If Bland was convicted of first-degree murder and jurors found any one of the special circumstances to be true, he would be eligible for the death penalty.

Lackie put together a ''Wanted'' poster with a color picture of Bland in a blue plaid shirt, listing his birthdate, physical description, vehicle description, last address, alias, and the fact that he was wanted for questioning in connection with the murders of Phoebe Ho and Wendy Osborn, and it stated that he could be armed with a handgun. Anyone who saw the suspect was urged to call Lackie at the Riverside County sheriff's department.

Months after ''Find Phoebe'' handbills blanketed the county, ''Wanted'' posters of her accused killer were plastered across the Southland.

Elaine Vernon had been trying to reach her mother, Ruth Ost, on the phone for days. Ruth's two sisters also had not heard from her. Worried, they'd called the apartment manager to open her San Diego apartment with a passkey.

She had been dead nearly a week. She was naked and bound with her hands behind her back, left for dead bent over a chair with her feet on the floor and her head on the seat. There was no sign of forced entry, but the tidy apartment had been heavily ransacked. The killer had pulled out her dresser drawers, littered the floor with girdles and undergarments, and emptied her closets of pantsuits, purses, and dresses looking for valuables.

On the floor next to her was an empty bottle of Irish cream liqueur, an open jar of Vaseline, a wire hanger that had been partially straightened out, and a pair of needle-nosed pliers from her kitchen toolbox. A cardboard box of chocolate-covered cherries had been pulled down from the kitchen cupboard and some of the foil-covered candies had tumbled to the floor. The eighty-year-old woman had been stripped of her jewelry and apparently had been strangled.

The bloating and discoloration of her body made identification difficult and painful for her sisters and made an examination for sexual assault impossible. The passage of time and deterioration also destroyed the possibility of recovering the killer's bodily fluids for identification.

The San Diego homicide detectives assigned to the case had never heard of Warren James Bland. It would take days before the detectives even realized that her telescope, binoculars, and other jewelry had been stolen, including a white gold watch with two dozen diamonds, a gold ring embedded with diamonds and opals, and a solid gold pendant sculpted in the shape of Jesus's face. Ost's sisters immediately knew that the three-carat diamond ring was gone. Before Ost had left to spend the 1986 Thanksgiving, Christmas, and New Year's holidays with her daughter, a jeweler had appraised the ring at $12,000.

It was Sunday morning and just as soon as Brett Cross and Frank Schroeder remarked that they hadn't seen "Thad" in quite a while, he walked in and ordered his usual hot chocolate and jelly donut.

"I have a new job at the U-Haul," Thad said. "I'm cleaning out the back of trucks for $4.50 an hour. Sure beats working in the grease pit," he added, referring to his term for McDonald's.

He said he got along with the boss real well, since both he and Thad were ex-Marines.

"I'd love to stay and chat, but I've got a lot of errands to do today," he said. "How about dinner tonight? I'd love to take you and your wife out to eat, say about six o'clock?"

Cross smiled and waved as he walked out the door, too timid to turn Thad down. He had been shaken up by spotting a girls' panties in the back of his car and he hadn't told his wife about it. She would hit the roof. Even without hearing about the panties, she made it clear she didn't want anything to do with him.

At 5:45 p.m., Brett and Joyce Cross shut out their lights and sat in the darkness, pretending not to be home. When Bland came knocking at their door at 6:30 p.m., they sat still and waited until they heard the sound of his car engine start up and they heard him drive away.

CHAPTER ELEVEN

"Our guys just arrested Thomas Kemp at home in Seattle."

Lackie recognized the voice of FBI agent John Kinard. Kemp was the escapee who had become pals with Bland while they were incarcerated years before at the California Men's Colony at San Luis Obispo.

"Any word on Bland?" Lackie asked.

"The agents up there confiscated a letter from Bland saying he wants to get together as soon as possible because he has some 'two-man operation lined up.'"

"He signs it Jim, but he gives an ..."

Interrupting and impatient, Lackie asked, "What's the return address?"

"San Diego," Kinard said, "It's a mail drop on Garnet Street. I already sent an agent from the San Diego office just to drive by and check the address. I wanted to call you first to see how you wanted to handle it."

"I think the best thing to do is to get San Diego PD

and CDC (California Department of Corrections) agents out there as soon as possible for a surveillance,'' Lackie said.

"Can you contact the postal service and find out who owns the mail drop and if Bland's been picking up his mail there?'' Lackie asked.

Within minutes Kinard phoned back.

"It's a residence that's been converted to a business called 'The Mail Box,' '' Kinard said. "It's actually in the city of Pacific Beach.''

"Thanks,'' Lackie said, then called the San Diego police department and got detective Mike Dean on the phone.

"We've got a line on Bland. He's got a mail drop in Pacific Beach on Garnet Street. Can you set up a surveillance?'' Lackie asked.

"No problem,'' Dean said. "I'll get someone out there right now to drive by to just get a look at the location so we can map out a surveillance plan.''

"Thanks,'' Lackie said.

The dark clouds that had threatened rain all day finally gave way to a meek drizzle when San Diego detective Patrick Birse hit the freeway and headed to Pacific Beach. He was among the stragglers catching the tail end of the evening rush hour, the remaining suburbanites having retreated to their homes in the wet winter night. A twenty-year police officer, Birse was part of the seven-month-old Fugitive Detail, established to track down and arrest dangerous people with outstanding felony warrants for bank robbery, murder, kidnapping, rape, and assault. Working odd hours, mostly at night, the unit had worked with Detective Lackie when Bland had paid a surprise visit to his girlfriend in Pacific Beach 2 weeks before. Last weekend, Birse and his partner had scoured Nester, a small town southeast of San Diego, close to the Mexican border, after the fugitive had been spotted there. A police sergeant in that city had seen a portly middle-aged man cursing and loudly arguing with someone at a pay phone outside a convenience store. When the sergeant got home and flipped on the TV, he realized the man he had seen was Warren James Bland, touted as "armed and dangerous" and wanted for questioning in the murders of Phoebe Ho and Wendy Osborn. By the time police got to the convenience store, Bland had vanished.

Birse rarely went into the office, communicating with his supervisor via pager and phone, spending time on the streets talking to friends, relatives, and associates of the targeted fugitive to find out as much about them and their habits as possible to increase the odds that their paths would cross. Aside from Bland's unexpected—and solitary—visit to his girlfriend, the mail drop was the only physical location tying Bland anywhere.

Birse exited the freeway at Garnet Avenue—it wasn't Garnet Street, as Bland had written—and headed west toward the ocean through the corridor of gas stations, supermarkets, fast-food restaurants, and other storefront businesses. He passed a McDonald's and a Thrifty's drugstore and drove slowly by the address, noting that it used to be a residence and had no parking lot of its own. The main sign read "Pacific Beach Mail Box." Smaller signs advertised parcel shipping, fax services, a notary, and packaging materials. It's next-door neighbor was Los Panchos, a casual Mexican restaurant, with white plastic outdoor tables and bright canvas umbrellas adorned with beer logos. Birse decided to park in the restaurant lot, which backed up to the business and was separated by a low brick wall painted white. As he slid his car into an empty stall, he noticed a blue 1970s Toyota in the space next to his. In the dimly lit parking lot under dreary skies, Birse sat in his car for a moment and stared out from his driver's side window at the Toyota, trying to make out the car's features.

That looks like the car, Birse thought to himself. As he sat looking at the car, the hair at the back of his neck stood up as he realized a man was standing on the driver's side. The veteran cop flashed back to the photograph of the fugitive.

It was Bland.

In one smooth motion, Birse grabbed his badge from his belt and opened the car door with his left hand while removing his 9mm gun from his shoulder holster with his right hand and scrambled to his feet. He was less than ten feet from the man wanted for the murders of Phoebe Ho and Wendy Osborn.

Leaning over the roof of the Toyota, Birse held up his badge, pointed the gun squarely at Bland's head, and yelled, *"Bland! San Diego police! Don't move!"*

Bland, his hair newly dyed black, hesitated, staring back at Birse. The chilling look on Bland's face was one Birse had seen thousands of times on criminals the instant they're confronted by a cop. It signaled that the cornered suspect was either going to shoot you or run. That look never crosses the face of someone who allows himself to be arrested.

Cops see it all the time but can't describe it any better than to call it animal instinct, the expression of a desperate person devoid of fear, deliberating whether to fight or flee. If Bland had a gun, Birse knew Bland would blow his head off without hesitation.

For the veteran cop, the world moved in slow motion. He was aware of the darkness of the dimly lit parking lot and the lack of spectators and cars behind Bland and painfully aware that he couldn't see Bland's hands to see if he was holding a weapon. In that fraction of a second, Birse thought that if they got into a foot chase and Bland somehow knocked him out, he could get his service weapon, kill him, and then turn the weapon on someone else.

Birse watched Bland thinking, knowing that he had been caught by surprise and knowing he was considering any option but surrender. Then the portly convict suddenly turned and ran, his reflexes surprisingly good for his age. Bland sprinted across the dark parking lot toward the back of the restaurant, his gait quick but unsteady in the light rain.

Birse ran a few steps, shouting, *"Police! Halt!"*

Bland ignored the commands and ran faster, heading toward the street behind the restaurant.

Birse stopped, assumed a shooting stance, aimed his sights at Bland's lower body, and squeezed off one round.

Bland collapsed instantly to the ground.

For a fraction of a second, after the sound of the gunshot reverberated in the neighborhood, dead silence served as a backdrop against the sound of the softly falling rain and the drone of traffic. Then pandemonium erupted as Bland screamed in agony and restaurant patrons stood up, aghast at the commotion, and looked out the restaurant windows in horror at the shooting victim writhing on the ground and at Birse holding the smoking gun. Birse holstered the gun, now warm against his chest, and walked over to where Bland was howling and holding his leg. Blood spurted from his inner thigh at the same frantic rhythm as his heartbeat, instantly turning his khaki pants a bloody maroon, forming rivulets and mixing with the rainwater as it abundantly flowed onto the wet pavement. Bland was losing buckets of blood. As Birse started administering first aid, a woman appeared at his side, explaining that she was an emergency room nurse.

Bland was screaming and incoherent, and both had to

hold him down. Patrons from the restaurant gathered in a half-circle, shouting that it seemed unjustified that an innocent man had been gunned down. Birse shouted back that he was a police officer and the man on the ground was wanted for murder and to step back into the restaurant.

Birse and the nurse could see the blood pumping from his inner thigh but neither could instantly locate the wound. They yanked his pants down to his ankles and saw the gushing wound. The nurse grabbed her purse, whipped out a large, padded feminine napkin, and slapped it on the wound, applying her body weight as direct pressure to the gaping tear on his inner thigh.

"It looks like his artery was hit," the woman said. "He could bleed to death out here. He has to get to the hospital soon."

Bland's screams had dropped to low moans as he started to lose consciousness. Birse ran back to the Plymouth for his radio and called for an ambulance, then ran back to Bland's limp form on the ground. Bland was silent and his eyes were closed, the raindrops splattering his silver-framed eyeglasses. His face was expressionless and bore the ghostly pale shade of death, and his mouth fell open. The minutes seemed like an hour as the familiar siren sound of the ambulance drew near. As soon as the ambulance slowed down, paramedics hopped out with their equipment kits and descended on the prone fugitive. Within a minute, police officers arrived, using their patrol cars to block the driveway of the restaurant lot. They wore rain slickers the same brilliant shade of yellow as the crime scene tape they unrolled, surrounding the parking lot.

Because the incident was an officer-involved shooting, a detective was assigned to investigate and interview Birse. The detective walked over to the blue Toyota and looked inside. He could see the snub nose of a small-caliber revolver sticking out of a red-and-blue jacket on the front passenger seat.

Paramedics worked feverishly on Bland, whose life slipped between their fingers several times from loss of blood before he barely stabilized for the ambulance ride to the nearest emergency room for immediate surgery to repair the severed artery. As Bland was strapped onto a gurney and loaded into the ambulance, a police sergeant flipped on a battery-operated tape recorder to capture any statements Bland might make on the ride. The detectives grimly realized any statement he made could be his last.

As the ambulance left, its siren blasting into the night, the detective walked around the parking lot looking for evidence, mapping out where the expended shell casing from Birse's 9mm handgun was ejected and where paramedics had cut off and tossed aside Bland's blood-soaked shirt and the stained pants Birse and the nurse had removed. As detectives worked, fat, heavy raindrops washed the blood clean from the asphalt.

The fugitive's dramatic capture made the top of the news on all state and local newscasts. When one enterprising reporter found out that Bland was being treated at Scripps Memorial Hospital, a private medical center, the remaining reporters quickly jumped on the bandwagon. In their reports from the front of the hospital, they noted that the captured felon might not survive surgery, turning the hospital stakeout into an all-night death watch. In the steady drizzle, TV reporters waited in heated trailers while radio and print reporters huddled under plastic canvas awnings and umbrellas or took the risk of waiting in their cars, knowing they would have to hustle a fifty-yard dash across a wet, slippery

lawn if anyone came out to give them an update or arrived
to visit Bland.

Eventually, a hospital spokesman emerged saying Bland
had been severely wounded and that surgeons had success-
fully removed a bullet from his buttock and repaired the
severed femoral artery. He was extremely weak and had been
near death, but he would probably survive. Soon afterward,
Detective Mike Lackie and San Bernardino Detective Billy
Arthur pushed through the crowd at the entrance.

On his first night in captivity, after weeks of alternately
sleeping in his Toyota and at Wanda's, Bland was drugged
and unconscious in the intensive care unit. As a precaution,
the detectives kept the tape recorder on while he slept off
the anesthesia. Hospital administrators, unhappy with the
unwanted media attention and the indigent patient, advised
the police that Bland would be transported to a public facility
as soon as possible.

At 2 a.m., after even the most persistant journalist had
left the grounds, Bland was moved from the private hospital
to a county-run teaching hospital at a local university. The
sixth floor of the hospital was set aside as the jail ward, but
there was no room for Bland. Instead, he was grouped with
other patients in a semi-private room in the trauma unit, but
Lackie was apprehensive about that arrangement. In his
present condition, Bland posed no escape threat, but he didn't
want to risk having a reporter or camera crew somehow gain
access to Bland, or have some vigilante seek out Bland and
extract vengeance. Because of the publicity, it would be
relatively easy for one of Bland's prison pals to locate him
and try to spirit him away from the hospital, which could
endanger nurses and other employees. Once Bland recovered, he would definitely pose an extreme flight risk.

To test security, Detective Patrick McManus entered the
hospital and asked for Bland at the second-floor nurse's

station without identifying himself. The nurse gave McManus directions to the trauma wing on the fifth floor. A uniformed deputy from the San Diego sheriff's department stood near the entrance to the trauma wing and asked for ID. McManus noted that Bland's room was close to both the nurse's station and the elevators and that no guards were posted outside the room or inside the room. After speaking to the deputy, McManus walked directly to Bland's bed.

Hospital security officials told McManus that Bland would be moved to the sixth-floor jail ward as soon as there was room. In the meantime, Lackie contacted the San Diego sheriff's department and was told that they had a staffing shortage and could provide only a part-time deputy. When he asked about making room in the jail ward, he was told that the security arrangements there consisted of handcuffing inmates to their bedrails. The sheriffs had a contract with a private security firm to staff someone outside the doors of any inmates being treated at the hospital. But since their county wasn't prosecuting him, San Diego authorities were planning to transfer him to the county with jurisdiction over him as soon as he was well enough to withstand the 2 hour trip to Riverside. That could be a matter of days or as long as 2 weeks, Lackie was told.

Deeming the security arrangements inadequate, Lackie assigned three detectives to watch Bland 24 hours a day in rotating shifts. While McManus and Lackie were making these arrangements, several news crews had made it to the nurse's station outside Bland's room. Later, a reporter bluffed his way to the hall outside Bland's room.

McManus started his shift that afternoon. Even though McManus was also an experienced detective, Lackie made it clear that McManus was not to initiate any conversation with Bland, just in case he said anything to implicate him in either of the crimes. If Bland had not been read his rights,

those comments could not be used against him in court,
unless he made unsolicited voluntary remarks. He could
listen but not encourage conversation from Bland. No one
but nurses or doctors or identified law enforcement was
allowed in Bland's room.

Bland was awakened at 2 p.m. to eat lunch, and he fell
asleep afterward. An hour later, he was moved to a sixth
floor security unit room shared by three other inmates. One
of the prisoners was handcuffed to his bed and was being
guarded by a plainclothes security guard in the hallway. Still
not satisfied, McManus asked that Bland be moved to a
private room because of the security risk to Bland, the other
patients, and hospital personnel.

Bland would awaken periodically, then settle back to
sleep. When dinner was served, Bland was awake and alert,
and he even discussed the TV programs with the nurses
tending his wound. After the meal, he finally was moved to
a private room with a door capable of being locked. Throughout the evening, Bland stayed awake more than he was
sleeping, and focused on the TV blaring the evening news,
still broadcasting Bland's dramatic capture, the surgery to
save his life, his recuperation at the hospital, and his immi-
nent prosecution for the torture-murders of Phoebe Ho and
Wendy Osborn. On every news cast, photos of the two
victims flashed across the TV screen along with the picture
of Bland before he'd fled, with a moustache and gray hair.

At 9 p.m., a San Diego reserve officer arrived and took
up a post outside Bland's room, then moved inside to watch
TV near Bland's bed. To McManus's surprise, Bland began
talking about life on the run, sleeping in the blue Toyota,
working at U-Haul, making friends, and using the alias
Thaddeus Sterling. McManus saw the tape recorder and
assumed it was continuing to record.

When the reserve officer left the room to assume his post

in the hallway, the local evening news was repeating the same story, and Bland turned to McManus.

"Officer, while we're alone, I want to tell you I appreciate your professionalism. This other girl," he said, as the photo of Wendy Osborn flashed on the screen, "you're going to find that I didn't do it. The time cards will bear me out."

Bland went on to describe more about his life in San Diego, his job working the counter and making biscuits at McDonald's, and discussing some of the people he had met. Bland said he had just made a phone call when Birse had found him and that the Garnet Avenue address served as only a mail drop. McManus expected Bland to deny his involvement in the Phoebe Ho murder, but he never did.

McManus simply nodded as Bland spoke, careful not to encourage him. In an hour, Bland dozed off again. When he woke up, he pestered the nurse for doses of morphine for pain. Despite his constant pleas to various nurses, they each checked his chart and administered morphine only at the intervals directed by the doctor overseeing his recovery. McManus waited until he was relieved by another deputy and then wrote down Bland's remarks in a report to hand over to DA McCarville, who was prosecuting him for Phoebe's murder. When Lackie later checked the recorder, he found that it had run out of tape.

For the seventh time, Warren James Bland was becoming entangled with the California criminal justice system that had kept him in custody, either in prisons or mental institutions, for 26 of the last 29 years. Now, as he lay in his hospital bed, a Riverside County judge was considering who, among the pool of experienced defense lawyers in the county, would represent Bland at county expense. For months, the public defender's office had declared itself "unavailable" for most death penalty cases. The drain on the scarce resources of the public defender's office from intense, complicated cases was too severe. At stake was a prosecutor hoping not just to lock Bland up, but to take his life. And for the first time, law enforcement agencies were standing in line to prosecute Bland.

Following Bland's arrest, San Diego police detectives presented a case to the U.S. Attorney's office to file charges on Bland for being a career felon in possession of a gun. A new statue, the precursor to the "three strikes" law that would follow years later, was the latest tool to slam shut the revolving door of prisons on repeat violent offenders. Prior to this new law, a felon paroled on a violent offense who carried a gun could be prosecuted either by citing him for a parole violation, or prosecuting him on charges of being a felon with a gun. The parole violation usually earned the parolee a 1-year trip back to prison after a brief hearing. The state offense carried a prison term between 16 months and 3 years.

The controversial federal law provided a strong deterrent for felons with three violent prior offenses caught with a gun—a life term in prison without parole. San Diego police didn't hesitate to approach federal prosecutors with the Bland case, and Assistant U.S. Attorney Larry Burns filed charges after verifying Bland's prior offenses.

At the same time, San Bernardino County was taking a close look at Bland. Detective Lackie had turned over the blue Toyota to San Bernardino homicide detectives because Bland had been driving it during the time Wendy Osborn was abducted and killed. If it contained any trace evidence, it would be linked to the abduction of Wendy, not Phoebe Ho, whose body had been discovered weeks before Bland had taken the Toyota.

As a courtesy, San Bernardino allowed Faye Springer and

Detective Sanchez to observe the search. In the back seat
of the car was a pair of flesh-colored girl's panties with the
seams cut out and clothespins pinching the crotch, candy,
a $17 pornographic magazine called *Oral Cravings,* a red
notebook, a handmade note holder resembling a school project, two different pairs of pliers, a tool box, various lengths
of clothesline and different kinds of rope, several sets of
out-of-state license plates, a set of ID for Leo Schroeder, a
telescope, a roll of nickels with a San Diego address and
the signature of Ruth Ost, and a credit card in another female
name. Bland had apparently also had a tooth removed and
there was a bill from a dentist in Pacific Beach and a prescription bottle of painkillers for ''Thaddeus Sterling.''

While the contents of the Toyota were nauseatingly typical
for an active sexual predator and consistant with his criminal
past, neither Sanchez or Springer saw anything useful for
the Phoebe Ho case. But homicide detectives from San Diego
did. Several weeks after the search of the Toyota, detectives
investigating the Ost murder finally located Florence
Kramer, who identified Bland as the kindly middle-aged
man who'd driven her from Pacific Beach to San Diego to
deliver the couch and pillow covers to Ruth Ost.

The telescope was identified by Ost's relatives as the
Christmas gift they had given her and the signature of Ost
on the roll of nickels. The jewelry was gone, but detectives
eventually found Wanda Schroeder and Brett Cross, who
recalled Bland showing off a solitaire diamond ring with an
enormous stone within 24 hours of the last time Ost was
seen alive. Wanda's nine-year-old son, who also saw the
unusual ring, drew a remarkably accurate picture of the huge
diamond, the unique setting, and the surrounding baguettes.
The boy's drawing matched a rendering created by the jeweler who had recently appraised the stone. Detectives also
made contact with Evie, who said Bland had promised her

a three-carat diamond ring for her birthday. The ring was never mailed and a check of local pawnshops failed to turn up the ring or any of Ost's other jewelry. However, the ex-con had $860 in cash in his wallet, far more money than he had earned at McDonald's and U-Haul combined.

The credit card caught the detectives' attention. It bore the name of a woman whose purse was snatched weeks before Bland's capture. Detectives learned that there had been a rash of strongarm robberies and purse snatchings during the time Bland had been in the San Diego area. Each of the victims described the thief as a portly middle-aged man with dark hair, using a small gun. When detectives put Bland's mug shot—with a moustache and gray hair—in a group of six other Caucasian middle-aged men, no one identified Bland or any other suspect.

The search of the Toyota had given authorities in San Bernardino and San Diego much work to do.

Deputy District Attorney Brian McCarville of Riverside County also realized he had a lot of preparation ahead to get the case ready for trial. Another prosecutor, Cregor Datig, was named as the assisting prosecutor and DA Investigator George Hudson was brought into the case. Two days after his lifesaving surgery in San Diego, Bland was chauffered by ambulance from San Diego to the jail ward of Riverside General Hospital.

Since Riverside had jurisdiction over Bland by virtue of the pending murder charges, they were first in line to prosecute him. McCarville estimated it would take at least a year or longer just to prepare the case for trial. Bland was easily the last person in line behind hundreds of other criminal defendants awaiting trial there. Some murder cases in Riverside County were tried within a year of charges being filed. A long and complicated scientific case like this one, and particularly a death penalty case, could linger 16 months to 2 years before it saw a courtroom.

Despite pressure from Lackie and the media, McCarville was cautious about filing murder charges against Bland. As a prosecutor, he had to satisfy himself that there was proof beyond a reasonable doubt of a definitive link between hairs and fibers from the victim and Bland, and that he could reasonably convince a jury to convict Bland. With Bland in custody, McCarville wanted the case against him nailed down as tightly as possible. He asked criminalist Faye Springer to get a second opinion on the hair and fiber analysis.

Springer knew exactly who to consult. She had trained with the best in the business: Skip Palenik, an expert criminalist at McCrone Associates in Chicago, Illinois, with whom she later consulted on other challenging cases. Palenik was considered one of the finest in the world at microscopy, spending the better part of every day looking into sophisticated microscopes, examining trace evidence. He specialized in "ultramicroanalysis," the examination of fibers, hair, soil, paint, and other substances too small to be seen with the naked eye. He was one of the experts consulted to examine the Shroud of Turin, which reportedly bore the burial image of Jesus Christ, and found it stained with an iron oxide pigment held in place by gelatin. Palenik worked on one of the Apollo missions in the 1960s, the Hillside Strangler serial murders in the 1970s, the Atlanta child murders, the Enrique Camerena trial, and the Holocaust war crimes case of John Demjanjuk, and he was regularly consulted by the FBI, the Department of Justice, Scotland Yard, Interpol, and hundreds of big-city law enforcement agencies.

While Springer could say the carpet fibers and paint taken from Phoebe's body were "similar" or "consistant with" those taken from the van Bland drove, Springer thought Skip

Palenik could button down the case by using his laboratory of
state-of-the-art equipment that the Department of Justice
laboratory lacked. While Springer could identify properties
of paint and fiber and do a visual comparison, Palenik, at
the helm of his whiz-bang machines, could do a visual
examination of molecular properties for a more definitive
identification, and if they carried identical properties, he
could testify to that.

But this would be time consuming. Palenik always worked
notoriously behind schedule because of the immense
demands on his time and the constant stream of law enforcement agencies needing emergency lab work. When Springer
phoned him in Chicago, he said he would be delighted to
help out.

If a defendant can't come to court in Riverside, then the
courtroom goes to him. The judge, his court clerk, the court
stenographer, a smattering of sheriff's deputies, Deputy District Attorney Brian McCarville, and Bland's two court-
appointed defense attorneys crowded around Bland's bed in
the jail ward of Riverside General Hospital for his arraignment. It took less than a minute for his two attorneys to
delay the proceeding until April. Given the attitude of the
public and press toward Bland, attorneys Steve Harmon and
Gerald Polis, appointed by the judge to represent Bland,
wanted to bring that momentum of public opinion against
their client to a halt. The experienced criminal defense lawyers knew the prosecution would need more than a year to
put the case together with additional detective and laboratory
work. Without the immense resources of law enforcement
or even the public defender at their disposal, the private
lawyers, both sole practitioners, needed time to mount a
defense in which their client's life was at stake. Harmon

and Polis juggled numerous cases and staggered one trial after the other. It would be many months, perhaps more than a year, before either attorney could clear his calendars to concentrate on this case, prepare for trial, and then devote the time to take it to trial. Neither knew how long it would take before Bland would recuperate and then actively participate in his defense.

Within the tight-knit circle of criminal defense lawyers and prosecutors, Harmon and Polis ranked on the short list of attorneys a prosecutor would hire if he or she found him or herself sitting in a defendant's chair.

Polis had been a prosecutor for several years in the early 1970s but had switched sides after a few years and soon proved to be a formidable opponent. Extremely bright, and a master at upturning a prosecutor's case to expose the flaws, Polis had handed the prosecution some painful losses on high-profile trials throughout his career. Bearded, and with the academic gruffness of a college professor, he extended dignity and cordiality to most witnesses but didn't hesitate to wring cooperation from smug prosecution witnesses with his intimidating intellect.

Harmon, the opposite of Polis, was more likely to charm witnesses into startling admissions on cross-examination. At 40, Harmon's boyish good looks and easygoing nice-guy attitude put jurors at ease, making them comfortable with rational, reasonable theories favorable to the defense. Prosecutors said he could sell the earth back to God.

Bland's lawyers wanted the public hostility against Bland to cool to a chill before this case got to trial. They genuinely liked their client, who, despite having been brought back from the brink of death, looked rather handsome, with dyed dark brown hair, still bearing the flush on his cheeks from being outdoors. They knew by the time this case got to court, Bland would bear the ghostly pallor common to long-term prisoners.

Unlike other clients who didn't appreciate their efforts, Bland extended his heartfelt thanks for their assistance and was cordial and soft-spoken. Harmon had been apprehensive about meeting the fugitive suspected of murdering two little girls and was excited to be involved in a high-profile case. The monster described by the media winced when he moved in his hospital bed as he discussed the case with his new lawyers. Polis and Harmon wanted to let the public's sharp anger dissipate and try the case in a neutral environment. They wanted to go slowly and leave no investigative stone unturned to defend their client.

By April, Bland felt strong enough to attend court for his arraignment. Public hostility against Bland registered so high, the sheriff's department offered to outfit both defense attorneys in bulletproof vests. The lawyers refused, not wanting to heighten the anti-Bland frenzy by wearing the vests in public. For security reasons, the arraignment was not held in Riverside Municipal Court, where all felony arraignments take place, because there was no secure way to transport Bland. The municipal courthouse was built without an underground tunnel to transport prisoners. Sheriff's deputies usually walked the chained-together prisoners down the block-long street from the jail to the courthouse. Even dropping Bland by a courthouse side door posed risks, so the arraignment was moved to the Superior Court, which had an underground tunnel from the jail.

Constructed at the turn of the century to resemble the Grand Palace of Fine Arts in Paris, the white marble edifice of the Riverside County Superior Court boasted life-sized Greco-Roman statues, stained-glass windows, vaulted corridors, and majestic columns ringing the exterior. Bland, now pale after months behind bars, wore a bright orange jumpsuit and handcuffs around the crutches on which he supported himself. With Polis on one side and Harmon on the other, Bland stood long enough to say ''not guilty'' after prosecutor McCarville read out the charges on the criminal complaint. The judge set a date for the preliminary hearing, but the lawyers knew that would be at least months, if not years, away.

CHAPTER TWELVE

There must be a special place in hell for someone like this.

George Hudson, the DA investigator assisting prosecutor Brian McCarville, felt sick.

Hudson reviewed the affidavit Lackie had prepared for Bland's arrest, outlining the circumstances of the abduction and the discovery of Phoebe's body. He paused at the opinion of the autopsy physician that Phoebe Ho had not been fed for at least two days prior to her death, that the pinching torture had left hideous bruises on her chest, and that her flesh had ripped and formed scar tissue after she was repeatedly raped and sodomized.

How could anyone get pleasure from doing this to someone? Hudson thought to himself. This was not a quick, merciful killing. This was a series of evil acts intended to cause a slow, painful death that only a vicious monster could inflict on a child. Torture cases were rare. The only other such case Hudson had worked on involved a pimp torturing a prostitute and leaving her for dead with a slit throat. The woman lived but was horribly scarred.

Bearded, with a thatch of salt-and-pepper hair, Hudson was a Navy vet who'd joined law enforcement because the money was good, he could work outdoors, and he could live and work in his beloved mountains where he loved to fish and hike. For the first few years in the early 1970s, he was the resident deputy and detective in Lake Arrowhead, a Southern California mountain town far east of Los Angeles with few year-round residents. He preferred to live there because it was a great environment to raise children and be close to nature. In the summertime, the population of Lake Arrowhead boomed as suburbanites retreated to their cool vacation cabins. They returned in winter to ski and spend the holidays in bona fide snow. Eventually, Hudson was pulled from the rural mountain roads to the streets of San Bernardino, where he worked narcotics, sex crimes, and homicide.

The Phoebe Ho case was not the first one that had brought tears to his eyes. He'd investigated serial killings, sadistic sexual murders, knifings, shootings, and drive-by killings and had come across just about every atrocity that one human being could do to another. He was also the parent of a girl Phoebe's age and got misty-eyed thinking of the agony and fright Phoebe must have felt and the neverending agony that would haunt her parents for the rest of their lives. Instead of becoming hardened to seeing the ghastly results of violent crime, Hudson found himself growing more sensitive to the suffering of the victims and the survivors, and seeing how an attack left victims stripped of the sanctity of feeling safe in their own homes or in their neighborhood streets, banks, and shopping centers. Over the years, he found himself wiping away his own tears as he comforted rape victims and the friends and relatives of homicide victims. Of all the gruesome and grisly incidents he'd seen, this case shook his beliefs. It was everything a parent feared.

He had joined the DA's office as a senior investigator seven months before, helping prosecutors polish cases for court and sometimes completely redoing entire cases because smaller police agencies had botched the investigation or lost evidence.

With Bland's trial potentially years down the road, McCarville asked Hudson nevertheless to start keeping track of witnesses. He was assigned to organize Lackie's reports and prepare the latter phase of the trial devoted to convincing twelve jurors to send Bland to the gas chamber. If the jurors convicted Bland of murdering Phoebe, evidence about Bland's prior convictions were fair game during the penalty phase of a capital trial. McCarville was planning to present jurors with testimony from the women and children Bland had assaulted and terrorized in his thirty-year criminal career. Hudson had the unenviable task of locating them.

Hudson wanted to send Bland to hell. He would have no qualms about activating the lever to extinguish Bland in the gas chamber. He'd even volunteer to shoot him. But Hudson had a better plan. He was going to work on killing Bland, but he was going to do it legally.

In one of his earliest photographs, a diapered Warren James Bland, his white-blond hair like peach fuzz, has two garden snakes wrapped around his neck, one fat little fist grasping one snake head and the other hand gripping the body of the second snake. His mother dutifully labeled the photo ''Jim and the snakes,'' as if there was nothing unusual about a toddler cuddling reptiles.

By the time Bland was born on January 21, 1937, his father's first marriage had long since dissolved in divorce and his new wife was not one to dredge up the past. His half-brother, Randall Bland, was the product of his father's former marriage. He was nearly an adult when Jim was born, and had married and moved to San Antonio, Texas, before the youngest boy was old enough to realize he even had an older half-brother.

Carl Odell Bland and Hava Kathryn Bland settled in Culver City, then a quiet working-class suburb of Los Angeles where housing was cheap and plentiful, affording Bland's blue-collar parents a stucco tract home and a Buick. Carl worked as a maintenance mechanic for the American Legion, and Hava worked at the local rubber plant. Despite their modest wages, the cost of living was low and they made sure their son had toys and a bike.

Family photos of Bland show a highly animated youngster in dramatic poses, bearing unusual facial expressions. In a summertime photo with his parents under a large, shady tree, a barefoot Jim, in long pants, his hair bleached snow-white by the sun, looks away from the camera in an odd, leering grin, his eyes wide, his hands behind his back as if he were hiding something. In another photo years later, Bland wears a Huck Finn-style straw hat and strikes a jaunty backyard pose, his legs apart, his hands stuck in his pockets, his lips pursed and staring directly at the camera. By the age of 12, Bland had sprouted nearly to his full height of six feet. The last photograph of him with his father, in front of the family car, shows Bland screwing up his face in a grimace and standing away from his father. One of the most telling photos shows Bland, in his usual grimace, standing next to his grandmother, who is wearing a fur car coat and stylish hat. She faces away from him, her jaw set, looking away, her ankles and arms crossed as she clutches her purse to her body.

Bland says he has no recollection of these grimaces but

admits he "goofed around" a lot as a youth and did things to get attention, like taking apart electrical appliances. He was mechanically inclined and felt happier taking things apart and putting them together again than going to school. For punishment, Bland would have to pick out his own switch from the pepper tree in the back yard. His father would yell at him while he whipped the back of his legs.

The only child of aging parents, Bland lost his father to a heart attack when he was 12. His mother took annual trips to see Bland's older half-brother in Texas to expose him to a male role model, but Bland didn't like the heat and the fire ants. Mechanics captivated Bland. In 1954, at 17, Bland was a senior at Culver City High School, but he spent most of his time sprucing up and racing motorcycles at the Saugus Raceway, a speedway 40 miles northeast of Culver City. His thirst for speed and love of performance cars earned him the nickname "Gearbox," which also became his first tattoo, on his right shoulder. He hung around a crowd of buddies, his hands blackened from dissecting car engines and putting them back together with considerably more muscle under the hood. He and his friends would street race the hotrods for quick cash on Culver Boulevard, taking turns behind the wheel and watching for cops.

At 17, Jim Bland had thick, wavy blond hair combed back into a natural pompadour, wore jeans rolled up at the cuff, and white T-shirts over his lean, muscular frame, a ringer for heartthrob James Dean. His tough-guy scowl was the perfect accessory for a daredevil motorcycle racer. Most teenaged girls didn't hang around noisy racetracks and back-yard garages, and Bland liked dating girls.

To meet them, Bland went to the local roller-skating rink. He started dating Sue-Ellen Sweeney, a fifteen-year-old junior with thick, wavy brown hair who attended his high school. The two, along with his mother, would take picnic

lunches to the Saugus track and Bland would race motorcycles. Bland was charming and romantic and he often sent
her flowers, but they never went on a formal date alone,
although they saw each other often at school. By the time
Sue-Ellen finished her junior year of high school, Bland had
proposed. Caught off guard, she said yes, but when the time
for the wedding rolled around the following summer, she
regretted it. Like any proper girl who was of marrying age
in 1955, she felt obligated to go through with the ceremony
after going through the trouble of asking her parents for
permission because she was only 16.

During that year, Sue-Ellen spent more time with Jim and
his mother and saw some disturbing behavior. She saw Jim
grab his own dog's genitals and squeeze them very hard
and watched the dog squirm in pain before the dog was able
to get away. One time, she saw Jim literally pick up his
mother, who weighed in excess of 200 pounds, spin her
around "like a helicopter," and then throw her to the ground.
Afterward, he made light of it, but Sue-Ellen was shocked
by the act and thought he'd done it out of meanness. He
also saw him crush his mother's hand with the backyard
gate as she was reaching to open it. Again, Bland made
light of it, but Sue-Ellen thought he did it intentionally.

On July 1, 1955, just a few weeks after graduating from
high school, they were married. Bland had dropped out of
high school the year before, three weeks before the rest of
his class graduated. By this time, Sue-Ellen had seen more
than she ever wanted of Jim Bland and didn't want to get
married, but she felt trapped and thought she couldn't back
out of the ceremony they had planned for an entire year.

She doesn't remember much of the wedding because she
was crying so hard. Afterward, they went to her parents'
home for the reception, where she was "kidnapped" as part
of a traditional wedding game of chivalry. In her wedding

gown and veil, she was put into the back seat of a car and
was driven away by friends, all of whom were laughing and
in a good-natured mood. Apparently, Bland didn't get the
joke. Incensed, Bland hopped into one of his hot rods, sped
around the block, and drove on the wrong side of the road,
aimed straight at the car containing his brand-new bride and
members of the wedding party. They swerved into another
lane to avoid a head-on collision.

That night the couple spent their honeymoon at an inex-
pensive motel paid for by their parents.

A virgin, Sue-Ellen was frightened and nervous about her
first evening alone with her new husband and spent a long
time in the bathroom, getting ready for bed. As a prank, her
bridesmaids had knotted her honeymoon gown and she had
a hard time untying it. Impatient, Bland broke the lock on
the door, pulled her out of the bathroom, and tried to get
her to drink some champagne. When she declined, he forced
her on the bed and consummated the marriage. Knowing
nothing about sex, Sue-Ellen didn't realize that she had been
raped until years later and thought the excruciatingly painful
assault was her obligation as his wife. She had bled considerably from his sexual assault and spent the rest of the weekend
in the motel pool to keep away from him, gritting her teeth
in agony from the chemicals in the pool water, which was
like an acid bath to her internal wounds. On Monday, she
was in so much pain she begged Bland to take her to see a
doctor, where she got a shot and required stitches. During
the following six weeks, the injuries never healed because
Bland continued to have sex with her whenever and wherever
he wanted. She allowed it because she was admittedly naive
and considered it her "wifely duty."

A few days later, after living in the "pigsty" of a home
Bland shared with his mother, the couple moved into a
rented home her parents had helped them find. One night,

Bland came home bragging about raping a woman, but she couldn't believe it. During the argument that followed, he became angry and blurted out the name of his victim, which Sue-Ellen recognized as a girl with whom she had gone to high school.

The rocky relationship never got better. One evening, while Bland was in the bathtub reading a comic book, he asked her to come in, then locked the door. He started talking about how much he liked to torture people and Sue-Ellen noticed that the comic book had a sadistic bent. Terrified, she struggled to get away, and in her panic, she could not unlock the bathroom door and was forced to listen to him fantasize about torture until he let her go.

Shortly after that, she woke up one night and found Bland kneeling in bed over her, tying her hand to the bedpost. He had already tied her other hand and both ankles in a spread-eagled position to the bedposts. Armed with a Bible and a knife, he started talking about being in "God's army" and mentioned killing someone, making Sue-Ellen think he was going to kill her. As she lay on the bed naked, her legs apart, her newlywed husband leaned close to her and traced the knife blade over her skin, across her neck, around her breasts and nipples, threatening to cut them out, then traced the blade over her stomach. When Bland left to go into the kitchen to get something, Sue-Ellen frantically untied one hand, then the other hand, then worked at the binding around her ankles.

When Bland returned, he had a large plastic bottle and he told her he was going to shove the bottle into her vagina and "suck her gizzards out." Sue-Ellen talked him out of it, explaining that God would not want him to hurt her, and he abandoned his plan.

After spending the wee hours of the night shivering in a nightgown curled up in a living room chair, she waited until

Bland left for work, then phoned her father and asked him to come and pick her up. She never went back to Bland, but Bland was not quite through with her.

He broke into her bedroom twice, once to threaten her and a second time to declare he would commit suicide if she didn't go back to him. Then Bland's mother phoned·to say that she would kill Sue-Ellen if Bland committed suicide. On September 11, 1955, Sue-Ellen filed for an annulment, citing grounds of extreme cruelty and grievous mental suffering. They had been married 2 months and 10 days.

On September 30, Bland walked into a Marine Corps recruiting center and enlisted for a three-year stint and was immediately shipped off to San Diego for basic training. Five weeks later, he went AWOL and was classified as a deserter. He was found at home more than a month later, claiming he needed to work in order to help his mother pay bills. He was sent to the brig for 6 months of hard labor, then brought back to finish basic training. On April 19, 1956, he went AWOL for a second time and was declared a deserter almost immediately. This time, the Culver City police department found him at his mother's house on August 7 at 10 a.m. When an officer tried to arrest him, Bland fled in a 1954 convertible Austin-Healy. By this time he had acquired another tattoo—a rose and dagger on his right forearm. He was court-martialed, sentenced to another 6 months of hard labor, and booted out of the Marines with a bad conduct discharge.

In his explanation at the time, Bland said, "the reason was for finance problems at home . . . at this time we are in pretty bad shape. My mother has lost two houses and her car. I'm very close to my mother and I do a lot of chores around the house to alleviate her burden.

"I have been no help to the military at all, and I feel as

long as this burden is there, I'll never be able to succeed back at duty. My father is deceased.''

Bland also told military officials that he took a job at a greenhouse, potting plants, planting orchids, and laying sod after leaving high school and claimed he quit high school to help his mother financially and that his ex-wife had run up debts that he had to pay off. Bland mentioned that he was engaged but claimed he was ''in no hurry to rush into marriage again.''

He was hospitalized briefly for what would be the first of a score of psychiatric evaluations. The military psychiatrist gave him a ''high average'' maturity level and an ''average'' potential for getting into ''disciplinary difficulties'' and deemed him to have problems handling his feelings of inadequacy and dealing with others ''who are doing better than he is.''

Two separate psychiatrists declared he was ''malingering.''

On July 12, 1957, when Bland was 21, he was released from the U.S. Marines. It was a little more than two years from the day he first married Sue-Ellen. About a year of that time he had spent in the brig, the military prison, doing hard labor.

In the meantime, homicide detectives from El Segundo, a suburb several miles south of Culver City, had been perplexed in the investigation of an unusual murder case—one of their own officers had been killed on duty. Just before he died, the officer had radioed in to report that he had stumbled across a man raping a woman. One of the suspects was Warren James Bland. He was never charged with the crime.

Two months later, Bland was back in custody in the adjoining city of Los Angeles for taking a 1956 white-and-green Thunderbird coupe for a test drive and keeping it.

Someone apparently tipped off the police about Bland, who
had gotten a job potting orchids at a greenhouse, driving a
spanking new sports car. The LAPD staked out the house
and saw Bland at the wheel of the T-bird, driving home at
5:20 a.m. The officers found that Bland had switched the
license plates of his mother's 1951 Chevy with those of the
T-bird.

The police arrested Bland as he was getting out of the
car.

Bland told the officers, "I went out to the (car dealer) lot
and talked to the salesman and talked him into letting me
take the T-bird out for a try. I didn't bring it back."

Bland gave his spouse's name as Sue-Ellen Sweeney,
though the annulment had become final 16 months before
that, and told them his hobbies were auto racing and "hanging out at the beach." His tattoo collection had grown. He
sported a heart with an arrow through it and "Love"
inscribed on his left shoulder and the word "Rose" written
in script on his left forearm. The LAPD officers noted Bland
had six teeth missing.

Bland pleaded guilty to grand theft auto and on October
18, 1957, he was sentenced to 30 days in the county jail
and 3 years' probation.

When Bland got out of jail in the winter of 1957, he was
hired by a man who operated a sand-blasting business out
of his home. Shortly after he was hired, he met a young
cousin of his boss's wife. Dorothy Cobb was a seventeen-
year-old high school senior who had just moved to Southern
California. Bland immediately started dating her as if he
had no time to lose. On Valentine's Day 1958, he presented
her with an engagement ring. She agreed to marry him but
said she wanted to wait until she turned 18. Though the
wedding date was several months off, Bland kept pressuring
her to have sex. A virgin, Dorothy refused his advances and

kept telling him she wanted to wait until they were man and wife.

After two months of badgering, Dorothy had had enough. When he took her out to dinner at a restaurant near Mount Baldy, in the local foothills about 45 minutes from Culver City, she decided to officially call off the engagement and handed the ring back to him after dinner.

Dorothy noted that he seemed "very cool" and did not make a fuss or appear upset. But when they left the restaurant, Bland started driving in the opposite direction of home, deep in the foothills. When she asked him where he was going, he didn't answer. Finally, he pulled over near a remote, dark hillside and asked her to get out of the car. Holding an M-1 bayonet he kept in the back seat, he then attempted to force her to the ground, but she turned and ran away. Bland called out after her: "You take another step and this knife goes in your back!"

She doesn't recall much of the rape except that he was on top of her with the bayonet poised over her throat and that it was extremely painful. When he finished, he kept holding her down for several minutes. Then he raped her again, telling her, "It won't hurt as bad this time."

After the rapes, Dorothy was in shock and felt as if no one would want her anymore. Coming from a strict Catholic family, she believed that once a man had had intercourse with her, she was compelled to marry him. Humiliated and feeling lost, she remained engaged to Bland, thinking that all she had ever been raised to believe about marriage was turned upside down. She continued having sex on demand with Bland, believing it was her duty to love and obey her husband-to-be.

One day in May, when she and Bland were supposed to go to the beach, he picked her up with his mother in the car and they started driving in the opposite direction, toward the desert. After they had been traveling for a while, Bland told his mother that he and Dorothy were on their way to Las Vegas to be married. Dorothy felt sick to her stomach, but believed she was obligated to marry him and could do nothing.

When he stopped to fill up the gas tank in Las Vegas, Bland opened the trunk of the car and pointed out one of Dorothy's dresses, which he had somehow taken from her closet at home. It was dirty and torn, as if it had been in the trunk for a while.

Hava Bland showed Dorothy a handwritten note, claiming Dorothy's parents had written it, giving their permission to allow their underaged daughter to marry, but Dorothy knew her parents hadn't written the note.

Immediately after the wedding, Bland drove them back to Los Angeles and he took Dorothy home. She hid her wedding ring and didn't immediately tell her father what had happened. Her father became enraged after learning she had married Bland, but she lived with her parents until she finished high school. By that time, she had become pregnant and the newlywed couple moved into a house near Bland's mother, who came over for dinner nearly every night. She noticed that Bland's mother did just about everything Bland asked her to do.

While they were in public together, Dorothy noticed Bland became extremely jealous when another man looked at her and became more angry if he noticed her looking at another man. After she got pregnant, he tried to scare her by saying he would make her have their baby at home instead of driving her to a hospital. He slapped her in the face one time when she got a ticket in a car Bland had stolen. She didn't know the car was stolen at the time but learned of it after he struck her.

On November 26, 1958, when Dorothy was 7 months

pregnant, she drove over to a Richfield gas station in Los
Angeles where Bland was working a second job as night
shift attendant. She arrived at 9 p.m., parked near the side
of the station, and scooted over into the passenger seat to
wait for him to finish up. That night, Ray Allen Blair had
been drinking at a local bar with a friend and had come to
the gas station because their car battery was dead. While
they were waiting for the battery to be fixed, Blair wandered
over to the car where Dorothy was seated and tried talking
to her. Incensed, Bland went over to speak with him, then
had to take care of a motorist who had just pulled into the
station for service. While Bland was gassing up the car,
Blair walked back over to where Dorothy was sitting and
kept talking to her. Dorothy was annoyed by the man's
incoherent babbling and moved to the middle of the car seat.
But Blair reached into the car to get Dorothy's attention and
this annoyed Bland. He walked over to the driver's side of
the car, grabbed his bayonet, and sliced the man's abdomen,
cutting it open. Dorothy saw Blair drop to the ground, bleeding profusely and trying to hold his split abdomen together.
Bland jumped into the car and drove Dorothy home, then
went back to the gas station after Dorothy insisted he return.

Bland told officers, "I didn't even know I had stabbed
him, but after hearing him make those lewd and indecent
proposals to my pregnant wife, I guess I saw red. I pushed
him with my left hand and I meant to show him the knife
in my right hand to scare him, but when I saw him fall
down, I knew I must have stabbed him."

Bland claimed Blair bothered him while trying to fix
Blair's car and said, "She looks like a fine chick . . . she
would make a good piece."

Blair's drinking buddy, who was closest to the car where
Dorothy was sitting, said he could not make out the words
Blair was saying because he was drunk and incoherent. The

LAPD officer who responded to the call said Blair was "belligerent and uncooperative" at the hospital.

Bland spent two weeks in jail until he could raise $2,000 bail. After losing his jobs, Bland got another job as a clerk at a manufacturing plant. He wrote out a ten-page statement explaining that he actually intended to hit Blair and didn't realize he had stabbed him. Much of the statement was devoted to showing the depth to which Blair had annoyed him, and saying Blair had given his wife, "sly, dirty smiles."

In the early spring of 1959, a jury found Bland guilty of assault with a deadly weapon, but on a motion of Bland's defense attorney, Judge Leroy Dawson vacated the conviction and found him guilty of a lesser offense: assault with force likely to produce great bodily injury.

Defense attorney L. M. Hunt spoke highly of Bland as a young man who had just been promoted and had "settled down with a wife and child."

"His wife was seven months along, he was on the job, this drunk (the victim) came messing around . . . I think he knows now when drunks come around he is to call the police and not do anything himself," Hunt said.

On April 14, 1959, Judge Dawson sentenced Bland, then 22, to a $250 fine, to pay all of Blair's medical expenses, and to 5 years' probation, then lectured Bland, saying it wasn't right to take the law into his own hands. Dawson opted not to send Bland to jail because the obligation "to preserve the whole social structure as far as your family is concerned" and supporting his wife and child were outweighed by society's interest in sending him to jail.

At the time of Bland's sentencing, Debbie Ann Bland was 2 1/2 months old. Dorothy was grateful Bland had been at work when she went into labor and had asked her father to drive her to the hospital. She recalled that her husband showed no emotion when the baby was born but later seemed jealous of the infant. When she cried, he would hit the wall out of frustration and anger. A second time, he struck Dorothy in the face and broke a tooth during an argument.

In mid-September 1959, when Debbie Ann was 9 months old, the infant was having a crying fit and Dorothy was doing her best to comfort her, knowing Bland's reaction to the baby's noise. But Bland calmly asked Dorothy to do something for him and Dorothy turned the infant over to her husband. She went about her task and saw that Bland had placed the baby on the floor, then put his bare foot on top of her body. Before she could rescue the infant, he reached down and hit her head so hard that her head bounced, snapping her neck back, hitting the rug and leaving a rug burn. The facial scar on her cheek stayed with the child throughout her growing years but finally dissipated as she reached adulthood. Dorothy decided at that moment to leave Bland but waited until he left for work the next day.

Afraid of her husband, she and the baby moved to Alaska and stayed for 6 months with her cousin, the same one who introduced them via the sand-blasting business. While she was there, a friend from Los Angeles gave her a newspaper article saying that her husband had been arrested for rape. Dorothy returned to Los Angeles to file for divorce.

The moment Iris Thompson stepped out of her car after pulling into her garage, she felt a hand clamp over her mouth and another around her throat. The forty-three-year-old woman froze. It was 10:20 p. m. on December 21, 1959 and she had just come home from work.

"Do as I say and I won't hurt you," he said.

The man forced her to give him the car keys and he pushed her back into her car. He sat in the driver's seat and drove around for a while, pulled over, and said, "We're going for a walk."

He forced her to walk up an alley and across a field and made her lay her coat on the field and take off her clothing, apologizing for the fact that she was shivering in the cold. He raped her on the field, warning her about making noise and watching for approaching cars. When he was done, he wiped his penis on her bra, made her get dressed again, and walked back to the car. He made his victim drive him back to the neighborhood near her apartment. Before he left the car, he took her money from her purse—about $6—and wiped his fingerprints from her purse and the car.

Thompson drove herself home and phoned the police, who took her bra as evidence. She took them back to the field, where they noticed footprints in the soil made by a ripple-type sole.

On January 4, in the same neighborhood, a forty-six-year-old secretary came home from dinner at 10:30 p.m. As she got out of her car in her garage a stranger approached from behind, put a hand around her mouth, and said, "Ssssh. Don't make any noise. I won't hurt you." He grabbed her by the arm, forcing her to walk through an alley toward his car when she broke free. The man got into a foreign-make sedan and drove off.

Minutes later, an eighteen-year-old model was walking home from a friend's house after seeing a movie when a man grabbed her from behind, put a hand around her mouth, and tried to put a cement sack over her head.

"Don't scream and I won't hurt you," the man said.

She screamed and he hurled her on the ground, fracturing her jaw on the sidewalk. She ran to a neighbor's home and phoned police, who were able to find the cement sack.

Five days later, on January 9, at 11 p.m., a forty-year-old woman was getting out of her car in her garage when a man came up behind her, covered her mouth with one hand, and shoved her back into her car. She kicked him in the groin and ran down an alley. She went inside her home and phoned police.

LAPD officers on patrol in the neighborhood heard the radio call and saw a green 1959 Renault leaving the scene. The registration showed it belonged to Warren James Bland at a nearby address. When officers went to his home, they found he was not there, but they checked the records of relatives and saw that his mother lived a short distance away. Hava Bland said she had not seen her son since 10 p.m. the night before. The officers searched her home and found Bland hiding in the shower.

As the officers pulled him out of the bathroom, he said, "Yes, I'm the one that was down there last night and spoke to that woman. When she screamed, I ran just as fast as I could. I just wanted to rob her. I've been really desperate for money. I have a lot of bills to pay."

This time in court, Bland faced higher stakes and multiple charges: forcible rape, robbery, kidnapping, kidnapping for the purpose of robbery, and three counts of attempted rape. Since he already had a prior felony conviction for stabbing Ray Blair, the filing enhancement was added to the charges.

At his preliminary hearing in Municipal Court on January 11, 1960, all the women identified him as the man who'd accosted them and he was held to answer on all charges. The case was sent to Los Angeles Superior Court for trial. This time, the judge set no bail for Bland, preventing him from getting out of jail before trial.

On February 8, Bland pleaded not guilty by reason of insanity and denied the prior offense. A trail was scheduled for March 17, 1960. Court records show a succession of attorneys appointed by the court, then fired by Bland, and even an attempt by Bland to represent himself. Superior

Court Judge Julian Beck appointed two separate psychiatrists to interview Bland to determine if he was sane.

The psychiatrists interviewed Bland separately one week apart in a visiting room in the Los Angeles County Jail in mid-February. They noted he was compliant, talkative, and eager to tell them details about his life, but vague about the details of his criminal acts. Bland told the psychiatrists that he got along "wonderfully well" with both parents and they never used any harsh words toward him, but he was a little closer to his mother.

Of his childhood, Bland said he was "left out" of games in grade school because he wasn't part of the group and the kids chased him home "because I was small."

As in his prior interviews with the Marine psychiatrist and with his former probation and parole officers, Bland said he didn't drink, smoke, or use drugs because he didn't "believe in any of that stuff."

Bland glossed over his work history, claiming he had continuous employment as a teletype clerk and a machinist. The reason he changed jobs, he said, was because of a steel mill strike, not his arrests and jail stints. Bland readily acknowledged his prison term from going AWOL from the Marines.

He told Dr. Karl Von Hagen, the first psychiatrist to interview him, that he started having left-sided throbbing headaches in September or October and "started to lose control of things," claiming that his wife accused him of going out with other women and of "staring at her." He admitted hitting his wife the first time because "I am the type of person that if something like this gets on my nerves, I lose control."

He told the doctor that Dorothy was "bickering" with him about seeing other women and he had struck her after he'd denied it.

"One thing led to another and she left me," he told the doctor.

Bland claimed his wife left on December 21, instead of the actual date in mid-September.

Bland told Robert Wyers, the second doctor to interview him, that he and Dorothy "got along very well sexually," but weren't having sex very much toward the end of their relationship just before she left him. Under questioning from Wyers, Bland said Dorothy left him before the criminal acts occurred.

When asked about those criminal acts, Bland insisted on telling the story "from the beginning," claiming it started with the bickering with Dorothy and the child crying and his headaches. He told his doctor the headaches began in November. Bland said he would lose track of time, such as fixing a friend's car for the entire day, then forgetting he had done it. He complained of being anxious and on the verge of a nervous breakdown. Bland told both doctors he was hit on the head with the butt end of a rifle while he was in the Marines and said he was knocked unconscious at least twice while he was racing motorcycles.

In response to direct questions about whether he had done the things the victims testified about during the preliminary hearing, Bland replied, "Well, I really don't know that I am the person involved in these things, yet they say that I am."

He claimed he intended to rob the last victim, but never meant to "bother her sexually."

All he recalled of the December 21 incident was stopping at a red light after mailing Christmas cards at the post office, then "walking on soft dirt." He said the second incident "sticks in my mind, like a dream, that I was running and it seems off in the distance a woman was screaming."

Both doctors concluded that the young man was physically

fit and intellectually normal, but suffering stress and anxiety from "difficulty at home," as well as spells of amnesia. He was perfectly sane.

On March 17, the date Bland's trial was to start, he abruptly withdrew his plea of insanity and pleaded guilty to kidnapping and raping Iris Thompson. Sentencing was set for April 19 and the judge ordered another round of psychiatric interviews to evaluate Bland as a probable sexual psychopath.

As was routine, a probation officer interviewed Bland in jail in order to evaluate him and help the court arrive at a reasonable sentence.

During the interview, the probation officer asked Bland to write down everything he could about the case and Bland complied—giving him seven single-spaced handwritten pages virtually repeating everything he'd told the psychiatrists about throbbing headaches, and a "happy" relationship with his wife, except for the times he'd slapped her after bickering over the volume of the TV and the squalling of his infant daughter.

Bland played up his responsibility to his wife and daughter and paying his bills on time and downplayed the assault on Ray Blair, claiming he'd stabbed him as he'd tried to "jerk" his pregnant wife out of their car.

He again claimed he couldn't recall anything of the Iris Thompson attack, except for walking on "soft dirt." Despite pleading guilty to kidnapping and raping her, Bland wrote, "I guess there was actual intercourse. I still can't believe it."

Bland gave a complete account of that day, including the fact that he "took it to heart" about "being yelled at" for doing two jobs wrong that day at work. He gave an idyllic account of coming home and having his wife kiss him at the front door—except that she had long before fled to

Alaska. Bland had even told one of the psychiatrists who had interviewed him 2 weeks before that she had left him at that point.

Nevertheless, Bland provided a heartwarming account of his home life, with his wife wrapping Christmas presents in the living room and his mother playing with the baby while he finished writing out Christmas cards in the kitchen.

Apparently insistent on getting an early postmark on the cards, he drove to the post office, dropped off his mother at home, and couldn't recall anything after that, except stopping at a red light and walking in "soft dirt." When his wife asked him the next morning what had happened, he said he didn't know what she was talking about.

Three days later, Bland claims his wife left him, which would make the day she walked out Christmas Eve, but he made no mention of spending the holiday alone. Bland also claimed he had known Dorothy's cousin for his entire life and she had been like a mother to him and introduced him to Dorothy, then inexplicably vowed to "do everything within her power to break my wife and I up," and lured Dorothy to live with her in Alaska and file for divorce.

Bland assured the probation officer in the letter that he planned to get a job and would eventually reconcile with his wife and child. If he was granted probation, he promised to go to a private hospital and get help, saying, "there is something definitely the matter with me . . . there are times when I just can't explain my feelings and I think I am more afraid of myself.

"I have heard people talk about this hospital, Atascadero, and even my lawyer told me about it, and I told them how I feel at times and they said I might be what they call a sex-psychopath and from what they say, I think I am one.

"If I cannot be helped here, when and ever I get out of prison, I intend to go to a state metal institution and declare myself as a Mental Abnormal Sex Offender and see if they can't help me, because the way I am now, I am not even any good to myself . . . I feel that I am a sick person and need help.''

Bland extended an apology to "this woman," meaning Iris Thompson, and hoped he'd be granted another chance on probation.

Deputy Probation Officer W. A. Howard didn't agree. He recommended that probation be denied, saying that Bland was, "in need of a long period of institutionalization and treatment" in order to protect society against his "antisocial tendencies," since he failed completely to live by society's rules.

When the second round of court psychiatrists started interviewing him on April 5, 1960, Bland had a new word to use in his arsenal, plucked from a psychiatric report—amnesia. He enhanced the reports of being knocked unconscious, reporting that he had been hospitalized for them and reported dizzy spells and additional bouts of amnesia on three or four different occasions.

But his amnesia regarding the attack on Iris Thompson miraculously improved—he recalled putting his hand over her mouth and that she did not scream during the assault and recalled asking her to drive him back to the neighborhood from which he'd abducted her. He added that he knew it was wrong.

Perhaps hoping to make a better impression on the psychiatrists, Bland claimed Sue-Ellen, his first wife, was a year older than he, claimed that they had "a rather extensive courtship through high school," and that her parents had their marriage annulled, saying they were "incompatible."

When Dr. Marcus Crahan delved into Bland's sexual history, Bland complained that Sue-Ellen was "frigid" during their entire marriage and wouldn't let him touch her on their wedding night, and that they didn't have intercourse until a week after they were married and had sex only 14 or 15 times during the 6 weeks they were married.

Bland denied having sex with his second wife until after they were married, then their sex life suffered because of "domestic strife."

"The TV was either too high (loud) or not high enough, or the child was crying," Bland explained.

Sex with his wife didn't satisfy him and he often would satisfy himself once or twice each night after having marital relations with his wife. To Dr. Crahan, he admitted peeping into a woman's window once.

Bland embellished the 1958 stabbing incident as well, claiming he had knifed Blair after Blair had opened the passenger door and put one hand on his wife's stomach and one hand behind her head.

Before his wife left him, Bland said he "found himself doing things and forgetting all about them; things happen to me that I can't remember. My wife brought up things to me that I couldn't recall and she even said once that I was insane."

To this examiner, Bland let loose more details of the rape of Iris Thompson—such as asking her to unbutton her dress and the fact that she was wearing a tight slip—but still claimed not to recall the actual rape.

To the third examiner, Bland recalled another detail— that he had apologized to her for the cold weather while she was undressing.

Bland also admitted that he was drawn to other women and would undress them in his mind.

Karl Von Hagen, the same doctor who'd interviewed him in February, was appointed again as one of the three psychiatrists to evaluate him as a sexual psychopath. Bland told him in February the headaches began in September or Octo-

ber and told the other psychiatrist they began in November.
In April, Bland said they started in 1954 and he was having
them twice a day. The psychiatrist made no note of this or
other obvious discrepancies. Bland apparently didn't recall
the date of his marriage to Dorothy, giving dates of April
17 and March 7, but he did recall in the second Von Hagen
interview that it was May 17, 1958.

But his memory seemed to have slipped—or he was intentionally untruthful—when he told Von Hagen that he went
out with Dorothy for 5 years before they married, as opposed
to the scant 2 months he knew her before he proposed. He
also claimed he never touched her before they got married,
then it took him a week until she began to respond to him.
He described his second wife, Dorothy, as a "nymphoma-
niac" he could not satisfy, in abrupt contrast to his prior
descriptions.

As in all former interviews and accounts to probation
officers and psychiatrists with the Marines and the two court-
appointed psychiatrists, Bland consistently stated he didn't
drink, smoke, or take drugs.

All three psychiatrists agreed Bland was a sexual psychopath who was wildly unstable, preoccupied with sexual matters, and a menace to society, with a hair-trigger trend toward
violence. Von Hagen, reflecting the philosophy of that
period, reported that Bland could not "control his heterosex-
ual desires in a socially acceptable fashion."

Their recommendation was for Bland to be hospitalized
"for observation and treatment," reflecting California's philosophy within the penal system to seek rehabilitative reme-
dies as opposed to simply punishing offenders. The
collective thinking was that society's interests were best
served by treating people and trying to cure their problems
as opposed to simply warehousing them in prisons.

The early 1960s were the dawning not only of great hope

for the presidential Camelot era and the precurser to Lyndon Johnson's "Great Society" of generous social welfare programs. Not only did scientists truly believe they could put a man on the moon, and young adults in the Peace Corps truly believe they could solve hunger in distant lands, there was tremendous optimism that rapists could be treated.

That approach took root in a society where sexual assaults against women and children were severely underreported and sexual attacks were thought to show just an inability to control one's sexual impulses, which doctors believed would disappear with treatment, as opposed to current thinking— that an attacker uses the sex organs to humiliate or to exert power and control over a helpless victim.

Psychiatrists and psychologists played powerful roles in the California penal system in the 1960s. Decisions to commit, retain, or release "patients" hinged on doctors' opinions as to whether a defendant posed a danger to the community or whether he had conquered his problem and would not reoffend. If one or two or three psychiatrists spent months or years treating a violent offender, the payoff would result in one less person hurting more innocent victims and a zero expenditure in prosecuting him through the criminal justice system in the future. The former inmate, if all went well, could return to society after therapy, education, and intensive vocational rehabilitation as a productive participant.

Judge Julian Beck, after reviewing the reports from the psychiatrists and the probation officer, made the legal finding that Bland was a "probable sexual psychopath" and committed him to the Atascadero State Hospital for a ninety-day observation period to allow the doctors there to evaluate him and determine whether he was a sexual psychopath.

In June, the same determination was made by doctors at Atascadero and the judge committed Bland to the hospital for "an indeterminate period." Bland found himself enveloped in a world of doctors and therapists probing his background, his thoughts and feelings, his understanding of his criminal behavior, and his childhood history.

Five years later, the head of the hospital recommended that Bland be sent back through the criminal justice system because he was not benefiting from treatment at the hospital.

"He remains a danger to society," wrote Dr. S. W. Morgan, the hospital's medical director. "He admits the rapes but not all the violence. He will now say, when asked, these were wrong, terrible, etc., but he also has said the offenses were not quite so bad.

"He claimed some of the women really enjoyed him."

While Bland attended therapy, Morgan reported, his sexual and aggressive conflicts appeared essentially unresolved. In five years of intensive treatment, the doctor and the staff found Bland glib, manipulative, and superficial, showing no emotion and no meaningful insight and intellectualizing excessively, concealing negative thoughts and feelings. He also broke rules by stealing hospital stationery and writing his own recommendations, which were supposed to be from hospital staff.

In fact, Bland admitted he had "raped a lot more than [I was] charged with."

"Instead of becoming less dangerous as a result of new insights gained, he distorts the new knowledge to give justification for his actions.

"If released to society, he would be assaultive and/or homicidal toward women," Morgan warned in his evaluation, dated July 19, 1965.

Two years later, Bland convinced a judge he had "buckled down" and "learned a lot about myself."

On September 19, 1967, the judge set him free.

CHAPTER THIRTEEN

Life at Atascadero State Hospital, on the outskirts of bucolic San Luis Obispo County in California, meant group therapy, individual therapy, and a constant search for the genesis of antisocial behavior among the patient inmates. There were educational and vocational programs and an emphasis on keeping pace with current business trends, such as the Junior Chamber of Commerce chapter at the hospital, of which Bland was a member. Bland learned how to operate a movie projector and became one of the hospital's projectionists.

Doctors there, however, feared Bland was not directly confronting the demons that drove him to rape women. At the direction of the medical staff they started to psychologically lean on him, perhaps to make him crack. An orderly verbally pushed him around, confiscated his hall pass, and took his job. Instead of making him buckle, the tactics simply shored up Bland's intestinal fortitude and the wall between his personal self and the outside world was bolstered by the stress, though he was uncomfortable.

This puzzled the doctors, who probed him more. What drove him to rape? His smothering mother? His distant dad? Rebellion against parental authority manifested through crimes against weaker females? His obsession with sex?

Increasingly unhappy, Bland, through his mother, filed a writ of habeus corpus. The writ demanded that Bland be released because he had been found sane and was being held in the hospital against his will. Despite the voluminous reports, memos, and evaluations of Bland's every thought, dream, feeling, and casual comment, two additional psychiatrists were appointed by a superior court judge to determine if Bland had been "cured" by the Atascadero staff and no longer posed a threat to the community.

Both psychiatrists found that Bland still posed a danger to society and recommended he remain hospitalized. To one of those doctors, Bland insisted that he'd pleaded guilty to only the kidnapping charge, not the rape.

Bland's lawyer, Donald Rosenstock, filed a subpoena in December for all Bland's records from the hospital, containing every report, memo, and evaluation written by the hospital staff about Bland, and asked that the psychiatrists review the entire file and render an opinion. That was done, and they felt he was not amenable to treatment at the hospital, which meant Bland could be sent to prison. After the records were turned over, the revolving door of lawyers representing Bland continued. Bland fired Rosenstock in court, then hired Eleanor Duncan, who happened to be in court on another matter.

On February 23, 1966, Bland appeared before Superior Court Judge Richard Hayden, who had read the entire file from Atascadero, as well as the various old and new psychiatric reports. The purpose of the hearing was to determine what to do with him—send him to prison, or return him to Atascadero. For this hearing, Bland took the witness stand and testified.

Duncan argued that Bland was no longer a danger to society and should be released on probation. Consistant with all prior reports, Bland didn't drink alcohol or take drugs.

But Judge Hayden zeroed in on the rapes and pointedly asked Bland to describe his actions. Reluctantly, Bland instead launched into a discussion of the causes, such as rebelling against a "mother image" and being a "confused, aggressive young man. I had no pattern of life whatsoever to really base myself on."

After being asked six times to discuss the details of his crime, he started to outline the details in approaching Iris Thompson, then said he "just became overly hostile and went after her . . . after my wife had left me . . ."

Judge Hayden interrupted to get him back on track. After his recitation about Iris Thompson, the judge asked about "the other ones. What about the one whose jaw you broke?"

Bland claimed to know nothing about it, saying that he "could" have pushed her and she "could" have fallen.

The judge also asked him about the 1958 stabbing of Ray Blair, and Bland embroidered the account, claiming Blair had one hand behind his wife's neck and one behind her head, trying to drag his screaming, pregnant wife out of their car.

The judge didn't buy it.

"I find it hard to believe that I really was hearing from him the truth of that offense," Hayden said about the stabbing, adding that he also didn't believe a man could break a woman's jaw and not know what he had done to her.

But Hayden made a distinction between a defendant lying to a judge in order to be released from custody and a defendant lying to himself about the known facts of a case. "What

I am afraid of is that I may be hearing what he believes to be the truth. That is what is disturbing."

In reviewing the abundant reports and evaluations, including one blaming Bland's mother for his criminal behavior, the judge found Bland an exemplary performer, aside from the fact that several of the women employees at the hospital were frightened of him and complained to the staff shortly after he arrived.

But his performance collapsed in the "area which is important, and that is the question of his commission of forcible rapes" the judge continued. One of Bland's doctors pointed out that "Mr. Bland can only be helped if Mr. Bland will start finding out why he raped those women, and he has been spending five years not doing it."

Of alarming consequence to Hayden was Bland's interpretation of an act of intercourse as "cooperation" and "agreement" from Iris Thompson, with whom he had no relationship. "This is not one of those ambiguous rapes where you buy a girl a couple of drinks at the bar and you misunderstand the agreement. These were good old-fashioned forcible rapes."

While the doctors at the hospital seemed eager to continue studying Bland, he had been there longer than most other patients and had long ago been expected to be released. The trigger that had brought him to court on the habeus writ came only after the hospital began the psychological pressure, Hayden noted.

"He is in a position where he has to make up his mind. Where does he want to spend the rest of his life? And he is not yet ready to spend his life on the street."

Bland's lawyer said Bland promised to continue his psychiatric sessions after being released on probation and the psychiatrist could have him recommitted if he thought he was becoming dangerous.

But the judge questioned how a psychiatrist or anyone, including a defendant, could possibly know the danger signs driving one to reoffend.

Bland, eager to be released on probation, offered to self-police his psychosexual behavior. "It happens when I start projecting hostility and I will start pulling away from everything and draw within myself. This is the first warning that I have for myself that I really notice and I have found the biggest cure I have for myself is just to get up and talk."

Hayden tried to explain: "We are talking about the fact that you do some things that you can't tell me about. I asked you about them and you couldn't tell me about them. I think if I were you, I would say, 'I have one life to live—I can either live it afraid that I am going to keep on raping people, or I can live it finding out why and what I can do about it.' You are not going to get out on the street . . . you have a chance to go back and get treated, or you have a chance to go to state prison."

Hayden pointed out that he might be out on the streets sooner if he simply went to state prison, but he would be no wiser as to his motivation for raping women.

"You will be out of prison afraid you are going to rape somebody . . . and with the danger that you may get scared enough when you rape them that you may kill them."

Having said that, Judge Hayden left it up to Bland to decide.

Bland chose to go back to the hospital, prompting the judge to deliver some advice: "This can be a dead-end street for you. This can be going in and not getting out. Do you understand that?

"If [the department governing the hospital] should change its policies, you might find yourself in an institution for the rest of your life.

"Your problem is getting to where you can tell somebody

why you raped somebody so they can really understand it and believe it.

"You have to be able to do that to yourself first."

Hayden legally found that Bland was still a mentally disordered sex offender (an updated term for sexual psychopath) and sent Bland back to Atascadero State Hospital, ordering psychiatric evaluations every six months.

On July 16, 1967, Bland sent a cheerful letter to Judge Hayden, crowing about his flawless recommendations from the staff and his new grounds privileges card, which allowed him to attend industrial therapy outside the hospital.

"When I was last in your Court, you told me on no uncertain terms for me not to come back from here with anything less than an 'A' recommendation from this hospital," Bland wrote.

"Well, sir, since that time, I have really buckled down and have learned a great deal about myself. And this knowledge I have worked into my everyday personality and apply it to everyday situations that arise."

Bland boldly asked to be released on his own recognizance until the hearing, "for the main purpose of enabling me to give their department a clear picture of my present and future plans."

This time, the reports from the state psychiatrists couldn't use enough superlatives. They praised his "excellent" personal hygiene, good appetite, regular attendance at therapy sessions, activity in the patients' self-government of the ward, and his position at that time as ward chairman.

He had again apparently rewritten his personal history. Where Bland again and again in countless psychiatric interviews described his childhood and family life as happy and loving, he for the first time described it as "Neurotic. Father beat on him excessively as a youngster, then was closer to him when he was a teenager and young adult.''

Perhaps Bland had been at the hospital so long that no one remembered that his father died when he was 12 years old.

Bland's therapist noted that he began receiving one-on-one psychotherapy in 1966, showing ''marked improvement and maturity,'' and described him as ''non-psychotic.''

''His personality became better organized and his controls appear to be well-stabilized. At the same time, he is more relaxed than ever before. Mr. Bland is always dependable and willing to help others.''

Because of his constructive change in attitude and behavior, Bland was deemed to be ''no longer dangerous on the basis of his cooperative attitude and behavior in this hospital.''

The report was signed by the Atascadero State Hospital medical director, the same doctor who believed in 1965 that Bland was potentially homicidal toward women. Bland was transported from the state hospital to the county jail to await a hearing.

On September 18, 1967, Bland walked out of his jail cell. Hayden, the same judge who wanted to hear that Bland understood his desire to rape, released Bland on his own recognizance with the understanding that he attend a hearing the next day. On September 19, 1967, Hayden gave Bland 5 years' probation and sent him on his way.

On November 21, 1968, Bland was behind bars again.

Two woman had been raped, two had fought off their attacker, and a fifteen-year-old girl was left for dead after a man slit her throat.

The attacks started in August and lasted until Bland was

behind bars. The suspect had a distinctive MO. He struck between 3:15 and 5:30 a.m. and the incidents were clustered in Long Beach, about 30 miles southwest of Los Angeles.

On August 8, 1958, in the first reported incident, a twenty-eight-year-old schoolteacher was awakened at 3:30 a.m. by a slap in the face. A man was shining a flashlight on her body and holding a four-inch curved-bladed knife to her throat.

"Do not scream and I won't hurt you," the man said to Leslie Fowler, pulling the sheets from her bed to expose her body. He told her to "move around" on the bed while he pinched and twisted her breasts. Then he asked her to kneel on the bed and openly display her genitals to him, then bend over and open her buttocks to him as he shined the flashlight.

"Are you a virgin?" he asked.

He then told the victim to move to the edge of the bed and said, "Do not raise your voice" as he forced her into oral copulation, then raped her. The chatty rapist told the frightened woman not to worry about getting pregnant because he had been "cut and tied," apparently referring to a vasectomy. The intruder said she knew him because he was the vice president of a local firm and promised to call her in a week for a date so they could get to know each other "on better terms."

Before he left, he made her turn over onto her stomach. "I'm sorry. Don't tell anybody," he said.

Police later found the rapist had entered her home through a window by cutting the screen.

Leslie Fowler described the rapist as being about five feet, seven inches tall, with white receding hair.

The next victim was a thirty-year-old business school student who was awakened by noises coming from her front door on October 29 at 3 a.m. She unlatched the door and saw a man in a crouched position lunge forward, forcing her backward onto her sofabed and punching her in the mouth. When she screamed, the man fled. She described him as being 35 or 40, about five feet, ten inches, 175 pounds, with a pot belly and balding.

Five days later, Darlene Carter, 15, biked to a local bayside park next to a golf course to watch the sun rise. She left the house just after 5 a.m. wearing bell bottoms, a Navy pea coat, and moccasins. After taking off her moccasins, she was sitting on the sand when she noticed a man crawl through a chain-link fence and approach her on the sandy islet.

Feeling apprehensive, she got up and started walking away, when the man grabbed her and said, "Don't scream." When she shouted out, he slit her throat, dragged her under a tree, unbuttoned her coat, and undressed her, pulling off her underclothes as she bled profusely. Choking on her own blood, she tried to cry out, but the attacker poured sand in her mouth. Even though she was about to pass out from loss of blood, she somehow got to her feet and stumbled away. Three golfers on the other side of the fence saw the scene and described a man about six feet tall, 175 pounds, with dark hair, running away.

One of the golfers, a nurse, scaled the six-foot fence and ran to her aid, applying direct pressure to her wound and saving her life. The emergency room doctor agreed that Darlene would have died if the nurse had not come to assist her. The attacker had carved a half-circle around her neck, then administered two additional gashes to the right side of her throat. Darlene, in intensive care for several days, was too traumatized to recognize her attacker and underwent psychiatric treatment.

The next morning, on November 4, 1968, Cheryl Lynn Morgan was awakened at 3 a.m. by a gloved hand over her mouth. Her eyes flashed open and she saw a man, wearing skin-tight black rubber gloves, leaning in through a window over her bed. "I have a knife and I'll use it if you make any noise," he said.

The intruder forced the thirty-one-year-old business manager to stand on her bed while he fondled her breasts and genitals, keeping one hand on her mouth. "I want to see what you look like," he whispered, still leaning in through the window.

He ordered her to remove a blanket from her bed, then ordered her to crawl through the window as he kept at least one hand on her, then prodded her to walk to the backyard of the house next to her apartment building and lay the blanket on the ground. He pinched and fondled her again, telling her, "you have a beautiful body," then put a gag on her mouth consisting of cloth, masking tape, and a small coil of white rope. Morgan pushed the gag away and begged him not to tie her up or gag her and he agreed, but only if she would not make any noise. She did not scream as he painfully tore and pinched her breasts. He forced her to kiss and fondle his genitals and buttocks and she noticed that he wasn't wearing underwear. After a few minutes, he told her to spread her legs.

When he had raped her, he asked if she had also reached a climax, and out of fear she stated that she had. He pulled his pants up and lay next to her on the blanket as if they were lovers and he asked her if he was "better" than her husband and if he could come back. Again, out of fear, Morgan stated that she would like to see him again and he promised to return but said he would not enter her home through the window again.

He ordered her to get up and as she shivered and wrapped herself in the blanket, he looked around the yard to make certain he hadn't left anything to link him to the assault.

Before he left on foot, he told her not to worry about getting pregnant because he had "gotten fixed."

Cheryl Lynn Morgan described her attacker as a thirty-five-year-old man, a little over six feet tall, with receding sandy or dark blond hair combed straight back, wearing thick glasses.

On November 21, Ann St. John, a twenty-two-year-old department store manager, was walking down the street at 3:10 a.m. when she noticed a man following her about twenty feet away. When she started walking faster, the man also started walking faster. She crossed the street, noticed he was still following her, then yelled out, "What are you doing?"

He grabbed her, threw her to the ground, and said, "If you don't say anything, I won't hurt you," and held a knife with a curved blade close to her body.

"I have a knife," he said, as he tried to cover her mouth by unfurling a roll of tan elastic, like an ace bandage.

The woman screamed and kicked the man hard on the leg. As he ran away, she ran screaming to the nearest house, where the occupants called the police. She described the man she saw—six feet, one inch tall, receding blond hair, 170 to 200 pounds, and between 20 and 30 years old—and the description was broadcast immediately over the police radio. St. John also said the man had on eyeglasses, a turquoise V-necked pullover sweater with no undershirt, and light-colored pants.

Long Beach police officers on routine patrol less than an hour later saw a motorist matching that description cruising through residential streets behind the wheel of a 1964 white Rambler sedan. When they stopped the car, Warren James Bland got out.

In his front pants pocket was a roll of ace bandage. Under the driver's seat was a 3 ½ inch curved-bladed tile-cutting knife and two pairs of skin-tight, black, rubber gloves. He also had a brown paper bag containing wire, rope, and miscellaneous tools, including pliers, and vise grips.

He chatted freely with the officers, who wanted to know what he was doing in the area. "I'm getting married and I have a lot on my mind," he said.

When asked if he had ever assaulted anyone with a knife, he said, "Yes, once a long time ago, I assaulted a man when he tried to rape my wife."

He denied assaulting anyone that night and said he "always" carried the gauze in his pocket because he had hurt his ankle "a long time ago."

The officers brought him to the police station and asked him to take off his pants so they could check his legs for bruises that might have been inflicted by an assault victim.

Officers discovered not only a "slight discoloration" two inches above his left ankle, they also noted that he wore no undershorts.

"I don't have any clean underwear," Bland volunteered.

He was booked on suspicion of burglary, rape, assault with a deadly weapon, and kidnapping.

Later the same day, Long Beach police presented a lineup for the four female victims, including the fifteen-year-old Darlene Carter, who had recovered enough from her injuries to attend. She had been unable either to give a description of her attacker or identify him. During the lineup, attended by Bland's newly hired defense lawyer, four of the women observed silently and sat apart from one another, separated by police officers. They were given the standard admonition that the suspect might or might not be in the lineup.

Cheryl Lynn Morgan and Ann St. John identified Bland. Morgan was so certain, she said she recognized Bland the moment he stepped on the stage.

Leslie Fowler was able to positively identify Bland's mug shot from a photo lineup.

* * *

During the months Bland was out of prison, he had been working as a forklift operator at a utility parts and equipment maker, making $107 a week and regularly seeing a private therapist and his probation officer. He began actively dating as soon as he was released and by June already had a steady girlfriend.

His probation officer, in regular reports to the court, noted that Bland's therapist termed Bland a "difficult" case, believed he needed long-term care, and was hopeful that he could someday "be made aware of his sophisticated and manipulative techniques . . . and that some realistic insight can be achieved."

After the arrest, the probation officer angrily wrote that Bland portrayed a "correct" attitude during interviews and was "seemingly cooperative," but "obviously sophisticated in his responses to interviewing techniques, and the real nature of his feelings remained unknown."

Bland was brought into court before Judge Richard Hayden, the same judge who'd implored him to do some meaningful self-discovery. Hayden set bail for Bland and he fled once he'd posted bond. Hayden issued a no-bail bench warrant and Bland was captured by a special fugitive unit on December 10. This time Hayden set no bail.

Bland proclaimed his innocence in vain. A jury convicted him in February on six counts: two each of kidnapping, forcible rape, and burglary.

Just as he had after the 1958 stabbing incident, Bland wrote a ten-page statement to his probation officer maintaining his innocence, complaining about how his lawyers had handled the case, and begging that they recommend probation instead of prison.

"I would like to point out to you, sir, that I am not guilty, although things have been turned around to make me appear so, and of course, the jury did find me guilty from what was presented to them.

"But I swear to you, that I did not betray the faith that both Doctor Morgan and Judge Hayden placed in me . . . I want to appear at your mercy and request that in my sentencing, you will recommend that I am sent to some hospital or place where it is quiet," he wrote.

In an bizarrely morbid note for a thirty-two-year-old man, Bland ominously wrote that he would probably not see his loved ones again, "as I will be, in view of the charges, what is termed a long-term individual.

"In fact, I'll probably pass away there. Therefore, I would like to further request a court order allowing me to make five telephone calls at my expense to my loved ones and to another attorney."

When the probation officer interviewed Bland he reiterated his innocence, saying he was convicted on mere "circumstantial evidence" and his psychological problems had been cured at Atascadero.

"The only thing that looks bad was the knife I had in my possession and the fact that I just happened to be in the area," he said.

The probation officer recommended that Bland be sent to state prison.

At the sentencing hearing on April 3, 1969, Deputy District Attorney R. Kelley likened Bland to "Dr. Jekyll and Mr. Hyde. Seven years at Atascadero have prepared him for every interview and diagnosis. He can play humility, remorse, open-faced candor, and sincere earnestness with Oscar-winning facility.

"He can be a model employee, punctual probationee, regular churchgoer, and doting sibling. But when alone at two a.m., he becomes Mr. Hyde. He has stabbed a man, raped at least three women, and tried to rape others. He has held a knife to the throat of some of his victims. He appears incorrigible, and his dangerousness has increased since his early crimes.

"Society is safe only while the defendant is incarcerated."

Bland spoke out at his sentencing, blaming the system for his woes and bemoaning the fact that he was to have been married at Christmas.

"I was convicted of breaking into two women's apartments for the purpose of rape—also of approaching a woman on the street and demanding that she come with me. I was tried in the Long Beach courts, where I found a great deal of hostility toward me.

"Previously, I was in the Atascadero State Hospital for a rape case, where I had been for some 7 ½ years.

"I—*because* of my past, was guilty, no ifs, ands, or buts. The detectives wouldn't even talk with me. The DA told me to confess or else! I didn't, and, consequently, many facts were turned around in court to fit what the DA wanted, even over the protests of my attorney."

Bland warned that he would present an appeal where "all the facts will come to light."

Judge Hayden noted that Bland's recent criminal acts had become more sophisticated and were "executed with more finesse than his first ventures. The only thing he seems to have learned is how to do it better.

"His pleasant disposition and his cooperativeness is disarming, but this Court can imagine no greater threat to society than to release him. There appears to be faint hope that he can be rehabilitated in view of the results of the Atascadero experience. Other crimes in his past indicate that he is dangerous and incorrigible."

Hayden sentenced Bland to 3 years to life for one rape count, 1 to 25 years on the kidnapping charge, and 5 years to life on one of the burglary counts, with all three sentences to run concurrently. Hayden gave Bland a break on the last three counts by waiving the sentence if he completed the term for the first three counts. Under California's complex tangle of sentencing laws, Bland's first opportunity to leave prison would be in less than 2 years.

Despite spending 7 years classified first as a "sexual psychopath," then a "mentally disordered sex offender," Bland was officially a first-timer in the penal system. He was shipped to the prison in Chino, a sort of clearinghouse for inmates where they are evaluated for their ability to interact with others in an institutional setting and for their vocational training potential, and classified for minimum, medium, or maximum security before being sent to another prison for long-term housing. Bland's prison photograph shows his once-blond hair thinning and darkened to dishwater blond, pleasant-looking eyes, and lips drawn straight across, as if he were about to smile for the California Department of Corrections camera.

Having spent nearly a decade being poked and prodded by institutional psychiatrists, Bland had perfected the art of the interview. Instead of being an only child, he became the last of seven children, explaining that all six of his siblings had died before he was born. In an astonishing revelation, Bland claimed he was "babied" as a child, forced to wear girl's clothing, then was made to wear shorts when other boys his age wore pants, leaving him with feelings of "masculine inadequacy."

As if straight out of a psychology text, Bland described his father as a distant dad, who was quiet and withdrawn, who taught him never to express his emotions. He played scary pranks on his son and was slow to anger, but frightening when venting. In another marked change from his previous interviews, Bland for the first time described his mother as the smothering, overprotective type who was very close to him and spent many hours going places and encouraging him to socialize with his friends. Bland opined that his father was jealous of his wife's affection toward his son and took it out on Bland by withholding affection.

Bland described himself and his first wife as "high school sweethearts." In an amazing bit of rewritten personal history, Bland said he was driven to commit the first rape after coming home to find his second wife in bed with another man, and claimed the victim was his then-wife's best friend. He couldn't keep up with his wife's desire for sex "every five minutes," Bland told the psychiatrist. It was only at Atascadero, Bland told the psychiatrist, that he realized that his second wife's fever-pitch sex drive, combined with his being forced to wear girl's clothes as a child, made him feel inadequate and drove him to prove his masculinity in violent rapes. The corrections counselor made the wary comment in his report that Bland "seemed sophisticated in the ways of institutions and interviews. He seemed alert, but evidently has never come to grips with reality and certain areas of his thinking."

Later that month, Bland was sent to Folsom Prison, a medium- to maximum-security facility in northern California where more psychiatrists and psychologists awaited him. Upon his arrival, there were more rounds of interviews and a battery of now familiar psychological tests, in addition to vocational and academic achievement tests. He scored 107 on his IQ test. His reading scores averaged at just beyond tenth-grade level, with his math scores a bit lower.

He was asked to fill out a sentence completion form. His job was to finish half sentences with the hope that the answers would somehow reveal his attitudes and feelings.

To the partial sentence "Sometimes sex. . . ." Bland filled in *"started arguments."* to "I was annoyed by people who . . ." Bland wrote, *"suck their teeth constantly."* "My body is . . ." *"aging somewhat rapidly."* "I don't like girls who . . ." *"smoke and use people."* "I like to make love when . . ." *"my partner is willing and in the mood."*

Next Bland was asked to draw a picture of his ideal female and write down four things about her.

Bland's cartoonish sketch shows a woman with pronounced cheekbones and full lips, a beehive hairdo, and cat-eye glasses, wearing a skirt and a button-front cardigan sweater and holding out one hand. Next to the drawing, he wrote, "Waiting for me, marriage, happiness."

The form also asked Bland to list his ambitions in life. He listed "success in business, marriage, and family and winning an appeal and a retrial to show them just how wrong about me the courts are." He described himself as "a man with great compassion and understanding of others," with the time and patience to listen to others "in some areas." To a question about what he would like to change about himself while in prison, he touted his 9 years' experience with psychotherapy and mentioned "continuing in that field" and using what he had learned to help others.

While psychiatrists and penal professionals were kicking Bland's tires once again, the California Department of Corrections mailed a questionnaire to Bland's then-fiancée, Francine Smith. She said Bland was with her during one of the rapes and was with friends another time. She listed their activities as church-oriented activities, watching TV, picnics, eating at her parents' house, and going to Knott's Berry Farm. She praised his sense of humor and patience. Hava Bland, in her written interview, reiterated that her son was a nondrinker and also supported the contention he was elsewhere when the rapes were committed.

In late 1969 and 1970, Bland twice appealed his conviction and his sentence to the appellate court and scored a partial but impotent victory. One count was tossed out, but conviction on five of the six counts was affirmed and his prison sentence remained unchanged.

At 32, Bland finally finished high school from the prison's adult school and obtained a General Education Degree by passing a high school proficiency exam administered by the state. His teachers fawned over his attitude and abilities and gave him straight A's in every subject. The head of the Folsom Prison education department remarked that he should be commended for working as a clerk typist while also keeping up his grades in each class.

Bland's good grades and dedication as a clerk paid off with a recommendation from the Folsom education supervisor that Bland be rewarded with a reduction in custody. Over the years at Folsom, Bland kept up his exemplary work record and his requests for reduction in custody were granted until he was at minimum security housing.

As was the practice in the California penal system at that time, Bland was evaluated periodically by staff psychologists to give the parole board a sense of the inmate's readiness for parole to the outside world. In one of the more notable reports, in August 1972, Dr. Alvin Groupe, Folsom's senior psychiatrist, observed that Bland had made the appropriate adaptation to institutional life, Groupe gauged Bland's psychiatric improvement as questionable and viewed further psychotherapy as useless because Bland had seemingly not changed between the time he was first interviewed at Folsom.

Groupe said Bland's continuing denial of the 1968–1969 rapes seemed convincing until Bland "committed a Freudian slip by stating, 'when I rape a woman I always see my wife's face in front of me.' "

Groupe concluded that Bland was saying "what he thinks

I want him to" and was interested only in pleasing the examiner. "His rationalizations and denial are glib and he apparently has learned all the psychiatric jargon from exposure to therapy at Atascadero."

In an August 1974 interview, Bland added that he had attempted suicide in 1953 by sniffing lacquer thinner. However, Chief Psychiatrist E.H. Harris said Bland appeared "optimistic." He said Bland's "violence potential" had decreased moderately and considered him "mentally able to refrain from repetition of his offensive behavior."

As the years passed, Bland apparently abandoned plans to pursue a career in psychology and instead received training as a sewage treatment plant operator through the University of California at Sacramento and even received on-the-job training. In July 1974, at the age of 37, Bland was certified by the California State Water Resources Control Board as a wastewater treatment plant operator.

The next psychological evaluation in October 1974 seemed aimed at launching Bland out of Folsom. His attendance record at group counseling was 100 percent, his teachers were laudatory, he posed no discipline program. But Harris also reported that Bland continued to deny his participation in the rapes and showed no remorse for his victims. In a remarkable turnabout, Bland made oblique references to a second psychiatrist in October 1974 that he was considering some kind of a confession to his crimes, but psychiatrist Robert Bolin remarked, "However, he was quite manipulative and one could hardly be impressed with his sincerity. [His] affective responses were rather superficial and his effort to be congenial and pleasing was quite deliberate."

A year later, Bland had "admitted" his guilt, saying he had discussed the issue with his fiancée and it had "strengthened [our] relationship." Bland was placed on a waiting list for group psychotherapy.

A corrections memo on May 15, 1975 mentioned the "rough" nature of his offense, but that he had "spent the past six years doing everything he could to work his way out of prison," citing "exemplary" behavior, work record, attitude, and school performance. Three months later, on August 22, 1975, Bland was paroled.

One year later, almost to the day, Bland was again behind bars for assaultive sexual conduct. For the first time, his victim was a young girl.

Donna Rogers was walking home from a party just after midnight on August 24, 1976, with her infant, her six-year-old son, and her eleven-year-old daughter in Long Beach when a man in a white-and-green car approached and asked if she wanted a ride home. She refused and he drove away. He came back and she refused again. When he returned a third time, she finally relented. When Rogers's daughter began to get into the back seat, the man said, "Why don't you get into the front seat with me? We'll all fit in the front."

She told him how to get to her house and he drove off in the wrong direction. She tried to tell him of the error and he pulled off into a dark alley, pulled out a ten-inch hunting knife, and said, "Don't give me any trouble or you'll get hurt. Do exactly as I say."

The man reached over her daughter, her son, and her infant in her arms to fondle her breasts and asked her, "Don't you ever wear a bra?" Donna Rogers, afraid to move, kept her children facing the other direction while the driver was touching her. He ordered her to get out of the car with the baby and her son. "I'm keeping the girl. I need her for insurance," he said.

He forced them out of the car at knifepoint and told them

to turn their backs to the car. If they looked, he would kill the girl.

Rogers caught a glimpse of the license plate and ran with the infant and her young son to a nearby home to call the police. Frightened and frantic, Rogers told officers the suspect was over 30 years old, six-foot-one, 185 pounds, with thinning brown hair. He had on a light long-sleeved shirt and blue or gray pants.

After the officers had interviewed Rogers and her son, they took them home to her husband. Soon after they'd arrived, the officers learned over the police radio that the daughter had just walked into a local hospital.

Vanessa Rogers said after her mother and siblings had left the car, the man had told her to lie down on the front seat of the car with her face in his lap, and to touch his pants between his legs, and had threatened to cut her unless she was quiet. The kidnapper drove for several minutes, then pulled into an empty garage, pushed the telescopic steering wheel up and out of the way, and told the fifth-grader to remove her pants. When she hesitated, he held the large knife up to her neck and threatened to cut her. He forced the young girl to orally gratify him, then told her to get into the back seat, where he had a number of tools in a plastic jug on the floor behind the passenger seat. He clipped clothespins on her buttocks, genitals, and tongue, then held her nose shut and tickled her, making the girl breathe heavily through her mouth. He also snapped a hemostat—a stainless-steel clamping device used by doctors—on her ribcage. He attempted intercourse but was unable to penetrate her. He reached into the bucket of tools and pulled out a long plastic tube with a point on it, resembling a turkey baster, and thrust it into the young girl, telling her he wanted to make her bigger for him. When that failed, he ordered her to fellate him again.

When the little girl cried out during the painful attack, he choked her to silence the sobs, then held a curved-bladed knife to her throat and told her to be quiet or he would cut her.

Afterward, he patted her on the head and said, "I would like to meet you again when you're eighteen," and told her to put her clothes back on and get in the front seat. He drove around, winding through various streets, then told her to get out and count to 100 before she left. Vanessa started walking and soon found herself near a hospital. She wandered into the emergency room and told a nurse that she had been separated from her mother.

Vanessa was treated at the hospital and interviewed by police, giving thorough descriptions of the suspect and his car. She described the man, wearing a moustache that ended at the sides of his lips, gold wire-frame glasses, a long-sleeved white shirt with a floral pattern, white dress pants, and tan loafers with a gold chain across the tongue of the shoe. When he took off his pants, she described blue swim trunks with a white design. The car was a two-door green 1970s Buick with a white vinyl top, bench seats, electric windows, green vinyl and cloth upholstery, a green vinyl contoured dashboard, green carpeting and floormats, and a steering wheel that moved up and down, and there were folded shirts in the back seat.

The next day, detectives pulled out 200 photos of known sex offenders and thirty sheets of mug shots, each containing six photographs of men who were registered sex offenders. Vanessa readily picked out a photo of Warren James Bland. In a separate room, Vanessa's mother was also given the photos to look through. She also chose the photograph of Bland.

The officers paid Bland a visit after he was done with work for the day. They found him at home in his garage with a green 1972 Pontiac. The description of the rugs, the dashboard and everything else matched the victim's description, right down to the folded clothing in the rear seat. In his room they found tan loafers adorned with gold chains and three shirts that were close to Vanessa's description of what her assailant was wearing.

Hava Bland said she had eaten dinner with her son that evening and she had brought him a glass of icewater while he'd worked out in the garage and that they both had gone to bed between 11 and 11:30 p.m. Bland waived his right to have an attorney and said during an interview that he had gone to dinner with a girlfriend at a Mexican restaurant in Lakewood, an adjoining suburb of Long Beach. They eventually parted company between 12:30 and 1 a.m., but closer to 1 a.m. Bland insisted he drove home on side streets instead of using the major thoroughfare, which was the same street from which Donna Rogers and her three children had been abducted. During this interview, the detectives recounted a report earlier in the month when a man answering Bland's description had tried to force a young boy into his car by brandishing a curved-bladed knife. Bland denied having had anything to do with that incident. But he agreed to take a polygraph test about the accusation of sexual assault and tried to convince the officers to allow him to speak to the victims, saying he was confident "the whole matter would be cleared up immediately."

The officers, of course, didn't allow Bland to interview Donna Rogers or her daughter. Bland took the lie detector test the next day and failed. When told of the results by the examiner, Bland asked, "Is this room bugged?"

Assured that it was not, Bland said, "between you, me, and the wall, I went out and celebrated being out of jail one year and got drunk. I picked up the people and the mother was good-looking, but the daughter was better looking and

I was attracted to her. I told the mother and the boy to get out of the car and they did." Bland then admitted some details of the sexual assault.

The examiner summoned one of the detectives and Bland repeated some of his statement, then added, "Oh, I just don't know why I did it, but I'm sure that's the only time it happened."

The detectives then interviewed Bland's date, who said he left between 11 and 11:30 p.m. the night of the assault and had not been drinking that evening.

Bland was prosecuted on four felony charges: assault with a deadly weapon, assault with intent to commit rape, oral copulation on a child with intent to commit great bodily harm, and kidnapping. Although the young boy identified Bland during a live lineup as the man who'd tried to drag him into his car at knifepoint, no charges were filed.

Almost as soon as Bland pleaded guilty to kidnapping and the intent to rape counts, he immediately declared that he was innocent of all charges and claimed he had accepted the plea bargain out of convenience. Bland told his probation officer that he didn't know why he had confessed. For the first time, Bland told Campbell that he was an alcoholic and said once he drank he could not stop, but then said he had completely abstained from alcohol during the year he was out on parole.

In an ominous note, Campbell wrote that police suspected Bland in a series of sexual assaults in Downey, Hollywood, and Long Beach where the MOs and the suspect's description matched. The police had trouble locating several of the victims because they'd moved out of the area and the others who'd looked at photos or live lineups including Bland described him as "very close."

"In another instance, there was apparently an attempted

rape that turned into a homicide when the woman's throat was slit,'' Campbell wrote in the March 1977 report.

As was the practice in California at the time, Bland was sentenced and given a release date of April 6, 1980. This time around, the forty-year-old savvy inmate took advantage of the free health care behind bars. As described by his victims, he had a noticeable paunch, the result of 190 pounds packed on his six-foot frame, and the cause of his high blood pressure. Nine teeth were missing and four were decayed. The cavities were filled, courtesy of the California Department of Corrections. He also had an ingrown toenail surgically removed and received medication and treatment for his high blood pressure.

Adept at the working within the penal system, Bland requested his old job as a clerk since he was unable to go to work at a wastewater plant. A dutiful worker, he made his way up to become the clerk for the captain of the prison, one of the highest-ranking authorities, and excelled, receiving commendations.

Bland married his third wife, Norma, in January 1981, after one of his court appearances, and requested conjugal visits in a trailer next to the prison. Those visits were approved. Aware of the credit possible for ''good time, work time,'' (credit for good behavior and credit for the amount of time he spent in the Los Angeles County Jail awaiting trial), Bland appealed to the parole board on March 21, 1980, complaining that he was ''overdue for release!''

His appeal was denied but he was released on schedule, according to the complicated parole computations that took his stellar behavior into consideration. On April 6, 1980, he walked out of prison again.

* * *

This time it was a little boy. The violence worsened, but the facts of the case were familiar.

Eleven-year-old Paul Corday was walking home at 8:30 p.m. when a man pulled up and offered to drive him home. He accepted and hopped into the green-and-white van. It was December 30, 1980. Instead of driving the boy home, the man said he was a tugboat pilot and offered to drive him to the docks to show him his boat. Paul said he didn't want to see his boat, but the man drove to the docks anyway and told him to open the van's side door. As soon as Paul turned his back, the man held a curved-bladed knife up to his face, put his other hand over his mouth, and forced him into the back of the van.

When the boy hesitated and said "No" to the commands to remove his clothes, the man struck him four times in the head with the handle end of the knife. Dazed, Paul removed his clothing and his attacker removed his own pants and tied the boy's hands behind his back with plastic rope, then wrapped the rope around his chest. Paul didn't struggle as the man ran his hands over his body, poked and scratched him in the face with wire, and clipped clothespins to his nipples, genitals, buttocks, and lips. The attacker removed some of the clothespins and used channel-lock pliers and vise grips to twist and pull his nipples and genitals.

"I get my fun this way," the man said, laughing as the boy writhed in pain.

The attacker took out the curved-bladed knife and held it to the boy's face.

"You know what this is," he said, then struck the boy on the head several more times, causing his vision to blur.

The man forced Paul to kiss him on the lips several times, then forced the boy to kiss his genitals and fellate him while alternately poking Paul in the face and body with the stiff wire and digging his fingers into the boy's rectum.

A gifted student with a near-genius intellect, the young boy never cried out during the torture and sexual assault, but instead focused on the man's face and the description of the van's interior in order to memorize all the details. After the assault, the attacker defecated in the back of the van, then wiped it up with a white cloth and tossed it out of the van. He promised to drop him off at home, but Paul diverted him to a neighborhood near his home instead.

Police didn't have such an easy time capturing the suspect this time. Using a sketch artist and hypnosis, the youngster tried to re-create the features of the man who'd assaulted him but could not focus on the license plate of the van. The artist drew a composite sketch of the man and refined it after the hypnosis session. It was distributed to local newspapers and TV stations. With their son's description of the van—green, with a horizontal white stripe around the middle—Paul's parents took the bold step of doing their own stakeout at the docks where their son had been assaulted.

For a month the Cordays spent 3 and 4 nights each week waiting and watching at the docks, sometimes staying until the early hours of the morning.

On January 27, 1981, they finally saw the van. They raced to a phone booth and called police only to see the van drive away. They managed to get back into their car and follow the van along city streets. Soon a black-and-white appeared behind them to take up the pursuit and pull the van over.

Warren James Bland was behind the wheel.

CHAPTER FOURTEEN

Bland was arrested that night on suspicion of child molestation and released on $35,000 bail. For the police lineup the next day, Bland dyed and curled his hair and walked with a limp. When each of the six men in the lineup was asked to say the words spoken by the assailant, Bland faked a southern accent. That was enough to dissuade Paul from making an absolute identification, but the boy said Bland was "the closest. [He] looks pretty much the same."

It was the van that Paul distinctly remembered. It was exactly as he'd described it—diamond patterns in the green vinyl upholstery covering the dashboard and the ceiling, green bucket seats, four windows on each side of the van that opened outward, and two windows on the rear doors. A search of the van revealed a .45-caliber gun with ammunition, a linoleum knife with a curved blade, four clothespins, a pair of vise grips, a crescent wrench, alligator clips, soldering wire, and a registration slip showing Bland was the owner.

On July 24, 1981, Bland pleaded guilty to two counts of

child molestation with the use of a deadly weapon and admitted his prior convictions. Bland was sentenced to 9 years in prison and sent to the California Men's Institution in Chino, a rural area of mostly dairy farms east of Los Angeles.

Bland's hunt for a wife had begun during his last stint in prison. He'd courted his wife-to-be at a church group for inmates. When he was released from prison in April 1980, he moved in with her and her three daughters, all of whom were nearly adults. Bland had explained away his prior record by saying that he had been railroaded by police and had pleaded guilty because he couldn't afford a good defense attorney and wanted to avoid embarrassing his friends.

As they were living together as a family, Norma had a hard time understanding her ex-con boyfriend's strange habits. He was out late almost every single night and never offered explanations about where he was. One day she picked up his personal address book and saw the names of "lots of women," including their measurements, their social security numbers, their birthdays, and the names of their daughters. Most names had between one to three Xs after them.

Norma never confronted him about his late-night escapades or why he kept a volume of women's names complete with his own rating system, but she assumed he was seeing other women. Although he enjoyed going to auto races, the beach, and amusement parks, Bland constantly pressured Norma to accompany him to see pornographic movies at the theater. She never went but assumed some of his late nights were devoted to attending porn movies.

She didn't understand until years later why her twenty-year-old eldest daughter was uncomfortable with Bland and had left to live with her natural father. She also didn't understand why her other two daughters, aged 17 and 18, disliked Bland. Norma never knew that Bland had attempted intercourse while molesting both of her younger daughters and had constantly pressured the older daughter for sex until he'd gone back to prison.

A stalwart Christian, Norma Williams believed she could turn Bland's life around through her faith and married Bland in January 1981 after he was jailed for the Corday offense. He had convinced her that police had framed him for child molestation because of his prior record. Norma stood by Bland for several years until she learned her daughters had been molested. She filed for divorce immediately.

This time around, penal psychologists were faced with a paunchy middle-aged multiple-term sex offender who was classified as a "sexual sadist." In his first psychiatric interview, the rapidly aging felon, surrounded by vastly younger inmates, claimed to be a diagnosed epileptic and reported to have low back pain and high blood pressure. No prison officials compared his claim of having seizures, in which one truly cannot account for one's behavior, with his prior assertion that he had suffered "amnesia" during a series of sexual assaults decades earlier.

For the first time, Bland also admitted to being a lifelong alcoholic, blaming his behavior on getting drunk and losing control. Corrections officials apparently accepted this admission without checking the reports of Bland's victims over the years, none of whom had ever reported that Bland was drunk or had the odor of alcohol on his breath during the commission of the crimes. In all his prior interviews, Bland had always prided himself on being a nondrinker.

Prison doctors immediately placed Bland on antiseizure medication and performed a battery of complex neurological tests to measure the electrical impulses in his brain. He was given blood pressure medication and pain pills for his lower back.

Months and many tests later, doctors concluded that Bland

was not suffering from epilepsy and he was taken off the antiseizure prescription.

Bland continued to encounter prison psychiatrists, one of whom was Freudian-trained and wrote that a lack of controls and restrictions in Bland's life on the outside allowed his "id," or his most primitive urges, to plague society. "When in free society, Bland is always locked in mortal combat with his id, and the id invariably emerges victorious. While incarcerated, he no longer has to contend and he leaves the supervision of the id to others," wrote William Swisher, a correctional counselor.

Months later, senior psychiatrist Sherman Butler reported that Bland "appears motivated for psychotherapy and can benefit from it" to come to grips with his self-destructive behavior and drinking problem. "Despite his long history of offenses, there does seem to be hope for him, in my opinion."

Truly excelling at institutional life, Bland asked to be returned to his previous job as a clerk, and the request was granted within a few months. But life was not as easy for Bland as it had been in his earlier trips through the prison system. The code of conduct, rife with unique rules existing only behind bars, allows thieves, killers, and violent offenders to coexist in close quarters with a fair degree of harmony. Rapists and child molesters, perhaps because they prey on women and children, must sleep with one eye open and constantly watch their backs for fear of violent retaliation from other inmates. Men in custody on those offenses typically either lie or say nothing about why they are in prison. In 1981, an inmate using a homemade prison shank sharpened from a metal bed spring attacked Bland while he was using the toilet in his cell, splitting open his neck from his ear to the collarbone. He nearly bled to death from the gaping wound. In-house doctors patched him up, but the gash left an ugly red scar. Bland believes he was attacked by a member of a prison gang.

After recovering from the slashing assault, Bland was befriended by a fellow repeat sex offender, Norman Felts, who broke the ice by joking to Bland that he was doing 13 years for "two lousy blowjobs." Even though the two became friends, Bland remained relatively secretive about his prior record as a habitual sex offender and was genuinely frightened about other inmates learning of his background. The only clues Bland gave was that the last offense involved molesting a little boy. Bland insisted he was not a homosexual and blamed the episode on getting drunk. Time and time again, Bland confided to Felts that he was afraid of getting out, getting drunk, and reoffending. He was a nice person most of the time, but when he drank, he described himself as a "sex monster" with sex drives that had to be gratified immediately.

With his past record, another prison sentence would be "like a death penalty" because additional time in custody for his prior offenses would be tacked onto the sentence for the crime he feared he would commit. Having spent most of his adult life behind bars, he didn't want to waste away in custody. A lengthy sentence would be like a life sentence because of his age.

The best way to prevent reoffending, Felts said, would be to quit drinking for good.

"You know, the first time you ever put a drink to your lips, figure you're coming back to prison," Felts told Bland.

"Well, if it . . . if I do, the best thing would be to minimize being caught. My idea is to stay out there as long as I can and minimize the chance of getting caught by eliminating the witness or the victim, that would be the best way," Bland said.

"Either way, if I get picked up for murder or if I get

picked up just for fooling around with a kid, either way, that's a death sentence for me. The chances are better that— you know—the odds are better of not getting caught for murder than for getting caught with some kid,'' he said.

''Well, you know, dead witnesses don't tell stories,'' Felts replied.

Bland's flawless work record and good behavior trimmed years from his sentence, but the aging ex-con faced release from prison for the first time without his mother to welcome him home. She had been hospitalized and died while Bland was in custody. Having spent 27 of the past 31 years socializing with inmates, Bland was approaching the sunset years of his life thoroughly institutionalized, having rarely experienced life without bars on windows and celebrating most birthdays and holidays in custody. Bland's ever-thinning hair was now predominantly gray, his weight had ballooned to over 200 pounds, he had been substantially weakened from the neck wound, and he was taking medication for chronic high blood pressure. Most prison psychiatrists, in their reports over the years, predicted that Bland's criminal sexual activity would fade as he approached old age.

On January 20 1986, one week before his forty-ninth birthday, Bland was paroled.

Hudson ran his hand through his hair and punched in the next phone number.

''Hello, my name is George Hudson. I'm an investigator for the Riverside County district attorney's office in California. I'm trying to locate Dorothy Cobb . . .

''No one by that name there? Okay. Well, do you have any relatives named Dorothy whose mother's maiden name was Hoover? No? Thank you very much.''

The list of people in the phone book with the last name

of Bland's second wife, Dorothy Cobb, and her mother's maiden name, Hoover, was getting smaller, and his prospects were getting dimmer. The energetic DA investigator had a full caseload of murders, assaults, and rapes to prepare for trial, but the Bland case was the most vexing. Hudson's job was to locate Bland's ex-wives and victims, some of whom would be in their early 70s and had not been interviewed by law enforcement for nearly 30 years. Police reports of 25 to 30 years ago were sparse on personal information from witnesses and victims. Most of them contained just a person's name and address. Without a birthdate or a place of employment or any other identifying information, trying to unearth a witness or a victim years later was proving to be very difficult, even with the vast resources and computer databases available to law enforcement. Hudson had already done the routine procedures, such as running the names through databases kept by local and state law enforcement. The computer databases turn up anyone with the same last name who had been a victim, a witness, a reporting party, or a suspect in any kind of case involving the police, but most of those databases had only been in existence for 15 to 20 years at the most.

Hudson got lucky finding some victims. Leslie Fowler, a victim of one of the 1968 rapes, found him first. Fowler was a schoolteacher who lived in Riverside County and had heard about Bland's capture and arrest for the Phoebe Ho murder and phoned prosecutors, offering to testify against him. The first time Hudson talked on the phone with her, she cried while describing the assault.

"Ever since this happened, I started gaining weight until I was obese because I didn't want to be attractive to men," she told him. "I went to therapy and I'm still in therapy and I'm still overweight. I'm married now but we have sexual problems. He's a very understanding man."

Hudson found that was a common link between Bland's victims. Many of them had suffered long-term psychological problems after being subjected to assault and rape, and many of them, including his ex-wives, had moved and changed their names to make certain Bland would have no way to find them. That made it extremely difficult for Hudson. Extensive computer searches of local and state police records, the FBI, utility companies, and Department of Motor Vehicle records of licensed drivers yielded him no clues as to the whereabouts of Bland's second wife. She apparently hadn't lived in California for quite some time.

To be thorough, Hudson checked with the vital records department in Las Vegas, where Bland mentioned that the two had been wed, and came up with some clues: her father's name, her mother's maiden name, and the fact that she had been living in Ontario, California, just before moving to Culver City in the mid-1950s. Hudson then contacted the high school in Ontario and confirmed the name of Dorothy's father and learned her father's hometown in Illinois. A check of that city's vital and police records led to another dead end. No one of that name had ever been a witness to a crime or a victim or had been arrested. Hudson finally asked one of the police officers there to fax him the pages of the phone book with the names of people bearing the last names Cobb and Hoover.

Hudson phoned every Cobb in the phone book, vainly searching for at least some distant relative. He'd begun placing calls to the Hoovers when he finally scored a hit. The second Hoover on the list was a cousin of Dorothy Cobb who was well aware of Dorothy's marriage to Bland but declined to give Hudson her phone number. Instead, she promised to call Dorothy and ask her to call Hudson. Dorothy called a few days later. It wasn't until he interviewed her that Hudson learned of the mountaintop rape, Bland's abuse of his own daughter as an infant, and the details of the Blair stabbing in 1958. Dorothy confirmed what was in the original police reports, which stated that Blair was drunk and babbling. She said Blair never said foul words to her, never touched her, and never tried to pull her out of the car, as Bland had claimed years later to justify his actions. Hudson had learned Blair had died, leaving Dorothy as the only living witness to the stabbing.

Hudson also had a tough time finding Sue-Ellen Sweeney, who had remarried and had tried to erase her tracks so that her ex-con ex-husband could never find her. When Hudson finally located her, she revealed for the first time the painful honeymoon rape and the strange threats Bland had made after tying her up and running a knife over her body.

Unable to find any victims of the 1959–1960 attacks, Hudson resorted to taking out a classified ad in the *LA Times,* listing the victims and their former addresses, the dates of the incidents, and the locations where the assaults took place. A private detective with extensive computer databases phoned him the next day and volunteered to prowl through the computer networks for free. The only woman he could find was the former model. Bland had approached her and thrown a cement sack over her head. The youngest of the victims, she was living in the state of Washington. When Hudson contacted her, she agreed to testify.

Every few weeks, Hudson set aside time to search for the women who had suffered violence from Bland decades before. With caring and compassion, he listened to the victims relive the nights of humiliation and pain at the hands of one man who'd triggered decades of self-hatred and therapy. He comforted Bland's ex-wives, who had buried the private agony of their former husband's assaultive behavior in their hearts and minds, remaining silent out of fear, naïveté, and ignorance that the acts committed against them were criminal, not part of a "wifely duty." In finally divulging their heartwrenching stories, Bland's ex-wives, together with the victims, filled out an unbroken string of violence against women spanning more than 30 years. It would be powerful testimony during the penalty phase of the trial, if it got that far. Even though some of the incidents had never before been reported to police and were considered uncharged offenses, they would be admissible during the final portion of a capital case in which a prosecutor asks a jury to render society's most severe punishment.

The months turned to years as Bland's case, in line with scores of others, languished in the criminal justice system. Criminalist Faye Springer, in California, and microscopist Skip Palenik, in Chicago, were each toiling behind microscopes and sensitive instruments analyzing the tiny bits of evidence painstakingly plucked from Phoebe's body. Prosecutor Brian McCarville had a long list of felony murders and other cases waiting to get to trial. He not only was awaiting the final reports from Springer and Palenik but was on the short list of attorneys who were being considered by the governor for appointments as municipal court judges. Defense lawyers Harmon and Polis were also in no hurry to get the case moving. Defense attorneys typically prefer if a case sits for a prolonged period of time. Within the criminal justice system, the defense lawyer's job requires him or her to put the prosecution's case to the test, poke holes in the case, and create reasonable doubt. The more time that goes by, the more the memories of prosecution witnesses fade, and the greater chance that a thread or a hair or tiny snippet of evidence will become misplaced or disappear in the great volume of evidence collected.

Also waiting for Bland's judgment day were the Hos. The pain of losing their daughter to violence tore at their marriage, and the couple plunged themselves even deeper into their work, finally fulfilling their dream of opening a shoe-store in a mall at the center of town. But their success seemed hollow with one of the most beloved family members gone. The couple worked themselves to exhaustion, vainly trying to quell the loss. A close family member said Phoebe's death had caused a virtual chain reaction of troubles and emotional upheaval for the Ho family.

To show their gratitude to the community while Phoebe was missing and after she was murdered, the couple offered the lowest possible prices on their shoes. "This is not a good place for a shoestore," Kenneth Ho told a reporter. "I just break even. But I think these people know opening this store is my way of saying 'Thanks'."

Neither Kenneth Ho nor his wife could understand all the delays in bringing Bland to trial. Justice had been swift in their former home in Taiwan. "In my country [murders] always get priority," he said. "This is very slow."

In October 1988, Hudson learned that Bland had made an incriminating statement to another inmate at the Riverside County Jail. Louis Boucher, jailed for vehicular manslaugh-ter, was processing fingerprint cards for three Mexican nationals on charges of child annoying and attempted kid-napping when he commented out loud that child molesters ought to be "castrated and executed."

Little did he know that Bland was standing in the area after coming out from the shower section across the hall. Boucher and Bland had become acquaintances and had exchanged magazines and talked every evening after Bland had showered and was waiting to be taken back to his cell. But Bland had never told any of the inmates, including Boucher, the full charges for which he was accused.

Bland had asked Boucher about the charges the three men had been brought in for and Boucher had told him, then repeated his comments about child molesters being castrated and executed.

Bland replied, "What I did to the kid was no different than what we did in Chu (Vietnam) Lai in 1968 to the women and children when we burned their huts."

Boucher said he was so angry, he was ready to pummel Bland, but Bland turned and walked out of that section.

"He took off in a hurry," Boucher said, according to the report Hudson was reviewing.

Furious, Boucher said he told a deputy about Bland's comments, then consulted his lawyer before phoning the prosecutor. Detective Phil Sanchez interviewed Boucher at the jail and wrote up the report.

Several months later, Hudson learned that sheriff's deputies in a routine search of Bland's cell, had found a pair of nail clippers hidden in his shaving kit. Clippers are a prohibited item for inmates and they were confiscated.

By 1989, two years had passed since Bland was first arraigned for the murder of Phoebe Ho. Assistant U.S. Attorney Larry Burns, aware of the scientific morass the murder case was embroiled in, offered to take Bland off McCarville's hands, estimating that he could be indicted and tried in federal court within about 6 months. McCarville gave the okay and Bland was whisked away by federal marshals from Riverside County down to San Diego for a three-day trial for being a felon in possession of a gun.

He was moved to new quarters in San Diego's federal prison awaiting trial. A search of his cell revealed 686 feet of bedsheets torn into strips and shaped into ropes, and a razor. The items were confiscated and the incident was recorded as a potential escape attempt.

During the federal trial Detective Patrick Birse, the officer who'd found the .22-caliber gun stolen from Celia Blake in her blue Toyota, and parole Agent John Blum testified at the first trial. Bland's federal public defender asserted that Birse was wrong to shoot Bland and had planted the gun to justify a "bad shooting." Burns argued to the judge that if the defense put Birse's frame of mind at issue, Birse should be allowed to tell jurors what he was thinking at the moment he'd shot Bland, such as Bland's heinous record as a violent sex offender, the outstanding warrant for the rape, torture, and murder of a child, and the fact that he'd weighed the danger of shooting a suspect against the danger of Bland going free and hurting someone else. The judge agreed. To soften the introduction of the information, the judge told jurors about Bland's criminal past and the subject of the arrest warrant during jury selection.

After a three-day trial, jurors took about 2 hours to convict Bland for the offense, making Bland the first ex-con in the region and one of the first in the country to be convicted using the controversial new law, the Armed Career Criminal Act. At his sentencing hearing, Bland read a lengthy statement to the U.S. District Court judge proclaiming, "I am just a simple man."

Bland blamed Burns for launching a personal vendetta against him with a "tidal wave of distorted misinformation" making him out to be a "three-headed monster" and inflaming the judge. Bland soft-pedaled some of his crimes, claiming the theft of Celia Blake's car was actually his "visit to an old friend's home. It was obvious because of her physical ailments that she would never drive again. I talked her into allowing me to borrow this car . . ."

The 1958 knifing of Ray Blair came about when "that man was virtually dragging my screaming, obviously very pregnant wife out of the car. When he saw me coming, he virtually (sic) dropped her on the cold concrete, making a run in front of the car to face me." Bland claimed he was the one who'd phoned for the police and called the ambulance.

The ex-con complained that the news media "had a field day with my past but never once addressed the positive things that I had realized and what I was doing with my life at that time" when he was under investigation for the Phoebe Ho murder.

He fled because he claimed Detective Mike Lackie had "destroyed" the contents of the Thayers' home and he was afraid of returning to prison, where a guard had once put him in an armlock that he claimed tore his abdominal wall.

Burns was mistaken, Bland said, for relying on old reports "prepared a long, long time ago. He does not even mention all the positive psychological reports. And he himself has never once attempted to sit down and talk with me. If he had, he would have found that I am a very caring and receptive individual," Bland told the judge.

He explained the roped bed sheets as raw material for rugs he was making in a prison handicraft program. "I was also the first inmate to introduce macramé to that program," he boasted.

While acknowledging he had spent the bulk of his adult life behind bars, Bland rattled off a list of fanciful, aristo-cratic hobbies. "I enjoy good classical music, various classic books, and live theater. I enjoy painting, power-boating, flying, and meeting people. I have enjoyed active participa-tion in motorcycle and sprint car racing since 1953 and have been involved in most kinds of motor-sport racing ever since that time."

Bland embellished his prison career as a water engineer and bemoaned having been "well punished" for his prior bad deeds.

"Your Honor, I still feel a lot of guilt because of what I have done with my past life, but I ask you, sir, when does a person get to a point when they stop paying for their past crimes?"

Prosecutor Burns said he was reminded of a saying, "Fool me once, shame on you; if you fool me twice, shame on me. How about if you fool me thirteen or fourteen times? The essence of this Armed Career Criminal Act and this prosecution is that there comes a point where we can no longer afford to let people like Warren Bland out."

Like others before him, Burns said one danger of Bland was his harmless appearance. "It's incumbent upon the justice system to protect the citizenry. In this case, the curtain ought to fall on Mr. Bland's career of crime."

The judge gave him a life sentence.

A *U.S. News & World Report* columnist, John Leo, applauded Bland's conviction and sentence under the federal statute. "Under this act, it took only thirty minutes in court for Larry Burns to accomplish what the state of California failed to do for thirty years—take Bland off the streets permanently.

"The state of California botched the Bland case for decades and is implicated by its incompetence in the savage murder of little Phoebe Ho. It has known for twenty-nine years that Bland is a violent sexual psychopath, yet it let him go five times."

For months afterward, defense attorneys in federal court representing clients under the "armed career criminal with a gun" statute used Bland as a yardstick against which their clients should be measured. "My client has a few prior convictions, but he's no Warren Bland," they would argue in pleas for leniency.

In the meantime, Bland's defense lawyers appealed and his conviction and life sentence were overturned.

Burns retried Bland in front of the same judge with the same defense attorney and a different jury. This time, the defense attorney questioned whether the car really belonged to Bland, given the fact that painkillers prescribed for

''Thaddeus Sterling'' and a dentist's bill for ''Thaddeus Sterling'' were in the blue Toyota.

In his rebuttal case, Burns subpoenaed the Pacific Beach dentist who had treated ''Thaddeus Sterling'' and asked him to identify ''Thaddeus Sterling.'' Without hesitation, the dentist pointed out Warren James Bland as his onetime patient.

This time, jurors took 10 minutes to convict Bland. The judge again sentenced him to life in prison without parole and shipped him back to Riverside County. Sharon Ho, interviewed the day the federal judge delivered a life sentence in prison, had just a few words for the man she believed killed her daughter: ''I only want him to die.''

''Get a life, Datig!''

With his coat off but his necktie neatly in place, Cregor Datig barely looked up from the police reports piled on his desk and nodded at the taunting from his fellow prosecutors. It was 7:30 p.m. and Datig didn't have a spouse and children waiting for him at home, leaving him time to start off the New Year in 1990 burying himself in the Bland case. While federal prosecutors had custody of Bland for the trial in San Diego, Brian McCarville won an appointment to the bench in January 1990 and was sworn in as a municipal court judge, leaving the case in the hands of Datig, who originally had been assigned to assist McCarville.

At 33, Datig's broad-shouldered build seemed better suited to the football field than the courtroom. Instead of physically tackling his legal opponents, Datig sought to overwhelm them with evidence so rock solid as to leave no cracks into which the defense could wedge a question of reasonable doubt. His strategy was to so immerse himself in the law and the facts of a case that he would anticipate the defense tactics and run interference against their every legal maneuver.

The son of an accountant, Datig grew up in southern California enchanted with TV lawyers on mid-1960s dramas like *Perry Mason* and *Owen Marshall, Attorney-at-Law*. He would play "court" by having friends play the roles of judge, defense lawyer, prosecutor, and witnesses. As he grew older, the lure of the stage and love of singing held his attention. But he later returned to the law bolstered with the dramatic skills necessary for commanding attention from a lawyer's most important audience—the jury. The success Datig enjoyed translated into a brisk pace of promotions. Like all deputy district attorneys, he started prosecuting drunk drivers and shoplifters, but he moved quickly through the department to become the youngest lawyer ever to earn entry into Riverside County's elite "special trials" section that handled murders, serial rapists, and high-profile cases.

Once at the helm of the Bland case, Datig plunged into the stack of boxes McCarville had left him containing police reports, evidence reports, and records of interviews with victims and witnesses, as well as records of Bland's prior crimes.

After sitting dormant for 3 years, the murder case had ground to a halt. The high-profile, high-status case had plummeted in popularity and had become the albatross of the DA's office. The energy and momentum that normally propels a case from arrest to conviction—the shock of the initial crime, the search for the killer, pressure from the press, and desire of the public to punish the offender quickly—had withered. The pinnacle of publicity came in the days following Bland's capture, when every prosecutor in the office wanted to sink his hooks into the meaty, high-profile case involving a depraved sex offender slaughtering a small child he had tortured for a week as his sex slave. Three years later, the glamor had long faded and the evidence seemed complex and intangible. Worse yet, the case had hung in limbo for so long that Bland was still awaiting a preliminary hearing. It is only after a preliminary hearing in municipal court that the judge deemed there was enough evidence to bind over a defendant for trial in Superior Court.

Except for Hudson's slow and steady progress at locating Bland's ex-wives and victims, no one had touched the case for years. Thousands of hairs and fibers were gathering dust in petri dishes stored in boxes at the Department of Justice crime lab. With other cases constantly demanding attention from criminalist Springer and Skip Palenik, the scientific analysis had ceased. Bland's conviction on the federal charge of being a career criminal in possession of a gun had garnered some attention within the legal community and judicial reform circles eager for a means to lock the revolving prison doors to repeat offenders. Other than modest interest from the legal press, there hadn't been a TV or newspaper story about Bland and the Ho murder for years.

The potential gaps in the presentation of evidence rang in Datig's head as he read through the reports. How would he clearly explain a hair-and-fiber case to a jury? How would he head off defense attacks on the trace evidence and their inevitable finger-pointing that there was no eyewitness? One of the biggest holes was finding out where the little girl had been kept. Fellow prosecutors shook their heads as Datig tried to pull together a logistical nightmare of a case with witnesses and scientific evidence scattered across the country and huge questions left begging.

Despite the murmurs in the office, Datig felt fortunate to be taking a fresh look at the case and dug into the reports. There were more than a dozen moving-sized cardboard boxes of paperwork. He met with Hudson, spoke with

Springer and Palenik, and set up interviews with the witnesses. Datig realized he needed to act as a catalyst to motivate the experts and freshen the witnesses' recollections.

At the bottom of one of the boxes Datig found one of the first reports delivered by Skip Palenik on the analysis of hairs, fibers, and paint chips. Palenik confirmed Springer's conclusions that a head hair from Bland and a head hair recovered from the bottom of Phoebe's foot were significantly similar, particularly the "troughing" that can be seen if one cut a cross-section of the hairs and examined them head-on under a microscope. Palenik described the "dramatic change in surface topography" which might be a mere curiosity if it was found in a single hair, but all of Bland's head hairs bore the same characteristic, which "greatly increases the likelihood that the questioned hair originated from the suspect's scalp."

Limb hairs plucked from Phoebe's pants and limb hairs from Bland were also unusually similar because paint was stuck to the tips of the hairs. After conducting an electron microprobe analysis, and using an energy dispersive X-ray to examine the contents within the paint, Palenik found the paint on the tops of both hairs contained equal amounts of aluminum and silicon, titanium dioxide (a white paint pigment), and calcium carbonate (white paint pigment and filler).

"This should be regarded as a significant finding," Palenik wrote.

Palenik plumbed the microscopic depths to examine the fibers and the dyes. The report was peppered with technical terms like "dichroism," "birefringence," and "anisotropic substances," all referring to the process of studying the geometry of the molecules within the dye of the fiber and measuring the fiber's response to light. Palenik analyzed the fibers with a microspectophotometer, which allows the study

of single fibers under various types of light. Palenik opined
that the blue polyester fibers recovered from Phoebe's body
and from the Thayers' van absorbed the identical dyes at
an identical rate of absorption and the rust brown nylon
fibers were dyed in the same fashion. As another means of
identification, Palenik also compared the melting rates of
the fibers and found they were "very close."

Datig was fascinated by the scientific detail. He was satisfied and proud at the thoroughness of the South Pasadena
detectives, Lackie, Springer, and Palenik. But he was
haunted by the very nature of trace evidence. Without a
fingerprint, there was no solid identity of Bland as the perpetrator, no confession, no eyewitness. Nothing definitively
put him there. The best that science could offer was the fact
that the fibers were "consistent" but not a "match." Datig
knew that experienced attorneys like Gerald Polis and Steve
Harmon would exploit that in trying to expose the weakness
of the scientific evidence.

Datig considered Polis and Harmon the finest of Riverside
County's criminal defense attorneys, peers to any of the
state's finest lawyers. The first time Datig met Polis was
two weeks after Datig passed the bar exam and was making
his first official appearance in misdemeanor court as a prosecutor. His supervisor had earlier instructed him not to allow
any defense attorneys to delay their cases. When Datig's
supervisor introduced him to the grizzled veteran of the
criminal defense bar, Datig's response was, "I'm Creg
Datig. No continuances."

"Who's Mr. Personality?" Polis had replied.

While Datig never lost his self-assurance or somewhat
stilted formality, the two eventually became friends and
enjoyed facing off on opposite sides of the counsel table in
court. He soon learned two things about the bearded defense

lawyer: if he made a promise, you never needed to get it in writing, and he always drove a nice new Porsche.

Datig had tried several murder cases against Harmon and won every single one of them, but it was an uphill battle. Harmon was so disarmingly nice that if Datig let his guard down, Harmon would seize an opportunity and twist the knife. Between the two of them, Bland had a ''good cop, bad cop'' defense team, Datig mused.

With every page he turned, Datig soon saw how important it was to make Phoebe come alive before jurors as a real little girl, not a remote, impersonal abstraction in a technical autopsy report. Against the inevitable defense arguments that the fibers didn't—and can't—indicate a finger-pointing match to Bland, he would breathe life into Phoebe. He wanted to convey the agony inflicted by a depraved criminal on this girl's tiny body. If the jury couldn't hear the murdered child testify, they would at least hear from her body via graphic photos of the torture marks and the voluminous hairs, fibers, and paint chips as thousands of silent witnesses. Some prosecutors shrug off the obligatory preliminary hearing as a necessary evil, but Datig wanted to prepare for it in earnest. It would be an important rehearsal for the trial and a chance to test his case. He would be very interested to see the response from the defense. Even though there is no jury at a preliminary hearing, Datig would also see how the gruesome evidence of the prolonged sexual attack, the torture, and the murder played out at the rather sterile pretrial hearing. Datig never wanted to forget the agony Phoebe had endured. After prosecuting child molesters, Datig was sensitized to the fear and the pain experienced by the young victims. He sorted through the piles of material for the photographs and finally found a color photo of Phoebe that had been reproduced for the house-to-house search in South Pasadena. Phoebe, celebrating her seventh birthday with a

cake and candles, was wearing the blue-and-yellow long-
sleeved shirt she'd worn on the day she was kidnapped.

Datig gently tacked the photo to a bulletin board directly
over his desk, determined to do everything he could to
remind jurors this was not an intellectual exercise.

It was a half-hearted rain, the kind of warm California
drizzle that drips from a confused skyline with threatening
dark clouds on one horizon and cheery blue skies peeking
though puffy marshmallow clouds on the other side. The
damp, cool air permeated the Riverside Municipal Court,
prompting Warren James Bland to don a dark blue jail-
issue sweatshirt underneath the neon orange jumpsuit with
"Riverside County Jail" stamped on the back. As was typical during his jail stays, Bland had put on a sizable paunch.
The dyed, black hair had long ago grown out, his wispy
moustache had grown in, and his hair was now predominantly white streaked with gray. Down to his twinkling
blue eyes and polite smile, Bland's kindly, grandfatherly
appearance was ruined by the jangling leg chains linking
his ankles and the handcuff encircling his left hand, clamped
to a second chain around his hips. Even as he approached
senior citizen status, Bland posed a dual security hazard as
an extreme flight risk and a death penalty defendant.

The last time Bland had been in court, a few months after
his arrest, TV cameras, reporters, and spectators eager for
a glance at the notorious child molester had jockeyed for
space in the majestic Riverside Superior Court a few blocks
away. On March 26, 1991, a single reporter sat in the dreary,
standard-issue courtroom of Municipal Court Judge Janice
McIntyre-Poe at the start of his preliminary hearing. While
the sheriff's department wasn't exactly comfortable walking
Bland across the street with the rest of the chained-linked

inmates headed for court, the fear of retaliation against Bland had shriveled and they simply drove him in a patrol car and escorted him into a side entrance of the building. The misdemeanor court was so nondescript it was often confused with other two-story office buildings and didn't even resemble a courthouse. Bland's pinstriped defense team, Polis and Harmon, sat on either side of their client. On the other side of the counsel table, Datig, in a conservative dark suit and tie, sat next to DA Investigator Hudson.

With the formal air of a Shakespearean actor, Datig rose to his feet and announced the name of his first witness. "The prosecution calls Gary Thayer." In succession, Datig called to the witness stand Thayer, Cindy Haden, and Lois Carver, Thayer's daughter. Bland, his right hand free to take notes on a yellow legal pad, gave quick nods and smiles to his former friends and acquaintances. The defense closely questioned the witnesses' recollections and sought to lock in their testimony about the dates Bland worked, when they recalled seeing him on the job, and when he'd borrowed Thayer's brown work van. If there was any change in their recollection at the trial, the defense lawyers could use that to impugn their credibility.

Datig arranged to have a videocamera mounted at the back of the courtroom to record the testimony of Maddy Jordan because of her age. Nervous and out of breath, she took several moments to walk past the bar, up the two steps to the witness stand and settle into the chair. The judge allowed her to take the oath sitting down. In a loud, clear voice from the podium, Datig gently questioned Jordan about her relationship with Bland as his former mother-in-law and how she had acted as a go-between to deliver his letters from prison to her daughter because she wanted nothing to do with him.

The elderly woman, wearing a bright red jacket and

brooch, paused several times to take a few deep breaths, sipped from a cup of water the bailiff had placed before her on the witness stand, and glanced several times at Bland, who appeared to have a small, frozen grin on his face. Jordan had trouble remembering exactly what Bland had said to her when she'd confronted him at Blake's house, and Datig had to remind her what she had told Lackie about Bland saying goodbye to everyone and claiming to be dying from bleeding ulcers. But she had no trouble recalling Bland's parting words when she'd driven him to the thrift store.

"He said, 'Grandma, I've done something awful.' I had already parked the car. He was crying. I didn't say anything, I just let him cry.

"I told him to go get on the bus, several times. Before he got out of the car, I told him, 'We need to pray.' I prayed, but I watched his face. I watched him and I saw his eyes going back and forth, looking at the key.

"It was a face I'd never seen before. It looked like something out of this world. It wasn't the Jim that I knew," she said, her voice catching in her throat. "He said he wouldn't be taken alive."

"What did you do then?" Datig asked.

"I told him to get out of the car, to get his things, and to go home. I told him not to go back to Celia's house anymore," Jordan testified.

Jordan continued that she was called again by her frantic friend, and she chased Bland out of Celia Blake's bathroom, where he had dyed his hair, and he'd leapt over the backyard fence.

On cross-examination, Harmon focused on the fact that it was several weeks before Jordan had told Lackie about Bland admitting "doing something terrible" and that she had told Detective Lackie that Bland had said "terrible" instead of "awful," as she had just testified.

"Did you take notes about what Mr. Bland told you?" Harmon asked.

"Oh, I couldn't forget that," Jordan said, perhaps anticipating the direction Harmon was steering her. "That's one thing I could not forget.

"There's a lot of things still stuck up in that old head," she said, pointing to her neatly coiffed white curls. Bland, his pen poised over his legal pad, looked up and smiled.

Still, Harmon pressed Jordan to recall whether Bland had used "terrible" or "awful."

"I don't remember, sir," Jordan answered.

On redirect, Datig had just one question. "Did anyone ask you to write down every single word Mr. Bland said?"

"No, sir."

"Thank you," Datig said, turning toward the counsel table. Then he paused and returned to the podium.

"By the way, ma'am, if you don't mind me asking, how old are you now?" Datig asked.

"I'll be 83 this year. I'm 82 now," Jordan said carefully.

"Congratulations," Datig said. "No more questions."

The next day, in preparation for Faye Springer's testimony, Datig and Hudson brought in charts and enlarged photographs of the crime scene, hairs, paint balls, and fibers, an unusual number of exhibits for a preliminary hearing. Datig expected that at the end of the prelim, Bland would be held to answer at trial. The defense, no doubt, expected it, too, since the burden of proof was slight for the purposes of a preliminary hearing. But Datig wanted Harmon and Polis to see that the evidence that Datig believed would send Bland to the gas chamber was more than a ragtag collection of odds and ends.

Skilled as an expert witness, Faye Springer dutifully raised her hand for the oath and gave her credentials in a practiced fashion, then outlined the crime scene as she recalled removing evidence from Phoebe's body. When the first exhibit board was placed on an easel containing a picture of Phoebe's lifeless form in the dirt, Bland looked up, put on his eyeglasses, and peered at the oversized photographs.

In response to Datig's questions, Springer gave a detailed analysis of the hairs, fibers, and paint balls, in addition to the semen stain on the leg of Phoebe's pants, explaining the different scientific methods to examine each type of evidence.

On cross-examination, Harmon pointed out again and again that there was not a single hair or fiber that conclusively identified Bland as Phoebe's killer to the exclusion of all other persons.

"If this fiber is consistent with Mr. Bland," Harmon asked, "that also means that it could also be inconsistent, isn't that right?"

"Yes," Springer said.

"You can't say that this fiber without question came from Mr. Bland, can you?" Harmon asked.

"Of course not," she said.

On the third day, Detective Lackie testified about carrying out the search warrants to collect hair and fiber from Bland's room in Gene Thayer's house and from the van and the dropcloths next to Gary Thayer's garage.

As the week wore on, Evie, who had married another man, testified about her and Bland's failed relationship and her efforts to persuade Bland not to flee as the police had closed in on him. Detective Pat Birse testified about shooting and capturing Bland. Sergeant Patrick McManus testified about Bland's statements to him from his hospital bed.

Finally, on the last day, the coroner testified about the autopsy on Phoebe in which her body bore the signs of sexual assault, torture, and the marks of death from strangulation around her neck.

The defense asked few questions of the coroner, apparently willing to concede that the young girl's injuries spoke for themselves.

A grim-faced Datig rose to argue before the judge in the near-empty courtroom. Earlier, he had filed an amended complaint adding a third special circumstance charge that the murder was committed during the course of torture.

"The defendant intended to kill this little girl and during the course of that he inflicted extreme and cruel pain and physical suffering," Datig argued, without looking at Bland. "I think it's obvious that what we're dealing with here is a brutally sadistic course of conduct. Based on all of her injuries, there certainly is sufficient evidence to warrant the court finding a strong suspicion that this child was murdered in the commission of torture, in addition to the other special circumstance allegations."

Polis and Harmon looked at each other.

Polis rose and said, "Submitted."

In what came as a surprise to no one, Judge McIntyre-Poe held Bland to answer for the crimes and ordered him to appear in Superior Court for trial.

CHAPTER FIFTEEN

For mid-morning arraignments in Municipal Court, about a dozen orange-jumpsuited inmates are handcuffed and chained together at the legs and escorted by sheriff's deputies in one big, clanking group from the lock-up to the jury box, where they sit and wait for their names to be called. When the judge leaves the bench in between cases, the stiff formality of the courtroom lapses into a casual coffee klatch atmosphere as prosecutors chat with the court stenographers, the wives of the inmates hold up their children for their in-custody fathers to see across the courtroom, and court clerks process the never-ending flow of paperwork. This is where most newly arrested suspects in custody meet their public defenders or court-appointed attorneys for the first time, exchanging handshakes and trying to have private conversations huddled over the manila folders containing their criminal complaint. In minutes, the lawyers typically discuss how they should plead to the charges, how to secure a release before their prelims and make arrangements to talk later at the jail.

The Municipal Court serves as the gatekeeper for all criminal cases, from minor misdemeanor offenses to the gravest of felony and capital cases. As the supervising deputy public defender for Municipal Court, John Isaacs oversaw the comings and goings of the men and the occasional women in custody and could usually guess the offense for which they were coming to court by sizing them up. He could pick out the sobered-up men in wrinkled street clothes on Monday mornings who were arrested over the weekend for drunk driving, the shoplifters, the armed robbers, and the men prone to indecent exposure. The one he couldn't place was the middle-aged businessman with the trim moustache sitting quietly near the others. Isaacs figured he was maybe a white-collar criminal or maybe a drunk driver who had run someone down and was facing more serious felony charges.

Every time he brushed past him to chat with a client in the jury box, they had a civil exchange of "Excuse me"'s. The bailiff later pulled him aside and told him that the distinguished man had chewed out one of his clients for not taking Isaacs' advice on his case. The next time Isaacs went past him, the man made a comment about Isaacs' masonic ring, which had belonged to his father, and asked for his business card.

Then he stuck out his hand and they shook.

"I'm Warren Bland," he said.

Bland started calling him from the jail on a regular basis to exchange pleasantries and talk about masonry and odds and ends, and then started asking him to do favors, such as giving people messages, but they never discussed his case. One day at lunch with his supervisor, the Bland case came up.

"Polis dropped out," his supervisor said. "The judge is kicking the case back over to the public defender's office."

The lunch table grew silent. No one in the office wanted

the case. The client was considered a monster and the crimes for which he stood accused were horrendous. The scientific evidence alone was confusing and seemed certain to lead to a conviction. Still, someone in the public defender's office would have to assist Steve Harmon, the lead lawyer on the case. As a death penalty defendant, Bland was legally entitled to two attorneys.

"I get along fine with Bland," Isaacs said to the hushed lunch-table crowd of fellow public defenders. "If it winds up on my desk, I don't mind."

Several months after Isaacs volunteered to assist Steve Harmon, Harmon was diagnosed with cancer and put his law practice on hiatus in order to undergo intensive chemotherapy treatment. It was decided that Isaacs would take the lead role in the guilt phase of the trial and Harmon would stay out of the footlights and handle the inevitable penalty phase.

At 10, John Isaacs had read all of Shakespeare's plays. At 12, he saw TV for the first time in his rural Virginia hometown. At 13, after becoming acquainted with Marxist and anarchist philosophies, he founded the Revolutionary Force of the True Virginians with another youthful proletarian and plotted the overthrow of the government by stealing World War II Mauser rifles and handguns and hoarding them in a cave. He joined the Marines at 14 but was kicked out when his commanding officer confronted him with his birth certificate. After starting a successful electronics business in his late teens, Isaacs shunned everything of material value and roamed the United States in search of the "ultimate truth" as a poet-philosopher, and then went to law school, convinced it would be a more effective way to change the world.

Isaacs' passionate stance against material things and his drawl eventually softened over the years, as his curly hair and beard became speckled with gray and his eyes were framed by laugh lines. The grandson of a top Virginia trial attorney who'd gotten for his last client an acquittal of capital murder a half hour before his death, Isaacs tried cases with the eloquent wit and profound graciousness of a southern gentleman. He was close to Bland's age, and they also shared the experience of losing their fathers on the cusp of adolescence.

As he did with all his clients, Isaacs spent hundreds of hours talking to Bland on the phone and in personal visits to the jail. Bland called constantly and demanded attention and visits from both Harmon and Isaacs. When Harmon fell ill, the duty fell mostly to Isaacs, but he didn't mind. He liked to get to know his clients. Even though many of his clients in serious cases were accused of dastardly deeds, he truly believed there was some good in everybody and always tried to find something to like. Part of that was his philosophical bent. Isaacs thought some people didn't willingly choose to do evil. He thought Bland and most other child molesters would give anything on earth to be kind, decent human beings and not be tortured by forces beyond their control, driving them to commit the unthinkable. The person that Isaacs got to know was a kind, generous, charming human being. But Isaacs knew Bland was likable now because he was caged and unable to commit crimes. If he ever got out, he would be subject to his evil drives.

In their conversations, Isaacs would ask him, "How could you do something like this? How did it feel?"

Bland confided that he had a "restlessness" that drove him to drink, to get in his car and cruise the streets, watching people. That would go on for several weeks until his drives would "get worse" and he would end up raping and molesting someone as if to release some internal pressure. When it was over, he would feel ashamed and scared and vow never to do it again. Bland insisted that every single one of his crimes was preceded by bouts of heavy drinking and that he had been molested as a youngster by a man and then by a woman in separate incidents.

Bland said his friend, Tyler Lowell, also an ex-con, had abducted Phoebe with the help of his Asian girlfriend, for their mutual exploitation. On the premise of stealing a motor home from a dealer's lot in a remote section of Riverside County, Bland met Lowell at a converted barn and saw him and his girlfriend molest the girl but denied ever touching her. He said he believed Lowell was responsible for her death, but that being in close proximity to the child could account for the hairs and fibers found on her body and clothing.

Isaacs knew this explanation of events would not diminish Bland's culpability for Phoebe's murder. If just one juror believed Bland was not in any way responsible for Phoebe's murder, a hung jury was possible. If Isaacs could convince jurors that Lowell, not Bland, had killed Phoebe, Bland could of course be convicted of murder, but it would be a non-capital offense if jurors believed Bland did not himself kill Phoebe. Bland was already serving a federal life sentence, so he was destined to die behind bars. For that reason, Isaacs wasn't entertaining any illusions about trying to win an acquittal. Bland had as much of a chance at an acquittal as a rebellious youngster had at mounting a coup d'état from the Virginia backwoods. Isaacs just didn't want Bland to die in the gas chamber.

By the fall of 1992, the Hos' pain of losing their youngest child to murder had not waned. With no trial and no punishment for the killer, the wounds seemed only to deepen, as if atrocities could be committed at will without retribution.

Finally, a trial date was set for early 1993 and DA Investigator Hudson told Sharon that she would be a witness. The couple continued to let their heavy work schedule distract them, and it again resulted in pain.

One Friday night in mid-October, shortly before he was getting ready to close the store, Kenneth noticed a white van with brown trim parked outside his store with three people appearing to look into his store. He thought this was odd but did nothing.

Three weeks later, on November 7, Kenneth and his wife closed up their shoestore about 8:15 p.m. on a Saturday to head home. Sharon drove their Toyota and Kenneth followed in their white truck which contained $45,000 worth of athletic shoes.

Barely one block from their home, a van cut in front of Kenneth Ho and bumped the rear of the Toyota. Sharon stopped the car and the van bumped her again, harder.

Kenneth parked the truck behind Sharon's car. He reached for his cell phone, a pen, and a gun he kept in the glove compartment. He put the gun in his jacket pocket and hopped out of the truck with the phone in one hand.

When he got close enough to see the license plate, he wrote it down on his hand. Sharon had also gotten out of her car and was standing behind Kenneth, close enough to touch.

The driver of the car, a male Hispanic, assured them that he would phone his insurance company.

Kenneth nodded and dialed 911 and told the operator the name of the street he was on. Someone from behind grabbed Kenneth's phone while a third man, also a male Hispanic, tried to pull him into the van. As he was struggling, Kenneth stuck his hand in his pocket, managed to wrap his finger around the trigger, and pulled once. The bullet hit the pavement. During the skirmish, Kenneth fired two more shots at the ground. A fourth man, a male black, grabbed Sharon and forced her into the back of the van. As two men were dragging Kenneth into the van, a neighbor who heard the shots came running out of his house, firing his handgun into the air as the van containing all four men and the captive couple squealed away.

Kenneth's hands were tied behind his back and he was stripped of his gun, his phone, and $184 from his wallet, then pistol-whipped. The two male Hispanics took turns kicking, slugging, and beating him. While he was being beaten, he could hear his wife screaming as she was being raped. The only thing Sharon recalled her attacker saying was, "feels good" as he raped her.

The couple was driven to an alley in Los Angeles and thrown out of the van.

Kenneth, nearly unable to see because of his injuries and the blood running into his eyes, still had his hands tied behind his back and could barely walk. Sharon's clothes were in tatters. The couple found their way to a house in Los Angeles, where paramedics and the police soon arrived.

Sharon was treated by emergency room physicians and released. Kenneth was hospitalized for one week with a broken nose, broken ribs, lacerations to both temples, a split lip, a fractured chin, and a crushed knee. His left thumbnail had to be surgically removed.

Within weeks, two of the men were arrested and charged with robbery, kidnapping for the purpose of robbery, aiding and abetting a rape, and assault. The other two men were still at large.

*   *   *

As the trial date approached, Datig worked feverishly, as if preparing for battle. Datig thoroughly reinterviewed each witness, Bland's prior victims, and his ex-wives. They flew Faye Springer back to Chicago to assist Skip Palenik in completing analysis of the scientific evidence. They worked with Hudson to prepare detailed exhibit boards displaying photographs of hairs and fibers plucked from Phoebe's body that were magnified thousands of times next to photographs of microscopically enlarged hair and fibers culled from Bland, the Thayers' van, and the curtain dropcloths. Within weeks of the trial, Hudson and Datig flew back to Chicago for a crash course in the complex scientific principles used to compare different elements of each fiber and identify similar characteristics in those Palenik and Springer said had come from the same source.

After becoming familiar with his evidence, and thoroughly versed in the scientific principles of trace evidence, Datig turned to the law books. Every day he gazed into the eyes of Phoebe Ho, whose photo was still tacked up near his desk, and prepared for what he thought the defense would do. For every piece of evidence or testimony to which Datig predicted the defense would object, Datig prepared a motion. For every anticipated defense protest, he assembled legal points and authorities to create a legal wall of impenetrability.

Datig predicted that the hardest-fought legal battle would be over Datig's motion to introduce evidence to jurors during the guilt phase of the trial about the torture and molestation of Paul Corday and Vanessa Rogers. Typically, criminal trials are sanitized and only the details of the offense at hand are introduced to jurors. But one section of the evidence code allows the prosecution to present evidence of a defen-

dant's criminal past as one means to prove the identity of
the perpetrator. Under California law, past-crimes evidence
can be admitted only if there are striking similarities between
the way the prior offenses and the present offense were
committed.

This was tailor made for Bland and his pattern of committing crimes against children, Datig thought. He laid out the
files of each of Bland's victims and marked all the similarities: Bland used a vehicle, he was cruising for children, he
sought out children who were walking, he abducted them
in a vehicle, he drove them to another place for the assault,
the method of sexual assault was similar, the pinch-torture
was nearly identical, the tool—pliers—was nearly identical,
Paul Corday and Phoebe Ho were both tied up, both were
abducted and held in an early-1970s Dodge van, both of
them were repeatedly hit in the head, Vanessa Rogers and
Phoebe Ho also had a torture instrument clamped to their
lips or tongue. In all, including the types of sexual assault
inflicted on the youngsters, Datig counted sixteen similarities
creating a distinctive pattern of abduction, molestation, and
torture.

This went beyond a *modus operandi*, Datig thought. Each
similar detail amounted to Bland's leaving his signature on
Phoebe's body, just as he had left his signature on Paul
Corday and Vanessa Rogers. Bland had created his own
style, Datig thought, the way an actor plays a part or a
gymnast performs a routine. Each person puts his individual
stamp on the acts he performs, and Bland had performed
these evil acts again and again in the same fashion. It was
a pattern of evil.

The phrase echoed in his head: *a pattern of evil.* That
would be the theme for the trial. Datig knew that repeating
this phrase would be a powerful tool, a drumbeat he would
sound during his opening statement, and it would resonate

with jurors as he presented evidence throughout the trial.
He had to win this motion. Datig was resolved to win each
battle. He didn't want the defense to score any points, either
in front of the judge or in front of the jury. This was a
showdown and he was not going to lose. If the defense
pulled a gun, Datig would shoot it out of their hands. There
was no mercy for this child killer. If anyone deserved to die
in the gas chamber, it was Warren James Bland.

A week before trial, in January 1993, John Isaacs and
Steve Harmon were pragmatic with their kindly client with
the grandfatherly smile. The dedicated lawyers were visiting
their jailed client more often than ever, sharing their strategies for defending him and getting his response. Isaacs and
Harmon pulled no punches with him. The last decision by
the judge in favor of the prosecution was going to hurt his
case. The jury—not picked yet—was going to hate him
after hearing of the attacks on Paul Corday and Vanessa
Rogers. During opening statements, they predicted, Datig
would solemnly wave the police evidence photos of Rogers
and Corday in front of the jury, showing that Bland had
tortured and molested two others before he'd gotten to
Phoebe. The only good thing about it was that it could
provide fodder for an appeal.

"The trial [was] over the minute that ruling was made,"
Isaacs told his client. Judge Gordon Burkhart decided against
their argument that the evidence was so prejudicial, it
amounted to convicting him before the jury heard any testimony. Isaacs had also unsuccessfully argued that it wasn't
all that unusual for child molesters to pinch or squeeze their
victims with tools such as pliers or clothespins.

"You have a choice, Jim," Isaacs said. "You can sit
silent at the counsel table and the jury will despise you and

condemn you to death. Or you can take the witness stand and tell your story. There's one chance in ten thousand that one juror might believe you.''

As difficult as it would be to put a client on the witness stand who had a record as long and violent as Bland's, it was their only hope to show jurors the nice side of Warren James Bland. They could see the human part of him, the man Isaacs and Harmon had come to like.

Isaacs was under no illusions as to what the likely outcome would be. They were preparing for a murder conviction. The goal was to convince at least one juror that Bland did not personally kill Phoebe. That was the only way to keep him out of the gas chamber.

Bland agreed to testify. He had told his story to both of his lawyers and they had assigned an investigator to check out the converted barn where Bland said Lowell and his girlfriend had brought the child to see if there was any evidence to shore up Bland's account.

In the meantime, Harmon had subpoenaed records from the prisons and mental hospitals where Bland had been treated. For the defense, the battle would not be in the guilt phase of the trial but in the penalty phase, where jurors would hear evidence from both the prosecution and the defense and decide whether to deliver a death sentence.

The records, Harmon and Isaacs believed, would give jurors every reason to spare their client's life. He performs superbly behind bars, unlike other defendants who continue to commit crimes during incarceration. The defense had their choice of corrections officers and perhaps psychiatrists who could testify about Bland's work ethic, his ability to get along with guards and other inmates, and his willingness to be treated.

Harmon and Isaacs knew they didn't have a great deal in their favor going into the trial, but they did have time on their side. In the few days before trial, Isaacs had performed his own informal survey in Riverside about people's recollection of the case. Whenever he was in a convenience store, a grocery store, a gas station, or a restaurant, he would strike up a conversation with someone there and ask if they recalled the Phoebe Ho case. He would say that he had just heard a snippet of news but had missed the rest of it. What was the Phoebe Ho case? Did the name Warren James Bland mean anything to them? Did they know what this was about, or why it might be on the news?

Almost to a person, no one recalled exactly what it was about. The names were vaguely familiar, but no one could directly name Bland as the offender and Phoebe Ho as the victim in a vicious child sex murder. The lapse of time had softened people's memories, making the selection of a fair and impartial jury who could weigh the evidence on both sides of a case more likely.

Isaacs was also buoyed by a recent win in a homicide case a few months earlier. It had also looked as dead-bang as this one and just as impossible to defend. His client had purportedly admitted the killing during a conversation with his longtime girlfriend. But every turn of events swung in favor of the defense. When the girlfriend got on the witness stand, she testified in elaborate detail about how her boyfriend had confessed to robbing and killing someone to her and how they had driven back to the scene of the crime, where he'd explained how it had happened.

On cross-examination, Isaacs had a bit of ammunition on his side. His investigator had found medical records showing the woman had been in the hospital for several days. In his trademark kind and gentle questioning, Isaacs probed the circumstances of her hospital stay and the girlfriend revealed she had suffered a miscarriage of the defendant's child. Looking over at her boyfriend, she said he had taken her to the hospital and never left her side for three days and three nights. Then Isaacs produced the record of her hospital admission showing the date and time was nine hours prior to the homicide. The jury, including the wife of a police detective, acquitted Isaac's client. The woman's brother later pleaded guilty to the murder.

As the date of jury selection drew near, Isaacs grew more confident. Like the protagonist in *The Rime of the Ancient Mariner,* one of his favorite pieces in literature, he felt optimistic and unstoppable. His adrenaline was pumping and he felt confident he could convince jurors that Lowell had killed Phoebe Ho. Bland was doing well in his practice sessions in preparation for his testimony and seemed able to portray himself as a likable man. Isaacs would fight his hardest to get evidence of Lowell's long criminal record introduced before jurors. And Isaacs would pour on his warmth and charm before jurors, not that he didn't already act that way in everyday life. He was too damned old to act phony. But he knew Datig came across with a stiff formality and a demeanor bordering on arrogance. That would work in his favor and he could seize control of the courtroom. He'd never approached a trial in his long career with the feeling that he was going to lose. This man was not going to the gas chamber.

They were the worst storms to hit Southern California in decades. The downpour that drenched the region flooded Riverside streets every day for weeks. A cattle call of 400 prospective jurors braved the deluge and showed up for jury duty on January 4, 1993, in the courtroom of Superior Court Judge Gordon Burkhart. So much time had passed between the time Bland was first arraigned in the turn-of-the-century courthouse that a gleaming new courthouse had been constructed across the way. The six-story courthouse of glass, terra cotta stucco, and teal metal accents was designed to comply with earthquake standards, create a more secure environment for felony prisoners, and essentially house all criminal cases, while all civil cases would be heard in the more stately courthouse.

Bland, his hair neatly combed back and his moustache trimmed, wearing a charcoal gray suit, blended in with the rest of the lawyers at the counsel table watching the jurors as they entered the courtroom. The court clerk and bailiff called out a list of twelve names and seated each person in the jury box for questioning. Another seventy-five remained in the audience and the others were scheduled to return to court in the afternoon or the next day.

To each group Judge Burkhart read the list of criminal charges and introduced himself, the lawyers, and the defendant. Jury selection allows lawyers to probe the hearts and the minds of prospective panelists and an opportunity to educate them about important legal precepts and the foundation of the case. Datig and Isaacs took full advantage of the opportunity to speak directly to the people who would decide the case and try to establish a rapport.

Datig, with a blend of professional detachment and a theatrical flair, introduced prospective jurors to the concepts of ''circumstantial evidence,'' such as fingerprints and hair and fiber evidence, and ''direct evidence,'' such as that of witnesses.

''If you take a jigsaw puzzle with two hundred pieces and pick up each piece one by one, you can tell what it's a puzzle of only after the picture grows and grows and finally you reach the point where you see enough of what you've put together and—boom—you say, 'That's New York City.'

''There may be pieces missing, like the place the child

was murdered or an eyewitness to the crime, but if you have enough pieces, you can see the Statue of Liberty in the harbor and the Empire State Building. If you're the kind of person that requires every single piece of the puzzle in order to tell what it's a picture of, that's not what the law requires. We use common sense.

"Do you think that as a juror in this case you can apply that standard, Mrs. Johnson?"

"Yes," the prospective juror replied.

Isaacs stuck to the basics. With philosophy and a low-key, folksy demeanor, he reiterated the tenet that all defendants are innocent until proven guilty and that just because someone was accused of a crime didn't mean that they were guilty of it. He cautioned them that they would be hearing some disturbing testimony but to keep an open mind. While the prosecution might try to shock them with other evidence, the key in the trial was to stay focused on the issue at hand, as hard as it was for them to do. They owed that not just to the justice system, but to Mr. Bland, he said.

"Will you be able to refrain from judging Mr. Bland, as bad as some of this evidence might be, and decide this case only after hearing evidence from both sides, Mr. Gabriel?" Isaacs asked.

"Yes," he replied. As each panelist was interviewed, Bland turned his chair toward the jury box, wrote notes on a yellow legal pad, and conferred with Isaacs. Harmon, still somewhat weak from battling cancer, drifted in and out of the courtroom during jury selection.

Datig and Isaacs very carefully questioned jurors about the death penalty and whether they could apply the law as delivered to them by Judge Burkhart. Jurors who could never apply the death penalty and jurors who would like to apply the death penalty for just about any crime were excused from the panel.

After a week of jury selection, the court clerk swore in a twelve-member panel and six alternates, including a school principal, a high school teacher, an elementary school teacher, a retired engineer, a college student, a supervisor at a navy missile base, a fireman, an accountant, and other retired professionals. All said they could stay on a case that would last 4 months.

The constant rain seemed an appropriate backdrop for the somber nature of the evidence. With twelve jurors and three alternates seated in the jury box, the other three alternates were seated in the first row of the courtroom gallery nearest the jury box. All eighteen rose and were sworn in by the court clerk to listen to the evidence and render a verdict based on the evidence and the judge's instructions. As they sat down, the courtroom grew quiet and Judge Burkhart asked Datig if he would like to deliver an opening statement.

"Yes. Thank you, Your Honor," Datig said. Wearing a dark suit and starkly white shirt and subdued tie, Datig rose from the counsel table in the silent courtroom and approached the podium. Datig knew this was the moment he needed to introduce jurors to Phoebe Ho and let them know she had once been a real little girl.

"Good morning, ladies and gentlemen. On December 18, 1986, the dead body of a little girl was found dumped in a ditch in the Glen Avon area of Riverside County. The body was crumpled, cold, lying down in an embankment near a freeway off-ramp in a sparsely populated area.

"The body appeared not to have been freshly dumped because it was cold and there was insect damage, where insects had started biting at the flesh of the body," Datig continued, noting that several of the female jurors flinched. "The investigators also noticed a deep ligature mark, a cord mark, so deep it was actually cut into the wrist, a terrible mark, a mark of evil,'' he said, allowing his trained voice to linger on the last word.

As DA investigator George Hudson worked the slide projector, Datig graphically described the marks the killer had left on Phoebe's body—the ''extremely painful'' bruises from pinching torture on her nipples, the backs of her knuckles, her ribcage, and her mouth, the blows to the head, the ligature marks on her wrists and around her neck. Some of the jurors seemed to grow pale at seeing the autopsy photos. Bland, in his charcoal gray suit, looked straight ahead.

''In her mouth here, the hard and soft palates, redness, abrasion, and irritation, indicating that something had been forced into her mouth. Next photograph, please,'' Datig continued, showing additional evidence of the sexual assault to her genital area indicating repeated forcible penetration.

''This is Miss Ho's anus,'' he said, showing the next photo, indicating that the coroner was expected to testify that the deep lacerations were in various stages of healing, indicating repeated forcible penetration by a large object and that such penetration hard enough to literally rip her tissues ''on a number of occasions is excruciatingly painful.''

Last, Datig said he expected the coroner to show that Phoebe's stomach and intestines were virtually empty, consistent with her not having been fed for several days.

''Ladies and gentlemen, these injuries to Phoebe Ho were horrible, but the evidence will show that they are part of and fit a pattern, a pattern spanning more than ten years, a pattern of evil, a pattern belonging to the defendant, Warren James Bland.''

Datig described the abduction, sexual assault, and torture of Vanessa Rogers, and then Paul Corday, noting the similarities how those attacks had taken place. He showed evidence

photographs of Corday with the scratches on his face and
the bruising on his nipples.

This was the moment in the trial Isaacs had feared. He
watched the faces of the jury change and harden. He saw
arms fold and legs cross, and barely concealed looks of
disgust. One woman in the front appeared to have a frozen
expression on her face. Many jurors could scarcely take
their eyes off the autopsy photographs to sneak peeks at
Bland, as if he were a monster.

Datig changed course, discussing Bland's anxiety, his lies
during the interview with South Pasadena detectives, his
failed marriage proposal to his girlfriend, the "dream" about
torturing Vietnamese women, his flight to San Diego, his
capture, and a summary of the hair and trace evidence.

"Ladies and gentlemen, this is the evidence that the People contend will identify Phoebe Ho's killer, the pattern of
evil of the defendant, Warren James Bland." Datig sat down
and it was Isaacs' turn to give an opening statement. Often,
defense attorneys prefer not to give an opening statement,
but Isaacs approached the podium.

"Ladies and gentlemen, there's only one true issue in this
case, and that is, who was the person who took the life of
Phoebe Ho?" Isaacs then discussed the time the body was
discovered and whether she had been dead for between 12
and 24 hours or between 12 and 48 hours, and whether she
had been kept alive for five, six, or seven days.

"Evidence will show that Warren Bland continued his
normal routine and everything he did throughout this time.
Early in the week, he learned that the police had been coming
around his employer, asking questions of people he knew,
and Warren Bland knew he was a convicted child molester,
he was a convicted sex offender, and the evidence is going
to show that Warren James Bland is not a person that you
would like, that you would want in your home.

"You'll find that he is a man who had spent most of his adult life ... in prison as a sex offender, that he had been released on parole some eleven months before, and he knew that the investigation had centered on him long before the body of Phoebe Ho was even discovered.

"The evidence you will hear will be consistant with, 'We cannot exclude Mr. Bland.' You will never hear any evidence which points definitively to Mr. Bland."

Isaacs asked jurors to look at evidence of Phoebe Ho being seventy miles away from where Bland was engaged in his normal work routine. "You will find that Warren James Bland did not abduct Phoebe Ho, he did not sexually molest her, and he did not take her life.

"The emotional content of the evidence that you're about to receive is the nightmare of every parent, of everyone who loves a child. I am asking you to objectively view the evidence through a pragmatic application of logic and not through the love of a child, but view it as a scientist would view it and render your verdict accordingly. Thank you."

"Mr. Datig, would you like to call your first witness?"

"Thank you, Your Honor. The People would call Damon Ho."

The little boy had grown to a strapping eighteen-year-old whose straight black hair framed a face with a haunting similarity to that of his younger sister. Damon told jurors where his family was living at the time she was abducted, the location of Arroyo Vista Elementary School, where he and his little sister were in school, and the last time he saw her alive as he raced off to school on his bike. He testified that his sister normally walked the five blocks to school and that she had not come home from school that day.

Datig then walked over to the counsel table and pulled Phoebe's thick, colorful jacket out of a brown paper evidence bag. Holding the jacket up so that the jury and the witness could see it, Datig asked Damon Ho if he'd ever seen that jacket before.

"Who did this jacket belong to?" Datig asked.

"My sister," Damon said, his voice tight as he swallowed a sob.

"Was that Phoebe Ho?" Datig asked.

"Yes," Damon whispered.

"Thank you, Mr. Ho. No more questions."

Isaacs declined to ask Damon questions and he was excused.

Next was Larry Scarberry, who testified about finding the body at Granite Hill Road and Pedley Avenue while collecting aluminum cans to recycle. For this witness, Datig displayed crime scene photographs showing the exact location of the body and asked Scarberry how difficult it was to see the small body lying in the steep gully unless one approached the edge of the embankment on foot and looked over, or unless one were walking along and looked from a distance at an angle. Both Datig and Isaacs questioned him closely about when he'd found the body.

Cynthia Haden testified about the hours Bland had worked at her home, including two-hour lunch breaks and short workdays. Gary and Gene Thayer talked about the hours Bland had worked and his trustworthiness as an employee. Lois Carver told jurors about the early-morning use of the van and the fact that Bland had turned to her after Gary Thayer had turned him down.

The focus of the trial shifted to the investigative stage with Lieutenant Joyce Ezzell telling jurors about the neighborhood canvass of South Pasadena, the detectives' dogged efforts to follow a confusing variety of different leads, and her eventual focus on searching for sex offenders in the area and their interview with Bland. Detective Mike Lackie picked up the trail when Phoebe's body was found and told jurors of tracking other suspects and looking at Bland's background as a likely candidate, among others, and doing a search warrant to collect hair and fibers.

Criminalist Faye Springer explained in detail how she'd culled hairs and fibers from the small child, comparing them under the microscope and finding the unusual troughing in Bland's hair, a trait she hadn't seen more than once or twice in over 20 years of examining thousands of hairs. Using the exhibit boards showing photographs of the enlarged hairs and fibers, Springer gave a thorough explanation of the similar characteristics she saw in the blue fibers, the rust brown fibers, and the paint chips. Isaacs let most of this testimony pass unchallenged, asking only whether the fibers prove a conclusive match. Springer said that it did not indicate a perfect match.

"So from looking at any of those hairs and fibers, you can't truthfully testify to this jury that Warren James Bland ever had contact with Phoebe Ho, can you?"

"No, I cannot," Springer testified.

Skip Palenik was next. A recitation of his qualifications threatened to consume the entire morning as he told jurors about the prominent cases in which he had been consulted as an expert to examine trace evidence, but jurors seemed fascinated by what he had done. As Datig guided his remarks, the mop-topped scientist, his lanky frame permanently hunched from a lifetime of peering through a microscope, enthusiastically explained his life's work to jurors. His testimony consumed nearly an entire day as Datig walked him through the complex scientific principles underlying the fiber and dye analysis and the monstrously complicated instruments he used for the comparisons, and then his results in matching similar qualities of the trace evidence. Datig's fine command of the confusing topics reflected his weeks of painstaking preparation, but jurors seemed dazed at the end of his testimony. Palenik, however, markedly narrowed the window for comparison by noting that the hairs, for example, were as close to identical as any he'd seen when looking first at the unusual troughing, then at the paint at the tips of both the hair plucked from Bland and the hair removed from Phoebe. In the paint, he told jurors, the components were exactly the same. In fiber after fiber, the dye and the fiber's reaction to different stimuli seemed the same and the cross-section of the fiber appeared to be the same.

When at last he was done, Datig held his breath for cross-examination, thinking Isaacs was reserving his sternest questioning for Palenik. It didn't happen. Isaacs had two questions for him and both of them were nontechnical. When Palenik stepped down, jurors looked over at one another with small smiles and heaved a collective sigh of relief.

Datig remained poker-faced, but he was pleased the scientific evidence would stand virtually unchallenged. He wanted the defense to win no points. He wondered if and when they planned to counterattack and whether he was adequately prepared. As each day began, either he or Isaacs would discuss odds and ends and some housekeeping matters. Sometimes Isaacs objected to testimony Datig wanted to elicit from a witness or an item on one of his exhibit boards. This is where the weeks of Datig's compulsive planning paid off. As the words would leave Isaacs' mouth, Datig would reach into his briefcase, pull out the appropriate motion, toss the paperwork on Isaac's side of the counsel table and hand a second copy to the clerk to hand to Judge Burkhart. Inevitably, the judge would read the paperwork and overrule the defense objection. Each day as they left the courtroom, Datig would ask Hudson if he saw the defense score any points. "No," Hudson would say. "No points."

Evie Kingston was next. She had since remarried and Datig purposefully focused her attention toward jurors and away from the man she'd once called her boyfriend to avoid getting her flustered. Datig was exceptionally gentle with her as he probed her relationship with Bland, the hours they spent together during the week Phoebe was missing, his anxiety as police detectives began taking a closer look at him, and his desire for her not to talk to police. Datig zeroed in on the troubles in the relationship and lingered at an apparently awkward moment in the relationship after they had become estranged when he'd chosen to seek her hand in marriage. After the proposal was turned down, Datig asked Evie to describe her boyfriend and she said he had begun to cry.

"Do you recall when Mr. Bland proposed to you and when you turned him down?" Datig asked.

"Yes, it was the first or second week in December, I think it was the second week, on a Tuesday night," Evie answered.

It was around the same time that Bland told her about a dream that he had of torturing Vietnamese women with pliers and inserting things into the women as a means of sexual assault.

On cross-examination, Isaacs probed Evie's recollection and whether she distinctly recalled the timing of the marriage proposal, his reaction to her turning him down, and the fact that she did continue to see him.

"You continued to see him because you had feelings for him, you loved him, didn't you?" Isaacs asked.

"Yes," Evie said, finally permitting herself to glance over at Bland.

After the police began closing in on Bland, he fled to San Diego, she testified, and unexpectedly showed up on the doorstep of a friend of hers.

The next witness was supposed to be Maddy Jordan, but her doctor felt that she could not withstand the rigors of testifying and cross-examination. Datig instead played the videotape of her testimony from the preliminary hearing. He also called Brett Cross and Frank Schroeder to testify about Bland's using makeup and hair dye to alter his appearance, wanting a bigger gun, and hiding from police in the bathroom.

Schroeder did not fare well on the witness stand. Exceedingly nervous and stumbling over his words, he bumbled through his testimony and had to be reminded several times what he had told Lackie and Hudson about Bland changing his name and getting the false ID with Schroeder's last name. Datig didn't mind. He wanted jurors to see how Bland had tried to manipulate a weak person.

Detective Patrick Birse testified that he was dispatched to scout out the location, instantly spotted his prey, and shot Bland when he ran. Detective Patrick McManus said Bland said he "didn't do" the other girl when the news reports of Wendy Osborn were broadcast on TV while he was recuperating from the hospital. Isaacs questioned McManus carefully about the medications Bland was taking and suggested he had been drifting in and out of consciousness after suffering a life-threatening wound. In fact, Isaacs asked, did McManus know that Bland had "died" on the operating table in the first few hours after the near-fatal wound? McManus said that he did not know, but he believed Bland had been near death.

During breaks in the trial, Datig would let Isaacs know the next few witnesses he had coming up and whether there were any scheduling problems. Datig had vacillated about calling Norman Felts, to whom Bland purportedly confessed that he intended to leave no witnesses if he reoffended, which Datig hoped jurors would interpret to mean that he fully planned to kill his next child molestation victim. But Felts's own background as a child sex offender, Datig thought, would soil his own case, and he chose not to call him. He felt he had enough evidence without him.

Datig did, however, call Steve Boucher, the inmate to whom Bland had said, "What I did to the kid was no different than what we did in Chu Lai in 1968 to the women and children when we burned their huts."

A pig farmer with a distinguished military career and a bad drinking problem, Boucher had served out his term for vehicular manslaughter, his sole criminal conviction. Like any prosecutor, Datig was loath to use any "snitch," as they are referred to in the criminal justice system, because inmates typically claim someone confessed to them and will testify to such a statement hoping to get leniency for their own cases.

But Boucher didn't ask for a deal in regard to his sentence; he had by this time served out his time and was back on the farm with his pigs. Datig believed jurors would not be as offended by a vehicular manslaughter charge as they would by a long history of violent offenses, such as Felts's record.

As his first witness the following morning, Datig called Paul Corday. The scared little boy Bland had molested in 1980 entered the courtroom as a twenty-three-year-old Navy seaman in his starched, pressed, and knife-pleated dark blue uniform, his black shoes polished to a brilliant shine and his bright white cap in his hand. Corday paused at the back of the courtroom and the room drew silent as Corday stood as if at attention, his eyes boring holes into Bland, who turned slowly to look at him. Corday then strode purposefully to the front of the courtroom, raised his hand, and faced the court clerk to be sworn in.

CHAPTER SIXTEEN

Corday laid his white seaman's cap on the counter in front of the witness chair, adjusted the microphone, and sat down a cocky sailor, no longer the frightened young boy in the photograph whom Bland had tortured and molested. Datig, milking the drama from the moment, asked Corday to tell the jury what he did for a living.

"I'm a private first class in the United States Navy, sir," Corday said, emphasizing the last word.

"And where was your last tour of duty?" Datig asked.

"I was in the Persian Gulf for Operation Desert Shield, sir."

Datig let that answer hang in the air as he languidly rifled through some papers at the podium while Corday sat ramrod straight in the witness chair. In matter-of-fact fashion, Datig asked him to explain the events of December 30, 1981, when he was 11 years old, when a man calling himself a tugboat captain in a green-and-white van picked him up and sexually molested him. Corday told the story with military precision, pausing only to sip water from a cup when his voice quavered slightly. He explained how Bland had clamped the vise grips on his nipples and twisted; poked his face with wire; and sexually assaulted him. Corday said he concentrated on committing to memory every last detail of the van interior and the face of his captor.

"Did you ever cry out in pain?" Datig asked.

"No, sir," Corday answered. "I studied the inside of the van pretty intently. There wasn't anything else my body could tolerate, so my body was shutting down, but mentally, I was awake and paying attention."

As he had with Evie, Datig stood to the far side of the courtroom away from Bland, keeping the witness's attention toward him. As he testified about the torture, Corday's twenty-year-old wife bit her lip and his parents sat in their courtroom seats with their arms around one another.

At the end of his testimony, Datig asked whether Corday, despite a dozen years' time, could identify the man who'd kidnapped, tortured, and sexually assaulted him.

Corday lifted his arm and pointed his finger like a solemn salute toward the ashen-faced defendant.

"That's him right there," the sailor said, staring at Bland while Bland stared back. As Datig again consulted his notes at the podium, Corday glared at Bland with his arm extended as Bland's face returned a cold look. Jurors, feeling the tension between the two men, glanced at Corday, then back at Bland, then at Corday again, as if watching a tennis match. The judge cleared his throat, hoping to get Datig's attention, and the bailiffs stationed around the courtroom shifted, poised for an incident, and kept their eyes on the witness and the defendant. After a long moment, Datig looked up impassively.

"Thank you, Your Honor. No more questions."

Isaacs declined to question Corday. Jurors could not take

their eyes off the man in the military uniform as he rose from the witness chair, picked up his bright white seaman's cap, gave Bland another simmering look, and walked out of the courtroom with his wife on his arm and his parents following behind.

Judge Burkhart called for the mid-morning break and it seemed as if everyone needed to breathe a sigh of relief.

After the break, a pregnant Vanessa Rogers took the witness stand. Tearful and distraught, but able to recall the most disturbing details, the young woman told her story of startling similarity to the abduction and attack of Paul Corday. In contrast to his crisp, precise testimony, Rogers testified as if she had a stinging lump in her throat from being forced to dredge up the night of horror she'd suffered at the hands of the defendant. Rogers testified with one hand clutching a pink tissue and the other rubbing her protruding belly. Isaacs also had no questions for her.

Datig rested his case at the beginning of February, about a month after jurors had been chosen. It was the defense's turn to present evidence, if they chose to do so.

"The defense calls Warren James Bland," Isaacs said, his normally soft voice rising slightly.

On February 9, 1993, Warren James Bland took the oath and climbed into the witness box wearing gold aviator-frame glasses, a dark blue suit, a starched white shirt, and a subtle paisley tie, his hair and moustache neatly trimmed. Extra bailiffs were called in to guard the two exits near the judge's chambers, the jury box, and the door to the public hallway outside the courtroom.

"Mr. Bland, do your friends call you Jim?" Isaacs asked by way of introduction.

"Yes," Bland answered.

"I'll be asking a lot of questions, Mr. Bland. We have a

long way to go. There's a pitcher of water there and a glass,'' Isaacs said.

"Thank you," Bland said, looking small and vulnerable in the witness chair.

"Now, you've heard some pretty terrible things said about you. You heard Mr. Corday and Ms. Rogers testify, is that right?" Isaacs said.

"I was guilty of those things so I pleaded guilty," Bland said.

Isaacs took Bland briefly through his criminal history, starting with his desertion from the Marines and his car theft conviction in 1957. Bland summarized each series of rapes by saying, "I committed a rape."

Bland's quiet, calm voice and meek manner seemed at odds with his history of thirteen violent felony convictions. Some jurors had to lean forward to hear him. Many of them scribbled in their notebooks.

"Would it be fair to say you've spent a substantial portion of your life in prison?" Isaacs asked.

"Thirty of the past thirty-three years," Bland said.

Isaacs delved into Bland's three marriages and the relationships he'd had with Maddy Jordan and Celia Blake. Bland explained that when he said, "Grandma, I've done something awful," he was referring to the fact that he had broken his parole, which meant an automatic year in prison.

Bland admitted dying his hair and leaving Blake's bathroom a mess but said he had asked her if he could borrow her car and gun.

"Why did you want her gun?" Isaacs asked.

"At the time, I felt I was cornered, I would put the gun in my mouth and pull the trigger," Bland said, looking down as his voice broke. Jurors seemed attentive, but Datig was leaning back in his chair, examing his nails as if he were bored. Hudson sat next to him, his expression blank.

When asked why he didn't pull the trigger when confronted by Birse, Bland said, "I didn't have the gun with me, sir.

"I made up my mind that rather than go back to prison for something I hadn't done, I would prefer death," Bland said.

"So you ran?" Isaacs asked.

"Yes," Bland said.

Bland admitted dyeing his hair and using makeup to build a new identify for himself "to be the person I wanted to be. Warren James Bland would just drop off the face of the earth."

Bland denied making the comments to Louis Boucher but admitted lying to McDonald's employees about his experience in Vietnam.

He also admitted dreaming about torturing Vietnamese women with pliers, saying that he had read everything ever written about the incident in which American troops had mounted a mutilation-massacre of a Vietnamese village.

Bland described his relationship with Evie as "a little rocky," but claimed he was honest with her about his criminal history.

From there, Isaacs walked Bland through his work schedule and his duties at the Hadens' as well as other clients for whom he painted and did minor repair work.

Isaacs asked Bland where he was and what he did on December 11, 1986.

In low tones, Bland said his friend Tyler Lowell had asked to meet him at a parking lot near the Thayers' home in Alhambra that night. When Bland showed up, Lowell invited him to get into the passenger seat of Lowell's white Honda Civic. Lowell's Asian girlfriend, Mary, was in the back seat, Bland said.

"I was told to look in the back seat," Bland testified.

"(Lowell) said, 'Surprise, surprise,'" Bland testified. "Mary was smiling and she pulled a white quilt back and I saw a little girl lying on the floor, a little Oriental girl. She was very small."

"I'm going to ask the jury to step back into the jury room," Judge Burkhart said, then waited until the jurors filed out.

"Mr. Isaacs . . ." Burkhart began.

"Your Honor, I know what you're going to say, and I want you to know that I've discussed this with my client," Isaacs said.

Burkhart looked hard at Isaacs. "This may very well be your defense, but I want to make certain that you understand the direction in which you are leading him. I just wanted to be sure."

"Thank you, Your Honor," Isaacs said.

When jurors were called back in, Bland described in somber tones how the young Asian girl was blindfolded, gagged, and bound with her hands tied in front of her.

"I got rather mad with him and asked what the heck he thought he was doing," Bland testified.

Lowell was apparently running out of gas, but the closest gas station was too brightly lit. Bland directed Lowell to drive to Gary Thayer's house in San Marino, unloaded the girl into Thayer's van with Mary to watch her as the two filled the gas tank, then Mary got back into the car and stowed the child in the back seat again. Bland said he agreed to meet Lowell at a converted barn next to a ranch house in a remote section of Riverside, purportedly to solidify plans to steal a large motor home from a dealer's lot in that area.

Bland testified that he showed up at the barn, went upstairs, and saw the young Asian girl sitting on a bed between Lowell and Mary, but Bland claimed he sat on a chair.

"What happened next, Mr. Bland?" Isaacs asked.

"How graphic do you want me to get, Mr. Isaacs?" Bland asked.

"Just try to answer the question," his lawyer said.

Bland said the adults began to fondle the small child, whom Bland began to refer to as Phoebe, while Bland claimed he just sat there in the chair, watching.

As Bland described Lowell and his girlfriend molesting Phoebe, he again stopped. "Do I have to continue?" he asked. Datig, who was leaning back in his chair, leaned forward and said something to Hudson and they both shook their heads.

Bland claimed he stayed in the chair and had sex with Mary there, then put his clothes on, ran a comb through his hair, and left. The little girl's clothes happened to be at the base of the chair in which he was sitting.

"Did you touch that little girl?" Isaacs asked with a hard edge to his voice.

"No part of my hand or my body ever touched that little girl," Bland testified.

"Mr. Bland, did you abduct Phoebe Ho?" Isaacs asked.

"No, sir, I did not," he replied.

"Did you kill Phoebe Ho?"

"No, sir, I did not."

"Mr. Bland, you admitted that lying is a way of life for you. Do you expect us to believe you now?"

"Well, I've done a lot of bad things and I've pleaded guilty to those, but I did not kill that little girl."

"No more questions."

It was Datig's turn. Most prosecutors relish the moment when they can put the screws to a reviled defendant and make him squirm in front of the jury. Datig's plan was to outpower this power rapist, outcon the skilled con, and manipulate the master manipulator. Datig planned to detonate Bland's attempt to con jurors into thinking he was too modest or old-fashioned to get into graphic detail on direct testimony and get jurors to laugh at Bland's ridiculous story about his ex-con buddy's capture of Phoebe as a "present" he'd refused.

Datig stood up and approached the podium. In a voice that went from easygoing to sarcastic, the prosecutor started to rub Bland's nose in the lapses of reason in his testimony.

"When you saw Mr. Lowell with the child in the car at seven p.m. that night, had he run out of gas because he'd been driving around Alhambra for eleven hours with that child in his back seat?"

"No," Bland said.

"You mentioned that you worked within a block or two of Arroyo Vista School. Had you told Mr. Lowell this was a good hunting ground from which to kidnap children?"

"No," Bland said.

"You testified that you pleaded guilty to many of these offenses. Isn't it true, Mr. Bland, that you plea-bargained for reduced sentences?"

"Yes," Bland said.

"You mentioned that you dyed your hair at Celia Blake's house. Wasn't it raining that day?"

"Yes, it was raining pretty hard. I took a towel and kept it wrapped around my head because the dye was running into my eyes," Bland answered.

"You were walking around Long Beach with a towel on your head?" Datig asked.

"Yes."

"You didn't want to draw attention to yourself, did you? Now, you said you already had Celia Blake's gun and you were planning to buy another, larger gun, isn't that right?" Datig asked.

"Yes, I was planning to commit suicide," Bland said solemnly.

"What were you planning to do, stick a gun in each ear?" Datig asked.

Jurors were trying to conceal their smiles.

"You would rather commit suicide than tell the police about Tyler Lowell?" Datig asked incredulously.

"He's a dangerous man," Bland testified.

"You would rather abscond on parole, risk a year in jail, and go to trial on a capital murder charge than tell the police about Tyler Lowell?"

"Yes," he said.

"You almost cried when you said you'd done a terrible thing. Are you telling this jury that you almost cried at the prospect of going back to jail?"

"I was almost killed the last time," Bland testified.

Bland also insisted that there was no discussion with Lowell about what to do with the girl and no talk between them about killing her, and he even claimed he didn't know there was going to be any sexual activity with the child.

"Are you telling this jury you drove seventy miles in the middle of the night not knowing there would be any sexual frolic with that young girl?" Datig asked.

"I assumed as much, but nothing was said," Bland admitted.

"You said that you'd dreamed of soldiers pinching the nipples of Vietnamese women and shoving things up their (genital area)," Datig said. "Did you adopt that as your personal method of child molestation?"

Finally, Isaacs, who had refrained from objecting to Datig's biting cross-examination, rose to his feet and meekly objected, but Burkhart overruled him.

"Yes," Bland testified.

"You mentioned that you suggested that this man Lowell

and his girlfriend, with a kidnapped child in the back seat, drive with an empty gas tank all the way to your employer's house to stow this kidnapped kid in your employer's van while you two got gas, is that correct?

"But you didn't want to pull into the gas station because the lights were too bright?"

"Well, none of Mr. Thayer's vehicles were there," Bland testified.

"Mr. Bland, what was the child doing while Mr. Lowell and Mary were fondling her? Did she scream or cry or ask for her mother?" Datig asked.

"She did not struggle," Bland said. "I saw no fear at all in that girl's face. She maintained a very stoic expression on her face."

Datig paused to allow the full impact of that answer to sink in. The jurors, who had seemed amused at Datig's unyielding cross-examination, stared at Bland.

Datig forced Bland to describe in prolonged, uncomfortable detail the sexual acts he'd performed on Corday and Rogers and explain the terror and fear he'd seen in their eyes as he inflicted the torture. Under oath, Bland was compelled by Datig to admit he'd become sexually excited by placing clothespins, pliers, vise grips, and a medical clamping device to pinch the nipples, tongues, and other body parts of the children he'd molested. Datig probed Bland's motivation in cruising around looking for children to sexually molest.

"Did this urge come over you after you laid eyes on Paul Corday and you thought to yourself, 'Gee, I think I'll kidnap and molest this kid?' " Datig asked.

"Yes," Bland testified. "I asked him what he was doing out so late at night and where he was headed."

"You expressed concern for his safety? You thought to

yourself a young boy shouldn't be out this late because . . . what type of danger were you afraid might befall this child?''

Bland hesitated, realizing he'd walked into another trap, and answered lamely that it was cold that night and Corday wasn't wearing a sweater. As Bland fumbled with his answer, Datig turned away to give a sly grin to a group of fellow prosecutors and deputy public defenders who were seated in the courtroom gallery observing his cross-examination.

Datig finally took Bland on an arduous explanation of the sexual acts he claimed Lowell and his girlfriend had engaged in, the acts he'd seen them perform on Phoebe, and Bland's reaction.

"You just sat there?" Datig asked.

"Yes," Bland replied.

"Did that ignite your urges to molest children?" Datig asked. "Wasn't this little girl offered to you?"

"Yes," Bland said.

"But you never touched this girl, is that right?"

"That's right," Bland replied.

Datig locked his gaze on Bland for his rapid-fire finish.

"It was you who kidnapped Vanessa Rogers and Paul Corday as they walked down the street, wasn't it, Mr. Bland?"

"Yes," Bland answered.

"But it wasn't you who kidnapped Phoebe Ho as she was walking down the street, was it, Mr. Bland?"

"No."

"It was you who made Vanessa Rogers and Paul Corday get undressed, wasn't it?"

"Yes."

"But it wasn't you who made Phoebe Ho get undressed, was it?"

"No."

"It was you who attached clothespins, pliers, and clamps to the nipples, tongues, and genital areas of Vanessa Rogers and Paul Corday, wasn't it, Mr. Bland?"

"Yes."

"But it wasn't you who attached clothespins, pliers, and clamps to Phoebe Ho's nipples, tongue, and genital area, was it?"

"No."

"It was you who forced Vanessa Rogers and Paul Corday to (commit a variety of sexual acts), wasn't it, Mr. Bland?"

"Yes."

"But it wasn't you who forced Phoebe Ho to (commit a variety of sexual acts), was it?"

"No."

"And it wasn't you who put a cable tie around her neck and ratcheted it down and strangled her until she was dead, was it?"

"No."

"You never laid a hand on Phoebe Ho, did you?"

"Yes, that's true."

"No more questions."

On brief redirect examination, Isaacs ignored the hours of testimony about Bland's prior sexual acts and zeroed in on Bland's fear of Lowell and his concern of returning to prison with a reputation as a "snitch."

Finally, Bland stepped off the witness stand. Isaacs patted him on the shoulder and spoke encouraging words. When jurors filed out of the courtroom, a bailiff approached, applied the handcuffs to Bland, linked them to the waist chain and the leg chains, and led him out of the courtroom, still wearing his blue suit.

"No points?" Datig asked Hudson as they walked out of the courtroom.

Hudson grinned and shook his head.

"No points."

For his closing argument, Datig pinned up the autopsy photographs of Phoebe Ho and the police photos of Vanessa Rogers and Paul Corday. In theatrical, thundering tones, Datig hammered home his theme that Bland's behavior constituted a "pattern of evil," bolstered by the hair, fiber, and paint evidence, his stress over failing in his relationship and being denied sexual contact with his girlfriend, the missing hours from work, and his admission that he "didn't do that one" when recuperating in the hospital.

Datig ridiculed Bland's story that a prison buddy he claimed to fear kidnapped a child as a gift, but then Bland turned up his nose at the child and declined to indulge his base urges. Having sex with the girlfriend of his ex-con buddy was just as ludicrous, particularly if Bland truly feared the man so much that he preferred suicide over revealing to police Lowell's purported kidnapping and molestation of Phoebe.

Datig said the suggestion that a few minutes in Thayer's van could not possibly account for the volume of fibers and literally thousands of paint chips found on Phoebe's clothing.

"Mr. Bland tried to explain away the semen, tried to explain away the fibers, but he never could explain why Phoebe's body and her clothing were covered with paint chips carrying fibers from those tarps Bland had been using as dropcloths," Datig argued.

But the defendant did offer an explanation as to one type of trace evidence, the prosecutor argued.

"What did Mr. Bland do after he had sex in a chair with his friend's girlfriend?" Datig asked, reaching into his suit coat breast pocket. Datig pulled out a small black comb and ran it through his hair.

"Why, Mr. Bland combed his hair, of course. You're supposed to believe that at least one of his hairs drifted over and landed smack dab on Phoebe's sock."

Datig probed the depths of Bland's sickness, his unholy use of sexual assault as a means of torture, his exploitation of youthful, vulnerable prey, and the physical and emotional carnage he'd wreaked. A true creature of habit, Bland repeated his pattern of evil on Vanessa Rogers, on Paul Corday, and finally on Phoebe Ho, Datig said, holding up the autopsy photo of Phoebe's delicate genital area, which had been literally ripped, partially healed, ripped, partially healed, and ripped again and again.

"Mr. Bland tore a hole in this young girl," Datig said, placing the photo uncomfortably close to jurors' faces. "Mr. Bland did this . . . to Phoebe Ho.

"Ladies and gentlemen, I ask you to find Mr. Bland guilty of murder in the first degree with special circumstances that the murder was committed during the course of rape, sodomy, lewd act with a child, and torture. Thank you."

Isaacs, in his characteristic low-key fashion, asked jurors to look deeper at the evidence for the holes in the prosecution's case. Bland could account for his time during the day. Where on earth could a child like that have been kept? Even if Bland was a half-hour late to work, that didn't give him time to drive seventy miles away to some secret hiding place and arrive at work by 8:30 or 9 a.m.

The reality was that there was no witness to Phoebe's abduction and there was no eyewitness to her murder. No one saw her being dumped, Isaacs argued. While the prosecution might find Bland's story nonsensical, only someone like Bland who has spent most of his life in prison could truly know the hard knocks behind bars and the revenge exacted from snitches.

The law doesn't require that it's possible that a defendant committed murder. The law doesn't say that if someone is a hideous child molester, it's probably certain that he also killed. The law requires a standard beyond a reasonable doubt, Isaacs argued.

He acknowledged that Bland had a lifetime of bad acts and said he had paid for that criminal behavior. It didn't make him a murderer.

Jurors took 4 days to discuss the evidence, then unanimously convicted Bland on their first ballot. On February 24, 1993, Bland was found guilty of all charges, including each of the special circumstance allegations triggering the penalty phase of the trial, where jurors would hear evidence and then decide if Bland should be sent to the gas chamber.

Many of the women were successful in business, real estate, motherhood, teaching, or medicine. Years ago, they were Bland's victims. In succession, the women who'd conquered a variety of hurdles to succeed in life visibly shrank as they once again confronted the man who had forcibly raped them.

During the penalty phase of Bland's trial, Bland's ex-wives came face-to-face with the man they had married and who had assaulted them, and from whom they had hidden in fear for years. Three of the women Bland attacked once again identified their assailant, this time to a jury who would decide whether Bland should live or die. The last time many of them had seen Bland, they were young women and Bland was at the beginning of his prolonged criminal career. Sue-Ellen Sweeney had not seen or spoken to Bland since 1955. She was the first of the ex-wives who appeared panicked at

spotting Bland in the defendant's chair, as if the fear was
still fresh after nearly 40 years. Sweeney, like the other
wives, had never before testified or told her story to police,
other than telling Hudson. Under Datig's kind questioning,
she turned toward jurors and told how her first husband had
brutally assaulted her on her wedding night when she was
16 years old.

"I was nervous and I was taking a long time getting ready
in the bathroom," she said, openly weeping. "Jim broke
down the door and pulled me out by my arm. He raped
me."

Sweeney explained how she'd endured the chemical sting
of the chlorinated pool to avoid being near her newlywed
husband, then had insisted she be treated by a doctor on the
following Monday. She told jurors how she'd left him after
waking up to find she had been tied spread-eagled to the
bed and he was "talking crazy" and running a knife blade
over her body.

Bland's second wife, Dorothy Cobb, told how Bland had
raped her after she had returned his ring, married him and
borne his child out of a sense of obligation and witnessed
him slit open a man's stomach at a gas station. She testified
that the cruelty to her infant child was the impetus for her
to leave him.

Norma Bland did not testify because she did not personally
witness the attempted molestation of her daughters and had
divorced Bland while he was in prison.

One after another, the women Bland had raped got on the
witness stand and pointed to him as their attacker. The court
clerk kept the box of tissues on the witness box and made
sure there was a fresh cup of water for each witness as she
recounted nights of horror.

Steve Harmon, handling the penalty phase, declined to
ask any of the women any questions.

Finally, Datig called Sharon Ho to the witness stand. As the mother of the victim, Datig sought once again to breathe life into the little girl whose life had been sacrificed for the sickness of a child molester. Phoebe liked dancing her way to school and loved buying cupcakes at her school on cupcake day, her mother testified somberly through a Chinese interpreter.

Sharon burst into tears as Datig showed her the enlarged photo exhibit showing Phoebe at her seventh birthday party, weeks before her disappearance.

"Is this your daughter?" Datig asked.

"Yes," Sharon answered, her answered muffled by tears. Datig walked back to the counsel table to allow Sharon to regain her composure and laid the photo facedown on the table.

Under Datig's questioning, Sharon described how Phoebe wanted to walk to school by herself and that she had called her back to "give Mommy a kiss." It was the last time she'd seen her daughter alive.

As Sharon left the witness stand, she walked past the counsel table and grabbed the photo of her dead daughter, clutched it to her chest, and swayed side to side with her arms wrapped around the photo. *"Phoebe! Oh, Phoebe!"* Sharon wailed, her voice filling the hushed courtroom.

Datig, the court interpreter, and one of the bailiffs gently guided her out of the courtroom and she briefly resisted as they pried the photograph, a court exhibit, from her arms.

Tears filled George Hudson's eyes and he saw most members of the jury fighting back sobs.

Isaacs objected, accusing the prosecution of staging the emotional moment and pointing out the "crocodile tears" of the DA investigator. The objection was overruled.

Harmon knew he was fighting an uphill battle to spare his client's life. His approach was to not challenge the prosecution's assertion that Bland had forfeited his right to live among the rest of society. He wanted to show jurors how well he had functioned behind bars by pointing up his stellar record as an inmate.

Harmon called corrections officials to give an overview of Bland's record, his dearth of disciplinary action, and his eagerness to work and be productive. He got along well with other inmates and all the guards and corrections officials. He was good at setting up conference tables and running the projector. He received a certificate to become a wastewater engineer. He was a model employee and a perfect clerk-typist.

On cross-examination, Datig pointed out that Bland's perfect record and work history was self-serving because it hastened the time Bland would be out on the streets.

A Riverside County sheriff's sergeant testified next that Bland had demonstrated his value by single-handedly fixing the jail's communications and paging system because no one else knew how it worked.

Datig ripped into the sergeant during his turn to question him.

"Can you tell this jury why a maximum-security inmate knows more about the jail communication system than the sheriff's department?" Datig asked.

The sergeant paused, then answered, "Now, I guess that's a problem, but I didn't think that at the time."

Datig also brought up the discovery of nail clippers hidden in Bland's shaving kit while in the Riverside County Jail awaiting trial for the Phoebe Ho murder and the razor and 686 feet of sheeting strips Bland had hidden in his cell while awaiting his federal trial in San Diego.

For the death penalty arguments, Judge Burkhart allowed both sides to argue twice, with the prosecution going first, followed by the defense, followed by the prosecution again, with the defense having the last word.

The linebacker-sized prosecutor, wearing a dark suit and a solemn expression, implored jurors to fulfill their duties and uphold their oath to impose the death penalty where appropriate.

"Ladies and gentlemen, the evidence has shown you that the death penalty is the only correct and appropriate verdict in this case.

"Now, there are those, I suppose, who would stand by and watch an innocent child viciously murdered because they don't want to impose themselves into this battle between good and evil," Datig argued, quoting World War II hero General Douglas MacArthur, who said the true soldier hates war but must do his duty.

Datig asked jurors to review the extreme suffering Bland had inflicted on Phoebe Ho and his other numerous victims with an eye toward deciding whether he deserved society's ultimate punishment.

"I ask you to consider the terror and suffering of a seven-year-old girl held captive, no food, no tenderness, no love. The only thing she had to look forward to was agony, pain, humiliation, and ultimately, death.

"Consider that, ladies and gentlemen—this is how the defendant, according to him, gets his jollies," Datig said, arguing that the hideous brutality occurred not in one momentary lapse of reason, not in one day, but was repeated day after day during an entire week. "This is upsetting, this is disgusting, but yet this is what he did to her."

To spare his life because he typed well or knew how to run a projector was to suggest society's values were horribly warped. Datig reviewed the past 37 years of Bland's criminal activity, starting with raping his wife on their wedding night, raping his second wife after she wanted to return the engagement ring, and inflicting the blow on his infant child. The evil that began with raping his newlywed wife never faded, Datig argued, not with his first conviction in 1958 for stabbing Ray Blair at the gas station and the rape he committed 8 months later. The evil continued as he conned the Atascadero hospital staff, and the evil continued in the rapes of Cheryl Lynn Morgan and the assault on Ann St. John.

"Had the evil gone away? No. It's the same evil that gut-slashed Ray Blair. It's the same evil that raped and kidnapped each of these victims. It's there. It doesn't go away, ladies and gentlemen."

After Bland indelibly imprinted his pattern of evil in a succession of violent sex crimes against women and children, the suggestion that the impact of a child torture-murder is somehow mitigated by a man's ability to set up a conference room or run a projector, Datig argued, was "incredibly callous."

Doing one's duty in battling good and evil means being "prepared to speak out and say that a murderer like this does not deserve to live. The death penalty is appropriate, and if there is a case that cries out for justice, this is that case."

When Datig sat down, Isaacs pulled the podium to the side and stood in front of the jury box.

"I stand before you to plead for Jim Bland's life. I've never been more acutely aware of my own inadequacies before in my life. How can I tell you, how can I communicate what's in my heart, what we have felt, what is right and what we want, what we need?"

Isaacs, in a brief and extremely personal statement, reassured jurors that their conviction of his client guaranteed that he would die in prison, but that the law permitted them to take his life for revenge "and you have to answer to no one except your own self and God.

"But you do not have to choose to kill Jim Bland. I'm asking you to spare his life because life has value, because all life is precious. The life of Phoebe Ho [was] precious. We should affirm life. There's been too much death and too much destruction all over the world, and we see the famines and the hate and evil, and sometimes there has to be an end to it. We have to say no to death," Isaacs argued.

He quoted the work of John Donne, "For whom the bell tolls," and implored jurors to take a stand against violence and killing and declare that they would not seek blood revenge, "even for this wretch.

"I am asking you to say yes to life, say yes out of the mercy of your hearts, the goodness of your hearts, the goodness of you. Let revenge be God's, not ours."

After a ten-minute recess, Datig returned to the podium and asked jurors to consider the choices Bland made in his life to become a rapist, a brutalizer of children, and a murderer. While it is unfortunate that jurors have had to delve into hate and cruelty and evil by virtue of serving on a jury, it did not make the jurors themselves evil. Putting an end to the cruelty and evil and preserving the values society has deemed precious means upholding the law, he argued, which does not put duty-bound jurors in the same shoes as "revenge killers."

Datig again returned to the last precious moments when Phoebe Ho was "naked, cold, hungry, cut, ripped, and tortured" at the hands of Bland—"evil incarnate. It doesn't get any worse than this.

"Common sense tells us what the appropriate punishment for this kind of evil must be. It's not a return to his cushy job as a typist in the captain's office, it is punishment, it is an affirmation of our values and our conscience. It is in this case the death penalty," Datig argued.

"Do we give him a freebie for this? Does her life come for free?

"Steve Harmon has the last word before you today, but ladies and gentlemen, Mr. Harmon doesn't really have the last word. Remember, he speaks for the defendant, and Warren James Bland wants you to fall for the ultimate con this time, to give him no more punishment than what he had received as a life sentence in federal court.

"Ladies and gentlemen, the last word in this courtroom belongs to Phoebe Ho. Thank you."

A somber Steve Harmon, the last lawyer jurors would hear before discussing the case among themselves, confessed to jurors that "this is one of those moments in life when it's almost impossible to know what to say.

"I will tell you now as directly and as bluntly as I can that you should spare the life of Jim Bland for two reasons— because there is still some value to that life, and there is no need, no reason, to kill him."

He compared Bland to a real-life Dr. Jekyll and Mr. Hyde character and urged jurors to look beyond Bland's savagry and see that he could live problem-free in prison.

"Do you kill Dr. Jekyll because of what Mr. Hyde has done, or do you put them both someplace where Dr. Jekyll can be of value and Mr. Hyde cannot ever be seen nor heard of again?

"The Mr. Hyde in Jim Bland is now dead. Detective Birse shot and killed him in that parking lot in San Diego. Detective Birse killed the Jim Bland who is that monster. Jim Bland will never, never, never be free again. He is caged now forever. The question, then, is do we need to stick a gun into the cage and shoot him dead?

"If Mr. Hyde is dead, do we need to kill Dr. Jekyll?"

Harmon then pondered the question of for whom the death penalty is best suited, such as the Hannibal Lecter character in the movie *Silence of the Lambs*, who cannot be trusted even behind bars.

"If you kill Mr. Bland, what you are saying is he has no redeeming value anywhere, and that's just not so. His prison record is not a sham. It's not a trick because he has lived that life for all of those years, and proved he can do it," Harmon said. "As a prisoner, he is good and has value and is worth something. Isn't that at least worth considering?"

Harmon next tackled the issue Datig raised of simply sending Bland "home."

"Well, you are not sending Mr. Bland home, you are sending him where he belongs. He never should have been released.

"Mr. Bland will die in prison. The only question is, will he die in prison at the hands of the executioner, or will he die in prison of other causes? You are not sending him home, you are sending him to die.

"Ladies and gentlemen, this is not an exercise. It's not like it used to be. People are executed. A vote for death means that you will put Jim Bland into that room; his life will end; he will breathe no more. God's work will have been done by you.

"God made Jim Bland; God, therefore, must have a plan for him. I have no idea what that is, but the point is, neither do you. So be careful and be sure. Don't do this if it's not necessary.

"Thank you."

In 45 minutes—about one-third the time it took for the lawyers to argue—jurors unanimously voted on their first ballot to send Bland to the gas chamber.

At his sentencing, Bland, as he had at his federal trial, read a long, rambling statement in which he profusely praised his lawyers as "humanitarian" and "compassionate," and then begged for the judge's indulgence while he "clarified" a few points, promising not to "retry the case."

With one hand handcuffed to his chair and the chain links around his hips and ankles, and deputies stationed around the courtroom, Bland read the twenty-three-page statement he'd written in pencil from his cell, sometimes stumbling over his own words.

"I am just a simple man," Bland declared in a flat, thin voice, appearing to have recycled most of his arguments from the federal trial.

He complained that jurors were not allowed to hear about Tyler Lowell's violent criminal record and decried the fact that he'd "bared his soul" in his testimony only to be beaten down by Datig on cross-examination.

"Your Honor, I have no reason to lie," he said.

Bland condemned Datig as a corrupt "master manipulater" whose "flagrant flagitiousness (depravity)," and "foulest, misbegotten flatulence" and "libelous drivel" had turned law-abiding jurors, news reporters, and even the judge into his innocent dupes.

"In the view of the public at large, it is painfully obvious that I have been cast in the worst possible light. In fact, portrayed as some kind of a three-headed demon—the personification of evil!"

Bland's remarks took a bizarre turn when he opined that Datig didn't really know "how vile evil is" or the "baseness of corruption," then declared that Bland did know and it was "much worse that anything Mr. Datig has ever imagined!" The defendant then said he doubted whether Datig was brave enough to call out "Glasyalabolas," which Bland claimed was Satan's personal name.

Bland claimed that the "evil" had died on the operating table, leaving the new and improved "productive and industrious Warren James Bland."

In a final slap at his ex-wives, Bland criticized their "narrow and pinpointed" version of the past.

"I know that there were some good memories there, but they seem to have forgotten them."

Taking another swipe at Datig, Bland crafted a disturbing metaphor using his training as a water treatment engineer by comparing Datig's arguments to foul sewage: "I am astounded by Mr. Datig's infatuation with his own pretentiousness and self-importance, when *anyone* with a smidgen of intelligence can see that his flatulent pomposity is of the rectal persuasion!"

As Bland read his notes with his head down, Datig turned to Hudson with a barely concealed grin. Judge Burkhart interrupted Bland several times for two reasons—first, to ask him how much more he had to read, and second, to remind him that his remarks weren't helping him make a decision whether or not to sentence him to death.

Bland then tried to read faster and tripped on his words somewhat. He disputed the contention that he was on his best behavior behind bars to gain early release and gave a discourse on sentencing laws, ending with an astonishing expression of dismay of the state prison system releasing dangerous criminals to prey on society.

Bland again lashed out at Datig for "emotionally raping" Sharon Ho and triggering her distress by leaving Phoebe's picture on the counsel table. He professed "deep sorrow and sympathy" for the Ho family and denied killing Phoebe but claimed he was "guilty" of not preventing her death. He did not elaborate.

Quoting from the Bible, Bland embarked on a lengthy discourse on the mistakes he had made in life and said that he fully expected that the death penalty would be the expected punishment for someone who caused so much "horror heartache, pain, and grief.

"As I reflect on myself, I know that I have no redeeming qualities. I have nothing left to offer. And rather than be a further burden or threat to all concerned, I would ask that you put an end to this menace! To take no further chances, for even in a prison setting, I would probably pose some kind of threat.

"I am confident that you will concur that the time has finally come to close the final chapter on Warren James Bland by handing down the requested and expected sentence that now lays within Your Honor's mind, heart, and hands."

Bland, like an actor prolonging his dramatic death scene by refusing to die, continued to read and Burkhart again interrupted, like a stage manager hooking him by the neck with a cane to pull him off the stage.

"Mr. Bland . . . ? Do you have much more? This is not helping me make a decision."

Bland said he didn't have much to go.

His last remark was to perform a dramatic reading from William Shakespeare: "Ah, Death, where is thy sting? O Grave, your Victory?

"I now stand ready for sentencing and I bid each of you, fare-thee-well," Bland said with a flourish and a rattle of his chains as he rose to his feet.

Burkhart directed Isaacs and Harmon to tell their client to sit down, and with businesslike efficiency, sentenced him to the death penalty.

The defendant shook hands with his lawyers, was handcuffed to his waist chain, and was led out of the courtroom by bailiffs.

In his final interview with a probation officer, Bland insisted that he be administered a lethal injection because he had heard death in the gas chamber would be too painful.

EPILOGUE

As a result of Bland's circuit through California's revolving-door criminal justice system, the legislature passed a law in which the state Department of Justice alerts local law enforcement when a repeat sex offender is released to their area. The law was passed as direct result of Warren James Bland's connection with the Phoebe Ho murder.

Two men were arrested and prosecuted for kidnapping, rape, and assault on Kenneth and Sharon Ho. The other two attackers remain at large.

In 1995, after sophisticated DNA tests, another sex offender was arrested and prosecuted for the murder of Wendy Osborn.

The Hos still own and operate a shoestore in South Pasadena.

Warren James Bland remains confined to San Quentin State Prison, awaiting a date for his execution. He continues to remain a model prisoner, although death row inmates are not allowed to have in-custody jobs.

To this date, the place where Phoebe Ho was kept during her seven days' capture has not been divulged.

INFORMATIVE—
COMPELLING—
SCINTILLATING—
NON-FICTION FROM PINNACLE TELLS THE TRUTH!

BORN TOO SOON (751, $4.50)
by Elizabeth Mehren
This is the poignant story of Elizabeth's daughter Emily's premature birth. As the parents of one of the 275,000 babies born prematurely each year in this country, she and her husband were plunged into the world of the Neonatal Intensive Care unit. With stunning candor, Elizabeth Mehren relates her gripping story of unshakable faith and hope—and of courage that comes in tiny little packages.

THE PROSTATE PROBLEM (745, $4.50)
by Chet Cunningham
An essential, easy-to-use guide to the treatment and prevention of the illness that's in the headlines. This book explains in clear, practical terms all the facts. Complete with a glossary of medical terms, and a comprehensive list of health organizations and support groups, this illustrated handbook will help men combat prostate disorder and lead longer, healthier lives.

THE ACADEMY AWARDS HANDBOOK (0258, $4.99)
An interesting and easy-to-use guide for movie fans everywhere, the book features a year-to-year listing of all the Oscar nominations in every category, all the winners, an expert analysis of who wins and why, a complete index to get information quickly, and even a 99% foolproof method to pick this year's winners!

WHAT WAS HOT (894, $4.50)
by Julian Biddle
Journey through 40 years of the trends and fads, famous and infamous figures, and momentous milestones in American history. From hoola hoops to rap music, greasers to yuppies, Elvis to Madonna—it's all here, trivia for all ages. An entertaining and evocative overview of the milestones in America from the 1950's to the 1990's!

Available wherever paperbacks are sold, or order direct from the Publisher. Send cover price plus 50¢ per copy for mailing and handling to Penguin USA, P.O. Box 999, c/o Dept. 17109, Bergenfield, NJ 07621. Residents of New York and Tennessee must include sales tax. DO NOT SEND CASH.